THE FALMOUTH FRIGATE

By James L. Nelson and available from McBooks Press

THE ISAAC BIDDLECOMB NOVELS
By Force of Arms
The Maddest Idea
The Continental Risque
Lords of the Ocean
All the Brave Fellows
The Falmouth Frigate
* * *

The Only Life That Mattered

THE FALMOUTH FRIGATE

An Isaac Biddlecomb Novel

JAMES L. NELSON

McBooks
Press

Essex, Connecticut

McBooks Press

An imprint of Globe Pequot, the trade division of The Rowman & Littlefield Publishing Group, Inc.
4501 Forbes Blvd., Ste. 200
Lanham, MD 20706
www.rowman.com

Distributed by NATIONAL BOOK NETWORK

British Library Cataloguing in Publication Information available

Library of Congress Cataloging-in-Publication Data

Names: Nelson, James L., author.
Title: The Falmouth frigate / James L. Nelson.
Description: Essex, Connecticut : McBooks Press, [2022] | Series: The Isaac Biddlecomb novels | Summary: "The year 1777 is bleak indeed for the cause of American Independence, with the British army twice defeating Washington and taking the capital city of Philadelphia and the Royal Navy sweeping aside the defenses of the Delaware Bay. And for Captain Isaac Biddlecomb and the men of the half-built frigate Falmouth, things are direr still. After managing to slip through a British blockade, they find themselves trapped in a desolate harbor on the New Jersey coast and menaced not by the British but by the outlaw bands that terrorize the countryside and see Falmouth as a potentially valuable prize. Deserter Angus McGinty steals Biddlecomb's most potent weapon, the captured British sloop Sparrowhawk, leaving him to face the ruthless Pine Robbers on his own, with only his diminished crew and the near-useless local militia to help. Meanwhile, Virginia Biddlecomb, trapped in occupied Philadelphia, sees her chance to play a clandestine role in the fight. In the course of her activities, however, she lets slip information that will put her husband, his ship, and his crew in mortal danger, leading to a desperate race to get the unwieldy Falmouth to a place beyond the reach of the Royal Navy"—Provided by publisher.
Identifiers: LCCN 2022017777 (print) | LCCN 2022017778 (ebook) | ISBN 9781493068562 (hardback ; alk. paper) | ISBN 9781493071241 (ebook)
Subjects: LCSH: United States—History—Revolution, 1775-1783—Fiction. | United States—History, Naval—18th century—Fiction. | LCGFT: Historical fiction. | Novels.
Classification: LCC PS3564.E4646 F35 2022 (print) | LCC PS3564.E4646 (ebook) | DDC 813/.54—dc23/eng/20220422
LC record available at https://lccn.loc.gov/2022017777
LC ebook record available at https://lccn.loc.gov/2022017778

To the Rigging Gang: Bob Ireland, David Bellows, Mike Foster, Stuart Gillespie, and Fred Gosbee. Well-done, gentlemen.

And to the good ship Virginia, *may she always find fair winds and deep water.*

ACKNOWLEDGMENTS

My deepest thanks to the many people who contributed to making this book happen. Thanks in particular to Helen Hollick, historical writer extraordinaire, for all of her help with horses and all things eighteenth-century equestrian. Thanks to George Jepson, longtime friend, longtime supporter, and now editor, and all the folks at McBooks Press. Thank you to Nat Sobel and Judith Weber, Adia Wright, Isabelle Fang, and all the great people at Sobel Weber Associates, who have had my back all these years.

And to my wife, Lisa, for everything else.

PROLOGUE

Ship Falmouth, Cpt. Isaac Biddlecomb, commanding. 30th Octr. 1777
To the Honb^{l.} The Marine Committee of the Continental Congress
Gentlemen:
I regret that I have not until this moment had the Leisure to take
pen in hand and inform the Committee of the events that have trans-
pired since my departure from Boston on 20th September of this year.
I trust that the following account will make clear why I have found
correspondence quite beyond my ability until now.

As aforementioned, I departed Boston on September 20 in com-
mand of the Continental brig-of-war Charlemagne with orders to
make the best of my way in said brig to Philadelphia, where I was
to assume command of the frigate Falmouth building there. I sailed
from Boston in the company of two privateers of that city, viz.
Horatio Gates and Vengeance. On 24th September with Great Egg
Harbor bearing west and about half a league distant, we encountered
a British sloop-of-war, which I believe to be the Merlin, since lost on
the Delaware River. Being as our squadron was of tolerable force, I
cleared for action and signaled to the privateers to engage the enemy.
This they did, up until the moment the very first shots were fired, at
which time they deserted us on a lee shore in the face of a much superior
enemy. Despite engaging in a spirited resistance for the length of half
a glass, I was forced to drive Charlemagne ashore, at which time we
burned the vessel to prevent her falling into enemy hands.

Not content with the destruction of our ship, the British sloop-of-war sent a party of Marines and Sailors in pursuit of our people, but they were driven off by a defense organized by Marine Lt. Elisha Faircloth, whose exemplary leadership and activity I wish to acknowledge. In the course of beaching the vessel and the subsequent fight, we suffered six men wounded and four killed. Among those killed was Lt. David Weatherspoon of the Continental Navy, a most promising young officer.

Subsequent to the loss of Charlemagne I acquired a schooner in Great Egg Harbor, and in said vessel, the ship's Company continued to make the best of its way to Philadelphia. Upon arriving in the Delaware River, we discovered that the city had been taken by Gen^rl Howe, and that a significant fleet of the Royal Navy was in the process of securing the Bay and River. This despite stiff resistance from Continental forces as well as state militia and Pennsylvania State navy under the command of Comm^dr John Hazelwood.

Through an unfortunate circumstance, the schooner in which we had sailed was lost, necessitating myself and the men under my command to take up one of the row galleys of the Pennsylvania State Navy, which had been deserted by its crew. In said galley we were able to render material aid in the effort to prevent the Royal Navy's progress toward the city.

While in the process of rendering said aid, word was received through sundry means that the frigate Falmouth had been safely launched and towed clear of the city before Gen^rl Howe's forces were able to claim it as a prize. This was accomplished through the efforts of one Malachi Foote, Master Shipwright, and a contingent from the Fifth Pennsylvania Regiment, who were assigned to protect the vessel (though truthfully they might also have been deserters, their status never having been made entirely clear). Mr. Foote was regrettably killed in action defending the frigate against an attempt by the Royal Navy to capture it. In addition to preventing the frigate's capture, my men and those of the Fifth Pennsylvania were able to make a prize of the Royal navy sloop Sparrowhawk in which the cutting-out party had sailed.

With Gen^{rl} Howe in possession of the city, and Admir^l Howe's incursion meeting with regrettable success, I considered it prudent to remove Falmouth from the river lest she become trapped in the like manner of the Continental frigates Effingham and Washington. To accomplish this, we undertook a ruse de guerre, viz. we took Falmouth under tow of the sloop Sparrowhawk, giving the frigate the appearance of a prize of war, and thus sailed and towed her through the Enemy's lines and clear of the Delaware Bay. The bearer of this report can inform you as to our present location, which I dare not commit it to paper lest this falls into the hands of enemies of this Country.

We reached this place on the 28th of this month in good order. The prize taken at Philadelphia, H.M. armed sloop Sparrowhawk, is currently...

Isaac Biddlecomb paused, his pen hovering over the page. He frowned and lowered the tip of the quill toward the paper, then paused again. He sighed in exasperation, tossed the pen on the desk, and leaned back.

Ah...damn...damn his eyes, he thought.

How to report the loss of *Sparrowhawk*? A well-armed, well fit-out sloop, of little consequence to the Royal Navy but a valuable addition to the Continental service. And worth a tolerable amount of prize money to Biddlecomb and the Charlamagnes.

Falmouths...Biddlecomb corrected himself. The *Charlemagne* was lost, driven up on a beach and put to the torch just a few miles from where he sat in the *Falmouth*'s great cabin. The men who had survived that, who had survived the fight on the beach and the trip up the Delaware Bay and the fight on the frigate's decks, who had sailed through the British lines back to Great Egg Harbor on the New Jersey shore, they were the Falmouths now.

That would take some getting used to. The loss of his beloved *Charlemagne* would take some getting used to.

Sparrowhawk...

She had been stolen from him, it was that simple. Angus McGinty, formerly sergeant of the Fifth Pennsylvania and, apparently, formerly of some naval service or other, British or Continental, Biddlecomb did not know, had taken command of the sloop during their clandestine run down the Delaware River and Bay. He had kept company with them right into Great Egg Harbor before putting the sloop about and standing out to sea, leaving Biddlecomb to shout impotently in his wake.

He could picture the big Irishman standing at the tiller, waving his hat in farewell, his thick red hair lashing in the wind, that stupid smile on his face. Biddlecomb had disliked McGinty from the start, distrusted him. He knew the man's sort: back-slapping, raucous laughing, as sincere and reliable as a French courtesan.

And yet...

When the British cutting-out party had come over *Falmouth*'s side, McGinty had fought like a demon. Biddlecomb had caught sight of him in the fray, wielding his bayonet-tipped musket like it was a rapier, cutting a swath through the red-coated marines. He had not shirked from that fight, not at all. And he had been genuinely grieved by the death of Malachi Foote, or so it seemed, which was not the reaction Biddlecomb would have expected from a callous lack-wit.

The very idea of sailing *Falmouth* through the enemy fleet as if she was a British prize was based on a trick McGinty had played to bring the men under his command out from behind enemy lines, a bold move when McGinty could have just as easily abandoned them all. And when they were underway, with Biddlecomb commanding *Falmouth* and McGinty and his men aboard *Sparrowhawk*, the whore's son could have deserted the frigate at any time, just dropped the hawser and sailed away. But he did not. He had waited until *Falmouth* was in safe harbor before...

"Before stealing my damned ship," Biddlecomb said out loud, the anger flaring up once again. But he was loath to write those words in his official report. If McGinty was caught, and found guilty of that offense, he would hang for sure. And Biddlecomb was not sure he wanted that. If they could get *Falmouth* to sea, there was always the chance that he could hunt McGinty down himself, reclaim his prize, and deal with the man as he, and not the naval committee, saw fit.

And, of course, Biddlecomb did not care to admit to anyone, and certainly not to the Marine Committee, that he had been played for a fool. In some dark and unexamined part of his mind, he understood that though he chose not to dwell on it.

He sighed again, picked up the pen, dipped the tip in the inkwell, and continued.

Sparrowhawk is now patrolling the coast hereabouts to prevent our being surprised, in our current vulnerable state, by British cruisers. At such time, as the officers of Falmouth and I feel she is no longer required for this duty we will apply to the Honb⁻ Committee as to their wishes regarding the disposition of the vessel.

Or I'll just tell the honorable committee that she's gone missing, Biddlecomb thought. *Captured... sunk...who knows?*

It is with pleasure I report that the Continental frigate Falmouth is currently in safe harbor, and has aboard her most of her rigging and sails, and is lacking only ballast and the remainder of her spars (her fore lower mast and foreyard being in place) to be in all respects ready for sea. That said, we are still lacking in a great many things required for the ship to be of any service to Congress and the country, viz. guns and powder, shot, victuals and water and all manner of gunner, boatswain and carpenter stores. As to men, we have now but a quarter of the ship's compliment. It is my intention to remain here, at the place indicated to you by the bearer of this report, until such time as the wishes of the Honb⁻ The Marine Committee are made known to me.

In closing I wish to recognize the outstanding service of the fine officers under my command. Lt. Elisha Faircloth, aforementioned, has done great honor to the service and acted with uncommon bravery and intelligence. The same may be said for Mr. Samuel Gerrish, Midshipman, and Mr. Benjamin Sprout, boatswain. All of the petty officers and men late of the Charlemagne did notable service in seeing Falmouth to safety, and I would recommend them all to your consideration. In particular I must mention Mr. Ezra Rumstick, first officer, whose courage, steadfastness and service in this late affair have been of more value than I can rightly describe. Mr. Rumstick has rendered greater service to these United States in her current struggles than any man known to me, and I would recommend him for promotion and command, which would be of inestimable benefit to the nation, if ever such opportunity presents.

Biddlecomb smiled at that. Rumstick would not be pleased to see what he had written. There was not an untrue word in it, but Rumstick was not a man on the look-out for promotion and glory. Still, Biddlecomb could do no less than recommend him for it. He put the pen to the paper once more and wrote, *I am, [&c.], Capt I. Biddlecomb.*

He set the pen down and stared blankly at the great stream of words he had scrawled down the length of the page; stiff, formal language put down in an untidy script. *Why doesn't anyone just write a report in the same way they speak?* he wondered.

He was not proud of his penmanship. He had had little formal schooling—educated by his mother when he was a young boy, and later on shipboard, where he had been taught by whatever master or mate had the time and inclination to help him further his studies. Such men looked on writing the way they looked on splicing rope or caulking seams: something to be done correctly and well, but not with any particular flourish.

In the years since, Biddlecomb had read widely, from Shakespeare to treatises on navigation or natural science, and had done much to compensate for that earlier lack of learning. But no amount of study could fix the habits of penmanship ingrained in his youth.

He shook his head slightly, pushing those pointless considerations aside, and turned back to his more immediate concerns. He had finally found the time to write a report to the Marine Committee, but he was not entirely certain where the committee was to be found. They, and all the Continental Congress, had been in Philadelphia when Biddlecomb sailed from Boston a month earlier. But they were certainly not in Philadelphia now, not with the Brothers Howe in all but complete control of the city. So where to send the report?

He had heard several rumors. Some thought the Congress had moved to Annapolis, some thought to Bordentown. Some said they were making for Boston and some that they had scattered in panic. Those were all possibilities, though Biddlecomb considered Bordentown to be the most likely, and certainly, it was the rumor he heard most often. So he would find some trustworthy soul among the local militia and pay him to carry the report to Bordentown, and if the committee was not there, then the man would just have to find out where they bloody were.

He moved his eyes from the paper to a silver locket that lay on the desk nearby, and without thought, he picked it up and flipped it open. Inside was a miniature of his wife, Virginia. He felt a minor convulsion inside as he stared at the portrait. She had given it to him a few years before, and with all the time he spent at sea, he wondered if he hadn't spent more time looking at that than he had looking at her actual face.

The tiny painting was well done. The artist had captured her flawless features, the lovely proportions of cheek and forehead and neck, the profusion of dark brown hair. He had caught a hint of her beauty, but Biddlecomb did not think any painting could ever catch more than just a hint. Her real beauty was in the vitality and spirit, which radiated out of her, and which could not be rendered in static oil paint and canvas.

Biddlecomb moved his eyes to the other half of the locket. At first, it had been blank, but now there was a second face there, baby Jack Biddlecomb, with his round, red cheeks and tuft of dark hair. It was a good painting of a baby, but whether it was a good painting of Jack, Isaac was not sure. It was hard to distinguish the portrait of one baby from another, and this painting of a dark-hair, pink-skinned infant might be his and Virginia's, or it might not. He was not sure he could tell.

But that did not diminish the pleasure he felt in looking at the picture. The pleasure, and the stab of loneliness and pain.

Biddlecomb pressed his lips together and snapped the locket shut. He set it down, pushed the report to the Marine Committee to one side, and picked up a fresh piece of paper.

Virginia was in Philadelphia, as far as he knew. He would write to her, give her a hint at least of what had befallen him over the past month, or so. How he would then get the letter to her, in a city occupied by the British, he did not know. But that was a problem for another time.

He dipped the tip of the quill in the ink and wrote, *My Beloved Virginia*, and he felt the stab again, the loneliness and pain. He stared at the words. There was only one thing that prevented him from going completely mad, he knew, and that was that the demands of his station, the constant tumble from one crisis to another, prevented him from dwelling too long on the misery of his separation from wife and child.

And as he stared at the name Virginia, written at the top of that blank sheet, and let those thoughts swirl around in his head, he heard footsteps on the deck above. He looked up. He heard a few sharp but muffled words, more footsteps, coming aft this time. And he knew that once again his private dwellings had come to an end.

CHAPTER ONE

They came down the long pier extending out over the tidal mudflats on the edge of Great Egg Harbor. They came on horseback and on foot, their way lit by a smattering of lanterns held aloft. In that uncertain light, Biddlecomb could not see how many there were, nor could he get any sense of their purpose in approaching his ship.

"Seen 'em in town. Their lanterns, anyway," Ezra Rumstick said. They were standing by the gangway amidships. From there, a gangplank ran down from the ship's deck to the end of the pier to which she was tied. "Didn't think much of it, until they started heading this way."

Biddlecomb nodded. He could hear a bustle from down below, voices calling, soft but urgent. Ezra had sent Midshipman Gerrish to the great cabin to alert Biddlecomb to the strangers' approach, but he had also ordered the other men to arms, and told Lt. Faircloth to turn out the marines. Rumstick was not the indecisive type, not the sort who shirked responsibility. And, after all their time together, the thousands of miles under the keel, the many treacherous and bloody encounters, he could well anticipate what orders Biddlecomb was likely to give.

It was a cold night, with October ready to yield to November. The air was crisp and it carried the scent of wood smoke and salt-water marsh. Biddlecomb buttoned his coat as he watched the people approach. Half a dozen horses, by Biddlecomb's count, and a dozen men. No more than that. A score of men? He could see light glinting off steel, the barrels of muskets, he guessed.

"What do you reckon?" Rumstick asked.

"Don't know," Biddlecomb said. "But armed men approaching at night…not generally a good thing." He turned to Rumstick and gave him a bit of a smile. "We best go see what they want," he said.

Biddlecomb stepped up onto the gangway and headed down, Rumstick behind him. The tide was near its height and the gangway was steep and Biddlecomb descended with caution. He did not care to go galley-west down the gangplank under the gaze of whoever was approaching. First impressions and all that.

He stepped onto the pier as the riders at the front of the untidy column pulled their horses to a stop and dismounted. Two of the riders stepped forward, and from behind, two of the men on foot hurried to join them. The men on foot Biddlecomb knew. The older of the two, a man somewhere in his forties, was Col. Richard Somers, commander of the local defense, the Gloucester County Militia. The younger, in his mid-twenties, was his captain, Noah Mitnick.

It was these men, Somers and his militia, who had come to Biddlecomb's aide on that nightmare day when he was forced to beach his beloved *Charlemagne* on the barrier island that formed Great Egg Harbor. They had secured wagons for the wounded, escorted the survivors to the ferry that bought them to the town of Egg Harbor, such that it was, and seen them ensconced safe in the town's one tavern. It was because of that help that Biddlecomb hit on the idea of bringing *Falmouth* there. It seemed a place where he could get the protection and assistance he needed.

That, and because Great Egg Harbor was the only deep-water port he knew of near the mouth of the Delaware Bay.

Somers and the rest had been surprised by the return of Isaac Biddlecomb, this time with a half-finished frigate, no less. Not pleased, just surprised.

"Colonel Somers, good evening," Biddlecomb said. "Captain Mitnick, to what do I owe this honor?" He addressed Somers, though it was clear that the man who had come mounted, and not the militia colonel, was playing the lead role in whatever drama was being staged.

The man had a rough look about him, to be sure. He wore a cocked hat, battered and scuffed, with some sort of cockade holding up one side. His coat was equally worn, dark blue with facings of a lighter color, a coat that might or might not be regimental dress. White breeches and white waistcoat, the dirt and stains visible even in the light of the few lanterns that illuminated the scene. A sword hung at his side, a sea-service pistol clipped to his belt. He was three days at least in want of a shave.

"Captain Biddlecomb, good evening," Somers said. He was a polite man, a cautious man, and despite his position in command of the Gloucester County Militia, he was not a military man, per se. He was a fisherman and cooper by trade, and seemed content with soldiering as long as the war was being fought on the far side of his state or beyond. And that, Biddlecomb guessed, was why he was not pleased by the arrival of *Falmouth*, which had brought the war to him.

"This gentleman here," Somers continued, nodding toward the man in the blue coat, "is Colonel Shadrach Barnett." If Somers meant to say more he did not get the chance. Barnett stepped forward as if the militia colonel was not even there.

"Captain...Biddlecomb, is it?" Barnett asked. "A pleasure." His voice was coarse, like a saw cutting through wood, and his tone was that of a man trying to not project aggression. Trying, but not succeeding entirely.

"Captain Biddlecomb, yes," Biddlecomb said. "Continental Navy. My first officer, Lieutenant Ezra Rumstick." Biddlecomb nodded toward the imposing figure of Rumstick who stood to his right. Barnett looked up at Rumstick and nodded, but showed no hint of expression on his face.

"Colonel Barnett...you would be a colonel of...what?" Biddlecomb asked.

Barnett frowned. "Detached unit," he said. "Headquarters."

Biddlecomb nodded. "I see," he said, though what he saw was likely not what Barnett wanted him to see. Not that Barnett was putting much effort into his subterfuge.

Some of the other men, those who had dismounted and those on foot, had shuffled a bit closer and Biddlecomb could see more of them in the light of the lanterns. They were in civilian clothes for the most part,

3

though some, like Barnett, wore clothing that might have once been part of some military unit. They carried muskets of various models; some French, some English, some locally made. Cartridge boxes of all sorts, and the occasional powder horn. Some had pistols, some had canteens, some had bedrolls slung over their shoulders. They might have been militia, but they did not look much like any militia Biddlecomb had ever seen.

Some of the others Biddlecomb recognized as Somers's men, and they did look like what Biddlecomb had come to expect of citizen soldiers. They were mostly farmers and fishermen, dressed in simple, rough, but clean clothing, working clothing, slop trousers or breeches, woolen stockings and homespun coats. They carried uniform muskets and uniform cartridge boxes that were issued from the local armory. They were tough-looking, not in the way of outlaws but in the way of working men. There were only half a dozen of them, and they did not look terribly pleased to be there. Nor did Somers or Mitnick, for that matter.

"Colonel Somers, you are acquainted with Colonel Barnett, I trust? Sure you gentlemen have met before."

"No, Captain, no, in truth, we have not," Somers said, making little effort to hide his discomfort. "The colonel here, he says he's just down from headquarters, you see, and he and his men just arrived and made their introductions."

"That's the right of it, Captain," Barnett said. "Just arrived here. From headquarters."

"I see," Biddlecomb said. "And…just who's headquarters, exactly?"

"Why, General Washington," Barnett said. "Who'd you think?"

"I had no notion," Biddlecomb said. "I'm surprised to hear General Washington even knows we're here."

Barnett looked at him for a long moment, then said, "You might be surprised to learn what General Washington knows."

"I reckon I would," Biddlecomb said. He heard movement on the ship behind him, footsteps on the planks. Barnett looked up but Biddlecomb resisted the urge. He had a pretty good idea of who it was: Mr. Gerrish, most likely, getting the men along the rail in a show of force. Gerrish would know to make it a casual display, nothing too forward. No reason to stoke any flames. What's more, *Falmouth* did not have very many men to defend her, and that was not a fact that Biddlecomb wished to show off.

Barnett gave the activity on *Falmouth*'s deck a few second's glance, no more, and then his eyes were back on Biddlecomb, his face still devoid of expression. "Sergeant Wilcox, get them men up here, pray," he said. From back in the shadows, someone—Sergeant Wilcox, presumably— gave a sharp order and a dozen men stepped forward, not the Gloucester militia but the hard-looking men who had come with Barnett.

And He will separate them one from another, as a shepherd divides his sheep from the goats... Biddlecomb thought.

"The thing of it is," Barnett said. "General Washington, he knows what he knows on account of men like us, who keep our eyes and ears open for him. He's expecting a report on the ship here, the...what's she called, now?"

"She's a ship," Biddlecomb said. "General Washington will know which one."

Barnett nodded. "Reckon so. But he'll want to know more. He's like that. So by your leave, we'll go aboard and have a look about. So we can tell the general."

"No," Biddlecomb said. "No, I think not."

Barnett nodded again and for a moment he and Biddlecomb just looked at one another. Then Barnett moved his eyes up to the ship's rail, a slow and deliberate motion, as if to make clear to Biddlecomb that he could see what force Biddlecomb had and he was none to impressed by it. He looked down again and the men behind him took another step forward.

"General's orders, Captain," Barnett said.

"I don't answer to the General, Colonel," Biddlecomb said. "I answer to the Marine Committee. And they say no."

Silence again, two men in a stand-off. One would yield, or there would be blood. Those were the possibilities, the only possibilities.

Then more sounds from behind, from *Falmouth*'s deck. More shoes on planks, but sharper now, the slap of disciplined feet moving with purpose.

Damn... Biddlecomb thought. He knew what would happen next. He heard feet coming down the gangplank, pair after pair. Barnett's eyes flicked over and up, then came back to Biddlecomb just as quickly. Biddlecomb resisted the urge to look, but he did not have to, really.

Lieutenant Faircloth appeared on the edge of his sight, his green regimental coat looking black in the dark. Behind him, his Continental Marines moved in a short column along the pier, not quite marching but not merely walking either. They fell in parallel to *Falmouth*'s side, muskets on shoulders, bayonets fixed, eyes straight ahead. Their perfectly uniform clothing was in bold contrast to the civilian garb of the Gloucester Militia, and even more so to that worn by Barnett's followers. Faircloth was a wealthy man, and he saw to it that his marines were well fitted out.

Biddlecomb's eyes never left Barnett's face. He saw the man glance over once again at Faircloth's marines, and saw the flicker of a smile cross his lips. There were nine marines who had survived the fighting on the beach when they had grounded *Charlemagne*, and survived the fighting on the Delaware Bay and the defense of the *Falmouth*. They were well-armed, well equipped, and well trained. Disciplined men. But there were only nine of them, and they did not frighten Colonel Shadrach Barnett.

The colonel, or whatever he was in truth, looked back at Biddlecomb. "Ship seems to enjoy some good protection," he said. "This all the men you have? All the marines onboard? General'll want to know."

Biddlecomb raised his hands in a noncommittal gesture. Faircloth's instincts were good, but he would have done better to just post a couple of marines at the base of the gangway, let Barnett guess at how many more were aboard. With the men lined up, it was pretty clear that those were all there were.

"Marines, sailors, it takes a host of men to man and sail and fight a ship such as this," Biddlecomb said.

"And you have a host of men?" Barnett asked.

"We sailed her here," Biddlecomb said. "And we can fight her."

Barnett nodded. He looked back at Faircloth's marines then up at the men along the ship's rail. He was not intimidated by what he saw, that was clear, but neither was he in a hurry to send his makeshift company against Faircloth's bayonets. And they did not look to be in a hurry to go.

He turned back to Biddlecomb and once again the two men regarded one another, silent and unmoving.

"Very well, then, Captain," Barnett said at last. "I reckon you decide who comes aboard your ship and who don't."

"I reckon," Biddlecomb said. "But pray, give General Washington my regards."

Barnett nodded again. "That I will, Captain."

"So," Somers broke in, relief in his voice. "Back to headquarters with you, Colonel?"

"No," Barnett said. "My boys are pretty well played out just now. Seemed there was a tavern in town that we seen. I reckon we'll bed down there for the night. Maybe stay in the neighborhood, see how we might help the cause. You know. Independency."

"Not sure the tavern has room for so many," Captain Mitnick offered, sounding a bit too helpful and apologetic to be genuine. "I fear you and your men would be none too comfortable there."

Barnett smiled at that. "Oh, don't you worry, Captain. We don't require anything too fancy. A roof over our heads, a warm meal. Cup of rum. That should do us fine." He turned his back on Biddlecomb and Rumstick and called to his men, "Mount up! Sergeant Wilcox, get the men ready to move!" He turned back to Biddlecomb. "Good night to you, sir. I trust we'll meet again soon."

"I suspect we will," Biddlecomb said.

With that Barnett strode back to his horse and swung himself up in the saddle. He took one last, long look around, then tugged his horse's reins and headed back along the heavy wooden planks of the pier, his mounted troops and his foot soldiers falling in behind.

Biddlecomb, Rumstick, Somers and the others watched in silence as they walked off into the dark, until there was nothing to be seen of them but the pinpoints of light from their lanterns.

Somers coughed and spit on the ground. "Sons of bitches," he said "Whore's sons, sons of bitches."

"I take it, Colonel, that you don't reckon they're really from Washington's headquarters?" Biddlecomb asked.

"Ha! No, I reckon not," Somers said.

"Pack of Loyalist dogs," Rumstick suggested.

"Maybe," Somers said. "The state's getting more lawless by the day. Law, government, it's what any bastard says it is. You got Loyalist gangs terrorizing folks, pretending to be King's men and legal for that reason. You got supposed Patriots preying on whoever they wish, figuring no one will object to them plundering King's men. But these bastards? I reckon they're just *banditti*. Pine Robbers. There's a plague of 'em, living in the Pine Barrens here, robbing anyone. Like we ain't got trouble enough."

Biddlecomb nodded. "They probably figure the ship and whatever's aboard is the richest prize they're like to find."

"Well, damn it all, Captain!" Somers said. "Do you see? You shouldn't have come here, and this is why. Ship like this attracts all sorts of attention. And we don't need attention here, not from the British, not from Loyalists, and sure as hell not from banditti."

"Look, Colonel," Rumstick said, his tone every bit as annoyed as Somers's, "fact is, you just might have to face some trouble, even here in Fragile as an Egg Harbor. Might be you'll even have to do some fighting. You know, like the rest of us."

"Thank you, Lieutenant. Colonel," Biddlecomb said, putting a stop to that altercation before it could gain any more momentum. "We can go fight them now, if you think it's wise. My men, your militia, we march right to the tavern and shoo them off. I'm sure we can be persuasive."

Somers was scowling, either from Rumstick's words or Biddlecomb's, or more likely both. "We don't need to start our own war here with them bastards," he said. "We got war enough. And I'm not concerned about this so-called colonel. I reckon he got an eye-full of your marines. He'll light off in the morning, him and his men. I'm just afraid of what comes next, and your ship drawing this vermin here."

"The thing of it is, Colonel," Biddlecomb said. "We don't much want to be here, either. No hope of getting the ship fitted out here, and totally vulnerable to the likes of Barnett and his pack of dogs."

"So…what will you do?"

"We'll get underway just as soon as we can," Biddlecomb said. "And the more help we get from you and your men, the sooner that will be."

Somers made a grunting noise. "Very well, Captain," he said. "You'll get every bit of help we can give, I promise."

Biddlecomb nodded. He did not doubt Somers's sincerity, because he did not doubt Somers's great desire to see *Falmouth*—and all the trouble she brought—well over the horizon.

CHAPTER TWO

Angus McGinty wore a cheerful aspect, generally. It disarmed people, he found, and was an excellent blanket under which to hide his true feelings. It worked well when playing cards, for instance. But now he had reached the limit of his patience.

He snatched his hat off his head and threw it to the deck and then stamped it with his foot, over and over, until it was all but flat. He was breathing hard when he looked up, and he imagined that his face was as red as his hair.

"There's not but two score ropes on this whole damned ship!" he shouted at the confused men forward. "And they're the same to larboard and starboard, so you don't have to learn but twenty of them! Is that too bloody much for you motherless simpletons?"

Overhead, the sloop *Sparrowhawk*'s square topsail was flat aback, the wind pressing on the wrong side of the sail, and the jibs and the mainsail were flogging even louder than McGinty was shouting. Over and over McGinty had drilled the men at what he himself considered the utterly simple task of putting the small ship about, and again and again, his crew of ham-fisted farmers made a complete hash of it.

"When I say, 'cast off the bowlines and haul away the weather brace', what the bloody hell do you think that means?" McGinty shouted, looking for some clarification.

Ten feet forward, Corporal Nathaniel Freeman, oldest of the men and least intimidated by McGinty, stood holding the limp brace in his hands, with three others backing him up. Freemen turned his head and spit a line of brown tobacco juice across the deck, which irritated McGinty at least as much as the bungled sail evolution.

"It don't means nothing to us, McGinty," Freeman said. "All that tarry, Irish burgoo comes spilling out of your mouth, it don't mean nothing to us."

McGinty gave a sigh, loud and dramatic. He bent over and snatched up his flattened hat and made a show of punching it back into some semblance of its former shape. He took his time, letting his anger settle, letting his sense of reason and fairness reestablish itself.

They're soldiers, boy-o, and they were farmers afore that, and you can't expect too damned much of them...

Angus McGinty had been a soldier as well, and many things besides. A fisherman out of his native town of Wicklow on Ireland's east coast; a private in the grenadier company of the Fourth Regiment of Foot, the King's Own; a sergeant in the Third Company, Fifth Pennsylvania, Continental Line. His occupations tended to be as fluid as his loyalties. But it was his time at sea, on a fishing boat or boatswain on a privateer (British or American, he had sailed aboard both) or a stint as fore topman aboard His Majesty's ship *Preston* that he truly loved. He had forgotten, after all the soldiering, how much he loved the sea, but he was remembering it now.

And that rekindled love was making this crew of farmers all that much harder to bear.

"Very well, lads," he said, forcing calm and good humor into his voice. "We'll go over it again, we will, and I'm sure you'll smoke it this time. If I was to use different words, would that help, at all? Say, if I was to call the topsail a 'heifer', or the main sheet a 'hayrick'?"

The men forward continued to stare aft. Often they did not know how to respond to McGinty because they did not know when McGinty was joking. Half the time McGinty himself did not know when he was joking.

He looked aloft at the flogging mess of canvas. His first job was to get that under control. He looked forward toward the bow, where three more of his men held the headsail sheets in their hands, the thick ropes twisting and thrashing with the sails. It looked as if the men were trying to keep hold of angry snakes.

McGinty opened his mouth. He meant to tell the men to take a turn around a pin and haul the headsails out to weather, but before he uttered a sound, he realized the pointlessness of that, the frustration he would invite by saying such a thing.

"Bellows, Foster, Asquith, take those ropes and pull them to…" he choked on the word 'weather' and then choked on the word 'starboard', afraid that either of those would be too much. "Pull them to the right side, there!" he called instead, pointing as he did. "Yes, like that! Hold 'em now, and don't you let go until I tell you!"

The men obeyed. What they lacked in seamanship they made up in strength, and so were able to hold the sails, back-winded, against the press of the breeze. Slowly *Sparrowhawk*'s bow began to pay off to larboard as the sails pushed the ship around.

"Good!" McGinty called. "Now, Corporal Freemen, you may pull on your rope, which we call a 'brace'. Foster, you may slack away as our good corporal pulls."

Freemen and the three men with him hauled on the brace while Foster, to starboard, eased away. Overhead the yards swung around until the wind was at last on the right side of the sails. *Sparrowhawk* heeled a bit and plunged as her speed built and the wallowing, dead-in-the-water motion gave way to forward momentum.

"That's well! Make fast!" McGinty cried. "By which I mean, tie your ropes off, figure eight around the pins, like I shown you!"

To larboard and starboard, the men made the lines fast, taking care to get them on the correct pins, which McGinty was at least gratified to see. Their sail evolutions were chaotic enough; if the lines were all misplaced, it would be a descent into madness.

"Hold her there, Pip," he said to the young man on the tiller. Charles Pippinger, youngest of the men who had come with McGinty aboard *Sparrowhawk*, had fished cod out of Marblehead for a few seasons and knew his way around boats. That was a great relief to McGinty, who would otherwise have had to steer along with doing every other thing onboard that required at least a passing knowledge of seamanship.

"Hold her there, aye," Pip said.

McGinty walked up to the windward rail and leaned against the bulwark, looking down the length of the deck, past the taut black shrouds and the long, elegant bowsprit and jibboom. *Sparrowhawk* was a lovely little ship, there was no doubt, and with her ten four-pounder guns arrayed along her sides, she could deliver a sharp peck if she wanted to.

He felt his irritation start to ebb. The sight of the handy little sloop, the feel of her steady rise and plunge as she plowed along, close-hauled, never failed to lighten his mood.

They had been underway for three days now, three days since they had towed the frigate *Falmouth* into Great Egg Harbor and then bid adieu to the officious Captain Isaac Biddlecomb and that great beast Rumstick. McGinty recalled the sight of Master Biddlecomb fuming and stamping and shouting from the frigate's quarterdeck as they sailed. The memory always put a smile on his lips.

Biddlecomb, no doubt, thought that absconding with the sloop had been McGinty's plan all along, but that was not the case. He had not put much thought into it at all, which was true of most things that Angus McGinty had done over the course of his wandering life.

They had been a couple leagues shy of the inlet to Great Egg Harbor when the notion of sailing off first began to stir. McGinty played with the idea, batting at it like a cat with a mouse, letting it run off and then catching it again. By the time they had come into the harbor and eased the frigate up to the warping posts, the plan was as fully formed in McGinty's head as any plan ever was, which was not to say very well formed at all. But enough, anyway, to act on. And what happened after that, well, he reckoned he would figure it out in due time.

Privateering...

That was what he had said to Biddlecomb, and it was still the main thing he had in mind. Privateering combined all the elements of everything that McGinty desired. It involved being at sea, but in the time and manner of his own choosing. Fighting when he wanted to, running when he didn't. A man could get rich, damned rich, in privateering. And on top of all that, the work even had a whiff of patriotism about it, for any who cared about such things.

Yes, privateering was just the medicine. And he had a good ship for it, at least, if not exactly the crew one might wish. A privateer wanted a large company of prime seamen, and most were able to get just that. *Sparrowhawk*, however, was manned by ten farmers and a nineteen-year-old cod fisherman. And that was a problem.

Well, there's time yet, McGinty thought. The lads may be a parcel of plow hands, but they're not fools. They can learn. And besides, they each of them know how to fight, and they ain't shy about it. If I have but a wee bit more time...

"McGinty, there! I see a sail!"

Ah, damnation! McGinty thought.

He had sent one of the former soldiers, a young man named Bobby Ireland, whose name alone inclined McGinty to liking him, aloft, up to the crosstrees, to keep an eye on the horizon. *Sparrowhawk* had problems enough without an enemy cruiser taking them by surprise. And as it stood, every ship on the American coast was their enemy.

"Where away?" McGinty shouted up to the man aloft.

"Over there!" Ireland replied, lubberly and unhelpful.

Over there? You bloody half-wit, what sort of damned... McGinty took a deep breath and smothered the reply that was forming in his throat. He looked up. The look-out was pointing to some place just abaft the larboard beam. McGinty turned and looked in that direction but he could see nothing but water. The ship was still below the horizon from deck level, which meant the look-out had seen it early.

"Well done, lad, well done!" McGinty shouted up. On any other ship he would have asked what the man could make of the strange sail: ship-rigged or otherwise? Larboard tack, starboard tack, running with the wind betwixt two sheets? Was she altering course? But he knew it was pointless to ask those questions now.

He stepped over to the binnacle box, pulled a telescope from the compartment there, tucked it into his coat, and swung himself up into the shrouds. He had spent the past half year in the Continental Army, marching back and forth across New York, New Jersey, and Pennsylvania, and he was about as lean and fit as he had ever been, which was admittedly not terribly lean. But he managed the shrouds with little difficulty and pulled himself up onto the crosstrees as easily as mounting a short flight of steps.

With the ease of long practice, he slipped his arm around the topmast shroud and pulled the telescope from his coat. He could see it now, the strange sail to leeward. A brig, he guessed, sailing on a southerly course. He put the eyepiece to his eye and twisted the tube.

*Brig, sure enough…*he thought. *Or a snow, perhaps.* They were running south under all plain sail, holding steady, not spreading more canvas or changing course at all. Either they had not seen *Sparrowhawk* or they had and she did not concern them.

What, do you think we're too small to do you any great hurt? McGinty thought. He found that a bit insulting.

He shifted his gaze to the west, but there was nothing in view but the gray-blue ocean. By his dead reckoning, they were somewhere off the coast of New Jersey, two or three leagues south of Sandy Hook and about fifteen leagues out to sea. It had been McGinty's intention to keep clear of the land and as much shipping as he could while he turned his men into prime seamen. The first part of that plan had worked out well enough, at least until now.

McGinty sighed. It was a blessing that this brig, whoever it was, seemed to have no interest in *Sparrowhawk*. A smart man would accept that gift, avoid any trouble, and continue on, leaving the strange ship alone. But McGinty knew full well that he was not going to do that.

"You keep an eye on her, lad," he said to the look-out. "She seems to change course, set more sail, take down sail, you let me know, hear?"

"Yes, Sargent," Bobby Ireland said.

"That's 'Aye, Captain,'" McGinty corrected.

"Oh, yes," the look-out said. "Aye, Captain. Sargent."

McGinty nodded. "Good lad," he said, then climbed back down to the deck. He stepped off the rail and walked aft, calling out to the men as he did.

"All right, lads, listen to your darlin' McGinty, now. I want you all to go and stand by them ropes you was standing by before, and get ready to do as I say with them. We're going the change course now, just a wee bit."

He took his place by the tiller and watched as the men sorted themselves out. "Very well, now, my dear Pip," he said, "put her head down if you would."

"Head down, aye," Pip said. He pushed the tiller away and *Sparrowhawk*'s bow began to swing away down wind. McGinty shouted his directions forward as he handled the mainsheet himself, and after a short but acceptable period of confusion, the sloop's stern passed through the wind and the vessel settled down on her new course, south by west, with the breeze over her larboard quarter.

"Well done, lads, well done, they couldn't have done better on Black Dick's flagship, I'll warrant!" McGinty lied, but he was content for now with their seamanship. "Bobby, what do you see of yonder sail?" he called aloft.

"Right in front of us, Sargent, and about two or three miles away," Ireland called down. "Nothing's changed about her that I can see."

"Very well!" McGinty shouted. "Keep your eye on her. But don't you fail to look around as well, keep a sharp look-out!"

"Yes, Sargent!" Bobby Ireland called down.

Freeman came ambling up and stood beside McGinty and the two of them stared off toward the horizon, which hid the brig from their view. Freeman leaned over and spit a stream of tobacco juice on the deck.

"Jesus, Mary and Joseph!" McGinty said. "You're not in some pox-ridden encampment, you know, you're on a bloody ship. You could have some respect, man!"

Freeman nodded but said nothing, just continued to work the wad of tobacco in his mouth and stare out at the horizon.

"So...what do you plan to do?" he said at last.

"Ah, I plan to get a nice, plump wife and a fine estate in the country and live out my life as lord of the manor, hunting foxes and such," McGinty said. "What about you?"

"Dumb arse," Freeman said. "You know what I mean. What do you plan to do about yonder ship?"

"Oh, yonder ship… Well, we know nothing of it, do we? So I figured we'd best go have a look, do you see?"

Freeman frowned. He leaned over to spit again, paused, then lifted his head and directed the stream over the side of the ship, easily clearing the bulwark.

"Well done, lad," McGinty said. "If you Yankee soldiers could fire your muskets half so well you'd have sent old Howe running back to England by now."

"The ship?" Freeman asked. "Kind of a risk, ain't it, just running right down on it? We ain't particularly well-armed or manned, and we don't have a lot of friends out here, in case you ain't noticed."

"Not so much of a risk, my dear," McGinty said. "You see, we have what sailors call the 'weather gauge.' That means we're upwind of this fellow. And the wind, well, it's like this wondrous invisible rampart. This fellow would have to climb up the rampart to get to us, you see, whilst we can just scamper away. We can fight or we can run, but either way the choice is ours."

"I see," Freeman said. "And if the wind shifts?"

"Ah, well, that can be a bit of a problem. But it's holding steady now, and promises to keep on that way."

And the wind did indeed keep on that way, to McGinty's great relief, blowing an easy twelve knots from the northeast, giving *Sparrowhawk* a point of sail that she liked very much. Two glasses turned and by then the brig was visible from the deck, her course and the set of her sails unchanged. McGinty stood on the bulwark, one arm around the shrouds, and studied her through his glass.

Fat bloody thing, he thought. Everything about her seemed to proclaim her a merchantman. And not just a merchantman, but a slow and fully laden merchantman. If *Sparrowhawk* was a shark, then here was an overstuffed, lumbering seal.

"Say, Foster, we still have that British flag aboard, don't we?" McGinty called to one of the men taking his ease on the main hatch. "The one we flew when sailing through Black Dick's fleet?"

"Yeah, Sargent, we do," Foster said.

"Well, pray, fetch it out and run it up the halyard there." He pointed to the thin line that ran up to the peak of the mainsail gaff. Foster nodded and pushed himself to his feet and ambled aft. He found a canvas bag by the taffrail and began to fish around in it.

"Say, Foster," McGinty called, "is that other flag in there as well? The Continental flag? With the stripes and the stars?" Once they had cleared the Delaware, Biddlecomb had sent the flag over, in case they met up with an American man-of-war—Continental Navy, State Navy, or privateer—and wished to display their true allegiance.

"Yeah, Sargent, it's here," Foster called. "You want me to run that up, too? One over the other?"

"No, no, just the British flag. For now."

A minute later it was set, streaming forward, *Sparrowhawk*'s *ruse de guerre* complete, though McGinty doubted they could see the colors aboard the distant brig. Nor could McGinty see any flag the brig might be flying; if they had one raised, then the wind was blowing it straight away from *Sparrowhawk*. But McGinty felt quite certain she was a merchantman, and quite certain she was British, a supply ship loaded with *matériel* of some sort, bound for Lord Admiral Howe's fleet or General Richard Howe's army.

McGinty collapsed his telescope and hopped down to the deck. Freeman was leaning on the bulwark a few feet forward. "Your invisible rampart still standing strong?" he asked.

"Can't you feel it, boy-o?" McGinty asked. "Wind's held steady as you might wish, just as I said it would."

"We're still just going to have a look at yonder ship?" Freeman asked.

"Just a wee look, to be sure," McGinty said. "Nothing more. Still, it's a wise man who's ready for whatever might come, be it misfortune or opportunity." He said nothing more, letting the words hang.

"Very well, you damned Irish rascal, what are you thinking?" Freeman said at last.

"Well, just that we would do well to load those guns now," McGinty said, gesturing toward the line of four-pounders along the rail, "while we have our leisure. And maybe have the boys fetch up their muskets and load those as well."

"So we can just have a look?" Freeman asked.

"Right, boy o, just so we can have a look."

He and Freeman had soldiered together for eight months, not a long acquaintance in the rational world, but a near-lifetime in the crucible of combat. Freeman was not stupid, McGinty knew that, and he was not so young as the others. They were likely of an age, he and McGinty, and unlike the boys under their command, Freeman was not easily taken in by what McGinty said.

But that did not matter. Because McGinty had already decided on what he would do next, and there was no one, least of all Corporal Nathaniel Freeman, who was going to stop him.

CHAPTER THREE

It was certainly a merchantman and it was certainly British. By the time *Sparrowhawk* was a mile distant, both those things were absolutely clear. The brig's merchantman's ensign, the red field with the Union flag in the canton, was flapping at the peak of her gaff. It was not easy to see— the wind was blowing it directly away from them—but there were flaws enough in the breeze that sent it flapping broadside to *Sparrowhawk*, giving them an unobstructed view.

The brig had cracked on more sail as *Sparrowhawk* started to overhaul her: a flying jib at first and then fore topmast stun's'ls and a ringtail. But it was not until McGinty had ordered the British flag down and the Continental flag up to the main masthead, where it was clearly visible, that the brig had really started to run. Main topmast stun's'ls, lower stun's'ls, even a main royal set flying from the deck, she crowded on every bit of canvas she had aboard in her race for the safety of the British fleet in the Delaware Bay.

Too late, boy-o, too bloody late, McGinty thought, watching the brig through his telescope. He had to marvel at the amount of sail she was able to fly. The wind was not terribly strong, but still, with the strain they were putting on the rig he had to wonder that some part of it had not carried away.

Let's have one of those topsails blow all to ribbons, he thought. *Or one of them fine topmasts go by the board. That would get this business done all the quicker.*

Sparrowhawk rose up on a swell and her bow came down and sent a spray of water up and aft over the deck, and the ten farmers-cum-sailors cheered with the thrill of it. McGinty shook his head.

Bloody lubberly plow hands, he thought. But he understood their excitement. *Sparrowhawk* loved that point of sail, and she was swooping down on the merchantman, fast and deadly as her namesake. The pounding of the hull through the water, the creak and strain of the rigging, only added to the tension and sense of drama.

It did not occur to any of them to wonder why they were chasing this brig in the first place. None except Freeman, and he was keeping his opinions to himself, for the moment.

"Fall off a bit more, Pip!" McGinty shouted and Pip pushed the tiller a bit more to weather. "That's good, there!" *Sparrowhawk*'s bow was aimed at a point just ahead of the brig, leading her the way one would take aim at a bird on the wing. Any direction that the brig turned now would only make it easier for *Sparrowhawk* to intercept her.

For half an hour, the two ships continued on their converging courses, the distance between them dropping away until McGinty could see movement on the other's deck even without the telescope.

"Corporal Freeman!" he called. "I think it's time we put a shot across her bow, what say you? Can I trust you to do such a thing without sinking her?"

Freeman took a few steps closer so he could speak without shouting. "Shot across her bow? And why are we doing that?"

"To get her to heave to, man!" McGinty said. "To get her to stop running away."

"Thought we were just having a look. Well, we've had a look."

"From here we've had a look, but ya can't see a damned thing worth seeing from here, now can you?" McGinty explained. "I mean to go aboard. Have a real look about. And for that, we needs she must stop, do you see?"

"I ain't happy about this, McGinty. I ain't happy at all," Freeman said.

"Ah, but you will be! And look at them other boys," McGinty said, nodding to the men crowding along the rail, staring out at the merchant ship, and cheering as *Sparrowhawk* plunged along. "Would you tell them we're going to give it up, and their curiosity never satisfied?"

Freeman looked over at the men. He looked back at McGinty. His expression, a mixture of disgust and resignation, did not change. He leaned over and spit a line of tobacco juice on the deck, then wandered off toward the bow to see to the forward-most four-pounder on the leeward side.

The former soldiers of *Sparrowhawk*'s crew had been infantrymen, not artillery. Nonetheless, they knew a bit about land-based field cannons, and there was not a great deal of difference between those and the sea-going sort, save for the tackle that held them to the ship's bulwarks and the stubby naval carriages. Put to it, the men were able to load the ship's great guns with a respectable degree of speed and coordination.

Still, McGinty hoped there would be no need for efficient gunnery anytime in the near future. A dozen men were not enough to man even *Sparrowhawk*'s small battery. More to the point, if they found themselves going broadside to broadside with another ship, that meant they had got themselves into more of a fight than McGinty was looking for. The use he had in mind for *Sparrowhawk* was legally questionable at best, even without throwing genuine bloodshed into the mix.

He looked forward. Freeman had a linstock with a length of smoldering match in his hand. He called a few men over to him, gesturing, pointing, and the men took up handspikes and trained the small cannon around. Freemen leaned down and sighted along the barrel, then gestured for the men to step back. He stood to one side and brought the match down on the priming powder in the touchhole. McGinty saw it smoke and he looked away, toward the frantically fleeing brig.

The gun went off with a sharp and impressively loud roar and the men cheered, as McGinty knew they would. He kept his eyes on the water just ahead of the brig and was rewarded with the sight of a white plume shooting up right in the merchantman's path and about a half a cable length ahead.

"Well done, boy-o, well done!" McGinty shouted. He turned and smiled at Freeman but Freeman was looking out over the rail at their quarry, his posture one of nonchalance, as usual, his face lacking any expression. As usual.

Ah, you're a cool one, Corporal Cucumber, McGinty thought. He turned his attention back to the brig. No change in her course, no alteration in the set of her sails. But there was no chance that they had missed the warning *Sparrowhawk* had sent across her bows. Even if the fall of the shot had gone unseen, the report of the gun and the jet of gray smoke would not have escaped their notice.

Cheeky bastard, are you? McGinty thought. *Do ya till think you can run clean away from ol' Angus McGinty?*

For another ten minutes, they stood on, their courses converging, the distance between them dropping quickly. The master of the brig most certainly understood by then that he could not outrun *Sparrowhawk*. He had to be hoping for a miracle, for *Sparrowhawk* to blow out a sail or lose her mast or a spar, but McGinty did not think God would be smiling on him that way.

"Corporal Freeman, have you reloaded your gun, there?" McGinty called out, his patience with the merchantman having run its course.

"Yeah," Freeman called back.

"Well, give this bastard another one, and if your shot comes a wee bit nearer to hitting him, I'd not be disappointed."

"Aye, aye, captain," Freeman called back with a thick dollop of irony. A moment later the gun went off again. McGinty did not see the fall of the shot, but he did see the ugly hole the ball made as it passed through the brig's staysail.

"Oh, that'll do it, lad, that'll do it!" McGinty shouted with delight, and a moment later he could see that his assessment was correct. Lower stun's'ls, topmast stun's'ls, ringtail, main royal, they all came in as fast as the merchantman's small crew could strike them. *Sparrowhawk* was just a couple of cable lengths to windward by the time the brig was down to plain sail, and McGinty ordered the sheets slacked away to slow her down.

"Now what are they doing?" asked Bellows, who was standing by the main brace a few feet from McGinty.

"Heaving to," McGinty said. "Rounding up with the main topsail aback." He looked at Bellows and could see he might as well have been speaking Hindoo for all the man understood.

"They're stopping their wee boat, lad, so we might call on them," McGinty explained, and Bellows nodded.

Heaving too, ah, damnation, McGinty thought, looking aloft. He had not thought this part through. They would have to heave *Sparrowhawk* to as well, and then get the boat they were pulling astern up alongside, man it with a boat crew, and row it over to the brig. None of those things would present much difficulty to a seasoned crew, or even a crew with just a handful of able-bodied seamen, but with his farmers, it would be a different matter.

He looked back at the brig. They had turned up into the wind and their mainsail was braced around until it pressed against the mast, effectively stopping the vessel dead in the water. Her broad red ensign was flapping as it was lowered to deck. But *Sparrowhawk* was still underway, still making for the merchantman, and if McGinty didn't do something soon, they would slam right into their ostensible prize.

"All right, lads, stop gawking like a parcel of fools and get your hands on them ropes, same ones you was manning before!" McGinty shouted and the men, who had been lining the rail and staring across the water, hurried off to obey, each going to the one rope they knew. McGinty looked back at the brig, then up aloft, then along the deck.

"Pip, my dear, swing her bow up into the wind, slowly now, slowly…" From behind Pip acknowledged the order and *Sparrowhawk*'s bow began to turn, swinging away from the brig, turning up into the wind. Overhead the taut topsail began to collapse and flog as the breeze came down the edge of the canvas.

"Foster, Asquith, you lot, let your ropes loose!" McGinty shouted. "Bellows, Tucker, all of you, haul away, now!" Overhead the main yard and the topsail yard began to swing around, turning to present the front of the topsail to the wind.

"Steady up, now, Pip!" McGinty shouted. He ran to the lee side, cast off the main sheet, than ran up the slanting deck to the weather side, and hauled the big fore-and-aft mainsail out to windward.

"Steady…" McGinty shouted again, looking aloft, looking out to windward. The sloop was stopped, he could see, hove too, the opposing pressures of wind and sail keeping her secured to that spot of the ocean.

McGinty let out a breath. He almost dared not move for fear of upsetting the balance. "Well done, lads, well done!" he called. "Now tie your ropes to the pins like your dear McGinty showed you and let's get that bloody boat alongside."

Twenty awkward moments later, they were settled in the boat and pulling for the brig, McGinty, Freeman—who, over McGinty's protests, had insisted on coming—and eight armed men late of the Third Company, Fifth Pennsylvania, Continental Line, and now a part of *Sparrowhawk*'s crew. Pip and a few others had been left aboard to mind the sloop, though what they could do if any real problems arose McGinty did not know.

"Now, listen here," McGinty said to the men at the oars, speaking in a harsh but low voice. "Everyone, lower your oar…pull…raise your oar. That's well. And again…lower your oar…" Every eye aboard the brig would be on them, he knew, and he did not want them to witness any gross incompetence on the part of the Sparrowhawks. If they saw that, if they thought the Americans were not up to the task, then they might start getting unwelcome ideas.

McGinty looked up from the rowers. The brig was just ahead of them now, and fifty feet away. As small a vessel as she was, she looked massive from the perspective of the boat.

"One more pull…" McGinty called. "Good! Now lift your oars straight up and set them down! Foster, get the boat hook, there at your feet, and grab hold of something as we come along side!"

McGinty pushed the tiller over and with the last of its momentum the boat glided up to the side of the brig. Foster reached out with the boat hook and grabbed onto the forechains, but McGinty was on his feet even before he did. He looked up. About a dozen men, sullen-looking and wary, were standing at the gangway, looking down.

"Clear the way, clear the way!" McGinty shouted as he climbed past the oarsmen and scrambled up the boarding steps to the deck. The crew of the merchantman stepped aside as he came through the break in the bulwark. McGinty had a cutlass hanging at his side and a pistol thrust through his belt, and he ostentatiously rested the palm of his hand on the butt of the gun as he stepped across the deck.

He stopped ten feet in from the gangway, panicked by a sudden realization: he had failed to tell the rest of his men to follow him aboard.

Ah, bloody damnation... he thought. He would look ridiculous going back and telling them now, but he would look equally ridiculous if they all remained in the boat. He was still wrestling with this when he heard more footfalls on the deck. He turned to see Freeman coming through the gangway, and the others behind him. The men carried their muskets, cartridge boxes slung over their shoulders, and some of them carried the pistols and cutlasses they had found aboard *Sparrowhawk*. They wore breeches and cocked hats and they looked like what they were—soldiers, not sailors. McGinty could see the confused looks on the faces of the British crew.

At the break of the brig's quarterdeck stood a man with a portly frame, a long blue coat and white waistcoat, a cocked hat on his head, and a most pronounced frown on his face. Captain McGinty had no doubt. He stepped over to the man, putting on a smile that he hoped would convey a kindly spirit and sympathy, though not too much sympathy, for the man's plight.

"I am Captain Angus McGinty, of the Continental privateer *Sparrowhawk*, at your service, sir," he said with a shallow bow.

"You're an Irishman," the captain said. It was not so much an observation as an accusation.

"I'm an American," McGinty corrected, the smile still fixed to his face. "Born in Wicklow, yes, but an American. And you, sir, are my prisoner."

The captain was still frowning as he looked around. "Queer damned lot of sailors you look," he said. "Privateer, is it? You'll show me your commission, I trust."

McGinty tapped the butt of his pistol with the palm of his hand. "This is all the commission I needs show you, sir," he said, and as the captain opened his mouth to further argue, McGinty turned to the men behind him.

"Mr. Freeman, pray see the crew are gathered up in the bow, under guard. Foster, Bellows, take a look through the wee ship, see there's none others lurking about. But take a care now, firelocks at the ready. I'll be down in the great cabin with the good master here, examining his books to see he's not a smuggler or some such."

"Smuggler?" the captain sputtered. "Damn your eyes, you..."

"Ah, I'm sure the Lord will damn me in good time," McGinty said, still smiling, as sincere as ever, "but as to you, I'd suggest your shut your bloody gob, unless you want to be sitting in God's judgment a moment, hence. My famous patience is quite near tapped out."

For a moment they just looked at one another, the merchant captain and self-appointed captain of a privateer. Then the merchantman turned on his heel and led the way up to the quarterdeck, then down the scuttle to the small great cabin aft.

The cabin was what McGinty guessed it would be: a room twenty feet side to side and fifteen feet fore-and-aft, with an expanse of windows across the stern that looked out to the west. When the ship rose on the seas, McGinty could catch a glimpse of the shoreline off on the horizon and he realized the chase had brought them nearer to the coast than he had thought. That was not good. Sea-room was his friend, just then.

A large desk, more of a table with drawers, took up much of the deck space, with a small sleeping cabin to starboard and a chest of drawers to larboard lashed to the side of the ship.

"We'll have all your papers, my good sir," McGinty said. "Manifest, bill of lading, whatever you will."

Once again the master hesitated, feeling the need to offer some bit of resistance to every demand, to save face if nothing else. McGinty understood that, and he let him have it. Finally, the master opened a drawer in the desk and pulled out several notebooks and sheets of paper and dropped them grudgingly on the desk.

McGinty picked up the first of them, the ship's logbook by the look of it. He flipped it open. *Brig Hopefleet, Jas Finch, Master*, he read at the top of the page. Cleared out of Portsmouth six weeks before, bound, as McGinty had guessed, for the Delaware Bay. He thumbed through a few pages of the log and then set it aside. He rummaged among the other papers until he found what he most wished to see; the cargo manifest. He held it up to the light coming in through the stern windows.

Jesus, Mary and Joseph... he thought as his eyes ran down the columns of neat writing. *It's not a bloody prize, it's a gift from God Himself.*

What he had captured was not a merchantman. It was an ordnance brig. She was not carrying the salt pork and barrel staves and bolts of canvas he had been expecting. She was carrying barrels of gunpowder and crates of muskets and bayonets and casks of flints and uniforms and naval ordnance, gun carriages, and rammers and sponges. It was a cargo of great value to the British army, of extraordinary value to the Continental Army. It was something that the former very much did not wish the latter to have, and, conversely, something the latter was desperate to acquire.

McGinty heard a footstep on the ladder and he startled as if he had been caught doing something he should not be doing, which in fact he was. He looked up as Corporal Freeman climbed down from the deck above, then stepped onto the deck of the cabin, and ran his eyes over the small space. He glanced over McGinty's shoulder at the manifest, then looked over at Captain Finch, who was glaring at the two of them.

"You," Freeman said to the master. "Get up on deck. Stand right by that hatch there, where I can see you. My men have orders to shoot you if you say one damned word to anyone."

Once again the master gave a moment of silent insubordination before stepping onto the ladder and climbing up to the deck. Freeman kept his eyes on the man until he was topside again but still visible from down below.

"Well?" Freeman said in a soft voice, too low for Finch to hear.

"It's manna from heaven, boy-o," McGinty said. He held up the cargo manifest and pointed to item after item. "Look here," he said. "And here, and here."

Freeman nodded his head as he ran his eyes down the list. He looked up at last. "This is piracy, you know."

"Piracy? We've made a prize of one of our enemy's ships. There's a war on, you understand. I'm surprised you ain't heard about it."

"War's one thing. Even I know you can't just go sailing around and taking prizes, no commission, no license, no bond, nothing."

McGinty waved his hand, dismissing such trivialities. "Paperwork, red tape, it don't hardly matter if we do all that nonsense before or after the fact."

"Think you can make this all legal-like? Before they hang the bunch of us as pirates?"

"They're going to hang us all as deserters anyway, so what does it matter?"

"We ain't deserters," Freeman said. "We were caught behind the lines and we escaped."

"And didn't try too bloody hard to get back to the army now, did we? You explain to General bloody Washington how we aren't deserters. And him loving to string a man up, to make an example."

Freeman was silent. He looked down at the manifest, and then up again. "We can't take this...prize, if you want to call it that, into any port. Not without the papers that say you're a legitimate privateer. They'd put us in jail directly. And that's if we're lucky."

"Ah, that's where you're wrong, Mr. Freeman!" McGinty said. "If the brig was carrying firewood, say, or salt cod, I'd say you're right, to be sure. But this cargo? An ordnance vessel? You think there's any prize court in the service of the Continental Congress that's going to refuse this ship? And what, give her back to Lord Howe? Don't be daft, man. If we go back to the army empty-handed, we hang as deserters. We go back with this beauty in tow, we're heroes. And rich men as well."

Freemen fell silent again, but McGinty could almost hear the wheels spinning in his head as he considered the argument. The corporal could be a hard one to read, but this time McGinty had a pretty good idea of which direction the man would go. It was generally easier, McGinty found, to convince someone of something when that something was true, and what McGinty had said was indeed true. Any Continental prize court would be willing to overlook a host of irregularities in order to keep a prize such as the one they had.

"Very well, you feel so sure of all this," Freeman said, "where do we take it?"

"Annapolis, in Maryland, would be our main chance, I'm thinking," McGinty said. He had been considering this question since they had first absconded with *Sparrowhawk*, knowing it would become an issue of the first importance if his plans for privateering played out.

"Why there?" Freeman asked. McGinty could hear the suspicion in his voice.

"Less chance of running into a British cruiser to the south of here than to the north," McGinty explained. "And down in Maryland, they're not a bunch of tight-fisted, Puritan old women. More likely to see the sense of ignoring such trivial concerns as commissions and such."

Freeman nodded, considering that. "Maryland's a fair distance off," he said. "We can sail this here prize, and *Sparrowhawk*, that far? With the men we got?"

McGinty had been thinking about that as well. Privateers generally carried big crews, in large part so they would have men to spare to bring their prizes into port. And those crews tended to be the cream of the sailor crop, thanks to the privateers' good pay and easy discipline.

Sparrowhawk, however, was barely able to sail with the men she had, and now they had an even larger vessel as prize to contend with, and prisoners as well. They would have to sail both ships hundreds of miles through seas patrolled by the British Navy.

McGinty let his broad, ingratiating smile spread over his face. "Ah, we'll have no problem at all bringing this little brig to market, have no fear, boy-o!" he said. "You know you can trust your sainted Angus McGinty."

Chapter Four

Virginia Biddlecomb was smiling despite the discomfort, the irritation, and the pain. It was not a genuine smile, more like a grimace she imagined, but it was the best she could manage. As a rule she did not like to let any discomfort show, be it physical or emotional, but with Susan standing there, scrutinizing her, she was particularly adamant on that point.

The family's sitting room, toward the back of the first floor, was quite warm, even on that chilly early-November day. Nonetheless, Mrs. Temperance Williams, widow, matriarch of the household, had ordered Nelly, the servant girl, to stoke up the fire in the fireplace. And when the girl had failed to do so to Mrs. Williams' satisfaction, Mrs. Williams had been brushed aside so that she could attend to it herself.

"Honestly, girl, do you want to freeze Mrs. Biddlecomb and her dear baby to death?" Mrs. Williams asked. Virginia could see nothing of her hostess save for the petticoats draped over her ample backside as she bent over the fire, her stout body framed by the blue and white Delft tiles that surrounded the fireplace.

"No, ma'am," Nelly said dutifully.

If you build that fire up any more, you're like to roast Mrs. Biddlecomb and her dear baby alive, Virginia thought, but she knew better than to say as much, or to even suggest, in less snide terms, that she was warm enough already. Such an observation would have been dismissed out of

33

hand, and followed up with a lengthy discourse on the proper temperature at which nursing mothers and their babes must be kept.

It had taken a while to acclimate herself to Mrs. Williams, her
household, and her daughter, Susan, but Virginia had made considerable
progress. She knew now, for instance, when to speak and when to keep
her mouth shut, and she was generally good about keeping her mouth
shut when necessary. For Virginia Biddlecomb, who tended toward
brash outspokenness, that was a steep hill to climb.

Virginia had been a guest for nearly a month now in the Williams'
lovely Philadelphia home, a four-story brick affair on Chestnut Street
between Fourth and Fifth. The Williams', formerly of Rhode Island,
were old family friends of Virginia's father, William Stanton, and her
late mother. Temperance Williams had stood as godmother to Virginia
at her christening, and her husband, Judge Joseph Williams, also now
deceased, as godfather.

The Williams' had moved to Philadelphia when Virginia was a
young child, but the families had always maintained their friendship.
When Virginia and Isaac had been married only a few blocks from the
Williams' home, Susan had acted as her bridesmaid. That, in truth, was
more the result of the family connection and the fact that Susan was the
only young woman Virginia knew in Philadelphia, and not because of
any mutual affection, of which there was precious little.

In early autumn of 1777 (which wags were calling the "Year of
the Hangman" thanks to the gallows-like appearance of the triple
sevens), Virginia and Isaac and baby Jack had set sail from Boston for
Philadelphia so that Isaac might take command of his ship, the new-built
frigate *Falmouth*. That was a voyage that had gone disastrously wrong,
and by the time Virginia had reached the city, escorted by Lt. Elisha
Faircloth, the British were already ensconced there. So Virginia had
made for the one place she knew she would be welcome for as long as
she wished to stay; the Williams' home. And there she remained, with
no idea of what she would do next, or how she would do it even if she
did think of something.

"There," Mrs. Williams said, satisfied at last with the height of
the flames and straightening with some difficulty. "Now you shall be

properly warm. You and that lovely little Jack. What a big boy! What a good, hungry boy!"

"Hungry, yes, he is," Virginia agreed. She had a blanket over her shoulder that covered the breast she had slipped out of her gown and Jack's head, which was the size of a twelve-pound cannonball, as Jack nursed with surprising vigor. For six months, Virginia had worn maternity gowns, sew from what seemed to her acres of fabric. Now she wore dresses that allowed her baby to easily reach his sustenance. She wondered if any of the gowns she had once worn, before her pregnancy, seemingly a lifetime ago, would still fit her.

The nursing had not come easy, and it was still not terribly easy. At first, Virginia was left sore and chapped by Jack's efforts, but that had improved in time. Now it was just occasional pain from engorgement, occasional back pain from holding the young man, stiffness from sitting, and nursing for hours on end that were a part of her daily routine.

That general discomfort was exacerbated by Mrs. Williams's chasing her around the house and stoking up the fire in whatever place Virginia found herself. No sooner would Virginia manage to find an unoccupied room still at a bearable temperature than in would come Mrs. Williams to toss cordwood on the flames to prevent imminent frostbite to mother and child.

Virginia had tried remaining in her own bed chambers, the one room in which she was safe, but if she remained sequestered there for too long, Mrs. Williams would come knocking, concerned about her health and well-being. Nor did Virginia feel it proper to hide from her hostess, so she endured the heat and forced a smile on her face.

"Come now, Virginia, dear," Susan said, her argument having been interrupted by the crisis over the fireplace. "You still haven't given me a good reason for being so backward."

Virginia sighed. Susan was standing in the doorway that opened out onto the main hallway but now she sailed across the room and sat in the armchair across from Virginia. She settled with a great flourish of silk and lace and wisps of blonde hair artfully escaping from under her mob cap, as if to say that she would not be leaving until she was satisfied.

35

"Dear Susan, I'm hardly in any state to be seen out of doors," Virginia said.

"Well certainly, not now," Susan countered. "But there's no reason you couldn't pretty yourself up. I'm sure you have some gowns that will fit you still, and if not we could have them let out a bit. Virginia, you're still a very lovely girl, you know."

Virginia smiled wider, hiding the fact that she was clenching her teeth. *You're still a very lovely girl, you know...* she thought, the words playing in her mind in a sing-song tone. At first, she had wondered if Susan said such things because she was a bitch, or if she was simply an idiot, and obtuse, but she had since realized that the girl was not obtuse at all.

"You're very kind to say so, Susan," Virginia said. "But I don't think I'm quite up to it."

The British occupation of Philadelphia, it seemed, had put no damper of the social life of the city. Anyone who had been part of the Continental government, or was a known and notorious rebel, had cleared out before Howe's men had come marching in. Of those left behind, the rougher sort still frequented the taverns and brothels, and if they did so in company with British soldiers and sailors, they were happy enough for the hard money their new friends had in their pockets.

The conquest had not deprived the elite of the city of amusements, either. Elegant afternoon teas, lavish balls, theater, it still went on, just as before. More lively than before, actually, with the addition of the hand-some and worldly young officers in their red and blue uniforms. Much of apolitical Philadelphia was taken with the sophisticated gentlemen from across the sea, and none more than the young, unmarried women of the city.

Among those was Susan Williams, who could play the part of a chaste maiden as well as any actor in the city's Southwark Theatre could play Desdemona, or Charlotte in *The West Indian*. Susan was anything but chaste, Virginia knew (and Faircloth had learned, to his delight), but she looked the part, with her demure face, flawless white skin and pink cheeks, the thin tapered waist and the great tumble of blond hair barely contained by her white linen cap.

Susan's father had been a well-respected judge who remained largely neutral in the growing conflict, and that meant that both Mrs. Williams and her daughter were not suspected of rebel leanings. Not that it would have mattered to the randy young officers in town. If Susan Williams had been caught manning the ramparts at Fort Mifflin, musket in hand, they would not have cared. Men were willing to overlook a great deal when it came to women who looked like Susan.

"Captain Cornwall will be calling again this afternoon," Susan said, "and he has a friend whom he's told about you, and the gentleman is very eager to make your acquaintance."

"I'm a married woman. You do recall that, Susan, do you not?"

"Oh, poo," Susan said. "You don't even know where your husband is."

Virginia sighed. *Stupid or cruel, which is she?* she wondered. It was certainly true that Virginia did not know where her husband was. She had not seen him for a month, not since she had made Elisha Faircloth bring her back to Isaac's ship so that she could apologize for the stupid fight she had picked with him, a fight that had sprung from her own fears of his going in harm's way.

They had made love in the tiny great cabin of the odd little galley Isaac was commanding. And that was the last she had seen or heard of him. When she lay in bed at night, with Jack gently breathing beside her, she replayed that scene in her mind, over and over—the only comfort she was able to find.

"I'm sorry, Virginia, my dear," Susan continued, perhaps realizing she had gone too far at last. "I know you're worried about Isaac. We all are. I just fear it's doing you no good, just sitting here and brooding. Sure having something to distract you would help. I'm certain Captain Biddlecomb would not want you sitting here with the blue devils."

"Captain Biddlecomb," Mrs. Williams said with a snort. "I'm sure I don't know what that young gentleman was thinking, bringing his wife and newborn babe into the middle of a war!"

It was hardly the first time the woman had expressed that opinion. The first half dozen times Virginia had pointed out that there had been no fighting around Philadelphia when they set out from Boston, that they had sailed in the company of two powerful privateers, and that she, Virginia, would not have tolerated being left behind in any event. But she soon learned that those arguments were less effective than simply not responding at all, since they only invited further arguments, so she remained silent and continued to smile.

"I'm not so sure these gentlemen will wish to meet me," Virginia said. "I'm hardly a Loyalist, or even neutral in my politics. And my husband has made himself one of the King's great enemies. Do they know that?"

"Of course not!" Susan said. "I told them your husband is a ship's captain, no more. I'm sure they assume he commands a merchantman of some sort, because I'd be a fool to mention it otherwise."

"Indeed you would," Virginia agreed.

"That blue gown you have, the one that sets off your eyes so beautifully!" Susan said, changing the subject with renewed enthusiasm. "I'm sure that would fit you famously. And we'll do your hair up the way you like it."

Virginia did not reply. She did not know how to reply, because she did not find Susan's suggestion so terribly awful, and that surprised her. She had always been trim and athletic, an excellent equestrian, a woman used to catching the notice of men. Being pregnant had made her feel like lumbering, ungainly a cow. She had grown heartily tired of it. And now she felt bloated and frumpy and about as vibrant and youthful as Mrs. Temperance Williams, thirty years her senior. And Susan's presence, pert and pretty Susan, did not help.

The thought of dressing up in nice clothing, doing her hair in some flattering manner, had its appeal.

"These gentlemen, they are just coming to call?" Virginia asked.

"Yes, that's it. Though there may be a ball in town tonight, I don't recall, exactly."

"Oh, Susan!" Mrs. Williams said. "Virginia can't go to a ball! And little Jack wanting to nurse on the hour, or near enough."

Virginia felt a little wave of disappointment. Of course, Mrs. Williams was right. Her baby seemed to want to nurse on a near continuous basis. She could hardly leave him for the evening.

"We could certainly get a wet nurse in," Susan protested. "Nelly, you know of a wet nurse available, don't you?"

"Yes, ma'am," Nelly said. "And she lives not more than two blocks away."

"Susan, don't be silly," Mrs. Williams said. "It's hardly the thing, for Virginia to be running all over the city."

"But the gentlemen will be so terribly disappointed," Susan said with a pout.

"I'm sorry to disappoint, but my situation just won't allow for such an evening," Virginia said.

"On the other hand, "Mrs. Williams said, "it would certainly do you some good to get out of this house, even at the risk of catching your death." It was very like her to argue the opposite of what she had just said a moment before, but Virginia had grown used to that as well.

"Oh, wonderful!" Susan said, apparently considering it settled. "Nelly, run and fetch the wet nurse! Virginia, come above stairs with me! We've quite a job ahead of us, getting you ready for this evening!"

It did take several hours, and all of Virginia's patience, which was far from endless, to accomplish the transformation. Susan insisted on helping with every aspect, and would not be dissuaded, try as Virginia might. Virginia was at least able to bathe in peace once the wet nurse arrived, the most luxurious moment she had experienced in some time.

Dressing was what Virginia dreaded most, and what she most wished to do in private. It had been a little less than a year since she had last donned any of her pre-pregnancy wardrobe. She had no notion of how the old clothing would fit now, but she was not optimistic, and she did not care to have Susan watching her squirm into a gown that fit like a sausage casing, if it fit at all. But Susan insisted, in the guise of being helpful, and since Virginia also did not want to admit to her concerns, she endured the help.

In the end, it was not nearly as bad as she feared. The blue gown, the one that set off her eyes, slid over her shift with little resistance, settling on her hips, and with the lacings eased off a bit enveloped her waist in such a way that she could still breathe with relative ease.

"Oh, that's wonderful!" Susan said, clapping with delight. "You fill that out so nicely, far better than you did before!"

Virginia smiled.

They moved on to Virginia's hair, and even Virginia had to admit to Susan's skill in that regard. She devoted well over an hour to the task, piling Virginia's thick, chestnut locks up on her head in a series of elegant swirls with wisps hanging just so, and adorned them with dried flowers and strategically placed pins.

She'll make me look pretty, but she'll take care I'm not prettier than she is, Virginia thought, watching in the mirror as Susan did her work. If there was one thing Susan would not tolerate if she did not have to, it was the presence of a woman more beautiful than herself.

Well, she couldn't make me more pretty than her even if she tried, Virginia thought next, studying her face in the glass. Susan was five years older than she was, but Virginia had spent far more time out of doors, riding, sailing in boats and ships, or just walking in the country. She had been through battles and she had had a baby. All of that, it seemed to her, was written on her skin, molded on her frame.

Susan took a step back, hands spread as if revealing a masterpiece. "There!" she said. "Done! You are the most beautiful woman in all of Philadelphia! I shall be envious of you all night!"

If that was true, you sure as hell wouldn't have said it, Virginia thought as she considered the result of Susan's efforts. And once again, she was surprised. Susan had done a good job. The dress, the make-up, the hair, it had all been done with skill and subtlety. Virginia smiled. A genuine smile.

"Thank you, dear Susan, it's wonderful," she said. And she meant it. For the first time in a long time, she felt a bit like the way she used to feel, when she was still the object of the young men's desires. Despite the damage she had inflicted on herself over the course of her two decades, she was still pretty. She could see that.

Susan was still straightening up when they heard a knock on the door from the floor below. The girls' eyes met, and Susan gave Virginia a conspiratorial raise of the eyebrows. They heard footsteps coming up the long staircase and Nelly knocked on the door and opened it.

"Beg pardon, ma'am, but the gentlemen are here," she said.

"Very good," Susan said. "Pray, seat them in the drawing room and tell them we'll be down directly."

Nelly nodded and disappeared. Susan sighed and seated herself in the chair opposite Virginia. For a moment they remained like that, sitting in silence. At length, Virginia spoke.

"Should we not go below stairs?" she asked. "And greet these fellows?"

"Oh, what a country girl you are!" Susan said with delight. "They must be made to wait at least half an hour!"

"They must?"

"Of course, they must! They can't for a moment think we're here at their beck and call. The less interested we are in them, the more interested they'll be in us."

"I see," Virginia said. "Mind you, I have no wish for any man's interest, save my husband's. This is an evening's diversion, no more, which I'm doing because you asked it of me. Pray, don't forget I'm married."

"I won't forget," Susan said. She gave Virginia her coy smile. "If you don't."

They passed the requisite half-hour in conversation punctuated with stretches of silence, and finally Susan stood and announced it was time to go below stairs.

"Virginia, dear," she said as they straightened their gowns, "I've known you...nearly all my life. And I know you can be...shall I say, headstrong? But I trust you'll be gracious to our visitors. For my sake, and mother's, if nothing else."

"Certainly I'll be gracious, I try always to be gracious," Virginia said, and thought *headstrong?* She had just been chastising herself for feeling nervous at the prospect of meeting this young gentleman from England, for worrying that she would stumble over her words and come off the Yankee Doodle bumpkin. For fearing that she had completely lost the ability to make civilized and intelligent conversation.

I wish I was headstrong, and not some blabbering fool, Virginia thought.

They left the room and walked and down the long, carpeted staircase, with Susan taking the lead. She turned left in the foyer and stepped into the drawing room with Virginia on her heels. The two gentlemen were standing near the fireplace and they turned as the women swept in and smiles spread over their faces.

Virginia took them in quickly, her eyes flicking from feet to faces. They were both somewhat above average height, lean and athletic-looking. In their mid-twenties, she guessed, with hair thick and long and tied back in queues. One had dark hair and an almost swarthy complexion to match, the other was fairer, with light brown hair that probably turned blonde in the summer's sun. Their faces were handsome, but with none of the softness of men who sat in offices. Rather they had the look of campaigners in the field. The sight of them made Virginia sick.

It was the uniforms. She had understood from the first mention that these men were officers of the British army. That was no surprise. But somehow in all the consideration of whether or not to socialize with them, she had lost sight of what that really meant.

But the uniforms—the rich, red regimental coats with their white facings and glinting buttons, the white waistcoats and breeches, the red sashes tied around waists, the swords hanging jauntily from polished leather belts—gave Virginia a visceral reaction that she did not expect, and one she was certain she failed to hide.

"Ah, Susan, as beautiful as ever, and that is very beautiful indeed!" said the fairer of the two, stepping up and taking Susan's hands in his. "Well worth the hour or two you made us wait!"

"You beast, it was nothing like an hour," Susan said, looking the man up and down. "And I should hope I'm worth it." She released his hands and turned to Virginia. "Gentlemen, allow me to present my oldest and dearest friend in all the world, Virginia Biddlecomb!"

The two made shallow bows. Virginia bowed as well and said, "*Mrs.* Virginia Biddlecomb."

The officers nodded and one said, "A pleasure to meet you, Mrs. Biddlecomb," and the other, "Delighted, Mrs. Biddlecomb," but Virginia was not sure who had said what, and they seemed to have no reaction to the addition of the title *Mrs.*

"Virginia, dear," Susan continued, "allow me to present Captain Nicholas Cornwall of the 17th Regiment of Foot, and Captain Richard Dexter, also of the 17th."

"My pleasure, gentlemen." Virginia said the words with no thought behind them. She wondered if either man would try to touch her, kiss her hand, or some such. She wondered what she would do if they did. She had no idea.

"So, Virginia, as I said, there is a fabulous ball being held at the Newsome house," Susan continued. "Not to be missed for worlds...and the captains have been so kind as to ask if they can escort us there."

Virginia felt the uncertainty take hold, the hesitancy that had been driven off right up until she had seen the uniforms.

"Oh, Susan, I'm not certain I'm quite up to this..." she said.

"Oh, come along, Virginia, you know it will do you good to get out of this dreary house," Susan said. "And the captains have a coach and four waiting for us. It would be terribly rude for us to refuse them, after all the trouble they've gone to."

Trouble? Virginia thought. *More trouble for the poor sod whose coach and four they commandeered.*

"Mrs. Biddlecomb?" the dark-haired one, Captain Richard Dexter, also of the 17th, spoke. "Forgive me. I certainly understand how dreadfully tedious these things can be. I'm no great fan of balls and such myself. And I assure you, Captain Cornwall and myself would be in no way insulted if you were to beg off. I probably would myself, were I able to."

His voice was soft, softer than Virginia would have guessed it would be, his tone gentle and sincere, and the sincerity worked strangely on her. It made her suspicious, put her on guard, but it put her at ease as well, like wind and current coming from opposite quarters.

She looked into his face, into his eyes. She knew that what she saw there would tip the balance. It would tell her if his sincerity was to be believed or dismissed. His eyes were dark, but there was a kindness in them, and they seemed slightly expectant, with no sign of arrogance or wile.

"Thank you, sir," Virginia said. "I would be honored, were you to escort us this evening."

CHAPTER FIVE

Isaac Biddlecomb and the men of *Falmouth* were harvesting rocks when Colonel Richard Somers of the Gloucester County Militia came riding up. They had been at it for several days. *Falmouth* needed an ungodly number of things: guns and gun carriages, powder, shot, masts and spars, food, water, bedding, paint, tar, cordage, all of the many tons of stores and equipment that went into a man-of-war, virtually none of which were to be had on the sparsely populated New Jersey coast.

She also needed ballast. And that, at least, could be found.

But, as it happened, not easily. The sandy soil of New Jersey's southern coast did not yield the abundance of rocks that could be found in, say, New England, and Biddlecomb and his men had to drive their two rented wagons inland to gather stones that could be sent down into *Falmouth*'s hold. They unearthed what they could find and loaded the stones into the wagons until the axles were groaning, then drove them back to the pier. There they loaded the stones into nets and swayed them down into the hold to be distributed along either side of the keelson.

It was tiring work, backbreaking and tedious. And it was all but pointless in light of everything else the ship lacked. But it was something that had to be done, and it was one of the few things they could do, so Biddlecomb set them doing it.

He joined in himself. He knew there would be grumbling no matter what, but there would be less if the captain took part, hefting his share of stones, wielding shovel and pick with the rest. Nor was there much else for him to do. *Falmouth* had no orders and no means of carrying them out if she did, and thus the running of the ship did not place huge demands on her captain's time.

His evenings were spent writing letter after letter to whomever he thought might do his men and his ship some good: the Marine Committee of the Continental Congress, the Continental Navy Board of the Eastern Department, the Continental Navy Board of the Middle Department, John Adams, Stephen Hopkins, William Stanton. In the morning each letter would be sent off in the care of whatever courier Somers could dragoon into the task.

Captain Biddlecomb did not write to George Washington. He did not bother. He had it on good authority that the commander-in-chief had a pretty low opinion of the worth of Continental frigates, and would just as soon see them scuttled or burned than lavish valuable resources on them.

He did write to his wife, Virginia, a single, ongoing letter that for some time he did not bother to finish because he had no means of getting it to her in occupied Philadelphia. It was not until a week after their arrival at Great Egg Harbor that Somers mentioned he knew a man who had family in Philadelphia and was thus able to enter the city, and was willing to bring Isaac's personal correspondence with him. Isaac dashed off a closing paragraph, signed it with love, sealed it, and sent it off.

Writing was done by candlelight; daytime was for hefting stones. Isaac was bending at the waist, lifting a chunk of granite the size of a small dog, a stone just at the edge of what he could manage, when he saw Somers approaching. He staggered over to the wagon and dropped the rock in the bed with a great thud, then wiped his hands on the old slop trousers he was wearing. He arched his back and groaned despite himself.

He was not entirely certain why he was groaning. It might have been for the numerous aches that throbbed in various parts of his body, or it might have been in anticipation of the latest disaster that Somers was about to deliver. Still, he was happy to pause in his labors to hear what Somers had to say, grim as that was likely to be. Biddlecomb was at least a decade older than most of the men working under his command and he was feeling every one of those years.

The Colonel of militia arrived almost daily with intelligence concerning this or that, and it rarely improved Biddlecomb's mood. Neither Somers nor any of the militia nor anyone at Great Egg Harbor wanted *Falmouth* there. They would not say it outright, lest they be accused of a want of patriotism, but they were not too subtle in their hints.

Biddlecomb waved at Somers as he approached and was surprised to see that the man was smiling. That, and his upright posture, and the quick pace at which he rode, suggested that, for once, there was good news, something he was actually eager to report. Isaac allowed himself to indulge in the possibilities: they had found a hundred men to fill out *Falmouth*'s crew; they had located a battery of eighteen-pounders to mount on the ship; they had found a shipyard with masts and spars suitable for the frigate, which were even then being hauled by a team of oxen to Great Egg Harbor.

"Captain Biddlecomb!" Somers shouted as he reined up and slid down from his horse. "I come with great news! Great news!"

Biddlecomb felt himself smile as he approached the man. "We could use some, colonel," he said. "Pray, what is it?"

"Gentleman Johnny Burgoyne! He's surrendered! Surrendered his whole damned army to General Gates. Just south of Lake George, a place called Saratoga."

"Oh..." Biddlecomb said. This took him by surprise, so much so that he was not quite sure what it meant. "Burgoyne...?"

"General Burgoyne?" Somers said. "Come down from Canada in the spring, took Ticonderoga? You heard how he got beat up in Bennington, I have no doubt, him and his German butchers. Well, now it's over for him. Surrendered his whole army."

"I see," Biddlecomb said. "That's excellent news."

"Excellent doesn't hardly describe it," Somers said.

"So, what does it mean?" Biddlecomb asked. "As far as the war and such?"

"Oh," Somers said, and paused to consider the question. "Well, I guess we won't know that for a while. It'll depend on how they take it in London, I suppose. Maybe they'll lose heart, and decide the Yankee Doodles are not like to be beat. Or maybe it'll convince the French we're going to win this thing, and they'll join in the fight. All sorts of things might happen."

"I see," Biddlecomb said again. Great as the news was in terms of the grand strategic vision, it made no difference at all to his current situation. And that situation was not so grand at all.

"So," Somers asked, "do you reckon Rumstick and them others will be back soon?"

"That I could not say," Biddlecomb said. "If they've met with luck, then yes." Biddlecomb had sent Rumstick and a dozen men inland to see if they could find a few trees suitable for masts or spars. If they could get just one more lower mast, or a couple of topmasts, it would make a very big difference in their ability to get underway.

Somers nodded. He was always interested in anything that would get the *Falmouth* out of Egg Harbor quicker. What's more, Rumstick had taken with him all the oxen and suitable carts that Great Egg Harbor could provide, and Somers did not tire of telling Biddlecomb what a hardship that was.

"I debated about sending those men off, you understand," Biddlecomb continued. "But I reckoned it was my best choice, because, as I said, it'll get us out to sea quicker. If they're successful. But it also slows us down here. We can't get underway until we're properly ballasted, especially not if we have more of the rig in."

"Uh huh," Somers said, nodding. He knew where Isaac was going with this.

"If we had more hands, maybe some of your militia, it would certainly help get this done all the faster," Biddlecomb continued.

"I have no doubt," Somers said. "But most of my men, they have families. Farms that need work, or they're fishermen, and out on the water. And, of course, now there's another problem," he added, and with that his tone changed for the worse.

Of course there is, Biddlecomb thought. It was too much to hope that Somers might show up bearing nothing but good news, even if that good news had nothing to do with *Falmouth*'s circumstance.

"And what's the problem now, Colonel?" Biddlecomb asked.

"It's that son of a whore Barnett. *Colonel* Shadrach Barnett."

"Barnett?" Biddlecomb said. "I thought he was gone."

Somers had predicted that Barnett and his men would leave after their encounter on the pier. He guessed the banditti would lose interest in the possibility of taking the ship after seeing how tough a nut *Falmouth* would be to crack, with a hard and well-armed crew and a contingent of marines who may have been few in number but were still formidable with their training, discipline, and long bayonets.

And he had been right. Once the ersatz colonel and his men had roused themselves the following morning they had left town, all but a handful who seemed to prefer the comfort of the tavern. But apparently that departure was not permanent, and Barnett was not done with them.

"He's back," Somers said. "And worse yet, he's got more men with him, and it seems there's more coming in. These Pine Robbers, they're mostly small gangs. A dozen men at most. But your ship, captain, it's drawing them like moths to a flame, and they're following this Barnett son of a bitch. They've all but filled the tavern. Ugly bunch."

"Damn his eyes!" Biddlecomb said. He thought he was done with that problem, but here it was again, another shovel-full on top of his ever-growing dung heap of problems. "What, by God, does he wants with *Falmouth*. There's not a damned thing aboard her of any particular value. Rigging, sails, that's about it. God knows I have no hard money."

"It's pretty clear he doesn't think so," Somers said. "Maybe you should have let him go aboard, see for himself, like he wanted when he first came here." The suggestion was largely rhetorical, but there was also a note of hope in the man's voice, as if this might be an easy and bloodless way out of this situation.

"Maybe," Biddlecomb said. "But I doubt it would solve anything at this point." Whether it would do any good or not Biddlecomb could not guess, nor did he bother considering the question. There was no chance he would let that son of a whore Barnett come aboard his ship. It was a matter of principle now.

The ship's too tempting, Biddlecomb thought as the two men stood in silence. *Falmouth* was unlike anything that was ever seen in a place like Great Egg Harbor. A massive ship, brand-new and vulnerable, its contents unknown, it was irresistible to the likes of Barnett. He would absolutely feel the need to possess it, and would not worry about how it might profit him until after it was in his hands.

Biddlecomb understood that, but he did not give voice to those thoughts: they would have just been oil on the flames of Somers' desire to see the ship gone. Rather, he said, "Might I count on you and your men to offer the ship some protection? And perhaps some help in fetching and loading ballast?"

"Yes, well, I'm sure there's some help we can offer," Somers said. "I can detail what men I can."

Biddlecomb did not push him further. He could not endure more talk of how the men of the local militia had farms to attend to, families to care for.

God forbid you actually take part in this war, Biddlecomb thought. He himself had not even had a home for the past three years and had spent less time with his wife and son that Somers had with his livestock. And there were plenty of fighting men who had it much worse. Plenty who would never draw another breath, including young David Weatherspoon, buried just a few miles from where they stood.

He did not think Somers was wanting for courage. He was not afraid of a fight. That Isaac would have found intolerable, and were it the case, he would have been more insistent that the man put himself and his troops in harm's way. No, Somers was not a coward. He just did not want to be bothered.

"Whatever help you can muster, Colonel, will be most appreciated," Biddlecomb said.

"Of course," Somers said. "And what of you? What will you do, now that Barnett's back?" There was that hopeful note again, the possibility that Biddlecomb and his ship might leave Great Egg Harbor.

Biddlecomb had been wondering that himself. Leaving was not a consideration, but another thought did come to him. It was not a terribly helpful thought, but it was a thought nonetheless.

"I guess I'll go talk to the man," he said.

"You're certain this is the wisest course?"

Lieutenant Faircloth was seated at the big table in *Falmouth*'s great cabin, a glass of brandy in hand, his posture relaxed. Faircloth looked relaxed, always at ease, wherever he was and in whatever circumstance. It was uncanny. Biddlecomb had often marveled at it, and wondered if it was a facade or if the man really was so genuinely untroubled.

He's bloody rich, no wife, no child, and in command of a full nine men. No wonder he's untroubled, Biddlecomb thought, but he made himself push such unkind notions aside. Faircloth might have been born under a lucky star, but he was also by nature bold and unflinching in the face of danger, as loyal and generous as any man could be. It was thanks to Faircloth that they were both enjoying that excellent brandy. Not only would Biddlecomb not have been able to afford it, he would not even have known how it could be had.

"No, indeed, I am not certain," Biddlecomb said. He was in his shirtsleeves, looking in a mirror, scrubbing away the last of the rock-harvesting dirt. "But here's the thing of it. We must see how many men Barnett has, and what sort they are. That'll give us a notion of how much of a fight we might have on our hands. And we can't have that bastard thinking we're cowering aboard the ship, do you see?"

"I do see," said Faircloth. "So, right into the lions' den, is it? Shall I have my marines turned out? We could make a damned nice show of it."

"I think not," Biddlecomb said. He remembered the last time Faircloth had made a show of it. Barnett had been something less than awed. And if Barnett's numbers had indeed swelled, as Somers said, then he would be even more underwhelmed by the marines.

"We're not trying to provoke a fight here," Biddlecomb continued. "Just the opposite, in fact. But I'm afraid that the presence of the marines might make things…tense."

"Of course," Faircloth said. "So who then will you bring on this daring mission?"

Biddlecomb turned, looked at Faircloth, and took a sip of his brandy. "I had hoped you would go with me," he said.

"Of course, I'm with you!" Faircloth said. "I had taken that as a given, my dear sir. I meant who else."

Biddlecomb shrugged. "Barnett is like to have a score of men. Maybe more. Two score, perhaps. So you and I alone should be enough."

Faircloth sported a wide mustache on his upper lip, more in the style of the Hessian mercenaries than American or British man-at-arms, and he was proud of it. Now Biddlecomb could see the mustache spreading side to side as Faircloth grinned.

"You and I should be more than enough," he agreed.

They considered pistols, they considered swords, but in the end, they decided to go unarmed. There was no chance that they would prevail in a fight, so it seemed pointless to bring weapons and possibly provoke one. Likewise, they decided that it would be civilian dress, not uniforms. Faircloth was disappointed by that decision, Biddlecomb knew—he loved his bottle-green regimentals—but gentleman that he was he said nothing.

They donned heavy coats, the night being cold, and Biddlecomb instructed Mr. Gerrish to take command of the ship. Gerrish protested, of course, protested about their going and then about his not going. But the midshipman knew his captain well, and he pushed the argument right to the point where Biddlecomb was starting the grow annoyed, and no then further.

This was one of the few times when Biddlecomb was glad that Rumstick was not aboard—the first officer would not have stopped short as Gerrish had, and he certainly would not have been left behind.

It was a mile or so over a half-frozen dirt road to the heart of Great Egg Harbor, and light enough from the quarter moon that they did not need a lantern to navigate. The town itself consisted of a smattering of buildings: a few houses, a small church, a blacksmith shop, and a dry goods store that was also a chandlery of sorts.

Most of the village, washed in the dull moonlight, was barely visible as they approached. But the big, three-story public house was brilliantly lit, the windows blazing from the massive fireplace in the common room and the numerous lanterns hung about, enough light that one might have thought the tavern was on fire. Even from a fair distance off Biddlecomb and Faircloth could see the crowd of men in the big room. They seemed to have the casual, unhurried manner of folks who set down their cares as they lifted their tankards.

They stepped through a gate with twin pineapples carved on the top of the posts and made their way up the narrow path, past a garden of raised beds filled with brown, twisted stalks. They paused at the big front door and exchanged smiles, a quick acknowledgment of the madness of what they were doing, then Biddlecomb swung the door open.

He had been in that particular tavern a dozen times at least, during his current stay in Great Egg Harbor and back when he drove *Charlemagne* ashore on the nearby barrier island, but he had never seen it like this. There were dozens of men in there, crowded at the tables, gathered in clusters around the room, standing near the bar. The air was dense with smoke, which hung like morning fog in the room and swirled and danced in the light of the fire. The cumulative noise of the crowd, raucous and well into their cups, was as thick and heavy and nearly impenetrable as the smoke.

Colonel Shadrach Barnett was seated at a table near the center of the common room, the biggest table there, and him at the head of it. The rest of the table was taken up by his men—Biddlecomb recognized the one Barnett had called "Sergeant Wilcox"—and the surface was strewn with platters, tankards, bowls, knives, and the debris of a meal inelegantly eaten.

Faircloth took the lead, pushing his way through the room, making his apologies with all the grace that that crowd warranted and no more, Biddlecomb following in his wake. Heads turned as they moved toward the bar, conversations dropped away. Biddlecomb's eyes were on Barnett, who looked up as he became aware that something was acting.

The quick run of expressions across Barnett's face nearly made Biddlecomb laugh. There was confusion at first, then recognition, then surprise, then anger, all in the time it took Biddlecomb to advance three steps. Then all of that went away, and Barnett forced a blank look on his face as he watched Biddlecomb cross the room.

He and Faircloth reached the dark-red painted bar and Faircloth called for the tavern keeper to bring them ale.

"This fellow's doing a good business," Faircloth said, loud enough to be heard over the noise and nodding toward the tavern keeper who was filling their tankards.

"As good as he'd do in six months of normal trade, I'd wager," Biddlecomb said. "At least he must be happy we're in town, and the custom we're bringing him, even if no one else is."

"The doxies above stairs are happy too, I should think. They have to be making their fortune as well," Faircloth said and Biddlecomb regarded him with a raised eyebrow.

"Not that I know about doxies above stairs," Faircloth insisted. "Just what I hear from some of my boys."

"Captain Biddlecomb!" Barnett called, his voice loud and jovial, cutting through the sound of the drunken men, which was building in volume once again. Biddlecomb turned to see the colonel on his feet and pushing his way through the crowd, a touch unsteady but still moving with authority, his way unimpeded as the others in the room moved quickly out of his path.

So this is how he wishes to play it, Biddlecomb though. *So be it.* He took up the tankard the tavern keeper had set on the bar and took a deep drink as he watched Barnett cross the room toward them.

"Colonel Barnett," he said once Barnett was close enough that he could speak without raising his voice overmuch. "A pleasure to see you again, sir. Pray, allow me to present Lt. Elisha Faircloth. I don't believe you had the pleasure, when last you visited my ship."

"Don't believe I did," Barnett said, his voice sounding like a shovel in wet gravel. He nodded at Faircloth and his eyes flicked up and down the two men, fast as a snake. They had unbuttoned their great coats on entering the tavern and the absence of weapons did not go unnoticed.

"I'll own I'm a bit surprised to see you here, captain," Barnett continued.

"Why is that, Colonel?" Faircloth asked, with just the right amount of faux curiosity in the question, just the right touch of irony in the word *colonel*, enough that Biddlecomb heard it but Barnett, through the noise and the rum, did not.

"No reason," Barnett said. "Just don't seem like the sort of place for a man of your breeding."

"Good enough for a colonel from George Washington's headquarters," Biddlecomb pointed out, nodding toward Barnett. "But pray, what brings you back? I had thought you had learned enough. You know, to make your report."

Barnett's expression darkened somewhat, his patience with that game wearing thin, his native wit faltering. "We're not done here, captain. Not done," he said. He looked slowly and meaningfully around the room, at the abundance of men. "Come back to finish it up."

"I see," Biddlecomb said, nodding. "Well, best of luck with that." He turned away from Barnett, leaned on the bar, and took a long drink from his tankard, and Faircloth did likewise. He waited for Barnett to leave, though he knew with certainty he would not. Barnett would not tolerate Biddlecomb's having the last word. He would not tolerate Biddlecomb's turning his back on him.

"Say, *Captain*, I give you high marks for courage, coming in here like this," Barnett said at last. "Maybe not for intelligence, mind, but for courage? Sure. Even if you did try to sneak in, leaving the fancy uniforms back on your ship. You and the toy soldier here."

Biddlecomb took another drink from his tankard. He did not turn around and he did not reply. A second passed, then another, then Barnett clapped a hand on Biddlecomb's shoulder and pulled, half spinning him around. The half-full tankard jerked sideways and with just a little assistance from Biddlecomb, a wave of ale hit Barnett square in the chest.

Barnett looked down at the ale and then up at Biddlecomb, and Biddlecomb could see the controlled rage boiling just under the surface. They looked at one another, unflinching, unblinking, as if each was holding a lit match, each waiting for the other to light the gunpowder that would blow the tavern to bits.

And then Barnett smiled. And then he laughed. "Clumsy, clumsy!" he shouted. "Both of us, clumsy, clumsy! We keep this up, there might be trouble."

He turned and addressed the common room. "Boys!" he shouted. "We have here a genuine captain of the navy of these united states! And I say we give him a big cheer! And the marine as well!"

The others, the banditti, half-drunk or more, fired up, eagerly took up Barnett's suggestion, shouting and raising tankards.

"Hip, hip..." Barnett shouted.

"Huzzah!" the crowd replied, tankards raised even higher. Biddlecomb watched the men as they cheered: young men, old men, dirty and rough-hewn. Fighting men, but men who fought for themselves, for their fellows, for the scraps they lived on, and the hope of riches. Half of them, it seemed to Biddlecomb, did not know if Barnett's cheer was supposed to be sincere or ironic, and they did not seem to care.

"Hip, hip..."

"Huzzah!"

"Hip, hip..."

"Huzzah!" they yelled again and the cheer broke down into random shouting, toasting, cussing, laughing.

"There, captain, a proper welcome!" Barnett said, smiling even wider now. "And I reckon it ain't the last you'll get from us!" He slapped Biddlecomb on the shoulder, nodded toward Faircloth, then turned his back and made his way back to the table, done with the officers of the navy of those united states.

"Well, that was damned friendly of them," Faircloth said, and unlike Barnett's men, Biddlecomb did not miss the irony in the words.

"Friendly, indeed," Biddlecomb said. He looked down into his empty tankard. They had managed to learn a few things, at least, in this ill-advised outing. They learned that they were indeed very outnumbered by some very bad men. They learned that Barnett had no intention of giving up until *Falmouth* was in his possession. And they learned that their situation was bleak, even bleaker that Biddlecomb had realized an hour before.

CHAPTER SIX

The two ships, the ersatz privateer and her prize, were sailing as fast and as well as could be hoped for, but that was not very fast, and it was not very well. McGinty's eyes were fixed on *Hopefleet*, that valuable prize. She was in *Sparrowhawk*'s wake and a cable-length astern. She had looked well enough a moment before, sailing full and bye under topsails, foresail, jib, and staysail. She had not been making nearly the speed she was capable of making in those conditions, but she had been moving fast enough.

But now she was not moving at all.

Angus McGinty was not the worrying type. He came by his calm naturally for the most part, though part of it was practiced as well. That aside, he was having a hard time remaining calm at that particular moment.

McGinty had tacked *Sparrowhawk*, nimble sloop that she was, turning her easily through the wind and settling her on a new course. His order to young Pip, now prize master of the ordnance brig, was to follow his lead, tack when he tacked, wear when he wore.

Pip had followed orders. At least, he had turned the brig up into the wind to put her about on the other tack. But he had mistimed the maneuver, keeping his headsails sheeted in too long and bracing his foresails around too early. The brig had failed to make the turn, and instead had stopped dead in irons with the sails aback and flogging.

Stupid, bloody stupid... McGinty thought. Part of that thought was directed at Pip, but mostly it was directed at himself. There was only so much that he could expect from the young man, whose entire sea-going experience had been as an ordinary seaman aboard a fishing schooner for a few seasons. He was hardly old enough to shave, probably still a virgin, and certainly was in no position to take command of a ship such and *Hopefleet*. But he was the best McGinty had.

Don't bloody tack, bloody wear ship you bloody fool, McGinty admonished himself. Pip had only tacked *Hopefleet* because he himself had tacked *Sparrowhawk*. If he had worn *Sparrowhawk* around, turning her stern through the wind, a slower maneuver but one that would not result in the ship being in irons, then Pip would have followed suit. And her sails would not be all a'hooy now.

"Humph. Damn poor show," said James Finch, former master of the *Hopefleet* brig. His tone was mostly critical, with a touch of amusement, and it put McGinty more on edge than any other sound on earth could at that moment.

Shut your bloody gob, or by God I'll be right up your arse with a belaying pin, boy-o, and never doubt it, McGinty thought. But rather than voicing that thought he smiled and said, "Ah, the lad's doing his best. Not easy, being in command of a vessel such as that. You should know, boy-o, you were in command of one yourself once." He looked Finch straight in the eye, smiled wider and added, "Once."

"Humph," Finch said and looked away.

McGinty did not care to have Finch onboard, but he wanted even less to have him aboard his former command, *Hopefleet*, getting up to the Lord knew what mischief. The man's presence was only one of many, many things that McGinty did not currently like, but found himself forced to endure.

He had been aware of the problem from the start: he could barely man one ship, how was he going to man two? The solution was to simply forego the value of the captured ship itself, off-load the cargo of any prize he took and then send the empty bottom on its way. Or so he thought.

He abandoned that idea as soon he read *Hopefleet*'s bill of lading. There was far too much aboard the brig than he could ever stow down aboard his little sloop, and every bit of it was too valuable to leave behind. So instead he went with his only other option, which was to find some way to sail two ships with a crew of greenhorns who could barely sail one.

"You want me to shut this bastard's mouth for you, Sergeant?" Bobby Ireland asked, nodding toward the still-fuming Finch. He was stationed aft with his musket loaded and a brace of pistols in his belt.

"No, let him bleat away," McGinty said. "Makes no never mind."

"'Sergeant?'" Finch said. "I thought you were supposed to be a captain, or so you said. Why do they call you, 'sergeant?'"

"You're a curious bugger, I'll say that," McGinty said, which was all the answer he would give the old man. "But see here," he added, "let me know if the chill's too much for you on deck. I'll be happy to have you stowed down in the hold." And that was all the warning he intended to give.

Sergeant... McGinty thought. These dumb bastard soldiers...boys... could never get it through their heads to call him 'captain'. He had given up trying, and he supposed it did not really matter. There was no one he needed to impress with a fancy rank or title.

He looked aloft where two of the ordnance brig's former crew, now *Sparrowhawk*'s crew, were laid out on the main yard, overhauling the buntlines. They had been pressed into service aboard the American sloop since the only possible means McGinty had of sailing both ships was to keep the men who knew what they were doing at their duties.

There had been fifteen men aboard the brig: a dozen foremast jacks along with the master, Finch, and two mates. The master and mates McGinty took aboard *Sparrowhawk* where he could keep an eye on them. He gave them their liberty on deck in exchange for a promise that they would not get into any mischief. It was foolish, he knew—he should have put them below in chains—but he could not bring himself to do it.

Among the foremast jacks, there had been two whose looks McGinty did not like. They seemed too self-assured, too confident. The sort who might lead the others in mutiny. Those two he took aboard *Sparrowhawk* as well and made them sit in the bow and speak to no one.

The rest of the crew he divided between *Sparrowhawk* and *Hopefleet*. He assured them they would not be made prisoners of war if they cooperated, a promise he really had no business making, and it was not clear the degree to which they believed him. He also left Freeman and five others of his former soldiers aboard *Hopefleet*, in part to help sail the ship, but more as armed guards to watch over the old crew, a task for which they were more suited.

McGinty looked astern once more, at the clumsy, uncoordinated way that the men aboard *Sparrowhawk* were backing the headsails to get the ship's bow to turn.

Treacherous bastards, he thought. McGinty was pretty sure *Hopefleet* had missed stays because her people had purposely made a hash of the maneuver.

Merchant crews tended to be small, but they tended to be prime seamen as well, since any sailor would take the merchant service over the navy if he had a choice. Only privateers had an easier time than merchantmen in filling out the ship's company. The five able-bodied mariners and the few landsmen aboard the ordnance brig should have been able to tack the vessel in those conditions with never a problem, even without orders from the quarterdeck.

Bloody silent insubordination…McGinty thought. He knew it well, that sullen lack of cooperation, nothing blatant, something that could be written off as a mistake or misunderstanding. He had seen it often enough on shipboard and in the army. He had been guilty of it himself, more than once. It was always amusing to trigger an officer's fury and yet give him nothing on which to pin his wrath. He was certain that that was what the British seamen aboard *Hopefleet* were doing now.

They kept at it moment more, a display of seemingly incompetent sail handling, and then *Hopefleet*'s bow began to turn and her sails began to fill once again.

"As I said," Captain Finch began, "if you put me back aboard…"

McGinty shot him a look that had not a trace of his Irish good cheer in it, and Finch shut his mouth and looked away. The man had made that suggestion several times: that he be put back aboard *Hopefleet* to take command and he would sail in company with *Sparrowhawk*, wherever

McGinty wished. McGinty had batted the suggestion away with a joke before, but he was done humoring the man.

Bloody British bastard, thinks an Irishman's dumb enough to fall for that...

He looked out over the starboard side. He could see a dark line low on the horizon, the coast of New Jersey. Or Delaware. He was not entirely certain. Angus McGinty was a good mariner but an indifferent navigator at best. His duties on shipboard had never included such lofty responsibility, and all he knew of the subject was what he had gleaned from overhearing the officers on the various ships he had sailed aboard, and what he had been told during tricks at the helm.

Ideally, he would have left the coast well below the horizon, stood out to sea, made a wide swing to the east before turning back toward Maryland. It would have given them the best chance of avoiding British cruisers. But he did not dare. He would have no idea when to change course and sail west again. Better to keep the shore in sight, make southing, and then stop some fishing boats to get their position. McGinty, like most men, did not care to ask for directions, but sometimes there was nothing for it.

He looked over at Finch. He had considered making the former master navigate, but he would have no way of knowing whether the old man was playing him false. Nor did he care to admit to his own ignorance. He felt the frustration building like steam in a pot.

You'll be a bloody rich man when this is done, boy-o, bloody rich, McGinty told himself, as he often did. It was good motivation when he found himself sinking under the weight of his myriad troubles.

And so far, at least, we haven't...

"Here, McGinty!" Foster shouted down from the crosstrees. "I see a ship out there!"

...seen another ship... McGinty completed his thought.

McGinty looked across the deck. Finch was looking at him, the first hints of a smirk on his face, but when he saw McGinty's expression, he wiped it off and looked away. McGinty looked up at the crosstrees above. Foster was standing there, one arm wrapped around the topmast shroud, and pointing to the northeast, almost directly astern, where *Hopefleet* was sailing in their wake.

He doesn't mean the bloody prize is what he sees, does he? McGinty wondered, but he was sure that would be too stupid even for this bunch of landlubbing farmers.

"How far off?" McGinty called.

"Three, four miles!" Foster called down. "I can just barely see it, and just when we go up on a wave!"

Bloody, bloody hell... McGinty thought. Once again there was no one aboard who could actually tell him what he needed to know. Foster wouldn't know a ship from a schooner from a damned herring gull. Any of the merchant sailors from *Hopefleet* could have given a proper report, but McGinty did not trust any of them. He sighed and snatched the telescope out of the binnacle and headed for the weather shrouds.

Five minutes later he was aloft, standing beside Foster, looking in the direction the man was pointing and trying to let his breathing settle.

"There! You see it there?" Foster asked.

"Aye, I see it now," McGinty said as *Sparrowhawk* rose on the sea and the flash of gray became visible in the distance. He extended the telescope and trained it in the direction of the distant ship, now lost from sight, and waited for the ship to rise again. A moment later it appeared in the lens and hung there for a moment as the long ocean swells lifted the two vessels at the same time.

Ship... McGinty thought. He could see the three masts, the topsails set on each, and lowers and t'gan'sls on the fore and main. Not massive, not a British two-decker or some such, but not tiny, either. Too far off to see if she sported gunports or seemed to be a man-of-war. Too far off to see any flag that she might be flying.

"Well, damn my eyes..." McGinty muttered. At least this strange ship was not chasing them. She was sailing a more southerly course than *Sparrowhawk* and *Hopefleet*.

"Well, sergeant, what do you reckon?" Foster asked.

"Ah, most likely a merchantman, bound for Bermuda, or the islands," McGinty said. Did he himself believe that? He was not sure. Either way, there was nothing he could do but alter course a bit to the west, open up the distance, and hope this whore's son took no notice of them.

"Take a look here, Foster," McGinty said, handing the man the telescope. He waited as Foster found the ship in the lens, not an easy thing to do while standing high on a swaying mast. "Do you see it, now?"

"Yes...yes, I do," Foster said.

"Well, fix her in your mind, how she looks, the sails she has set and such. If anything changes, if she puts up more sail or takes some down, let me know. If the shape of her seems to change it likely means she's changed course, so let me know that as well."

"Aye, sergeant, I'll do that," Foster said, nodding as he continued staring through the glass.

"Good lad," McGinty said. He swung outboard on the topmast shrouds and reached down with his toe to find the ratlines below. He stepped down onto the lower shrouds and headed down toward the deck.

He had not made it halfway down before Foster called, "Sergeant! I reckon he's changed course, by the looks of it."

Ah, bloody, bloody hell! McGinty thought, as he paused in his descent, sighed, and climbed back aloft once more.

McGinty's last hope was that Foster was mistaken, or, if the ship had altered course, it had altered course away from *Sparrowhawk* and *Hopefleet*. But neither was the case. Once McGinty was back on the crosstrees, once he had the distant ship fixed in the lens of the telescope, he saw that Foster was indeed correct, the ship had altered course, and she had altered course such at that she was making directly for his little squadron.

Bloody, bloody hell! he thought.

If she was coming in pursuit, then she had to be one of four flavors of ship: British Navy, Continental Navy, or privateer, British or American. That was it. There was no other sort of ship that would go out of its way to pursue two strange vessels.

McGinty considered these things, and what they implied, as he climbed down from aloft and walked slowly aft, looking back in their wake, past *Hopefleet* and out toward the place where the distant ship was now hidden by the horizon.

If it was a British man-of-war or privateer, then capture meant losing everything, becoming prisoners of war and a slow death aboard the prison hulks. If she was Continental Navy or an American privateer, it meant losing everything and hanging for either desertion or piracy. A prize court might be willing to overlook the extra-legal capture of the ordnance brig in order to get their hands on her contents, but a man-of-war would not. Quite the opposite. If McGinty and his men were found to have taken *Hopefleet* illegally, then she would become the prize of her new captors, and *Sparrowhawk* as well.

Bloody, bloody hell, he thought.

He looked up at the sun, just visible through the thin overcast of clouds. They were approaching the first dogwatch: it would be full dark in just a few hours. That would help, to be sure.

In the best of worlds, he would wait until dark and then drastically alter course, and send word for *Hopefleet* to follow suit. But it was not the best of worlds and he did not believe young Pip and his questionable crew would be able to keep on station, and once separated, they would never find one another again.

He could heave to instead, take all his men off *Hopefleet*, restore *Hopefleet*'s crew to their rightful vessel, and sail off, hoping this strange sail would not pursue them. But he was not willing to abandon the fortune that *Hopefleet* represented, not that easily. Success, he knew, did not come without risk, and he was willing to risk a lot for the fortune the brig represented.

Set more sail, perhaps? he wondered. He looked aloft. The sloop would bear the small t'gan's'l they could set from the deck, but that was about all the extra canvas they had to spread. He had no way to tell Pip to set more sail, nor did he know if he would be able to. It might be just another opportunity for his surly crew of prisoners to muck things up.

"The sails don't bloody matter," he said out loud. The other vessel was ship-rigged, longer on the waterline, faster than either *Sparrowhawk* or *Hopefleet*. Setting more sail would just delay her overtaking them by an hour or so, no more. There was nothing they could do but keep on the way they were and hope that the ship in their wake lost them or abandoned the chase in the night.

The five sailors formerly of *Hopefleet* were clustered on the starboard side, near the base of the mainmast, and McGinty did not like that. It would not do to have private gatherings such as that, even if they were not able to talk to their former officers aft, or the two possible trouble-makers who were under guard in the bow.

"You there, the lads from the brig!" he shouted forward and the five turned and looked aft. McGinty scrutinized their faces for looks of guilt but found none. "Clew up the main course and the topsail! Bellows, Ireland, bear a hand with that."

The men moved to the lines but none of them with any great turn of speed, the British sailors because they did not want to, the Americans because they did not know what to do. But soon enough the two square sails were hauled up like curtains to their respective yards. The speed came off *Sparrowhawk* and *Hopefleet* came surging up alongside.

"Set the topsail! Set the course!" McGinty called, once the ships were nearly side by side, and the sails came down again and the two ships plowed along together. McGinty took up a speaking trumpet and called to Pip across the stretch of water between them. He instructed him to see that all lights aboard *Hopefleet* were extinguished, save for a single light in the bow, shining forward. He told him to follow in *Sparrowhawk*'s wake and a couple of cable-lengths astern, as best as he could in the dark. He told him *Sparrowhawk* would show a light astern, just for a second at every turn of the glass. It was the most he dared do.

He did not tell Pip about the ship astern. He did not need his men to worry, or the British sailors to get any ideas. Their chances of avoiding capture were not great, even without interference from the prisoners.

For some time, the two ships continued within hailing distance, but slowly *Sparrowhawk*, the quicker of the two, began to draw ahead, until at last she was a few cable lengths ahead and McGinty ordered the main course clewed up again.

The first dogwatch came to an end as the sun dropped down toward the western shore, a gray and ugly day lapsing into a dark and tense night. The men of the second dogwatch, British sailors and American soldiers, took the deck. McGinty sent Finch and his two mates and the two troublemaker foremast jacks below and had them locked in the first officer's cabin. They would be cheek to jowl there but at least they would be out of his hair, and unable to cause any trouble.

He himself fetched his heavy coat and a thick scarf he had found aboard *Sparrowhawk* and a pair of gloves he had liberated from Captain Finch and took his place on the quarterdeck. He knew he would not be sleeping that night. It did not even occur to him to try.

He looked at the compass, lit by a candle in the binnacle box. He looked aloft but could not see even a hint of the sails. Still, the wind was steady out of the southwest, blowing twelve to fifteen knots he reckoned, and if it remained that way, the sailing would not be terribly taxing. It was the first bit of luck he had encountered since taking *Hopefleet*.

Lucky, was it, taking that cursed brig? he mused. *Hopefleet* might make his fortune or spell his doom. It was too early to know which one it would be, but he knew he might find out in the next few hours.

He spent the rest of the second dogwatch standing by the helmsman, making certain he maintained the proper heading, that he did not overcorrect when the sloop's bow began to turn one way or the other. At the start of the following dogwatch he took the tiller himself, since it was easier than constantly supervising.

At midnight, the watch changed again, and since the wind had held steady and McGinty did not think there would be a need for sail handling, he ordered one of the British sailors to come aft and take a trick at the helm. It was a relief to step away from the tiller, to lean against the bulwark for a moment. The motion of the ship, the feel of the wind on his face, was enough to tell him if the helmsman was keeping a true course, and he knew that he was.

He walked back to the taffrail and looked astern. *Hopefleet*'s bow light was just visible in their wake, swinging up and down and side to side as the ship pitched and rolled. McGinty took hold of the shutter on the lantern mounted on *Sparrowhawk*'s transom and flipped it open, counted to five, then shut it again. If the unknown ship was still behind them, they would not see *Hopefleet*'s light shining forward, but they could possibly see *Sparrowhawk*'s light shining aft, and that McGinty wished to avoid.

They plowed on through the night, the glass turning on the half-hour, McGinty flashing the light astern so that Pip could follow in his wake. The watches changing after eight turns of the glass and the wind held steady and McGinty found another of the British sailors to take the helm. He stared out toward the west, looking for any sign of land, any warning that they were standing into danger, but he could see nothing. The cloud cover that had been with them all day blotted out stars and moon. They were driving on through a great void, with only the motion of the ship and the creak of the rigging and hull to give any hint that they were moving at all.

The middle watch ended, the morning watch was well underway and McGinty was leaning against the bulwark when he felt the warmth and comfort spread over him like a thick blanket. He embraced the sensation, let it smother him, felt himself sinking under the weight. And then his body jerked and he startled awake.

No one had seen him drift off, it seemed, and he was glad of that. He stood upright and arched his back and looked around. It was still night, still dark, but he thought he could detect the darkness lifting just a bit, the complete blackness yielding to something less complete.

About bloody time, he thought. He turned his gaze outboard and made a slow scan of the dark, looking for whatever he might see out there in the night, but he could see nothing, which was exactly what he wanted to see. He looked astern. *Hopefleet*'s faithful little bow light was still bobbing away behind them.

He looked forward. *Sparrowhawk*'s main course had been clewed up to prevent the sloop running away from the brig, and now the sail was no longer blocking McGinty's view in that direction. But there was nothing to see there either, nothing but blackness. And then a flash of light.

Oh, what the hell? McGinty thought. It was just the briefest of flashes, like a lantern opened for a second, or a flint hitting steel. Almost nothing. But too low down to be a star peeking through the clouds, or some such.

Eyes are playing tricks, boy-o, McGinty thought. It was common enough at sea; strange lights or other things that fooled the eye. McGinty knew better than to think that one tiny flash of light meant anything at all. He assured himself that it was nothing. But he did not believe it.

And he was right, right to not believe it. Because as the darkness began to recede McGinty became more and more certain that there was something out there in the night, something off the larboard bow. Now and again he was certain he could hear the sound of a sail slapping or masts creaking or water on a hull that was not *Sparrowhawk*'s. The more he peered into the dark, and the more the dawn approached, the more certain he was.

Then Bobby Ireland called out from forward. "Sergeant, I think I see a ship or some damned thing, right out there!" And that was followed by a host of other voices, all calling their agreement. And then, from out beyond the larboard bow, appeared the unmistakable form of a ship under sail, half-seen in the predawn light.

It was another half-hour before they could make out any details, but slowly the strange vessel revealed itself. Ship-rigged, about eighty feet on deck. Ten gunports on her starboard side that they could see, each open and the guns run out. She was no more than a couple hundred yards away, sailing a course parallel to *Sparrowhawk* and *Hopefleet*. She must have overtaken them in the dark, and once she did, the light on *Hopefleet*'s bow would have made it easy enough for her to keep on station, just as *Sparrowhawk* had.

The three ships continued on for some time more, sailing their southeasterly heading. No one on *Sparrowhawk*'s deck spoke or even moved. Rather, they remained fixed where they were, staring at the mysterious vessel emerging from the dark. There was a flag flying from the peak of her gaff. It was difficult to discern at first, but as the light gathered they could make it out at last.

"Continental flag, boys!" Bellows shouted and that was met by a general cheering along the deck. It was still too dark to see the stars in the blue canton but there was no mistaking the canton itself and the red and white stripes. It was the flag that the Continental Congress had decided on half a year earlier.

Dumb bastards, McGinty thought, but, of course, they would see it as a relief that this ship belonged to their countrymen, and not bloody Black Dick Howe. None of them, save Freeman, understood the danger that an American ship-of-war presented. And maybe these men would not be found responsible for the illicit privateering. After all, it was McGinty who had been in charge, and had assured them all that what they were doing was perfectly legal.

It was quite possible that McGinty alone would be hanged for piracy. The rest would be acquitted of that charge. And then hanged as deserters. It was their lucky day.

CHAPTER SEVEN

There were only a few times in her life that Virginia had consumed enough wine to be what one might consider intoxicated. But she knew the feeling, and she felt that way now—head spinning, slightly sick, slightly confused, somewhat remorseful, and also very much not. This, despite the fact that she had not consumed a drop of alcohol. She had not even reached the ball where she might be offered such a thing.

She was seated in the coach and four, an elegant vehicle driven by a somber Black man who wore a heavy wool coat over what appeared to be fine livery. Its interior was heated to a comfortable temperature by the foot warmers on the floor, and it moved easily over the half-frozen, rutted roads of Philadelphia, its fine suspension tossing the occupants gently about.

Virginia did not know from whom the British officers had borrowed the vehicle, or how voluntary the loan might have been, but she was sure she would have known the name of the owner if it was mentioned. There were only a handful of people in Philadelphia with money enough for such a coach, and Virginia had met them all at some point or other.

When Virginia had accepted Captain Richard Dexter's invitation to the ball, the gentleman had smiled at her—nothing gaudy, triumphant or over-eager—and inclined his head by way of acknowledgment. Susan had squealed with delight. That, in turn, led to another twenty minutes of preparation before leaving the house.

Virginia and Susan went off to fetch their cloaks and gloves and hats, which took all of five minutes. That done, Susan insisted that they remain in the family room for another quarter of an hour while the officers waited for them.

"Absence makes the heart grow fonder, my dear Virginia," Susan explained, "And waiting makes the young gentlemen so very much more eager."

"I suggest the young gentlemen not get overly eager where I am concerned," Virginia said. "I'm doing this as a diversion, and a favor to you, nothing more. I'm a married woman, you'll recall."

"Of course, I recall," Susan said. "You never tire of reminding me. But it all seems so very tedious, marriage and babies and such."

Once the requisite time had passed, the officers were freed from the purgatory of the sitting room and Captains Dexter and Cornwall were allowed to escort the women down the granite steps to the brick sidewalk that fronted the house and up into the coach, which they did with European grace and chivalry. The four of them settled into their seats and Cornwall thumped the roof and with a lurch the coach was underway, iron-bound wheels grinding over the hard dirt.

Virginia tried to bring the reality into focus, like twisting the tube of a telescope. But like someone with too much drink in her stomach, she could not make it sharp, could not keep it all from spinning.

What in hell am I doing? she wondered. But the question was disingenuous. She knew perfectly well what she was doing, why she was there.

Her husband had gone off to fight his war and left her and her baby to the smothering ministrations of Mrs. Temperance Williams and the constant goading of her daughter and it made Virginia angry and resentful. Her baby son (whom she loved desperately, she assured herself) seemed to want to nurse nearly continuously, and cry or puke when he was not, and, despite herself, she felt angry and resentful about that as well.

Once she had been on fire for the cause of the Revolution but now that had all changed, her priorities and values had been turned upside down, and it seemed as if there was nothing solid under her. She had felt young and beautiful not so long ago and now she felt none of those things. Susan's occasional half-hearted reassurances notwithstanding, she felt like a fishmonger's wife; fat, frumpy, and old.

And then Captain Dexter had shown her that genuine smile, a gentleman's courtesy.

She sighed and her head spun and she wanted to puke just like little Jack. Vomit had become such a regular part of her day that she was quite indifferent to his tossing up on her gowns. She wondered if Cornwall, seated across from her, would feel the same if she heaved on his uniform.

"This is my first visit to Philadelphia, I'll own, and I find the city a delight," Captain Cornwall said, breaking into Virginia's reverie and smiling at her and Susan.

"You'd have been welcome at any time," Virginia said, her tone more biting than she intended. "You need not have brought an army with you." The words were out of her mouth before she could check them, though she was not sure she would have done so in any event.

"Virginia!" Susan said but Captain Dexter laughed out loud.

"Quite right, Mrs. Biddlecomb, quite right!" he said. "Though I fear our invitation to visit the City of Brotherly Love was lost in the post. I never received mine, at any rate."

Virginia smiled, despite herself. A clever riposte, and not a hint of offense at her words. She turned toward him so he could see her smile, see that she could take it as well as hand it out. Captain Dexter smiled back at her, that same disarming half-grin. And then she wanted to puke once again.

That damned uniform, she thought. *That hateful red uniform.* Every time Captain Dexter made her feel just a bit of her old self, the uniform was like a slap across the face.

What in hell am I doing?

They rolled on through the city, the red brick buildings and sidewalks lit with the streetlights that stood like sentries along the road. They spoke of the city and the people who lived there and the architecture and how it compared (favorably) to many cities in England. They did not talk about the declaration that had been drafted blocks away, or the Continental Navy that had sprung to life on the city's waterfront or the Congress that had fled just ahead of Lord Howe's approach.

Virginia joined in, tentatively at first, but then with more enthusiasm as the talk built in tempo. Dexter was a droll and witty man, Cornwall nearly so, and Susan much more clever than she generally let on. Virginia enjoyed the repartee, enough that she was soon able to look at the men's faces and not their regimental coats. She felt the whirling in her head settle, the upheavals in her stomach subside.

After some time, the coach came to a swaying stop outside a three-story brick home not unlike that of Mrs. Williams. A streetlamp spread light over the brick sidewalk and the two servants who stood waiting; one to open the door and hand the occupants down and the other to set a portable step on the ground for their convenience.

Captain Cornwall was first on his feet and out the door, brushing the servant aside so that he might hand the women down. He reached up and took Susan's hand and in a most solicitous manner helped her to the sidewalk.

He reached up for Virginia's hand next, but she hesitated, unsure that she wanted his help, certain that she did not need it. Various biting remarks flashed through her head, but she kept them to herself, with some effort, and took the proffered hand, stepping down onto the smooth brick.

Last, Captain Dexter stepped lightly from the carriage and gestured toward the house. They climbed the granite steps and went in through the big front door, held open for them by yet another servant. The entry of the Newsome house was brightly lit by a chandelier high overhead and numerous candles burning in sconces on the walls, and the warmth was striking after the cold November night.

There were half a dozen people seated in the sitting room to the right, and more ascending and descending the wide staircase that rose up from the main hallway: women in beautiful silk gowns, their hair piled elegantly on top of their heads, men in embroidered suites and brilliantly polished shoes and glinting silver buckles. More than a few wore the red coats of the British army, or the deep blue of the navy. From above stairs, they could hear to the sound of the musicians playing and the people dancing and the muted sound of a hundred different conversations.

"Oh, this is delightful!" Susan said as she yielded her cloak and hat to a servant girl who stood ready to collect them. "The Newsomes are famous for their balls, you know, Virginia! You will be ever so happy you came!"

"I have no doubt," Virginia said, but she failed to muster much enthusiasm. She had been warming to the whole thing during their ride in the carriage, but now she was less sure.

"Ladies, shall we go above stairs?" Dexter said, gesturing toward the staircase. "Ride to the sound of the guns, as it were?"

Susan took the lead, Virginia a half a step behind, and the two captains forming the rear guard as they climbed the carpeted staircase with its beautiful carved banister on the left and various portraits of Newsomes living and dead on the wall to the right. The top of the stairs opened onto a landing where more of Philadelphia's elite, at least those of a Loyalist or apolitical bent, mingled with the men of British arms.

At the far end of the landing, a door opened into what Virginia guessed was the ballroom. Through the crowd, she could see people in chairs along the wall and she could catch the occasional glimpse of the swirling dress or well-shod foot and silk stocking of those dancing. The warmth and the sound were double what they had been below stairs.

"Susan, may I please have the first dance?" Captain Cornwall asked with an exaggerated bow.

Susan gave him a curtsey and a coy sideways glance. "I'd be delighted, sir," she said and with that, Cornwall swept her off into the ballroom, leaving Virginia and Dexter alone among the crowd.

"I fear I am not much of a dancer," Dexter said, turning to Virginia. "But if you wish…" He gestured toward the ballroom where music had come to an end and the dancers were clapping their approval.

"I am not much of a dancer myself, Captain," Virginia said, though it was not true. She was an excellent dancer and loved to dance. But they were dancing minuets just then: complex, precise, and performed by each couple, in turn, in front of the entire ballroom. Virginia was woefully out of practice, having not danced at all for more than a year, and she felt awkward and clumsy as well. What's more, she was still wrestling with the fact that she was attending this ball with a man, and British officer no less, while her husband was…she did not know what he was doing, or where.

"That's a great relief to me, Mrs. Biddlecomb," Dexter said. He craned his neck to look into the room behind them to the right. "They seem to have refreshments in the other room, here," he said. "Would you care for something? We should make an effort to devour all of our host's most expensive offerings. They might think us rude otherwise."

Virginia smiled. "I'd be delighted," she said. Dexter took her by the elbow and guided her into the nearby room. She thought, as he reached for her, that she might recoil at his touch, she did not. In fact, she found something comforting in the firmness of his grip, the gentle pressure of his arm, as he directed her toward the door.

The room was crowded, as was all the Newsome home, but not as crowded as the ballroom or the landing, and they were able to find a free corner in which to stand while Dexter gathered a plate of pastries and two glasses of wine. He handed one of the glasses to Virginia and she took a sip. The wine was lovely, tart with just a hint of fruit.

"Do you ride, Mrs. Biddlecomb?" Dexter asked.

"Ride?" The question took Virginia by surprise. She was passionate about riding, about horses in general. She had been a fearless rider since her youth. It was one of the few places where she and Isaac differed. Isaac was the master of anything afloat, but he disliked horses.

"Yes, I do ride," Virginia said. "Why do you ask?"

Dexter shrugged, a disarming gesture. "People who ride…they have a way of moving. A sort of confidence, I guess. A certain grace. I can always tell."

Virginia smiled. "You ride as well, I take it?"

"Oh, yes!" Dexter brightened with the question. "Hunting, mostly. Back home. My father maintains a prodigious stable. I have a Cleveland Bay, which is a particular favorite. I raised her from birth, a magnificent hunter. Are you familiar with the breed?"

"I am not," Virginia said.

"Much like your thoroughbred, but stronger, in the long run. More tireless, I find, if one sees to their feeding properly."

And with that, the conversation sparked, like an ember dropping onto a train of powder. There was little Virginia enjoyed more than discussing horses, but it was rare indeed that she found anyone who could match her depth of knowledge, a knowledge born of passion, and all out of proportion to her years.

But Dexter was a worthy partner in equine discourse and seemed to have as much passion as she did for the subject. Even when they disagreed, which was seldom, she had to admit that his arguments were well-founded.

They drained their wine glasses and finished off the plate of pastries and Dexter replenished both and the conversation continued. Then Susan and Cornwall came stumbling into the room, flushed and glistening with perspiration and smiling, and Virginia wondered if they had been dancing this whole time, or if Susan had managed to find an empty bedchamber somewhere.

"Ah, Mrs. Biddlecomb!" Cornwall said, "I do hope my dear Dexter has not been boring you to tears with this and that."

"Not at all, sir. We've been discussing…horses."

"Ha!" Susan shouted with delight. "Of course you have! You are the only woman I know, Virginia, who would come to such an affair, with a handsome gentleman such as our Captain Dexter here, and discuss horses."

"It was my doing," Dexter said. "I broached the subject, and I dare say I'm glad I did. Mrs. Biddlecomb is among the most knowledgeable people I have ever met in that regard. It's been a delight to speak with her."

"Well, time for speaking is past, I think," Susan said. "I insist you dance the next dance, when the musicians are done with their respite."

Cornwall and Dexter went off to fetch more wine and returned with four brimming glasses. "A toast!" Dexter said, raising his glass, and Virginia felt herself tense, felt the good cheer teetering on the edge.

A toast to what? she wondered, bracing. *The King? Lord Howe?* This could all turn ugly fast.

"A toast to friendship," Dexter said. "Let us be united in that."

Virginia smiled and thought *I can drink to that, I suppose.* She raised her glass and knocked it against the others and listened to the dull ring it made.

They had all but drained their glasses, and Virginia was most certainly feeling the effects, when they heard the sounds of the musicians tuning up and making ready.

"Oh, come, let's dance this next, the four of us!" Susan said, and now Virginia found that she was ready to dance. Eager, even. The thought appealed to her.

"Captain Dexter, I don't wish to discomfit you…" she said, turning to Dexter.

"Not at all," he said. "If you can endure the humiliation of partnering with me, I would be delighted."

"Oh, come now, Richard!" Cornwall said, turning to Virginia. "My friend is a perfectly fine dancer, don't listen to his false modesty!"

"We'll let Mrs. Biddlecomb be the judge of that," Dexter said as the four of them moved from the sitting room like soldiers advancing in a square formation.

The ballroom was an elegant space, running the full width of the house, with ceilings twenty feet above the floor. The walls were painted a brilliant white and interspersed with windows surrounded by rich velvet draperies and massive canvases depicting idyllic country scenes. Four chandeliers hung at intervals down the length of the room, giving considerable light and adding to the warmth generated by the press of dancers. A marble fireplace, thankfully devoid of fire, took up the middle third of one wall.

The minuets were done, to Virginia's relief, and the simpler country dances starting, with couples lining up opposite one another on either side of the room. Captains Dexter and Cornwall took their place in the far line, shoulder to shoulder, facing Virginia and Susan across the floor. The musicians finished their tuning and fell silent. The men bowed and the women curtsied and the musicians began to play in earnest.

With the first steps of the dance, the butterflies that Virginia had suffered flew clean away. Her feet, her legs, her arms, knew what to do from many hours on the dance floor, and she took joy in the strength in her body and the elegance of the practiced steps as she moved toward the center of the room, hand outstretched.

And there was Captain Dexter, his hand outstretched as well. Her fingers lighted on the top of his and neither could resist smiling. With the first steps, Virginia could tell that Dexter was a skilled, experienced, and graceful dancer. They whirled around one another and again formed into lines, now on the opposite sides of the room from where they started. They paused for half a measure of music and then stepped to the center of the room once more, skirts swirling, shoes shuffling on the polished wood.

So unlike Isaac... Virginia thought. Her husband was a tolerable dancer, and he was willing to dance for her sake, but he was no great enthusiast. So many years on a ship's deck, and so few in a ballroom, had done little to hone his skills.

Once again she and Dexter whirled around one another, their arms crossed, their eyes locked. A wisp of hair was falling down over Dexter's forehead and his face wore that half-grin that was in no way unappealing. They came apart, arms outstretched, and Virginia spun around, feeling the silk of her dress lifting with the momentum.

Again they separated, moving to opposite sides of the room. Virginia could feel the smile on her face, the pleasure she found in this simple thing, this civilized thing, this bit of a life she had once enjoyed. She and Susan came side by side in the line, looking across the floor at the soldiers who had brought them.

Susan leaned close to Virginia and whispered, "I *promise* I won't tell Captain Biddlecomb what a fine time you're having!" The tone was playful but the words were like a sword-thrust in the gut. Virginia felt her good mood collapse, the pleasure drain away.

The girl to Virginia's right stepped toward the center of the room, and Susan to her left did the same, and Virginia moved with them, her feet stepping by rote, her mind and spirit no longer in the dance. She met Dexter midway. She laid her fingers on his extended hand and circled around him. She could see the change in her mood registered on his face.

They continued the dance, advancing down the room, Virginia's arms and legs moving flawlessly despite her lack of interest. Dexter moved beautifully as well, but the concern was evident on his face.

Then, finally, the music stopped, and Virginia curtsied again, and Dexter bowed.

"Forgive me, Mrs. Biddlecomb, but are you well?" Dexter asked and his concern seemed genuine. "You seemed to…I don't know…"

"Fine, sir, I'm fine, thank you," Virginia said, waving his concern away. "I think the wine has gotten to my head."

"Pray, come, let me find you a seat," Dexter said, gesturing toward the door that led out to the landing. Two of the chairs against the wall were unoccupied and Virginia settled in one, Dexter in the other.

"Might I get you something? Some water? A bite to eat?" Dexter asked.

"Water, please," Virginia said.

"Of course," Dexter said, springing to his feet and disappearing into the room where the refreshments were laid out. Virginia did not necessarily want water, but she wanted a moment to herself, and sending Dexter on an errand seemed the most expedient means of getting it.

"What in hell am I doing?" she asked herself, speaking out loud. She felt like a fool, trying to reclaim something long past. Play-acting that she was not a married woman, and a mother. Staging this silly drama in the company of a British army officer, of all things. She felt disloyal. A traitor.

Susan, damn you to hell, she thought, but she knew that Susan's wheedling was only in part to blame. And probably not the biggest part.

Dexter was back with a glass of water. He handed it to Virginia and sat beside her and Virginia dutifully took a sip.

"Thank you, Captain," she said.

"How do you feel?" he asked.

"Better, thank you," Virginia said. "Sitting helps."

"Good, good," Dexter said. For a moment, they sat in silence, staring at the floor. Just as it began to grow uncomfortable, Dexter spoke again.

"I can't tell you what a pleasure it is to be in so fine a house as this," Dexter said. "Cornwall and I are quartered in rooms above a hatter's shop. I had no notion of the horrid smells that a hatter's work creates."

"Indeed?" Virginia said, trying to sound interested. "Are there no better quarters for you?"

"For us, no," Dexter said, smiling. "Colonels and above are finding very agreeable quarters, but for such as us, no."

"And your men?"

"Well, it's worse for them. They're still bivouacked on the Northeast Square, the sorry buggers. We're searching out winter quarters, but little luck so far."

"I thought half the city ran off when your army arrived," Virginia said. "Aren't there quarters enough?"

"It might seem half the city ran off, but in truth they didn't," Dexter said. "The wealthier sort did, certainly, the ones who have no love for the king. But I don't think the common folks had the means to flee. And they're the ones in the homes we need for our men."

"I see," Virginia said, and she could feel the glow of a new thought coming to life. "You don't think your regiment will be called away? It would be nice to think I might have your company for some time more."

"Oh, I shouldn't think we're going anywhere soon," Dexter said. "We're attached to Fourth Brigade. At Germantown, we saw some bloody hard fighting…beg your pardon."

"Fear not," Virginia said. "I was raised around sailors, you know."

"Ha!" Dexter said, smiling. "Well, after Germantown, we were sent into the city, and I dare say we'll be here for the winter, at least. There's some talk of the Forty-Fourth Foot going off. A reconnaissance in force of some sort. But I'm not certain."

"A reconnaissance in force?" Virginia said with feigned confusion. "Whatever is that? Would they really send the poor fellows of this Forty-Forth off in such cold?"

"They might, indeed," Dexter said. "Lord Cornwallis, he's not so concerned for the men's comfort as you, I fear."

Virginia smiled as she listened to Dexter discourse on the possible movements of British troops in the country around Philadelphia. Men, she knew, loved to talk. And now, she realized, she could do her country some good by listening. And taking note.

CHAPTER EIGHT

Do something, just bloody do something, damn your eyes, McGinty thought. It was maddening, maddening in the extreme. For an hour and a half, since the first hint of dawn, the three ships had been sailing a parallel course, *Sparrowhawk* heading south by west with *Hopefleet* in her wake and the strange ship two cable lengths to weather.

The newcomer had not changed course or altered the set of his sails in any way. He just stood on, his ten guns jutting out from the gunports, ready to tear *Sparrowhawk* apart in a single broadside, if he so chose.

"Sergeant, what the devil are they about?" Foster called from the larboard rail where he and the rest of the ship's company were leaning and gawking out across the water. Their initial excitement at seeing the American flag had turned to confusion as the minutes rolled past and nothing seemed to happen.

"They're having their breakfast...writing love songs to sing us...how should I bloody know?" McGinty snapped. He, too, had run through the gamut of emotions, with more twists and turns than those of the men under his command who did not appreciate the precariousness of their position.

He had been furious at first with his ill-luck, to have a fortune within his grasp only to then have it snatched away. But that feeling had faded and the fear had set in as he began to truly appreciate that he was likely to lose a great deal more than a valuable cargo. Then the fear had turned to resolve as he reminded himself of the many tight places he had managed to wriggle out of over the years. And with that thought, he was suddenly eager to get to it, to grapple with these bastards in whatever way they meant to grapple, to match wits with the Yankee Doodles, which he did not figure would be much of a match at all.

But the captain of this ship seemed to be in no such hurry, and as the minutes crept by in their petty pace, McGinty found his resolve turning to frustration and anger. He looked aloft at the peak of *Sparrowhawk*'s gaff for what he knew was at least the fourth time. The Continental flag with its stars and stripes was flying there, the wind blowing it over to leeward making it clearly visible to the ship off their larboard side. That being the only Continental flag they had, *Hopefleet*, per McGinty's orders, was flying no flag at all.

Despite his wanting to appear cool in front of the men, McGinty was ready to start cursing out loud by the time the ship finally made a move: a slight turn to starboard and her yards here hauled around a bit and she turned on a heading more directly toward *Sparrowhawk*. Now their courses were converging, and the two of them would collide eventually if no one altered course again.

It did not come to that, however, because the stranger, when she was still two or three hundred feet away, turned back to her original course and hailed. McGinty heard the voice come over the water, amplified by a speaking trumpet: "What ship is that?"

He was ready for the answer because he had been turning it over in his head for the past hour or so, had been going down one rabbit hole after another, trying to find the passage that would lead him to freedom, at a bare minimum, and to possibly holding onto his prize as well.

"Continental sloop *Sparrowhawk!*" McGinty called back. "What ship are you?"

There was a pause before the answer came. "*Oliver Cromwell*, Connecticut State Navy!"

Connecticut State Navy? McGinty thought. He was only vaguely aware that states had navies, and he certainly did not think any of them had cruisers of this size.

Bloody far from home, aren't you? he thought next. But then he realized it might be a stroke of luck that this ship was part of a state navy, and not the Continental service. He wasn't entirely sure how it might work to his advantage, but he had an idea that it might.

He lifted his speaking trumpet, ready to make some haughty reply, to throw this state navy blockhead onto his beam-ends, but the master of *Oliver Cromwell* beat him to it.

"Where are you from, and where bound?" he called.

"We're late of the Delaware Bay, on Continental business," McGinty replied, conveying in his tone that men such as him did not have time to waste with the Connecticut State Navy. "If you wish to escort us, you're welcome, but otherwise pray don't hamper us!"

He lowered his speaking trumpet and waited for a reply, waited longer than he expected he would. There seemed to be some discussion going on aboard *Oliver Cromwell.* That was not good.

"What is the brig astern of you?" the voice called back.

"She is our prize. Continental business! We must make all haste!" McGinty called back.

Again there was a pause, with only the familiar sound of the creaking of the hull and rig and the slap of water to fill the air. McGinty could see the looks of confusion on the faces of his men, and the British sailors as well. They must have thought this would be a simple matter: a ship of a state navy meets a ship of the Continental Navy and her prize, they wave to one another and then everyone goes on their way. It's how McGinty felt it should play out. The only one who seemed to feel differently was this whore's son aboard *Oliver Cromwell.*

It was a minute or two before the master of *Cromwell* replied, and when he did, the words were exactly what McGinty did not wish to hear. "Heave to! Heave to, we mean to come aboard you!"

Damn you, you impertinent rascal, McGinty thought. He lifted the speaking trumpet to his lips. "I told you already, captain, we must make all haste! Not a moment to lose! Continental business of a most urgent nature!"

This time there was no hesitation in the reply. "Heave to immediately, or we'll fire into you!"

85

Damn... McGinty thought. *These bastards don't seem overly impressed by this 'Continental' horse shit. Maybe it's actually worse, them being Connecticut State Navy.* He looked around the deck, looked at *Hopefleet* in their wake, and then looked out to the shoreline to the west. He sighed.

"Hands to the braces!" he called. "Cast off them damned bowlines. Make ready to heave to!" There was nothing for it, he could see that.

Ten minutes later *Sparrowhawk* was stopped dead in the water, as was *Oliver Cromwell*, a hundred yards to windward. Pip, happily, had been alert enough to see what was going on, and his men cooperative enough that they were able to heave the brig to before she slammed into *Sparrowhawk*'s transom. Now both vessels waited as a boat from *Oliver Cromwell* pulled away from that ship's side and made its way over the swells to *Sparrowhawk*.

"Bellows!" McGinty called to the nearest of his men. "Go below, fetch up the prisoners locked in the mate's cabin." He would have liked to keep those men hidden, but if he was caught doing so, which he likely would be, it would be very difficult to explain.

A few moments later Finch and his two officers and the two foremast hands appeared on deck looking noticeably worse off for having spent the night jammed together in the small cabin. The sailors headed forward, the officers came aft.

"I trust you had a comfortable night," McGinty said as they approached.

"Comfortable?" Finch said. "Damn you, you..." His voice trailed off as he noticed *Oliver Cromwell* hove to weather. He stared at the ship for a moment and then turned back to McGinty, but McGinty cut him off before any questions could be asked.

"Now, see here, boy-o," McGinty said. "This ship, she's a Yankee Doodle, just like us. It ain't the bloody Royal Navy come to save your miserable hides. So you'll all keep your bloody gobs shut, or it'll go hard on you after they leave, depend on it."

Finch frowned and McGinty could see that he was wrestling with making reply. But finally he settled for a "Humph," and said no more.

The *Cromwell*'s boat closed the distance quickly, the oars expertly manned by twenty sailors in blue jackets, three officers sitting in the sternsheets. Along the centerline, between the rowers, sat a company of marines. McGinty could not help but feel a pang of jealousy at the sight of them, and of so many experienced, able-bodied American seamen.

Ah, damn my eyes, give me them men and I'll sweep the seas clean, he thought, but then the boat swooped up under the transom and came along the leeward side and McGinty knew it was time for him to go to work.

He strode across to the gangway and stood back as the first of the officers stepped through the bulwark and onto the deck. McGinty did not greet them and he did not smile. His expression, his stance, conveyed the notion that he was not at all pleased with this interruption of his voyage, that he did not have time to waste, and that these upstarts from a mere state navy were making a grave mistake interfering with Continental business.

"Gentlemen," he said when the last of the officers had come aboard and the first of the marines came up behind them. "It's regrettable that you chose to delay us in this manner. As I said, I'm on business that won't admit of delay, and…"

"That'll do, captain," the first of the officers said. He was looking around *Sparrowhawk*'s deck, not really paying attention to McGinty at all. McGinty knew full well what the man was seeing: a ridiculously small crew for a naval vessel, men dressed as soldiers, not seamen, men carrying muskets on deck. And he knew what the man was thinking: something was not right aboard *Sparrowhawk*.

After a moment of uncomfortable silence, the officer from *Cromwell* turned to McGinty. "And you, sir, are…?"

"Captain Angus McGinty. Continental Navy." He kept his tone formal, made it clear he was offended at having to answer impertinent questions.

"Continental Navy?" Finch huffed behind McGinty's back. "You said you were a privateer! You're a damned pirate, sir, and nothing more."

The officer from *Cromwell* looked at Finch and then looked back at McGinty, an eyebrow raised.

"Master of the prize we took," McGinty said, nodding toward Finch. "He'll say what he will to try and worm out of being made a prisoner of war. And who are you, sir?"

"Lieutenant John Little, first office of the ship *Oliver Cromwell*," the man said, making the words sound almost like an afterthought.

Oh, Little John, is it? McGinty thought. *And is Robin Hood the master of the ship?* But he kept the jibe to himself, which for him was no easy task.

"You have your commissioning papers, I assume?" Lieutenant Little said. "Your orders and muster book and such? Ship's logs?"

"No, I don't, and bloody thanks to you," McGinty said. "You start chasing after us, and sure we can't see your colors. You might have flown them from the masthead, where they'd do some good. We reckoned you were Royal Navy, reckoned we'd be taken for sure, so we threw the lot overboard."

"All your papers? You threw them overboard?"

"It's customary, you know, to keep such things out of the hands of the enemy."

The lieutenant regarded McGinty for a moment, and his face showed no hint that he believed this story. "It's customary to throw signal books and orders and correspondence overboard," he said. "Not commissioning papers and muster books and ship's logs."

"You may have your ways in your Connecticut State Navy," McGinty said. "When you sail under orders of the Continental Congress, you do things a wee bit different, boy-o."

Lieutenant Little sighed a deep sigh. "I can see we won't get this straightened out here," he said. "Captain Parker is master of *Oliver Cromwell*, we'll let him sort this out. Pray, get what papers you have remaining, if any, and join me in the boat." He turned to Finch. "You had best come as well. I'll warrant you have an interesting tale to tell."

McGinty retreated down to *Sparrowhawk*'s tiny great cabin. He found a canvas bag and stuffed all the paperwork he could find into it, which included the sloop's logbook from her days as His Majesty's armed vessel *Sparrowhawk* and the logs and sundry papers from *Hopefleet*. Since taking command he himself had not kept a log of any kind. He did not see the point, and he did not feel it would benefit him to have any official record of his activities.

He made his way back on deck and down into the boat alongside. Finch was already seated in the sternsheets, while one of the officers and the company of marines remained aboard the sloop.

They crossed over to *Oliver Cromwell* in silence, and when the boat hooked onto the chains Little and the other officers went up the boarding steps first, then Finch and then McGinty with his sack of documents. He was met at the gangway by more marines, standing in two lines, and gun crews standing idle at each of the twenty great guns.

"This way, gentlemen," Lieutenant Little said, leading McGinty and Finch up a short ladder to the quarterdeck aft. There they were met by a man in a blue uniform coat with white waistcoat and breeches and a most serious-looking expression.

"Captain Parker," Lieutenant Little said, gesturing toward McGinty. "May I present Captain Angus McGinty of the Continental sloop *Sparrowhawk*?" He put just the slightest emphasis on the words 'captain' and 'Continental', enough to suggest that those designations were not to be taken as a given.

Captain Parker gave a perfunctory nod and Lt. Little said, "And this is Captain James Finch, formerly master of the brig *Hopefleet*, which Captain McGinty took as a prize. Gentlemen, I give you Captain Timothy Parker of the Connecticut State Navy ship *Oliver Cromwell*."

"An honor, sir," McGinty began, "but let me say, as I tried to inform the young officer here, I..."

"You have your papers, sir?" Parker interrupted. "Ship's log, commissioning papers, and such?"

"I've some," McGinty said. He was still trying to project an air of importance, of a man not to be trifled with, but this Parker was making the task considerably difficult.

"It seems he threw most of them overboard, sir," Lieutenant Little chimed in. "Or so he says."

"Threw them overboard?" Parker asked.

"And well I did," McGinty said. "Given the position you yourself put me in, sir, I would..."

"Yes, yes," Parker said with a wave of his hand. "We'll see about that. Here, is that what you have?" He pointed to the canvas bag in McGinty's hand.

"Aye, it is, and…"

Parker reached over and before McGinty knew what he was doing he took the bag. "I'll see what you have here, sir. Pray remain on deck and I'll send for you. Lieutenant Little, with me, if you please."

"Sir, I must protest this outrageous treatment…" Captain Finch said, stepping forward, but Parker waved him off as well.

"You'll have your chance, sir, depend on it. Now, pray, forgive me." He nodded again, turned, and he and Little disappeared below, leaving McGinty and Finch to wander the *Oliver Cromwell*'s quarterdeck in silence.

McGinty sauntered over to the rail at the forward end of the quarterdeck and looked down at the waist below, and then up at the rig and the sails. Everything was tidy and ship-shape, the guns and the rigging blackened down, the sails in good repair, the men properly fitted out. The deck was white from scrubbing and the masts neatly painted a buff color. A ship of the Royal Navy would not have looked any better.

Ah, this Parker's a right tartar, I see, McGinty thought. *Pushing him about will take some doing, you'd best believe.* It had been his plan from the first to brass it out, to show sufficient confidence and outrage that he could bowl over any martinet of a naval captain, smother him in horse manure and be on his way. He had done it often enough and found it generally worked. But it would only work on a certain type of martinet, and it seemed this Captain Parker was the wrong type altogether.

Well, we'll see now, won't we? McGinty thought. And he knew he was right about that. One way or another, he would see.

For a few moments more, he remained at the break of the quarterdeck, staring idly across the water at *Sparrowhawk* and rehearsing his story in his mind. He had to have it fixed, he knew, had to repeat every element exactly the same way. Any change in the tale, any misspoken words, were the death of deception.

"Captain McGinty?" he heard Lieutenant Little call.

McGinty turned to find the officer standing behind him. Little was still putting that note of doubt in the word 'captain' and McGinty considered giving the man a verbal back of the hand for his impertinence, but decided against it. Better that Little not know he was getting under his skin.

"Captain Parker will speak with you now, sir," Little continued. He led McGinty down the ladder to the waist and then aft under the quarterdeck to the door of the great cabin, the scuttle being reserved for the captain and first office alone.

A marine sentry stood at the door to the great cabin and as they approached he knocked on the door and called, "Lieutenant Little, sir!"

Bloody thinks he's bloody Admiral George bloody Rodney, McGinty thought as Parker called "Come!" The marine opened the door and McGinty ducked into the spacious cabin—spacious at least in comparison to that of *Sparrowhawk*.

Parker was seated behind the table that took up a good part of the cabin's deck space, the various logbooks and papers McGinty had brought spread out in front of him.

"Captain McGinty," he said, looking McGinty in the eye, "we seem to have a…complicated situation here." His tone was less brusque, less officious, and dismissive than it had been on deck. More reasonable. McGinty found that encouraging. And suspicious.

He glanced down at the table. *Hopefleet*'s bill of lading was on the top of the pile, sitting at the captain's right hand.

Ah, you greedy bastard! McGinty thought. *You see how valuable that prize is, don't you? And you want it, all legal-like.*

"Complicated? I suppose you might say so," McGinty said. "Though not so different from what we Continental Navy fellows encounter, often enough."

"The thing of it is," Parker continued, "I see here that your sloop, *Sparrowhawk*, was part of the Royal Navy but a month ago. And that's about all I see. No indication she was taken into the Continental service. And I dare say I've never heard of any vessel of that name captured or adjudicated or commissioned. And I generally hear of such things."

"As I explained to your Lieutenant Little," McGinty said with a note of weariness, "Most of the papers went overboard, on account of me taking you for a British cruiser. And as to *Sparrowhawk*, she was taken into the navy in an informal way, sort of a brevet promotion, if you will. We took her on the Delaware River, right in the middle of the worst of it, trying to hold Black Dick Howe at bay. It was Captain Biddlecomb, of the *Falmouth* frigate…"

"Hold a moment," Parker said, leaning back. "Captain Biddlecomb? Captain Isaac Biddlecomb, of Rhode Island?"

Ah, that's struck a spark! McGinty thought. "Yes, Captain Isaac Biddlecomb, of Rhode Island," McGinty said. He had no idea if Biddlecomb was from Rhode Island or the far side of the moon, but he reckoned he had best play along. "Do you know that worthy, sir?"

"Met the man once," Parker said, "but I know him by reputation well enough."

McGinty could not miss the tone of respect in Parker's voice, and thought, *Maybe old Biddlecomb isn't quite the silly blockhead I took him for.* Here was an unforeseen path opening up before him.

"I've no doubt you do know his reputation," McGinty said. "Any man-of-war's man would, who's served on this station. So you must know, he was given command of the *Falmouth* frigate, building in Philadelphia. Problem was, the damned British took the town before the ship could sail clear. She didn't even have her ballast in her. My lads and me, we were assigned to her protection, do you see? Sent to keep her out of the hands of Billy Howe and his German butchers."

"Assigned?" Parker asked. "By who?"

"By General Washington, of course!" McGinty said as if the answer should have been obvious. "We were with the Fifth Pennsylvania, Continental Line. The general sent me because he needed a man who knew his way around a ship, and I've been to sea all my life, man and boy. Commanded a privateer in the first year of the war. My lads, to be sure, are not sailors. Lieutenant Little here might have mentioned as much."

Parker looked at Little and nodded and Little nodded as well.

"There's the reason, do you see?" McGinty said. "We were sent to protect the frigate, not sail her. But when the British sent *Sparrowhawk* to cut her out, me and Captain Biddlecomb, we took *Sparrowhawk* instead. And he puts me in command of her, and my men as crew, because he has not a real sailor to spare."

"I see," Parker said. "And how do you happen to be out here? And taking prizes?"

"Well, we managed to get the *Falmouth* frigate to Great Egg Harbor in New Jersey. But she's got no spars, no stores, no ordnance. So Captain Biddlecomb sends me out in command of *Sparrowhawk* to see what we could take from the British to fit her out. Hunting for prizes, you know, and us being a commissioned Continental vessel, and all. And damn my eyes if I didn't hook exactly what the good captain was fishing for!"

"Hmm..." Parker said. Like McGinty, he was seeing great riches slipping from his fingers. "The sloop's not, in fact, a commissioned vessel. And she's not a privateer. You're not a commissioned naval officer. And yet Captain Biddlecomb sends you out to cruise against the enemy? Smacks of piracy, what?"

"He did it on his own authority," McGinty said.

"I'm not sure he has that authority, *Captain*," Lieutenant Little chimed in.

Sorry, Little Lieutenant, but you won't get your slice of this pie, McGinty thought, but rather than voice his sympathy, he said, "You'll have to take that up with him, Lieutenant. And General Washington, who give him his orders."

For a long moment Parker was silent, staring blankly at a point just past McGinty's left shoulder, considering all of this. "So, Captain," he said at length, "you say you left Captain Biddlecomb and his frigate at Great Egg Harbor?"

"Aye, Captain, that's where we were bound," McGinty said.

"Yet you were heading south when we spotted you."

"We were heading north when *we* spotted *you*," McGinty said. "Making for Great Egg Harbor. We put about when we saw you and took you for a British cruiser. As I have explained. Several times."

Parker nodded slowly. "I think perhaps the best course of action here is for us to escort you back to Great Egg Harbor," he said. "I trust Captain Biddlecomb will then be able to set this all straight."

Ah, damn your eyes! McGinty thought. Parker was still hoping to catch him in a lie and keep *Hopefleet* and *Sparrowhawk* for himself. The fact that McGinty was in fact lying would not help matters. Nor could he expect to receive much aid and comfort from his old comrade in arms Isaac Biddlecomb.

"I have to agree, Captain Parker. Back to Egg Harbor, and Captain Biddlecomb can give you the truth of the matter and put this all to rights," McGinty said, though it was in fact the very last thing he wished to see happen.

He pictured the chart of the coast in his head. If they were anywhere near where he thought they were, and the wind held steady the way it was, then Great Egg Harbor was about two days' sail away.

Ah, Angus, boy-o, you know you're in no danger of drowning on this passage, he thought. *If ever there was a man born to be hanged, it's you.* But the hangman had been put off once again, and now he had another forty-eight hours to come up with some other means of keeping that worthy at bay.

CHAPTER NINE

Shadrach Barnett was pacing. Six paces to the southwest, six paces to the northeast, six paces to the southwest, back and forth. His room on the third floor of the tavern was small, but it was the only private room to be had. The rest of his men were crammed into various communal bed chambers, the fortunate ones, anyway, the ones who had arrived first. The others slept in the tavern room where they bedded down on the floor or passed out at the tables.

Barnett had no complaints about his room. Small as it was, it was dry, and being on the upper floor it was fairly warm. It was vastly better than the miserable hut that he occupied up in the Pine Barrens. It was there that he and his men mostly lived, hiding out, keeping watch for opportunity, and for any authorities who might come looking for them, though as the war dragged on they were finding fewer and fewer of each.

They had come from all over the area, the sundry refuse of the villages and the poor, hard-scramble farms of southern New Jersey. Barnett himself had farmed a few acres some miles north of there, supplementing his not quite subsistence living with a bit of petty larceny here and there.

He tried to keep clear of the war at first, and politics in general, in part because he had bigger worries, and in part because he did not care. But, of course, the war had found him. Loyalists sacked his farm and took what little he had. Pathetic, really. Even he himself would not have bothered to steal the worldly goods that he had possessed.

With few options left to him, he joined the Continental Army and spent an unpleasant year marching back and forth across the state until he was caught liberating a few chickens from a farm near camp. For that, he received a dozen stripes. He could still feel the rough scars left in the wake of the cat o' nine tails where they brushed against the fabric of his shirt. He was drummed out of the service and left with nothing but a burning hatred for all of them, Loyalist and Patriot alike. He drifted into the Pine Barrens where, through cunning and unflinching brutality, he became a leader of sorts. The Prince of Thieves.

But he was not thinking about the Pine Barrens now, or his men, or the tavern, as he kept up his pacing, from one corner of the room to the other. He was thinking about the ship. *Falmouth.* That was her name, or so he understood. He was thinking about what might be stored away in her depths. Food. Rum. Weapons. Specie. He was thinking about Captain Isaac Biddlecomb.

"Ah! Damn his eyes!" Barnett paused in his pacing and cursed, and since he happened to be next to the washstand, he picked up the basin and flung it across the room. He watched it hit the wall and shatter, but it was not as satisfying as he had hoped it would be.

"Damn that bastard," he said, softer, letting his fury settle. His eyes rested on the dull patch of light on the floor. The sky outside was thick with cloud, but there was enough late morning light coming in through the window to illuminate that section of boards.

Barnett had spent a good part of the past few days alone in his room, drinking, pacing, throwing things. He was not a patient man, but he did not like to put that impatience on display. He did not want anyone to think he was anything less than calm and in command; in command, both of his men and of his own temper. He did not care to have company when he was in a rage, and worse, when he was not certain of what he should do next.

"*Falmouth…*" he said out loud. He was fixated on the ship, obsessed. He knew it and knew there was nothing for it.

His interest at first had been purely mercenary, figuring the ship might be housing something of considerable value. He still thought that, but there was more to it now. Now he wanted the ship simply because he did not have it. He wanted it because others were keeping it from him. He wanted it because getting his hands on the ship meant getting his hands on Isaac Biddlecomb, and getting his hands on Biddlecomb was the only way he was going to release the pressure inside.

For a moment more Barnett looked at the shards of basin scattered on the floor, then he walked over to the window, leaned on the window sill, and looked out at the frozen ground spreading out beyond the tavern yard. He could see a few buildings from there, homes mostly, and a smith's shop. Trails of smoke were coiling up from their chimneys. Beyond that the countryside was bleak and lifeless, with patches of bare trees reaching up to the leaden sky and brown fields of dirt and dried stalks. He could not see the wharf or the ship from his window.

It had been many days now since he was down to the waterfront. He had been waiting patiently for the right moment to return, but his patience was like a rope under great strain, slipping bit by bit from his grip. But still he waited, waited for all the pieces to be set in place.

Men had been streaming in from the countryside, dozens of men. When Shadrach Barnett sent word, men responded. He had far more men under his command than that bastard Biddlecomb had, and they were tough men, and used to fighting. But they were not so used to taking orders, or obeying without question, and that was the problem.

A frontal attack on the ship meant charging down the long wharf and fighting their way up the ship's side in the face of men with muskets hunkered down behind the rails. There was no question that Barnett and his men would win in the end—they had the numbers to guarantee it—but there was also no question that many of them would die in the effort, and none would be willing to pay that price.

Faircloth, Biddlecomb's toy soldier, could order his marines to make a forlorn assault such as that, and they would do it, because all thinking had been drilled out of them. But Barnett knew he did not have that luxury. His men, the pine robbers, as they were called, were not puppets, and there was only so much authority one could wield over folks such as them.

So…hostages. Word reached Barnett that part of Biddlecomb's crew had gone off to the Pine Barrens in search of trees for masts, and once he heard that, the plan was obvious. He sent Wilcox, the only man he trusted, and him just barely, and two dozen others off to hunt the woodsmen down and make them prisoners. He gave careful instructions: as many of Biddlecomb's crew as possible must be taken alive.

Hostages. That was what was needed here. Trade the ship for the prisoners. Or, if Biddlecomb was not willing to do that, set a gallows up on the dock and hang the bastards, one by one, until the whores' sons on *Falmouth* had to come out and fight, just to stop it.

And if they didn't, if they just let the prisoners die, then at least there were a dozen fewer men defending the ship.

That was the plan and it was a good one and Barnett had been waiting for Wilcox and his men to return with the prisoners in tow. He had been waiting for days, which he knew was not an unreasonable amount of time. Neither he nor Wilcox had any idea of where that big bastard Rumstick and the others had gone. Might be another few days before he even got word. All he could do was wait.

He stood upright, so quick and so involuntarily that he felt as if he had been jerked back by a rope around his neck. But it was not a rope. It was his own resolve, come on him like a blast of grapeshot. He was done waiting.

"Damn the lot of them," he said as he turned and grabbed his coat from the hook on the wall and shrugged it on. And he knew when he said *the lot of them* that he meant exactly that: the lot of them. Wilcox and his men, and the hostages, and Biddlecomb's men, and even his own men, damn all of them, he was ready to take action and he would make them all dance to the tune he called.

He slung his sword over his shoulder and hooked his sea-service pistol on his belt and left the room with long strides, not bothering to close the door behind him. There was nothing in there that he really cared about, and one way or another he did not think he would be coming back.

He took the narrow steps fast, his boots loud on the worn wooden treads. On the first floor, he strode down the narrow hall and into the surprisingly large tavern room. Some of his men were already starting in with the day's drinking, some were having their breakfast, some were still asleep on the floor. Barnett might have chaffed at the waiting, but these men were enjoying it, and getting much too comfortable in the process. But their days of ease were done.

"The lot of you, up and to arms!" he shouted. "Move it now, shake a leg!" He looked into the dumb, surprised faces of the men, mouths hanging open as they stared blankly up from their plates and tankards, and he wanted to plant a fist into each one of them.

Finally one of them spoke. "What?" he said. "Are we to…"

That was as far as he got. Barnett half turned and looked at the man, and the look on Barnett's face was enough to stop him in midsentence, enough to inspire him to shut his mouth, leap to his feet and grab his musket and cartridge box in silent obedience, and the others in the tavern room did likewise.

Good… Barnett thought. The men were getting lazy and fat, but not so dull that they forgot the price they would pay for disobeying him, or even being too slow to obey.

"Get above stairs," Barnett called to a knot of men by the hallway door. "Roust out anyone still abed, or whatever they're doing. Whoring, whatever. Get them down here, now." He turned to another man. "Fetch the stable boy and tell him to bring the horses around the front."

The men by the hallway turned and raced for the stairs. Barnett crossed the tavern room and stepped through the big front door and out into the yard with its small raised bed garden, which looked as sorry and dead as everything else out of doors. He walked down the path and through the gate with the carved wooden pineapples on top.

Never seen a pineapple, Barnett mused. *Wonder if they're good.*

As bleak as the countryside was, the air was bracing, sharp and fresh, a great change from the smoky, fetid air of the tavern. He breathed deep and felt the haze in his mind get swept away.

"That son of a bitch," he said out loud. He understood, suddenly, what had sent him to that low place where he had been those last few days. It was that son of a bitch Biddlecomb and his little stunt, walking right into the tavern as free as you please. Barnett realized he had been knocked back on his heels by that bold move.

He had been surprised at the moment, to be sure, looking up and seeing Biddlecomb and Faircloth come marching into the tavern. But he had recovered his wits, mocked them with three cheers. He thought that had settled it for him, restored his balance. But he could see now it hadn't. Biddlecomb's effrontery had shaken him deep.

"Well, we'll set that whore's son straight," Barnett said.

The tavern door opened again and his men began to spill out into the yard. They looked hastily dressed, hastily armed, half-drunk or hung over. But that was fine. They had not tarried, but rather turned out in their sorry state because they were afraid of him. As they should be.

"Listen here, you miserable pukes," Barnett called so all could hear. "We're going to march down to that wharf and we're going to give those bastards on that ship one last chance to give it up. And if they don't want to come off the ship now, then by God they don't ever come off. We'll set up camp right there, right at the end of the wharf. No one comes or goes. No food, no water, no poxed militia comes or goes from that ship. And we'll see how long they care to put up with that."

He watched the men exchange glances. Some of them, the less stupid ones, understood what he was saying: they would be giving up the comforts of the tavern for bivouacking on the hard ground by the water's edge. He waited for someone to object, but no one did.

A moment later the stable boy and the innkeeper came around the side of the building leading the four horses that the pine robbers had to their name. Barnett took one and three of the other lead men took the others. Wilcox would have had one, had he been there, but he was not. He was, Barnett hoped, at that moment marching Rumstick and his band back along the road from the Pine Barrens to Great Egg Harbor.

Wonder if we should set up the gallows first? Barnett thought as he climbed up into the saddle, but then decided against it.

Let ol' Biddlecomb decide about surrendering the ship before I play that card.

He reached around and grabbed the reins and nudged the horse with his heels. The hooves made a soft thudding sound on the hard ground as the animal gathered way. The three other mounted men walked their horses alongside him, and behind him, he heard the shuffle and clatter and mutterings of a good three dozen men falling in behind.

They moved down the frozen road, through the cluster of buildings that made up Great Egg Harbor and on toward the waterfront. The local folk at work stopped to watch them parade past, and some frowned and shook their heads as they watched. No one said anything. No one would dare. Barnett's company was by far the most powerful force within fifty miles.

He swiveled around in his saddle and looked behind him. The column stretched back for fifty yards, and though there was nothing uniform about the men, still they were walking in something like a straight line with muskets resting on shoulders, troops on the march. Barnett had seen units of the Continental Army that looked worse than his men.

*Colonel Barnett...*he mused. That had been pretty much a joke when he thought of it, but now he was starting to like the idea. He liked riding at the head of a column of soldiers.

Once we take this ship, that'll set us up, he thought. *I'll keep this lot together, maybe hire us out. Whig, Tory, it don't matter. Whoever has hard money, that's the side we fight on.*

Barnett's mind wandered off into that happy land as he rode, and he became so lost in those thoughts that his arrival at the end of the wharf took him by surprise. He held up a hand to stop the column, then slid off the horse and onto the ground.

He looked down the length of the dock at the frigate tied there. A thin column of smoke was rising up from the forward end, from an oven, he guessed. Breakfast would be done but maybe they were keeping it stoked up to provide some warmth below.

How much wood you got onboard? Barnett thought. *How much food and water? Not so much, I reckon.*

He turned around and strode back to the men gathered on the road. He walked down the line, pointing to those who looked the least disreputable, the least like the bedraggled, sorry outcasts that they all in fact were.

"You lot, come with me," he ordered. "And try to look like proper soldiers, much as you can." Then, seeing the hesitancy on the men's faces added, "Oh, don't you worry, you sorry bastards. Ain't no one going to shoot you. Except me, that is, if you make a hash of this."

He headed down the wharf and the picked men fell in behind him. They would not make the same martial impression as Faircloth's marines, but they would do. Barnett kept his eyes on the ship and he could see the activity now, men hurrying fore and aft, no doubt turning out under arms. The arrival of the Army of the Pine Barrens had not gone unnoticed, nor was it a threat that could be ignored or dismissed.

He stopped fifty feet from the ship, crossed his arms, and looked up at the quarterdeck rail. The ship was not particularly high-sided, but empty as it was it was riding high, and the wharf was low to the water, so Barnett could not see the deck from where he stood. Nor could he see anyone on the deck, not Biddlecomb or anyone else. The men he had seen scrambling before were now hidden from sight.

He considered calling out but decided immediately against it. He could see the game that Biddlecomb was playing here, and he could play it too, by his own rules. He would wait.

A minute passed by, and then another. Barnett felt his anger rising, despite his determination to play it cool. And just as he was thinking that he would have to act, the call out, or march back down the wharf or fire a musket ball into the side of the ship, a head appeared over the rail. Not Biddlecomb or Faircloth, but one of the other officers. Barnett recognized him—a little portly, round eyeglasses, not particularly awe-inspiring—but he had never met the man.

"May I help you?" the officer asked.

"No, I reckon not," Barnett said.

The man nodded. There was another moment of silence, and then the man said, "May I enquire as to your purpose in visiting us?"

"You can," Barnett said. "But I reckon it's your captain I should talk to."

There was another moment of silence, as if the officer was weighing whether or not this was worth disturbing the captain for, and then he said, "Very well. Pray, wait a moment."

He disappeared from sight. Barnett rested his hands on his sword hilt and the butt of his pistol and waited. He wondered if Biddlecomb was down below, or if he was standing just on the far side of the deck, out of sight. Barnett decided it was the latter, that they were just making a show of having to go and fetch Biddlecomb, pretending that the bastard could hardly be bothered.

Faircloth and his marines, he suspected, and the rest of the crew were under arms and also skulking on the other side of the deck, or down in the waist. They could pretend that the presence of Barnett's men did not warrant any concern, but everyone there knew that it was not true.

Play make-believe all you like, Biddlecomb, Barnett thought. *I know you're scared of me.*

A moment later Biddlecomb himself appeared at the quarterdeck rail. He was in uniform now, a blue coat and red waistcoat under his boat cloak, a hat, considerably less battered than Barnett's, perched on his head.

"Ah, Colonel Barnett," he said. "Just back from headquarters, I imagine. Are you bringing me the latest orders from General Washington?"

"I am," Barnett said. He had not actually thought through what he would say, he was just acting on his gut, and so he gave his gut free rein. "General says you should let me and my men come onboard, have a look around. He says, it'd be the healthiest thing for you and your men."

"Does he, now?" Biddlecomb asked. "Well...I think not."

"You think not?"

"That's what I said."

Barnett nodded. He ran his eyes over the ship. Nothing had changed since the last time he had been there, as far as he could see. She might be sitting a hair lower in the water for all the rocks they had been humping onboard, but that was about it. And even that he could not tell for certain.

"Don't look like you're getting too much done," Barnett observed. "You ain't much closer to sailing off."

"It can be hard for a fellow like you to tell," Biddlecomb said. "You know, a fellow that knows nothing about such things."

"Still, I reckon it'd be a fine thing to get some masts in her, huh?" Barnett said. "Say, if you was to send some men up to the Pine Barrens to cut you some spruce. That sound like a good idea?"

That, at last, provoked a reaction. It was subtle, and Biddlecomb checked himself quickly, but Barnett saw it. The words had struck home, the threat had landed.

Barnett would say no more. In truth, he had said more on the subject than he intended to. He knew all about the dangers of counting chickens before they hatched, or flaunting hostages before they were actually in your possession. But he could not resist taking that verbal swing at Biddlecomb's smug face, and he had the pleasure of seeing it land. And the further pleasure of seeing Biddlecomb struggle for a response, and fail to find one.

"Any event," Barnett said, "you probably don't need my advice about masts and such. So here's what I come to tell you. I'm concerned, you see, about the safety of this fine ship, here. There's lots of bad folk around these parts. Banditti and such. So what I'm going to do, I'm going to post my men at the head of the wharf there. Got about fifty or so, and more coming in. We'll see to it no one comes near your ship. Understand? Like the way the great Washington himself had them British stuck up in Boston. No one come in or out. That way you'll be good and safe. You understand?"

"Yes," Biddlecomb said. "Yes, I certainly do understand. I just hope you understand how this might not work out so well for you."

Barnett nodded. "Oh, I think I understand how this will work out for me," he said. "But if there comes a time when you want to discuss the situation, like if, say, you and your men were out of food, well, you know where I can be found."

He turned then without another word and walked back up the wharf, his men falling in behind him. He was pleased. Pleased that he had the discipline to shut up just at the right moment, just when he had landed that last jab. Pleased that he had thought to come now and box Biddlecomb in before the poxed bastard found some means to get away. Pleased that the frigate would soon be his, and there was not much in heaven, earth, or hell that Captain Isaac bloody Biddlecomb could do to stop him.

Chapter Ten

It was just before breakfast, four days after the ball at the Newsome house, when the first letter arrived. Nelly brought it to Virginia on a small silver plate: a crisp white bit of parchment, neatly folded and sealed. Across the face, in a bold and elegant, though not at all feminine hand, the words *Mrs. Virginia Biddlecomb*.

Virginia thanked Nelly and took the folded paper, perfectly aware of who it was from despite the lack of any return address. She broke the seal and unfolded the page.

*Mrs. Biddlecomb...*she read.

> *I thank you again for the honor you did me in accompanying me to the ball at the Newsome's house the other night. If you found even a fraction of the delight in the evening that I did, I shall count it a success. The chief of my conversation these days is among my fellows in the military line, and it can get tedious in the extreme, I assure you. I found our discussions to be like a warm spring breeze on the heels of a cold winter's gale.*

"Indeed, sir?" Virginia said out loud, her eyebrow cocked in skepticism, but she read on.

I hope that I properly expressed to you the pleasure I took from our discourse in matters equine. Your knowledge and insight in most remarkable indeed. That said, I wonder if you would not be interested in some actual riding, rather than the mere theoretical consideration of it? I know the weather is not all what one might ask, but I can easily procure for us most suitable mounts and it would be my sincere pleasure to escort you through some of the less settled parts of this city.

If this is agreeable to you, and tomorrow mid-morning an acceptable time, then you would do me further great honor in accepting my invitation. I will send a man by later for your reply, but whatever it may be, please believe that I remain,
Your obedient, humble servant,
Richard Dexter, Esq.

Virginia put the note down and regarded herself in the mirror, then picked up her brush and resumed brushing her hair, which she had been doing when Nelly knocked on the door.

Oh, dear... she thought as she stared at her reflection. She felt like a woman sitting in a window and looking out at a storm building on the horizon. She could see all of the roiling emotions inside her like black skies in the distant, but they felt far off, something to observe but not feel.

Her mind moved to the practical, as it usually did: it was who she was, and thinking about practical things spared her from thinking about the other, much more complex and potentially troublesome matters.

She looked over at baby Jack, mercifully asleep in his crib. The wet nurse they had brought in so that Virginia might attend the ball seemed willing enough to come when needed, and Jack seemed to take to her admirably. That thought gave Virginia a stab of guilt, just one more of dozens such pinpricks. It was absurd, she knew, no reason at all to feel guilty for turning her baby over to a wet nurse for a few hours—many women of her station did not nurse at all—but guilt and logic were rarely bedfellows.

Next, she considered her wardrobe. She had riding clothes, and breeches as well if she had to opportunity to ride astride, which she preferred, to riding aside on a side saddle. So there was no concern in that regard.

This is a most excellent opportunity, she thought. Most of the British troops, those for whom they had yet to find more suitable housing, were bivouacked on the outer fringes of the city. Troop logistics would be a natural point of discussion. From there, Virginia could find out more about victualing, supply lines, potential troop movements, offensive maneuvers, where Lord Howe most feared an attack. A ride with Dexter could be very profitable indeed, from an intelligence standpoint.

She sighed. "You are such a damned liar," she said out loud. She knew perfectly well why she was tempted by Dexter's invitation, and it had nothing to do with victualing or troop bloody logistics. She enjoyed his company. She would never, ever, even entertain the notion of being unfaithful to Isaac—and she knew that to be the truth—but she nonetheless enjoyed the company of Richard Dexter; droll, urbane, and intelligent.

I would never rut with another man, she thought as she drew the brush through her hair, *but am I not still being unfaithful? Allowing myself to be charmed by Richard Dexter?* Captain *Richard Dexter, of His Majesty's Seventeenth Regiment of Foot?*

She threw the brush on the table and looked away from her reflection in the mirror. She missed her husband terribly. There was no question in that regard. But she was lonely. And bored.

And there was yet another aspect to this. She really, genuinely, wished to go riding, whether it was with Captain Dexter or Beelzebub himself. She sighed again, then stood and crossed over to the small desk on the other side of the room. She spread a sheet of paper in front of her and dipped her quill into the ink.

*Captain Dexter...*she wrote, *I would be very pleased to accept your kind invitation to an afternoon of riding in the city...*

Virginia hurried through the reply, eager to be done with the task of which she was still uncertain. She blotted the ink, folded and sealed the note, and was half finished with dressing when Jack woke, his gurgling escalating quickly to the sort of demanding cry that only his mother could satisfy. She scooped him up from the crib and settled down to nurse, letting her mind wander off to the autumn fields and well-bred stallions of her home in Bristol, Rhode Island. Fine times. Simple times. When war had not yet come to those United Colonies.

Once Jack was done, Virginia stood with him in his arms, a familiar bundle, and stepped out into the hall. She moved three doors down the carpeted hall and rapped lightly at Susan's door.

"Come!" Susan called and Virginia swung the door open and stepped inside. Susan was still at her mirror, still hard at work on her hair.

"Oh, Virginia, dear, don't you look particularly beautiful this morning!" Susan gushed, regarding Virginia in the mirror. "And you've had a letter, I understand!"

"Indeed," Virginia said. She had long suspected that Susan slipped Nelly the odd guinea to keep her informed of everything that transpired in the house, or wherever the girl was able to insinuate herself.

"From that handsome Captain Dexter?" Susan asked.

"Yes, from that handsome Captain Dexter," Virginia agreed. "He asks me to go riding with him on the morrow."

"Oh, marvelous!" Susan said. "Even something so loathsome as riding a horse might be tolerable in that gentleman's company."

"The thing of it is," Virginia said, "I had quite hoped you would join us. Perhaps you and Captain Cornwall. I don't think it would be quite the thing for Captain Dexter and I to go off on our own."

"Oh, my dear, you are such a country mouse!" Susan said, turning and looking at Virginia directly. "Of course, I would never make so bold as to ask Captain Cornwall myself, but if he were to ask me to go along on your little outing, I will promise to accept. Even if it means getting on top of some beastly horse."

"Thank you," Virginia said. "And do you think he might ask?"

"I'm all but certain of it," Susan said with a knowing smile.

Breakfast passed pleasantly enough. Virginia knew better than to wear any sort of shawl or bed jacket to the meal, as Mrs. Williams was certain to have the fire built up to a great inferno to preserve Jack's apparently tenuous life, which indeed she did. There was considerable talk concerning which officers were quartering with which families, and of upcoming balls or theatrical productions, or who stood the chance of marrying whom, and the price and scarcity of groceries, but it passed right through Virginia's head as if there was not the least impediment between her ears.

She was back in her room, rocking a sleeping Jack with her foot and working a piece of embroidery on a hoop when Nelly knocked again.

"A letter has come for you, Missus," she said when Virginia called her in. Again she held out the small silver tray with an envelope sitting on top. Virginia frowned. Captain Dexter's man had not yet come for her reply, she would not expect further word from him. But she could see that this letter was considerably more battered and road-weary than the crisp note that Dexter had sent.

"Thank you, Nelly," Virginia said and she picked up the envelope. Across the face of it, she read, *Mrs. Virginia Biddlecomb, c/o Mrs. Temperance Williams, Chestnut Street, Philadelphia.* That was all, but she gasped when she saw the writing.

"Isaac..." she said, her voice just a whisper.

"Missus?" Nelly asked.

"Thank you, Nelly, that will be all," Virginia said, but her eyes did not move from the faded ink. She heard the servant cross the room and close the door and for a moment more, Virginia just sat, rocking her baby—their baby—and staring at the envelope.

"Isaac..." she said again, and she felt a flush of guilt, a sensation of confusion and uncertainty. Then with a sudden rush of need, she tore the seal open and unfolded the letter.

My Beloved Virginia, she read, and from there her eyes flew over the words, racing along the familiar handwriting, barely taking its meaning as she did. She was eager, desperately eager, to consume every bit of it, in the same way she would have torn at Isaac's clothes, eager to consume his person, had he been there in the flesh.

She reached the end of the text, the letter half-digested, and only then did she understand the other reason she had read it that way—she was looking for bad news, for some word that he was hurt, captured, sick. She was frantic to know, but the letter contained nothing like that.

"Oh, Isaac..." she said softly. She closed her eyes for a second, let her thoughts settle, then began again from the salutation, reading slowly and carefully, letting the images her husband had crafted with his pen form in her mind. The fight with the cutting-out party on the river, the desperate gamble sailing through the British fleet, the race up the coast, fearful that any moment a British cruiser might appear over the horizon.

I dare not tell you where we are now sheltered, for fear that this letter will go astray, Isaac had written. *We are vulnerable in the extreme, and there are many who are very eager indeed to gain possession of this fine ship, not least the King's officers under whose very noses we slipped away. I dare say our escape caused some considerable consternation in the great cabins of His Majesty's ships at anchor in the Delaware Bay. I will say only that we are now at the place where poor David Weatherspoon met his untimely end last autumn. Dear Lord, it seems a hundred years ago.*

Virginia stared off into the distance. *David Weatherspoon...* She remembered it perfectly, as if the fight was a painting, she had been staring at all her life. *Charlemagne*'s final act, driven ashore to keep her out of British hands. The red-coated marines and British sailors landing on the beach, her husband's men hunkered down behind the dunes. The bursts of gun fire, the hand to hand fighting. Her attempts at surgery in the aftermath.

Young David Weatherspoon, midshipman, shot down in the sand, a pistol ball through his throat.

Great Egg Harbor, Virginia recalled. That was where it had taken place. They had lodged at the tavern there, after the British had been driven off and the local militia had come to their aide. Virginia could picture the waterfront where they had purchased a half-rotten schooner, which Isaac's men had christened *Lady Biddlecomb*. She could imagine the great bulk of the *Falmouth* frigate tied up at the end of that long wharf.

Virginia looked back at the letter, her eyes resting on the words but not reading them.

So there it is... she thought. Word at last, nearly two months since she had heard anything from her beloved Isaac. As of that writing he was safe and all but trapped at Great Egg Harbor. But was he still there? Still safe? She did not know. The letter was dated October 30 and it was now the twenty-sixth of November. Everything Isaac had written might already be moot.

She was vaguely aware of something going on below stairs, someone at the door, it seemed, but she gave it no thought. And then she realized who it must be – Captain Dexter's man come for her reply. And with that realization came the understanding that she could not possibly accept Dexter's invitation now, now that she had received word of Isaac, now that her husband was suddenly no longer an abstraction but a real presence in her life once again, even if only through his written word.

Virginia jumped to her feet, raced across the room, and pulled the door open. Ten strides and she was down the hall and at the head of the stairs. Four steps down the staircase and she could see the front entrance at the end of the foyer on the first floor, just in time to catch a glimpse of a red uniform on the stoop outside as Nelly closed the heavy door. In Nelly's hand was the small silver tray, empty.

Damn it... Virginia thought. Her mind raced through the options: chase after Dexter's man, send another note rescinding her acceptance, feign illness when Dexter arrived.

Damn, she thought again. It was too late. There was no gracious way out of it now. She would have to go.

She could still, of course, gather intelligence that might be of use to the Patriot cause. And she might even find some pleasure in being on horseback once again. That last part, she suspected, would be the one most easily accomplished.

The wet nurse arrived the following morning at 9:30 promptly, and Virginia was able to act pleased at how easily Jack took to her, despite the fact that she found it vaguely annoying. With the nurse and Jack ensconced in a chair at the far side of the room, Virginia dressed herself in her riding clothes: breeches worn under a skirt, which looked perfectly normal but was in fact divided into two legs for riding astride, if Captain Dexter were to bring a mount with such a saddle. She wore as well a short, padded riding jacket and a small cocked hat, pinned to her hair.

When she was done dressing, she made her way down the hall to Susan's room. Mrs. Williams had thankfully gone out for the day, sparing Virginia her cloying concern about the prudence of a young mother going riding on a cold, late fall morning in the city. Susan had not yet emerged from her room, and Virginia assumed she too had been making ready for the day's activities.

"Come!" Susan called in her sing-song voice at Virginia's knock. Virginia opened to door to find Susan at work at her hair, still wearing her shift and bed jacket. On the bed was a blue and white silk gown, a lovely garment but hardly one fit for riding.

"Susan, dear, the gentlemen will be here directly," Virginia said, "and you don't seem quite ready." The words were a formality, nothing more. Virginia knew from the moment she walked in the room that Susan had something in mind that did not involve horses. In truth, Virginia had suspected from the moment Susan agreed to go riding that she would find some means of slipping off that hook.

"Oh, Virginia, dear, I'm so sorry," Susan said. "When I woke this morning, I could just feel the beginnings of a wicked cold coming on. I swear it would be the very death of me if I were to go riding on so bitter a day as this. You hardy country gals can endure such things, I know, but I'm sure I could not."

"Captain Cornwall will be ever so disappointed when he gets here," Virginia said.

"Oh, never fear. I sent him word earlier. When I realized that I felt unwell."

"I see," Virginia said, and she did. She would be out of the house for most of the day. Susan's mother was out of the house. Susan was spending a lot more time on her hair than one would expect for a woman taken with illness.

Undoubtedly her note to Captain Cornwall did not suggest that he stay away, but simply that he wait until the coast was clear.

"But Captain Dexter will be here, certainly," Susan said. "And you should never cancel your plans with him out of any concern for me! I know how much you've been looking forward to this."

"Indeed," Virginia said. "So you'll be taking to your bed when I'm gone?"

"Oh, I should think so," Susan said.

"I would think so as well," Virginia said. With that, she left Susan to her hair and made her way below stairs. In the back room found her cloak and riding gloves.

There was a knock at the door at exactly 10:30. Nelly opened it to reveal Captain Richard Dexter, a wool cloak partially obscuring his flawless red uniform with its white facings, his waistcoat and breeches also white, like new-fallen snow. He gave the servant girl a courteous nod of the head and looked past her to where Virginia stood under the arch that marked the foyer's end.

"Ah, Mrs. Biddlecomb!" he said, bowing more formally. Nelly opened the door wider and Dexter came sweeping in. "I was sorry to hear that Miss Williams is ill disposed," he continued. "If you would like to forgo today's excursion, I certainly understand."

"No, no, Captain," Virginia said. "We'll soldier on, as it were, and leave Miss Williams to whatever entertainments she manages to find."

Dexter smiled. "Excellent," he said. "If you're ready, please come and inspect the mounts I've brought." He half turned and gestured toward the open door. Virginia crossed the foyer and stepped out onto the stoop. Three horses stood on the street below, their reins held by two men in the uniform of privates of the Seventeenth Regiment of Foot.

"Three horses and two foot soldiers," Virginia commented with a raised eyebrow as Dexter stepped up beside her. "It seems one too many for the two of us."

"Well, here's my quandary," Dexter said. "Generally, most woman of my acquaintance prefer to ride aside on a suitably quiet mare. But seeing as you are a rider of such experience, I thought perhaps you would prefer to ride astride." He indicated two saddles resting on the ground. "So I brought mounts with either saddle, so that you might choose."

Virginia nodded. She was impressed with the thoughtfulness. Very impressed. All the same, she was aware of the necessity for respectable behavior – even if dear Susan was, apparently, not. She smiled, indicated her clothing. "I thank you for the courtesy of choice of saddle, sir, but as you see, I am suitably dressed for riding aside. Perhaps the temperament and conformation of the horse will decide me?"

Dexter also smiled, nodded. He too was impressed.

Virginia approached the first horse, a striking dark bay gelding of about sixteen hands. She patted his neck and ran her palm across his shoulder and down his foreleg, picked up his foot, inspected how well he had been shod. Nodding satisfaction she straightened, stood back a little and assessed him. Quality breeding, good conformation, but he looked strong—a man's horse.

She smiled and went to the next, a gray mare with a silver-black mane and tail, slightly smaller than the bay. Large, kind eyes, good feet. The mare nudged her with her muzzle and Virginia laughed, rubbed the mare beneath her forelock.

Dexter chuckled. "She's always liked being scratched just there!"

The third horse, another mare, the smallest of the three, stood around fifteen hands. A chestnut, nearly the same color as Virginia's hair, with a diamond-shaped white star on her face and one white sock on her near hind. The mare snorted, tossed her head, and laid her ears back as Virginia approached.

Virginia ignored the grumpy temper and scratched with her nails along the gleaming coat of the mare's neck, crooning quietly under her breath as she did so. The mare twitched her ears forward, then back again, listening. Running her hand along the topline of the horse's rump, Virginia made to walk behind the mare intending to inspect her offside.

Dexter started forward, anxious. "Careful," he said, "this one's a bit touchy about her rear end; she's been known to kick. I didn't actually want her, but..."

"But," Virginia answered, and left it at that. She stepped back a few paces to assess all three horses from a yard or two distant. "There are scars on the chestnut's legs, and one on her flank. She has not been well treated." Virginia turned to Dexter. "Not, I trust, by you, sir!"

"Not by me, I assure you!" Dexter said. "We do our best for them, but they're army mounts, after all, and they can see some hard use. There's nothing for it."

Virginia nodded, cocked her head slightly to one side, patted one finger against her chin, considering. The bay was obviously his horse. Would he mind if she chose that one? She was a good rider, could control a strong horse—but a good rider also knew her limitations. The gray was a pretty, willing-looking mare who would go for miles without falter or fuss, but the chestnut...?

Virginia smiled. The chestnut was full of spirit and capable of standing up for herself: an 'I'll kick you before you kick me' attitude. Virginia could appreciate that.

"The chestnut, with the side saddle, please," Virginia said, decisively. She looked at Dexter, curious as to how he would react, but the young officer just smiled slightly and indicated for one of the men to saddle the horse.

He knew I would pick the chestnut, and that saddle, Virginia thought as she pulled on her riding gloves. She was not certain whether she was annoyed or flattered by that.

"Excellent choice," Dexter said with no hint of coyness in his voice. He stepped over to the chestnut's side and cupped his gloved hands to assist Virginia to mount. She thanked him as she put right boot in his hands, and as he effortlessly boosted her upward, settled herself sideways into the saddle.

The chestnut shifted nervously under her, a little unused to the lighter weight, but Virginia, holding the reins and the riding cane in one hand, scratched the animal's neck once again and made her soft crooning sound and the horse seemed to calm a bit.

Virginia smiled at the private holding the horse's bridle, brought her left leg back slightly. "Might I trouble you to shorten the stirrup leather one hole? It's a little long for comfort." The private blushed slightly as he moved aside the skirt of her habit, and altered the stirrup quickly. Again Virginia thanked him and settled the reins in both hands, ensuring the extra loop flicked over to the right-hand side of the horses neck so that it would not catch in the toe of her booted foot.

She looked around as Dexter mounted the bay with practiced ease, and she had the sense from the way he sat the horse that he was indeed as good a rider as his talk suggested he was.

"Is all well, Mrs. Biddlecomb?" he asked.

Virginia shifted slightly in the saddle to correct a slight feel of imbalance. It had been a long time since she had seen the world from the height of eye that a horse provided, a long time since she had felt a spirited animal moving under her. All of those sensations, so familiar and yet so removed from her life this half year past, all came flooding back. And despite the uncertainty she felt, the gnawing sense that this was all entirely inappropriate, the guilt and worry, and the hundred other conflicting feelings, she smiled.

"Yes, Captain," she said. "Very well, indeed."

"Excellent!" Dexter said, smiling back at her. "Then let us be off!"

CHAPTER ELEVEN

The sky was an ugly gray, the November air sharp and cold. Of the many smells carried on it, some were a regular part of Ezra Rumstick's life, a life lived out mostly on salt water, and some less so.

Rolling down from the Pine Barrens, they could detect the tang of the sea, or at least the salt marshes that bordered them. There was wood smoke in the air as well, and Rumstick caught of whiff of it now and again. It was not so prevalent as it might be in a town or village. They were moving through sparsely populated country now, with struggling farms scattered at odd and distant intervals and random woodcutters' huts and other rude shelters. The smell of nearby woods and the fresh-cut stumps and limbs of the massive logs they were hauling was stronger than the wood smoke. Strongest of all were the oxen and the deposits they left on the hard, frozen road.

"Whoa, whoa, whoa, there!"

It was Tommy Sullivan who yelled, Tommy who was handling the reins on the lead team. He was one of Faircloth's marines, and getting Faircloth to agree to let him go on the hunt for masts had been a job of work. It would have been easier, Rumstick imagined, to separate Faircloth from his own right hand than to take one of his men. But Sullivan, unlike most of the men under Biddlecomb's command, had spent more time on a farm than a ship, and he was adept at driving teams of any sort. That was something that Rumstick decidedly was not.

"What is it?" Rumstick called. "Problem?"

"No, no problem," Sullivan called back. He was at the head of the lead train, while Rumstick was a dozen paces back, nearer the middle, where he had a better view of the whole. "The big fellow, he likes to get ahead of the rest, and I need to keep him back, is all."

If that dumb cow is eager to get back to the ship, well, I'm with him, Rumstick thought. He lifted his musket a little higher and rested his thumb on the top of the hammer and looked around. The country was low, sandy, and bleak. They had left the more wooded area a few miles back and now were rolling through open fields dotted with stumps and dry, brown stalks, past the occasional farmhouse, which were mostly sorry-looking affairs. The few hardwood trees still standing had lost their leaves and looked skeletal now, and the evergreens looked dark and colorless under the overcast sky.

They saw people on occasion, men out in the fields who would stop for a moment to watch them pass, or women in the dooryards of the farmhouses. They would see small knots of men on the road, usually far off, who seemed to purposely avoid meeting up with Rumstick and his men. Banditti. Pine robbers, Rumstick guessed.

He was not too terribly concerned about them. He had a dozen men with him, well-armed and tolerably well disciplined. They were clearly not men who would be easily robbed, nor they did they appear to have much worth stealing. These pine robbers, he imagined, were like pirates, or vultures. They would not want to put themselves at risk or work terribly hard for their prey.

He had seen that already. Shadrach Barnett, *Colonel* Shadrach Barnett, had arrived with a gang of men, an unusually large gang for pine robbers, or so Richard Somers of the Gloucester County Militia had informed them. The *Falmouth* frigate was a tempting target, apparently, and Barnett seemed to envision considerable wealth stowed down in her hold.

But one show of strength—the marines parading on the dock, the men armed and lining the rails, Isaac Biddlecomb refusing to flinch—had been enough to make the man give up. He and most of his banditti had headed out the following day, and Isaac had felt secure enough that he was willing to send the woodcutting party, a quarter of the men aboard *Falmouth*, away.

Rumstick swept the countryside to his left, then looked over the top of the massive tree trunk and swept the countryside to his right. Nothing that he could see gave him cause for concern. He looked ahead, down the dark, frozen, dirt road. He had sent two of his men out ahead, a couple of foretop sailors named Manning and Ewald, to serve as pickets of sort, to make sure there were no surprises. He realized that he had not heard from them or seen them in some time.

That fact did not worry him, however. The road ran over a series of low hills as it meandered down to the sea, and the two men were likely hidden behind one of them. It would be easy enough to get well ahead of the lumbering train of oxen.

The boys are fine, doing just what you told them to do, Rumstick thought. And he believed that. To a degree. But, truth be told, the two were not particularly well suited for that job. They were not soldiers, after all, not light infantry. They were sailors, more accustom to moving nimbly through the rigging than stealthily down a road. That was true of all the men under Rumstick's command.

There was nothing stealthy about the rest of the party from *Falmouth*. Eight armed men, a dozen oxen, and three massive trees rolling along on six pairs of loggers' wheels. *Falmouth* had been launched with an admirable amount of gear stowed down in her hold. Most of the standing rigging, much of the running rigging, and all plain sail had been built while the hull was being raised on the ways. All of it had been put onboard before the ship had gone into the water. The ship's builder, Malachi Foote, had had the good sense to realize that sending it off with the ship was the only way to keep it out of British hands.

But rigging and sails were useless without masts to hang them on. While anchored in the Delaware River, they had managed to get a fore lower mast and a foreyard in place, but that was it, that was all the sticks they had available. *Falmouth* could make a little headway with that rig if the wind was strong and abaft the beam, but they would need more if they hoped to sail her to someplace of safety.

There was little timber to be had near Great Egg Harbor, but just inland a ways was a stretch of country known as the Pine Barrens, and the name seemed to offer possibilities. There was, of course, only so much they could do when it came to securing masts and yards: serious mast-cutting required dozens of men and many dozens of oxen, snow-cover ground to drag the trees from the woods, iced-over roads on which to haul the timbers by sled, and mast landings where the great trees could be launched into the ocean and towed to where they needed to be.

The men of *Falmouth* had none of those things. But after much cajoling and distribution of hard money, they were able to coax the oxen and loggers' wheels and axes from the farms around Great Egg Harbor. Rumstick had led his band of ad hoc loggers up into the Pine Barrens to see what they could find.

They went looking for white pine, that most admirable of trees, but they found none. What they did find was mostly cedar, which was useless for their purposes. They found spruce as well: not their first or even second choice, but it was serviceable. A few decent spruce trees could double their sail area, enough to hopefully drive them past the Royal Navy-infested waters off New York and clear to the more amenable seas around Boston.

On the first ridge, they located a few spruce trees large enough that they might have served as lower masts. But they were too big for Rumstick's small crew, with their handful of oxen and dubious gear, to haul back to the ship. They moved on, and finally located three trees big enough to serve as topmasts, certainly, and perhaps as somewhat stunted lowers, but were still small enough for them to manage.

Those trees they felled and limbed, and with considerable effort and ingenuity positioned the loggers' wheels under them and hitched up the teams. Sullivan took the lead and they headed back down the road, a road that would have been impossible to traverse if it had not been frozen solid.

"Ten miles, you reckon, Mr. Rumstick?" Woodbury asked. Woodbury, like Rumstick, had been bred to the sea, and like Rumstick had no great love for this sort of thing.

"About," Rumstick said. He looked back over his shoulder, toward the hills to the west. There was no sun to be seen, but from the light in the sky, he guessed that sunset was a few hours away. Under the thick cover of clouds, the day was growing dark already.

"We won't make it tonight," Rumstick added. He turned back and looked out over the country ahead of them. "Maybe find a barn or some such to bed down in."

They continued on in their ponderous way along the road to Great Egg Harbor, the oxen occasionally bellowing their displeasure, the men under Rumstick's command muttering theirs, quiet enough that their growling was not so obvious, which allowed Rumstick to ignore it. They rolled down one of the several hills and the oxen strained to pull the logs up the far side and Rumstick continued to scan the country ahead of them.

"There, Woodbury, that look like a farm to you?" He pointed off to the south. There was a light, it seemed to be a window against a darker shape. The evening was coming on quick, the low areas already lost in shadow.

"Yeah, I think so," Woodbury said, squinting in the direction that Rumstick was pointing. "Farm has to mean a barn."

And food and maybe ale, Rumstick thought. He knew that was what Woodbury was thinking because he was thinking it himself. They had been living on cold meat and bread. What ale they had carried with them was long gone and they were reduced to water for the duration.

"Manning and Ewald, they're probably there already," Woodbury said. "Sons of bitches, probably having a smoke by the hearth as we speak."

Rumstick nodded. He considered making some quip about the possibility of a farmer's daughter, but he was too cold and weary to think of anything particularly clever, so instead he said, "Wish those two would show themselves, let us know what's ahead."

They crested the next hill and started to roll down the other side and Rumstick was certain now that it was a farm they were looking at, and not some miserable woodcutter's hovel. He could see light in a few windows, and behind the house another building that seemed to be a barn of some sort. A barn would mean straw and some degree of shelter from the cold. If they drove the oxen inside, it would warm the place up some. Rumstick could comfort himself in the knowledge that he had slept in worse company.

The voice came from his left and from somewhere ahead. It came sharp and loud and unequivocal. "Hold!"

Rumstick frowned and looked in that direction and his first thought was that it was Sullivan calling out, that there was some problem with the team.

*Not Sullivan...*Rumstick realized. The voice was not Sullivan's. Then there was another shout from the right and a cry of surprise, a loud curse, and that last one was most certainly Sullivan. The curse was followed with a dull thud and the sound of something dropping to the road.

Rumstick tried to see what was happening but they were in a dip between two hills and it was hard to make things out in the deep shadow. He raised his musket to chest height and cocked the firelock.

"What's acting? Sullivan?" he shouted. There were more cries of alarm behind him and then a dozen men came swarming up from the ditch beside the road, a ditch that Rumstick had not even realized was there. He could see muskets in the men's hands and he swung his own musket around level, finger on the trigger.

"Son of a bitch!" Rumstick shouted and he pulled the trigger. The priming hissed and the charge lit and the musket jerked back in his hands as it fired. In the muzzle flash, he could see the men coming at him, some with muskets leveled, some with pistols. He could see that his one shot had struck no one.

He flipped his musket around, grabbed the warm barrel and swung the gun like a club, because that was the only sort of weapon it could be now. A broad, wild swing, but if he connected he might be able to take out one of two of them.

"Hold!" the voice shouted again. "Don't fire, none of you, don't fire!" The command was loud and emphatic. It cut through the confusion created by the bold attack, the frantic defense. Rumstick could see the men from the ditch stepping back, lifting muskets to shoulders, aiming at him and the others, but not firing. Up and down his column he could hear the struggling and the shouting give way to quiet.

"Put your muskets down, the lot of you!" the voice, calling again. "Rumstick, you son of a whore, where the devil are you! Tell them to put their muskets down."

Rumstick frowned and looked in the direction from which the voice had come. He did not lower his musket. He did not reply.

"Rumstick, damn your eyes," the man called again, then said, "Abbot, bring that damned lantern over here." For a moment there was a shuffling, a clanging of metal on metal, and then a spill of light where someone unshuttered a lantern. He held it high, walking down the length of the log that was mounted on the loggers' wheels.

"There you are, Rumstick, you bastard," the man said. He stopped five feet away, holding the lantern up so its light fell on his face and Rumstick's as well. It was a face Rumstick recognized. Not a face he knew well, but one he recognized.

"You're that poxed bastard Wilcox, styles himself a sergeant or some such," Rumstick said, remembering at last where he had seen that unpleasant face before. Only once, and standing beside the other whore's son Barnett, the one who styled himself a colonel, from *headquarters*, of all things.

"Sergeant...that's right," Wilcox said. "Don't make no never mind, in any event. I might as well be the pope, for all the difference it'll make to you."

Rumstick's first impulse was to demand an explanation, to ask what Wilcox thought he was doing, but he kept his mouth shut. It was pointless. He knew what Wilcox was doing: he was eliminating a dozen of the men defending *Falmouth*, a quarter of the ship's company, and when he was done, he would doubtless rob their corpses for good measure. Maybe he was acting on Barnett's orders, maybe acting on his own, but that was what he was doing.

"Where are my men? The ones I sent ahead?" Rumstick demanded instead.

Wilcox actually smiled at that. "Them two idiots, come strolling along like they was going to a Sunday picnic? That the best you got? Lord above, if that's true I'd be doing you a favor by killing you now."

"If you killed them, then you are one dead son of a bitch," Rumstick said. "With my own hands, I'll kill you."

"Uh huh," Wilcox said. "That would be quite the trick, seeing as you'll likely be dead yourself soon enough. But don't fear. They ain't hurt. For now, the lot of you are worth more to me alive. For now."

Wilcox looked up and down the length of the train, at the men on both sides with muskets raised, then looked back at Rumstick. "Seems like we have a bit of a stand-off here," he said. "But I got two dozen men to your…ten, maybe? Which means if every one of us kills his man, I still got more than a dozen standing."

"You got a hell of a head for figuring, I'll give you that," Rumstick said.

"Thank'ee," Wilcox said. "So…why don't you tell your men to put their damned firelocks down before I tell my boys to blow all your damned heads off?"

Rumstick nodded slightly as he considered the demand. At this range, it was likely that every shot on either side would tell, and the Falmouths would certainly come out on the losing side of that exchange. He could not dispute Wilcox's arithmetic. Loathe as he was to surrender, he knew there was a better chance of escape if they were not dead.

"Very well," Rumstick said, then in a loud voice called, "You men of the *Falmouth*, lay down your arms! Lay them down, I say!"

He could hear grumbling and cursing in the dark, and the thud of heavy muskets tossed to the frozen road. He hoped none of the weapons would misfire: one accidental discharge and he and his men could be on the receiving end of a firing squad.

The last of the muskets hit the ground with nothing louder than a thump and Wilcox ordered his men to bind the hands of Rumstick's crew. This they did with admirable efficiency because, Rumstick saw to his annoyance, they had the lengths of cordage in their coat pockets, ready to go.

Pretty damned sure of yourself, weren't you? Rumstick thought, but he had to admit, to himself at least, that Wilcox's self-assurance had been well-placed.

"Here now, the lot of you, get a move on," Wilcox called once Rumstick's men were bound at the wrists. "Form up there and get a move on."

"What, ho? You're just leaving the oxen?" Rumstick asked. "And the logs?"

"Sod the oxen, and sod the logs," Wilcox said. "We got no use for them, and neither do you." With that, he and the others herded Rumstick and his men to the front of the train and gathered them together, surrounded on four sides by the musket-wielding banditti. With another shout and various curses, the rag and tag parade moved out, shambling along the dirt road, which was becoming increasingly hard to see in the gathering dark.

They marched up the next hill and down the other side and Rumstick called, "Hey, Wilcox, we marching clear to Great Egg Harbor? Kind of far to cover, and night coming on, ain't it?"

"Shut your gob," Wilcox said, and he offered no more enlightenment regarding his plans. But it was clear soon enough what he intended. Near the bottom of the next hill, he directed the men away from the road and down the beaten way that led to the farmhouse Rumstick had seen from a distance. They did not pause at the farmhouse at all, but marched on past toward the barn. A couple of men stood at the big, open door, lanterns head high.

"In you go," Wilcox said, gesturing toward the door with an exaggerated sweep of the hands. "They got cows and swine in there, but I reckon they won't be too offended by you lot."

Rumstick led the way in, followed by his men and the men with the lanterns and Wilcox's men. The barn was what Rumstick imagined it would be—not terribly large by the standard of barns, but large enough for the animals and the prisoners. A loft overhead, all but lost in the shadows, was spilling over with hay, and more hay and straw lay in a great heap on the floor. Manning and Ewald were sprawled side by side on the straw, hands bound, mouths gagged.

"You gentlemen make yourselves comfortable," Wilcox called. "Too damned late to kill you lot tonight, we'll take care of that little thing in the morning. Unless any of you want to try and get away. In that case, we'll kill you where you stand."

"Hey, Wilcox," Rumstick said, "my men need food and drink. Since you're being so hospitable, and all."

"I told you, you dumb bastard, I'm going to kill you all in the morning," Wilcox said. "Ain't gonna waste food and drink on you now."

With that, he and his men pushed Rumstick and the rest onto the pile of straw. Wilcox posted four guards at various places around the barn and issued sundry threats for them to stay vigilant, and described what would happen to them if they did not. The rest of his men he took with him as he headed back out to the farmyard, closing the big doors behind him.

"Lieutenant..." Tommy Sullivan whispered. He was lying on the straw beside Rumstick. In the initial fight, he had taken a blow from a musket butt to the side of the head and he had been pretty wobbly through most of the march to the barn, but he seemed to be doing better now.

"Yeah?" Rumstick said.

"Do you reckon they truly mean to kill us? In the morning?"

"They won't kill us," Rumstick said.

"That son of a bitch, he said he was going to kill us," Sullivan insisted.

"He won't kill us," Rumstick said. "If he meant to kill us he'd have done it out on the road. Left us in the ditch. No reason to go to the trouble of marching us all the way here."

Sullivan nodded and was quiet for a moment. "So...what then?" he asked.

As to that, Rumstick had a pretty good idea, and nothing he could think of suggested he was wrong. "They want the *Falmouth*," he said. "This Wilcox bastard, or him and Barnett, doesn't really matter. They want the ship but they sure as hell don't want to fight their way onboard. That would be a slaughter if they tried it. But an exchange—hostages for the ship—that wouldn't be too much trouble."

"Huh," Sullivan said. "But, you reckon Captain Biddlecomb..."

"Here, shut your damned mouths!" one of the guards called from across the barn. "We got to be stuck in here with you sorry sons of bitches, we don't need to hear you yapping away, to boot."

"Don't need to stay here," Rumstick called. "Wilcox and them others, they're all getting a hot meal, a cup of ale. Rum. And they left you out here. Ain't fair. Go join them. We can watch ourselves, it's no problem."

"I said shut your damned mouth!" the guard said in reply and so Rumstick shut his damned mouth, deciding he had pushed that far enough.

Very well, he thought. *This son of a bitch Wilcox has his plans. So I guess it's up to me to make a hash of them.*

And that was just the thing Rumstick intended to do. There were, of course, a few obstacles he had to overcome first. He was unarmed. He and his men were vastly outmanned. He was laying on a pile of straw with his hands bound and a guard who was eager to blow his brains out standing not fifteen feet away. But beyond that, he was ready to go.

CHAPTER TWELVE

Biddlecomb and Gerrish spent the remainder of the day taking shifts as look-out at the top of the lower foremast, the highest point on the sparsely rigged *Falmouth*. They stood watches of fifteen or twenty minutes, once every hour. It was about all they could endure with the cold wind coming off the water, but it was enough. They could see clearly what Barnett was doing, which was exactly what he said he would do.

It was two bells in the first dog watch and the sun was setting behind the heavy clouds to the west when Biddlecomb called a council of his officers in the great cabin. Earlier he had found a small brazier tucked in a locker, a square iron box intended as a field cookstove for one or two men. He built a fire in it, and it was enough to give the cabin a modicum of heat, so that they could remove their cloaks and scarves and gloves and still be tolerably comfortable.

The council was as sparse as everything else aboard the frigate. There was only Biddlecomb, Mr. Midshipman Samuel Gerrish, and Lieutenant Faircloth of the marines. Biddlecomb asked Mr. Joshua Sprout, the boatswain, to join them as well. Sprout was a warrant officer, of course, not a commissioned officer, but he was good at his job, he knew a great deal about the ship, and Biddlecomb had come to trust the man's opinions.

"Well, gentlemen," Biddlecomb began after he had filled wine glasses all around. The wine, as usual, was excellent and courtesy of Mr. Faircloth. "Mr. Gerrish and I have spent an unenviable amount of time aloft with a glass today, watching the goings-on on shore. I would not reckon this Colonel Barnett for an honest cove, but he does seem to be doing what he said he would do, which is bivouacking his men right at the end of the wharf and setting a guard on the road and on the wharf itself. Seems to have near fifty men, again, as he said. They've pitched tents and have campfires going and from what I can hear they're into the rum already."

That was met with a general silence. No one was entirely sure how to respond.

"Might we hope they drink themselves into a stupor?" Gerrish suggested. "Enough that we could launch a surprise attack?"

"Like Washington at Trenton, wrought small?" Faircloth suggested.

"Exactly," said Gerrish.

"Perhaps," Biddlecomb said. "But not tonight. We'll keep a weather eye on them, try to get a sense for how vigilant they are. They'll probably get less so as the days pass. But it would always be a risk. They outnumber us. By quite a bit."

"And more so now, with Mr. Rumstick and his lot gone," Sprout offered. Heads nodded in reply.

"That's another thing," Biddlecomb said. "Barnett, when I was talking with him this morning, just before they made camp at the end of the wharf, he made some veiled reference to Rumstick's column. Didn't come out and say he knew the men were off looking for spars, but he dropped enough of a hint that it's pretty clear he does."

"So he knows we're weaker still," Faircloth said.

"He does," Biddlecomb said. He did not say anything further, but in truth Barnett's knowing they were weaker was not his first concern. Rumstick had only a dozen men with him. Barnett seemed able to conjure up many more than that. If he sent some of his banditti after Rumstick and his men, it would not end well, not for the banditti and not for Rumstick.

He felt like an idiot, ordering Rumstick off on his ill-conceived woodcutting venture. He had done it because he thought Barnett was gone for good, and that made him feel like an even bigger idiot. And now he lacked the moral courage to admit any of that to these men, even though they had likely cottoned to it already.

All in all, not my finest hour, Biddlecomb thought.

"Well, damn it, what about this damned militia?" Gerrish said, letting his frustration spill over. "Somers and his lot? Don't they exist just to deal with this sort of thing?"

"Perhaps," Faircloth said, "but they never struck me as being terribly enthusiastic about it."

"To say the least," Biddlecomb said. "Look, I've been down this road with Somers, several times now. It's his contention that Barnett hasn't actually done anything yet to warrant the use of force." This brought sundry chuckles, snorts, and guffaws from the others and Biddlecomb held up his hands in resignation.

"I second those sentiments," Biddlecomb said. "But here's the simple fact. Barnett has a lot more men than Somers, and they're a dangerous bunch and the militia are not. And there's no will among the militia to take up this fight, because they reckon they'll all be killed. And they're probably right."

More nodding all around. No one could disagree with that.

"If we could act in concert," Faircloth said. "Coordinate an attack with the militia…"

"I'll stop you there, lieutenant," Biddlecomb said. "I think we had better all understand … Barnett has cut us off. We can't talk with Somers, we can't warn Rumstick, we can't stroll into town for a bowl of flip at the tavern. There's no way off the ship. Barnett had blocked us by land and we have no boats. And we sure as hell can't swim."

"We have no boats, sir, but we could build one," Sprout said. "Doesn't even have to be much of one. Just something to float some men to shore in the dark of night."

"Good," Biddlecomb said. "Pray start on that immediately. Now, who can tell me how much food we have onboard?"

"Three and a half barrels of salt pork, sir," Gerrish said. "The better part of a barrel of dried peas. Three sacks of ship's biscuit. Four sacks of oats. There's no ale and rum aboard, which is probably just as well, but there's plenty of water. Enough for a week at full rations."

Biddlecomb nodded. "Very well. Mr. Sprout will build his boat. We'll keep watch, look out for some opportunity to rid ourselves of

Barnett and his banditti sons of whores. See if Rumstick is able to effect something on his return. I can think of nothing we might do beyond that. Any of you gentlemen have any suggestions?"

"If we can get a man ashore," Faircloth said, "it's but a few day's ride to Washington's headquarters. We might get word to them and get some real damned troops down here to help."

"I think not," Biddlecomb said. "Washington, as I understand it, has no great love for the ships of the Continental Navy. Thinks they're a waste of resources. He's just tell us to do with *Falmouth* what he recommended be done with the other ships, which is to sink it."

That was greeted with expressions of muted outrage and disbelief. "Well," Gerrish said, "That certainly is not going to happen."

"No," Biddlecomb agreed. But in truth, if things did not go well, and it did not look like they would go well, then that was exactly what he intended to do.

He did not mention it to the others.

They were changing out the guards every two hours. That was Rumstick's best guess. He had no way of knowing for certain: he had no watch, and no way to reach it if he did, and he could not see the moon or stars at all, despite the wide gaps in the boards in the barn's walls.

There were two lanterns hanging from the heavy beams and they gave just the weakest illumination, two desultory pools of light falling on the hay and the dirt floor and a few of the crude wooden stalls that held the livestock. In that dim light, the guards could not see that Rumstick was watching them, gauging how alert they were, how attentive to duty. From what he could observe, they were not much of either, and that was good.

For some time, they could hear muffled sounds from the farmhouse across the yard, loud laughter and shouting and the bang of the door as men went in and out to relieve themselves, or so Rumstick imagined. The farmer, apparently, had a copious supply of rum, or the pine robbers had brought their own, but either way the noise suggested they were well into it.

It seemed to Rumstick he had spent an ungodly amount of time sprawled on the hay before he heard the bar on the barn door lift and the big door come creaking open, but on further reflection, he guessed it had not actually been that long. Two hours. It just felt considerably longer.

Four men entered to replace the four who had been on watch. The on-coming watch seemed to have been enjoying their time, judging from their loud talk and unsteady gait. Conversely, the off-going watch, with their clipped and belligerent tones, seemed resentful of having missed the fun. Once relieved they left quickly, and the new men settled in. They were in no condition to stand for their entire watch, so they found seats on barrels and carts. Rumstick doubted they would even stay awake for their full two hours.

Damn it... he thought as he struggled with the bindings on his wrist. If he could get free, then it would be no problem to overcome the men set to guard them. Most likely he would be able to just amble over and cut their throats once they had passed out on the floor. But the lashings on his wrists were well-tied, and he knew he would not get out of them on his own.

The barn was filled with ugly, guttural, snorting sounds, which might have been mistaken for the livestock but Rumstick knew were actually his own men, fast asleep where they had collapsed.

Unbelievable, he thought, but he was not terribly surprised. It was the mark of a sailor, to be able to sleep wherever, whenever. A small concern like the promise of being killed on the morrow was not enough to trouble their slumber.

He reached back tentatively with his foot until he found Sullivan's shin and gave it a little kick. Sullivan made a grunting noise but did not wake, so Rumstick kicked him again.

"Huh? What?" Sullivan said, a bit too loud, as he came partially awake. Rumstick did not reply. He lay still, listening for any movement among the guards, any sign that they might have heard, but there was nothing. As far as he knew, they were part of the snoring contingent.

"Here, Sullivan," Rumstick said in a breathy whisper. "Lay back to back with me and see if you can untie the bindings on my wrists. Quiet now." He did not wait for a reply, but rolled over on his side, back toward Sullivan, unsure if the man was even awake. But a moment later, he heard Sullivan roll over as well and felt the man's fingers moving over his hands and wrists until they found the bindings. He pushed his hands away from his back to make them easier for Sullivan to reach, and lay still as Sullivan pulled and prodded and searched for a way to loosen the ropes.

He worked at it for some minutes without the least bit of success, as far as Rumstick could tell. The cordage had a light coating of tar, which made it sticky and difficult to untie in the best of circumstances. To make things worse, the bindings were so tight that Rumstick's fingers had grown numb, and he imagined Sullivan's were as well. There was little chance, he realized, that Sullivan's efforts would succeed.

But the man kept at it anyway, and as he did Rumstick started thinking on other ways to get free. He had a folding knife in his coat pocket. To get it out himself, if that was even possible, would require rolling around and thrashing in a way that would certainly have attracted the guards' notice. But perhaps he could roll over and position himself so that Sullivan could fish it out. It might work, certainly if the guards had enough courtesy to pass out drunk.

Laying as he was on the straw, looking out into the dark, concentrating on Sullivan's efforts and thinking about the knife in his pocket, he did not see or hear the guard approaching. He was not aware of the man's presence at all until he felt the butt of the musket slam into his gut. The breath was knocked from him and he doubled over, as much as he could, laying on his side.

"What the hell you think you're about?" the guard growled.

Rumstick lay still for a moment as he sucked in air and regained his breath. Then he rolled on his back and looked up, seeing the man for the first time, a squat, ugly brute who was much in want of a bath and a shave.

"I was counting on my finger all the times I rogered your mother," he said. "Ran out of fingers so Sullivan here was helping."

"Oh, funny man," the guard said, and stepped closer and drew his musket back again. He drove the butt at Rumstick's stomach once more but Rumstick swung his leg sideways and knocked the gun away as it came at him, then cocked his leg and drove his shoe into the man's gut. The force of the kick tossed the guard back onto the floor, sending his hat flying off in one direction, his musket in another.

That was probably a stupid thing to do, Rumstick reflected as the man landed hard, sprawled out on his back, then scrambled awkwardly to his feet. He grabbed up his musket, which had landed a few feet away, then turned back toward Rumstick. The look on the man's face, even in the dim light, and his hunched posture, suggested that he was furious, humiliated, and ready to dole out a beating.

If you're going to knock me on the head, I'll make it a job of work for you, Rumstick thought as he jerked his body forward and used the momentum to carry himself up onto his feet. This was all foolish, he knew, counterproductive. It would not help them escape. Just the opposite. But he did not care. Anger was driving him now, an unwillingness to just take the abuse, a hope for some degree of vengeance if he could wring that out of the situation.

The other three guards, who had been asleep, or nearly so, were on the move, coming closer, moving cautiously, muskets ready. Rumstick could hear his own men stirring behind him.

"Wirt, what the devil are you about?" one of the guards asked as he stepped closer.

The ugly one, whose name was apparently Wirt, had his musket in his hands, held like a club, butt up, as he took a cautious step toward Rumstick.

"This big bastard, this Rumstick, he thinks he's a funny man," Wirt replied, his eyes never leaving Rumstick's. "I'm gonna teach him he ain't."

"All right," said the other guard. "But don't make too much of a mess of him."

"And don't you kill him, dumb ass," another of the guards chimed in. "Barnett'll do for all of us if you do."

"Aye, pray, don't kill me, Wirt," Rumstick said as the man took another cautious step in his direction. "Though I don't reckon you could if you wanted to. You look mighty scared for someone fighting a man who's got his hands tied."

Rumstick watched with satisfaction as the scowl on Wirt's face deepened, and listened with pleasure as his own men hooted and even Wirt's compatriots laughed. The angrier old Wirt got, the better.

"Scared, huh?" Wirt said. "How's this for scared?" He brought the musket back over his shoulder, ready to swing it around and deliver a powerful blow, but before he could even start the swing Rumstick dashed forward, three steps, until he was inches from Wirt and looking down into the shorter man's startled eyes.

Wirt was just starting to utter something when Rumstick smashed his forehead down on Wirt's face. He felt the sharp impact and the jarring pain in his skull, and then felt something of Wirt's give way under the blow. He looked up as Wirt staggered back. Blood was gushing out of the man's nostrils. It looked black in the dim light of the lanterns.

"Son of a bitch!" Wirt shouted, but the words sounded comical coming through his broken nose. He started to level his musket and thumb back the hammer of the firelock but Rumstick was on him again, this time kicking up between the man's legs, his foot connecting with that end as solidly as his forehead had with the other.

Wirt crumpled over, bent at the middle, and Rumstick took a step back and cocked his leg to deliver the blow to the man's head that would end it all. He was just starting the swing when the three other guards stepped up, muskets leveled, muzzles just a few feet from Rumstick's face. The click of the hammers snapping into the cocked position was loud in the confines of the barn.

"That's enough," one said. The other guards might have no great love for Wirt, but they were not going to let one of their own take such a beating.

Rumstick checked the kick and stepped back. He was breathing hard. Behind him his men were on their feet, he was sure of it. The three guards still standing had their muskets at their shoulders and they were swinging them side to side, pointing at each man in turn, as if daring them to take a bullet for their shipmates.

"Stand down, men, stand down," Rumstick said. "It's done here." He glanced quickly to his left and right. He did not see anything, or anyone. Still, he had a sense that the men around him were not the only men in the barn.

Let them put their firelocks on half-cock, Rumstick thought. Wilcox and the others back in the farmhouse might be dead drunk, or near enough, but a gunshot could well get someone running.

"Sit your arses down!" one of the guards called, gesturing toward the hay stack with the end of his musket. "The lot of you, down!"

"You heard the man," Rumstick said, keeping his voice calm, no threat in his tone. "Sit down, nice and easy. No rush, plenty of time… don't want one of them muskets going off now, do we?"

He heard the shuffle and crunch of the men behind him settling back down in the straw. He took another step back and felt the edge of the pile under foot and began to ease himself down, not a simple thing with his hands lashed behind him. He came down on one knee and paused.

"There we are now, all down and safe," Rumstick said to the guards. Wirt was on the floor, on his side, his hands between his legs, rocking side to side and moaning, but the others were formed in a semicircle, muskets still aimed at Rumstick and his men.

"Very well, you great whoremonger," one of the banditti said. "I don't care to hear anything more from you. And get back on that damned hay pile." He looked over at the other men behind Rumstick. "Any one of you stands up again, or says one damned word, and by all that's holy, I swear I'll blow your rutting head off."

He lifted his musket and pointed the muzzle up toward the roof. He eased the hammer down to the half-cock position and the other two guards did the same. But they did not step back and they did not take their eyes off Rumstick and his men. And, because of that, they did not see James Ferguson, fore topman, and Ephraim Kirby, also of the fore-top, moving in behind them, from left and right, keeping to the shadows, stepping as quickly and silently as they could.

*Good lads, good lads…*Rumstick thought. Just as he had sent Manning and Ewald ahead of the column to scout things out, he had told Ferguson and Kirby to hang back, half a mile at least, to keep a weather eye out for anyone following, and to serve as reinforcements if any trouble came to the main body. Rumstick had considered this rearguard to be of even greater import than the pickets, so he had chosen two men more seasoned and able that Manning and Ewald, and it seemed to have paid off.

"Now see here," Rumstick said in a loud voice, addressing the guard who had ordered him to be silent. "We ain't looking for trouble, or any such thing, we were just…"

"I told you to shut your damned mouth," the guard said.

"I know, I know, but you'll want to hear this," Rumstick said, letting his voice get louder still. "Because there's money hidden on the ship, hard money. I know where it is. And I'm willing to make a deal here, my life and my men, and I tell you where it's hidden."

The guard was not buying it. Rumstick could see that in his expression. But words like "hard money" and "deal" were enough to make even a skeptical man willing to listen, at least for a short while. And a short while was all Rumstick needed. Seconds. He forced himself not to glance over at Ferguson and Kirby, who were now moving across the floor behind the guards.

"The thing of it is," Rumstick continued, "Captain Biddlecomb, he…"

That was as far as he got. The guard to the right caught the movement in the corner of his eye and swung around and shouted in surprise. He started to bring his musket up, his thumb moving to the hammer, when Kirby leapt at him, his own musket held high. Kirby drove the musket forward, butt-first, slamming the heavy wooden end into the man's head. The guard went back and down, crumpling to the floor as the other two whirled around in surprise.

Ferguson was there, right in the face of the man to the left, driving his musket home the way Kirby had done. The guard in the middle, the one who Rumstick had been addressing, was still standing, bringing his weapon up, when Rumstick launched himself forward. He hit the man shoulder first in the back, driving him forward and off his feet. The priming in his musket's pan flashed as he fell and the weapon fired with a blinding and deafening report, illuminating the barn in a lightening flash as the guard and Rumstick went down in a heap.

Damn it! Rumstick thought as he fell on top of the man. His nose was filled with the sharp smell of burned powder and filthy clothes and unwashed body, and he heard a *puff* as the air was driven from the man's lungs.

For a moment he lay there, trying to get his legs under him, thrashing like a fish in the bottom of a boat. Then he felt hands grab his arms and Ferguson and Kirby lifted him back to his feet. Ferguson opened his mouth to speak but Rumstick said, "Shush...quiet..."

They stood in silence, the only sound the guard on the floor kicking and gasping, and Wirt, who was rocking slightly side to side and making soft whimpering sounds. The other two guards made no sound at all, nor did they move; knocked out by the blows from the muskets or dead or on their way to being dead.

Ferguson stepped around and pulled his sheath knife from his belt and cut Rumstick's bonds away. It felt so good that Rumstick wanted to sigh out loud but he kept his mouth shut and cocked his ear toward the barn door. He listened for any change: voices raised in the farmhouse, shouts of alarm, running feet. The musket shot had sounded so loud in the confines of the barn it seemed impossible that they had not heard it clear to Great Egg Harbor.

They stood that way for a full minute as the guard at their feet caught his breath and began to stir, pushing himself up. Rumstick reached over and took Ferguson's musket and pressed the muzzle to the man's head.

"Quiet," he whispered. "And don't move."

The guard eased himself back down to the floor, motionless and silent. Rumstick and the others continued to listen to the sounds of the night. They could hear a slight moaning from the wind and the occasional creak of the barn and the sounds of the sleeping animals. But beyond that, nothing.

"Good," Rumstick said at last, just loud enough to be heard. "Guess the lot of them are too drunk to hear much of anything. Ferguson, Kirby, cut the rest free. Quiet now."

Behind him, Rumstick heard the crunching of straw underfoot as the Falmouths moved off the pile and one by one their bonds were cut away. Kirby knelt over the one conscious guard and bound his wrists and stood him up on his feet. Rumstick took the man by the collar and pulled him close.

"What was the plan?" he asked. "I know you lot weren't gonna kill us, 'cause you would have killed us on the road if you were. So what was it?"

The guard scowled. He tilted his head back and let the defiance show on his face. Rumstick did not react, just held his hand out to Ferguson and Ferguson put the hilt of his sheath knife in Rumstick's palm. Rumstick took the knife and laid the tip gently on the man's face, a half inch below his left eye.

"Very well, let's try again," Rumstick said, but still he got nothing.

"Lieutenant," Ferguson said, "you know he's gonna scream like a bastard when you take that eye."

"You're right," Rumstick said. "Better gag him first." With that Kirby stepped up and grabbed the tail of the man's coat and cut a strip of cloth away. He stepped behind the man and drew the cloth around his head, forcing it in between his clenched teeth.

"All right, all right," the man said, the words muffled by the gag. Rumstick nodded and Kirby pulled the cloth away. Rumstick pressed the tip of the knife a little harder against the man's skin to further inspire him.

"Barnett, he wants that ship," the man said. "Reckons there's something worth a hell of a lot onboard. Least that's what he says. Me, I think he's got it in his head he just has to have it. He ain't one for anyone defying him, you understand?"

Rumstick nodded. "So?"

"So, he knew you lot were up here, up in the Barrens, so he sent Wilcox and the rest of us up here to grab you. Figured, best case, the captain of the ship would make a trade, you bastards for the ship. Worst case, we kill you all and that's a dozen less we got to fight later."

Rumstick nodded again. It made sense. In Barnett's shoes, he probably would have done the same. Splitting up *Falmouth*'s company had always been a risk. Biddlecomb had only done it because he needed the spars, and because he thought Barnett had given up.

"Well, I reckon you're telling the truth, or close to it," Rumstick said to the man. "So I guess I won't kill you." He removed the knife, to the man's evident relief, and handed it back to Ferguson. "But I will gag you now, and bind you good." He nodded to Kirby and Kirby slipped the gag over the man's head once more and jammed it in his mouth before he could utter another word.

Rumstick looked around him. The rest of his men were gathered near, their hands free at last. They had collected the muskets and cartridge boxes from the guards on the floor.

"Better tie and gag that sorry bastard Wirt," Rumstick said, gesturing toward the man on the floor. "How about the other two? Any need to tie them up?"

Woodbury knelt down by the closest man, prodded him a bit, then stood again. "No. No need to tie these ones up," he said.

Rumstick nodded. "Ferguson, how'd you two get in here?"

"Door. Around back," Ferguson said, nodding toward the back of the barn, lost in shadow.

"Bar that door there," Rumstick said, pointing to the big doors in the front of the barn, and when that was done, he turned to Ferguson. "Lead the way."

They moved quietly around the piles of hay and straw, Ferguson leading, the lanterns giving off just enough light that it was not utterly impossible to see. Ahead of him, Rumstick heard the sound of a bar lifting and the soft groan of a door moving on hinges, and then he could see the pale light on the ground outside and he felt a blast of fresh, cold air.

They filed out of the barn and into the November night. The moon behind the clouds illuminated what little countryside they could see in a pale, bluish light. They stood there for a moment, letting their eyes adjust, and more and more of the barnyard and the hills beyond resolved out of the gloom.

Once again Rumstick concentrated on the sounds in the night, and once again he heard nothing beyond what he would expect to hear. No shouts of alarm. No armed men turning out to prevent an escape.

"So far, so good," he said softly.

Ten miles. They had about ten miles to go to reach Great Egg Harbor, and an hour or so's head start before the new guards found the old ones sprawled out on the floor. Rumstick stepped to the front of the column and marched off south, leading his men over the frozen ground.

Chapter Thirteen

The weather was crisp, but not terribly cold, on the morning that Virginia Biddlecomb and Captain Richard Dexter took their first ride together. Once they were mounted, Dexter dismissed the two privates who led the dark bay gelding away. He asked again if Virginia was content with her mount, and when she assured him she was, he turned his own horse and led the way north.

They rode along Chestnut Street, their horses' hooves making a sharp clacking sound on the cobblestones, past the tall brick homes that lined the way, weaving through the crowds of tradespeople and servants and red-coated soldiers. Virginia wondered if Dexter would turn left on Fifth Street to avoid passing the State House where, a year and a half earlier, the seditious Continental Congress had signed the declaration that proclaimed the Colonies free and independent, and where, until just a few months ago, they had met to administer those united states. She wondered if he would try to avoid any awkwardness that might arise from seeing that potent symbol of the present conflict.

But Dexter did not turn, he continued on, which was, in Virginia's mind, to his credit.

There were considerably more soldiers there than there had been even a block south: red coats with white facings and yellow facings and blue facings and the regimental drummers, young men, Black and White, with their colors the inverse of their regiment. The soldiers wore cocked hats or the leather hats of dragoons or the lofty fur hats of the grenadiers. There were German soldiers as well, with their blue coats and tall brass-plated hats and their impressive mustaches. So many soldiers, so well equipped.

"The State House has been taken over as a barracks," Dexter said, nodding toward the imposing brick building and the hundreds of tents set up on the open ground to the west. "But I imagine you know that already. Second story is a hospital for American wounded. Mostly poor fellows from Germantown. A bloody business, I dare say."

"I've heard as much," Virginia said, eyeing the British soldiers as they rode past.

He's never asked me about my loyalties, Virginia mused. Dexter had not shied away from mentioning things in the military line, but he had never asked Virginia where she stood on the question of fidelity to the Crown, or made even the slightest attempt to ferret out an answer.

He reckons I think the same as Susan does, most likely, she thought. *Meaning I don't think anything at all.*

Susan had no discernable opinions about the war that Virginia was aware of, or about politics, or anything beyond fashion and the potential of this gentleman or that to make a suitable husband. But Susan could be an enigma, too. It was entirely possible that she thought very deeply about such things, but kept her own council.

Still, Virginia did not think so. Nor did she think Captain Dexter believed that she, Virginia, was quite as shallow as Susan Williams. More likely he did not care where Virginia's loyalties lay, or did not care to know. Whatever designs he had on her, she did not think they involved politics.

"Are these all of General Howe's troops?" Virginia asked. "Quartered here?"

"No, no," Dexter said. "A fraction of them, really. The General was concerned about having the bulk of his army in the city, leaving the country unguarded. That's why we were at Germantown, you know. Howe pulled the men back after the battle, and they're quartered in various places in the city, or just outside. The Queen's Rangers are north of there, covering Swede's Ford. A few regiments have been sent to deal with the fortifications on the river below the city. The Seventeenth was to remain in Germantown at first, but happily we were pulled back into the city as well."

"Happily?" Virginia asked with a teasing tone. "Do you fear the wilds of America? Would you be bored in the countryside?"

"I would not have made your acquaintance," he replied.

"Indeed," Virginia said. She was not impressed by such flattery, but found herself flattered all the same.

They crossed Sixth and then Seventh Street and the building began to thin. They turned east and crossed wide Market Street and soon found themselves in the North East Square with its park-like fields and stands of trees. Virginia had been to the square only once before, when the grass was green and the trees still sported leaves and there were no tents lining the western end, as opposed to the hundreds that were there now. Small cook fires burned here and there, and men in red regimentals huddled against the chill.

"These poor devils!" Virginia said, gesturing toward the men and tents. "Will they be here all winter?"

"I shouldn't think so," Dexter said. "We're finding proper quarters as quick as we can, and having some luck at last. Within a week, we hope these men will all have roofs over their heads."

"So they're in the city for the time being?" Virginia asked as casually as she might. "Boredom is the only thing they'll have to fight?"

Dexter laughed. "Boredom is a dangerous enemy," he said. "It can be more destructive than battle or smallpox. But we'll see the men are not bored, I assure you."

"Drills?" Virginia asked. "Marching?"

"That's the chief of it," Dexter said. "Something more, perhaps. It seems General Washington has encamped at a place called Whitemarsh, about twelve miles east of here. There's some talk that General Howe might pay a call."

"Is that so?" Virginia said. "I hope the Seventeenth would not be called away for such a thing."

"And I would be very disappointed if we were not," Dexter said. "But I doubt that I'll be disappointed. Washington's army behaved very well at Germantown. Sir William won't underestimate his opponent, and he won't take half-measures in attacking him."

"I see," Virginia said, wondering as she spoke why Dexter was willing to share so much of this information. *Is he lying?* she wondered. *Does he think me a loyalist, or of such little consequence that it doesn't matter what I know?*

Regardless of the answer, she could see this was potentially important intelligence, a line of questioning well worth pursuing, but with care and subtlety.

They rode north over the short, brown grass of the open ground, a much more pleasant sensation than riding over cobbled streets. "I hope this Whitemarsh business will not happen any time soon," Virginia ventured.

"Hard to say, really," Dexter said. "One hears rumblings, but it's so often the case in the military line that we seem on the verge of some great thing, only to be told to sit on our hands once again."

"But you hear hints of something…imminent?"

"Hints," Dexter said. "But forgive my prattling. This sort of talk must be so terribly dull for you. On the other hand, I've heard you wax eloquent about the joys of a good gallop, and here we are on open ground and we're still walking our mounts as if we were bound off for Sunday service."

"Oh, indeed?" Virginia said, smiling wide at the challenge. "How's this for walking?" She gave the horse's offside a meaningful tap with her cane and flicked the reins. The small chestnut bolted forward with an explosive energy, but Virginia had anticipated that sort of reaction from the spirited animal and she took the acceleration with grace, maintaining her place in the saddle and her control over the horse as its hooves dug into the frozen ground.

She heard Dexter shout in surprise, heard him urge his own mount on. She heard the pounding of the bay as it closed the distance between them, and soon they were galloping hard, side by side, with the open ground flying by under them. Virginia felt tears streaming down her cheeks and she laughed out loud with the sheer delight of the thing.

They spent the next few hours that way, alternately galloping and trotting and walking their mounts over the open country to the north of the city. Virginia did not mention Whitemarsh again, or try to wheedle any further intelligence from Captain Dexter, for fear that he would grow suspicious if she did. And, in truth, she soon found herself so taken the riding and the talk of horses and the pure pleasure of being on horseback once again that she forgot all about her ostensible reason for accepting the captain's invitation.

Daylight was growing short when they finally walked the horses off the fields and back onto the streets of Philadelphia, which happily were not cobbled so far from the city center. They returned by the same route they had come, with the tradesmen trudging home after their day's work and the shops shuttering their windows in the fading light.

They reined to a stop outside the Williams' house on Chestnut Street and Captain Dexter dismounted and offered Virginia a hand as she slid down from the chestnut's back. She gave the horse one last scratch on the neck and then turned to Dexter.

"I thank you, sir, for a most enjoyable afternoon," she said, and she meant it, most sincerely.

"It is I who must thank you, Mrs. Biddlecomb," Dexter said. "Such gracious company is a rare thing in my profession, you know."

"No doubt," Virginia said, and she paused, considering her next words before she spoke. "And please, Captain, call me Virginia."

Dexter smiled, not an arrogant or triumphant smile, but one with a hint of pleasure. "You do me great honor, Virginia," he said. "And I would be more honored still if you were to call me Richard."

"Richard it shall be," Virginia said. "And now, good night to you, Richard." With that, she left him on the street and made her way up the granite steps and through the big front door of her temporary home.

It was three days later when Virginia next saw Captain Richard Dexter: three days of wrestling with the ebb and flow of feelings, the guilt over having enjoyed her time with the officer while her husband languished in some frozen purgatory, her sense that the information she had gleaned about Whitemarsh was potentially important and should be shared—but with who?—her desire to ride with Dexter again, her need to terminate all contact immediately.

Added to that was an unfamiliar soreness in muscles she had not used in some time, and all together it made for an awkward and confusing three days indeed. She had all but decided that she was done with Dexter, riding and intelligence-gathering be damned, and that she would decline his next invitation and the next after that (for certainly he would not be so easily dissuaded) when Susan announced that the gentlemen would be calling on them that very evening.

"Forgive me, Susan," Virginia said. "They'll be doing what?"

"I had a note from Captain Cornwall," Susan said. "Nicholas," she added coyly. "He asked if he and Captain Dexter might call for us in that lovely coach and four they took us to the ball in. A tour of the city, I believe they had in mind. I told him that would be agreeable."

"Agreeable for you...and for me?"

"I know that you and Captain Dexter got on famously," Susan said. "I assumed you would be happy to see him again."

"But I can't leave Jack..." Virginia said, grabbing on to the first excuse to float by. "Oh...let me guess...you already sent for the wet nurse?"

"Of course, I did so directly," Susan said. "But never fear, I took care that my reply to the gentlemen did not sound too eager. They're perfectly aware of how great a favor we're doing them."

"As long as Captain Dexter does not expect the sort of favors Captain Cornwall might, then I suppose I can go along," Virginia said, too taken by the suddenness of it all to think of further ways to beg off.

"I'm sure he'll be grateful for whatever courtesies you show him," Susan said.

And indeed, when the two officers arrived at the Williams' home a few hours later, dressed in their ever-immaculate regimentals, the same fine coach they had procured earlier parked on the street outside, they did seem genuinely grateful for the company. They were, as ever, the picture of gracious courtesy, though Virginia could see that something had changed between Susan and Cornwall, some level of intimacy and silent communication that had not been there before.

She made good use of an empty house, I'll warrant, Virginia thought as Richard Dexter helped her on with her cloak.

They descended the stairs to the street where the officers handed the women up into the coach, made tolerably comfortable by tin foot warmers filled with hot stones and set on the carriage floor. Once they settled into place, Cornwall thumped on the roof and the carriage lurched into motion.

"I had thought perhaps we would have a tour about the city," Cornwall said, "and then maybe some supper after? There's a tavern that's reopened on Second Street under the name the King's Arms and I hear it's tolerably good."

"Oh, that sounds delightful!" Susan gushed, though Virginia suspected she would have reacted the same way if Cornwall had suggested they muck out the city stables. She did not think Cornwall could say anything that Susan would not find delightful.

"Would that be agreeable with you, Virginia?" Dexter asked, and try as she might Virginia could not stop herself from glancing over at Susan, who met the look with a smile and a raised eyebrow. She had not missed the use of Virginia's Christian name.

"That would be most agreeable...Richard," Virginia said, and she graced the officer with a smile of her own.

The coach rumbled down Chestnut Street toward the water, past the various meeting houses, the shops and the fine homes. The officers had invited the women on a tour of the city, but in truth, Susan was the only one among them who knew anything of Philadelphia, and she quickly took on the role of guide and embraced it. She named the families who lived in the elegant houses and many who lived in the lesser homes, she explained who among them were still there and who had fled when Howe's army had arrived. She pointed out the various shops and explained who was to be trusted and who was a criminal, and which to patronize and which to avoid.

Susan was a lively and entertaining narrator, with a fine ear for detail and gossip, and she kept them quite amused as they rumbled along. Cornwall and Dexter were able to add their part to her narrative, pointing out which houses, abandoned by their owners, were now occupied by which general officers of Sir William Howe's army. Virginia took silent note, in case that information might be of use to someone who was no friend of General Howe or his army.

Cornwall leaned over and unbuckled a leather bag on the floor at his feet. He pulled out a bottle of claret and four glasses, uncorked the bottle, poured, and distributed the glasses around. They toasted friendship and drank.

At the waterfront the carriage turned west and continued on. The moon was nearly full and it cast its light over the river, enough to illuminate the various ships at anchor there, from tiny sloops and cutters to the massive men-of-war of Lord Richard Howe's fleet.

"Do you know what ships those are?" Virginia asked, nodding toward the water. She had finished her glass and allowed Cornwall to pour another and she could feel the wine in her head.

"Well, let's see," Cornwall said, turning in his seat and looking out at the river. "I know the big one ain't *Augusta*. Bloody navy burned that one to the waterline. And I don't mean the rebel navy. The Royal Navy managed that one on their own."

"Is that true?" Susan asked. "I know she burned but...the navy burned their own ship?"

"Perhaps," Dexter clarified. "She was aground and caught fire. No one is quite sure how. Might have been a bit of wadding from one of her own guns."

Virginia had heard that as well. One of the Royal Navy's greatest losses and it seemed the Continental Navy had played no part in it. In truth, there was no longer any Continental Navy, or State Navy, anywhere on the Delaware. What ships had survived Howe's push up-river had been burned a few weeks back.

She thought of Isaac slipping *Falmouth* past those powerful ships. She thought of him in the near-empty great cabin of his beloved frigate. Was he thinking of her just then?

"The big one there, that's *Roebuck*, Hammond's command," Dexter continued, pointing. "And the frigates, one is *Liverpool* and one is *Pearl*, but I can't tell one from the other. Even in broad daylight, I doubt I could tell. Bloody ships all look the same."

"The other one, just down river," Cornwell added, "the fifty-gun ship, that's *Experiment*, Captain Wallace's command. Beautiful ship, just three years old, copper-bottomed. But I heard she won't stay here all winter. Underway soon, I understand."

"Nicholas, please," Dexter interrupted. "You'll only bore the ladies if you try to impress them with your vast knowledge."

"Wallace?" Virginia asked. "James Wallace, who used to command the frigate *Rose*?"

"Sir James?" Dexter said. "Yes, I believe so. Not entirely certain. Army and navy, we can be a bit like oil and water, you know."

"I see," Virginia said, staring out at the great bulk of the ship, just visible in the moonlight. "I didn't know Captain Wallace had been knighted."

"Just earlier this year, as I understand it," Dexter said.

"Hmm," Virginia said, and she said no more. She did not care to seem overly curious.

The coach turned and left the waterfront behind, heading back toward the city's center. It came to a stop in front of a tavern, well-lit with various lanterns hanging from hooks along the sidewalk and busy with men and women flowing in and out. Virginia drained the last of her claret and handed the empty glass to Cornwall.

"Here we are, ladies, the King's Arms, finest tavern in Philadelphia, I'm told," Dexter said. Whether that was true or not, Virginia did not know. The City Tavern had long been considered the finest tavern in Philadelphia, but that impressive building had been turned into housing for prisoners of war, first by the Americans and then by the British. Whatever fare they were serving there now, Virginia did not imagine it was up to the standards of well-bred British officers.

Cornwall and Dexter stepped out of the coach and helped the women down, then escorted them up the few steps and through the tavern's front door. The big dining room into which they stepped was warm, loud, and smoky, well-lit by candles in sconces mounted on the walls and several elaborate chandeliers hanging from beams overhead.

The place was crowded, the tables nearly all taken. There was a smattering of civilians there, men and women whose clothes reflected their status in the upper echelon of Loyalist Philadelphia, but the preponderance of the dress was uniform: the red coats of the army and the blue coats of the navy. They were young men mostly, lieutenants and army captains, and some older men as well, colonels and post-captains, and the like. Many of them, like Dexter and Cornwall, were in the company of women.

Cornwall gave a subtle wave, to who Virginia could not tell, and a moment later a heavy-set man in green waistcoat and breeches approached, gave a shallow bow, and allowed Cornwall to slip something discreetly into his hand.

"This way, please, ladies, gentlemen," the big man said, and a moment later, the four of them were seated at one of the few empty tables in the room. They had hardly settled in their chairs before cups of hot flip were set in front of each of them.

"You seem to be well regarded here, Captain Cornwall," Virginia said.

Cornwall smiled. "I wish I could say it was due to my charm, or my good looks, but alas, it has more to do with how one spreads one's money about." He lifted his cup for a toast and the others followed suit.

Virginia took a sip. The drink was warm, just on the edge of hot, a sweet and potent mix of ale and brandy, sugar and nutmeg, with a few raw eggs stirred in, a perfect drink for a cold autumn night. Virginia could feel the slight burn of the alcohol on her throat, but it went down as easily as chocolate.

"Oh, this is delightful!" Susan said.

"They do an excellent flip here," Cornwall said. "As well as a lamb stew that cannot be bested." And so, on the captain's recommendation, they ordered the lamb stew, along with roasted potatoes and asparagus, which was all the more fashionable for being so far out of season. They finished their cups of flip before the food arrived and four more appeared as if by some conjurer's trick.

Susan and Cornwall were soon deep in a discussion about a colonel of the Thirty-Third Regiment of Foot, seated on the far side of the room, and the young woman with whom he was dining, who looked as if she could be his daughter or his niece, but clearly was not. Virginia was about to interrupt, and change the subject, when Dexter turned to her.

"Forgive my asking," he said, leaning close so as to be heard without shouting over the din of the room, "but I understand you're from Newport, Rhode Island, originally?"

"Bristol," Virginia said. "North of Newport."

"Of course," Dexter said. "I know Bristol tolerably well. I spent quite a bit of time in that area, Newport, principally, before…the present situation."

"Perhaps we know people in common," Virginia said, speaking with care. She had felt the effects of the claret even before leaving the coach, and now the flip was announcing itself.

"Perhaps so," Dexter said. "Let me see…do you know a gentleman by the name of John Wanton? A merchant in Newport?"

"Oh, yes, certainly!" Virginia said. "My father is a merchant as well, you know, and he's friends with most of the prominent men in Newport. And so, perforce, am I."

My father is also a great rebel, she thought, *and a financier of the effort to drive you lot of Redcoats into the sea,* but she still had control enough to not speak that part aloud.

"Ha!" Dexter said. "Mr. Wanton is a friend of my father's as well. It's a wonder we didn't run into one another in his sitting room! Do you know a lawyer in that town by the name of Daniel Lyman?"

"Yes, I believe I do," Virginia said, pushing her way through the fog of wine and brandy until she could recall the man's face. "Yes," she said with more certainty. "Yes, I certainly do."

"An excellent fellow!" Dexter said. "I know the whole family well. How about Jonathan Weatherspoon? Do you know that worthy, at all?"

"Weatherspoon…" Virginia mused. "I knew a David Weatherspoon. I believe he was from Newport, though in truth I'm not certain."

"Jonathan had a son named David," Dexter said. "Middling height, brownish hair. He's a few years junior to me, but I knew him fairly well. Might he be the same fellow?"

"Could well be," Virginia said. "It sounds like him, to be sure."

"Have you heard from him of late?" Dexter asked. "I haven't seen him or his father since…oh, I should think not since '71. Is he well?"

"I couldn't speak to the father," Virginia said. "As to David, well, I'm afraid he was killed. Last fall."

"Killed?" Dexter said, frowning. "Oh, dear, I'm sorry to hear that. Do you know...perhaps I shouldn't ask...but do you know the circumstances?"

"He died fighting," Virginia said. "At a place called Great Egg Harbor." She looked at Dexter with an expression that she hoped would indicate that she did not wish to speak more on that subject. She did not wish to discuss which side David Weatherspoon was fighting for, and which against.

"I'm sorry," Dexter said. "Sorry to have brought it up at all. Pray, let us move on to some more pleasant topic."

And with that, Dexter was able to nimbly steer the conversation back to a happier place, and soon he and Virginia and Susan and Cornwall were all laughing and raising their cups of flip and enjoying a lamb stew that was every bit as excellent as Cornwall had promised.

Virginia could feel her head was light with the drink, and when at last they stood to leave, she could feel it even more profoundly. But she managed to remain steady, or so she thought, and make it out the door, down the steps and up into the coach without embarrassing herself.

They soon arrived back at the Williams' home, where the officers helped the ladies down and saw them to the door. They bid their goodnights, and Susan graced Cornwall with a less than discreet kiss.

"Oh that was a dream of an evening, was it not, Virginia?" Susan gushed once the front door was firmly shut.

"A dream," Virginia agreed, but the effect of the alcohol on her head and her stomach, and the constant twist of emotions, had her feeling something less than dreamy at that moment. She made her excuses and with some effort mounted the stairs and made her way to her room. She quickly undid the lacing of her gown and let it slide to the floor, relieved to be free of the weight and the confines of the silk.

She crossed the room and sat down at her mirror and began pulling pins from her hair. She saw behind her, reflected in the glass, the small writing desk on the other side of the room. She turned and stared at it. Something there was nagging at her, but she was not sure what it was.

On the top of the desk, right where she had left it, sat the letter from Isaac. She had not bothered to hide it, or even put it away. Why, indeed, would she? It was not as if anyone, save for herself and the family or the servants, was ever there on the second floor of the house.

Then she felt the sudden rush of realization, like a gust of cold wind.

"Oh, you son of a bitch," she said out loud.

CHAPTER FOURTEEN

Rumstick led his men through the barnyard and over a rail fence at the far side, then across a field of frozen grass where a few sorry cows stood huddled off in the far corner. He moved quickly, his feet making crunching noises on the ground. That, and the similar crunching of the other men, was the only sound he could hear over the light wind.

"Lieutenant?" The voice came from his left and almost alongside and Rumstick turned his head as he walked. It was Sullivan, the farmer turned marine.

"Yeah?"

"Well, sir...are you planning on just walking across this field, like we're doing?"

Rumstick frowned. It seemed like a stupid question. "We're heading east. That's the way we want to go."

"It's just that...walking across the field like this, it'll be damned easy for anyone who knows anything about tracking to follow us," Sullivan said. "And I reckon among them pine robbers, there's like to be someone who knows that business."

"You know about tracking?" Rumstick asked.

"Some," Sullivan said. He paused, and then added, "Truth be told, a lot."

"And you can lead us so they can't follow?"

"I can lead so's it'll be damned hard to follow, sir," Sullivan said. "Impossible, unless they're very good."

"Very well," Rumstick said, gesturing to the spot in front of himself. "You take the lead."

Sullivan moved to the front of the column, and at first he did not alter the direction of the march. But when they came to the edge of a plowed field, he turned sharply right, which was not at all the direction Rumstick wished to travel, and he passed the word back for the men to walk in a strict single file. They followed the edge of the field for some time, moving nearly at a jog, then Sullivan turned again and led the line down a plowed furrow in a direction that was more southeasterly, closer to the rhumb line course to Great Egg Harbor.

For some time, they continued on like that, zigging and zagging from one section of difficult ground to another. It reminded Rumstick of trying to beat a ship to windward, tack after tack, covering so much ground but making so little progress toward their goal. Still, when looked back, he had to admit there was no track to be seen, whereas when he had been leading them, they left a path in their wake as visible as a post road.

The farm was well behind them by the time Rumstick noticed a general lifting of the darkness. The fields emerging in the dawn light appeared as gray-blue stretches of open ground, with stands of trees off in the distance. He looked up. The cloud cover had not broken up in the least, but somewhere behind it the sun was rising and soon it would turn the near-black sky to a leaden wolf-gray.

"Halloa, Sullivan," he said in a loud whisper. "Sun's coming up. What do you reckon…keep on going or find some place to hide?"

With that Sullivan stopped and turned and the rest of the men stopped and Rumstick imagined they were as grateful as he was for the respite. Sullivan looked back over the country they had just crossed.

"Reckon they've found the guards by now, and they're coming after us," he said. "They might think we took to the road, so they'll just follow that. Or they might try to track us, but that won't be easy. It might be best to find a place to hide. Or it might be best to press on. I don't know."

Well, that was damned unhelpful, Rumstick thought, but he did not say anything, because it was not Sullivan's job to make that decision, it was his. He considered the options and tried to reckon what Wilcox's priorities would be.

That fellow Barnett seemed to inspire a lot of fear among these people, meaning Wilcox would not want to return to Great Egg Harbor empty-handed. Rather, he would try to hunt his escaped prisoners down. Or perhaps he would shirk all blame and head back to the Pine Barrens, but Rumstick doubted he and his men would get that lucky. Luck had not been their companion of late.

"We'll press on," Rumstick said. "Right for Great Egg, and less tacking and wearing. I reckon if they're trying to follow, then we've thrown them off our trail. But if they're heading straight to meet up with Barnett, then we've got to beat them to it."

"Yes, sir," Sullivan said.

"We'll rest another couple of minutes," Rumstick said. "Then we'll shove off."

Some of the men crouched on their heels, some remained standing. No one sat on the frozen ground. They would have all dearly liked a drink of water or a bite of food, but they had neither. Then, after a few moments of a largely unsatisfying break, they were up and moving again.

Sullivan kept the lead, but he did as Rumstick wished and took a more direct route toward Great Egg Harbor. He still veered in one direction or another, keeping to ground that would help cover their tracks, but not with the same care as before, and they made much quicker time over the rolling hills and the long, flat, plowed fields.

"There's smoke," Sullivan said at last as they came up on the crest of a hill. Off to the east, they could see a few columns rising at an angle from unseen chimneys, the scattering of houses, and the tavern that made up the little town. Rumstick paused and turned back and looked over the countryside they had just covered.

"Sir?" Sullivan asked. "What...what are you doing, sir?"

"Looking for Wilcox and his men," Rumstick said.

"Best not to stop on the crest of the hill, sir, where we're easily seen against the sky," Sullivan said.

Rumstick grunted and continued down over the hill, then stopped when he was mostly concealed behind the high ground. He turned again and looked back and Sullivan did the same. The two men ran their eyes over the land to the west.

"Don't see anything," Rumstick said.

"There, sir," Sullivan said, pointing. Rumstick looked off in the direction the marine indicated. He could see men moving about, or so he thought. Not a group of men but a few scattered individuals. One was on a road that seemed to parallel the main road through the countryside, a few others were moving across the fields.

"Very well…" Rumstick said, drawing out the last syllable. "I think I see them. You sure they're not just farmers or such? Men at work?"

"Might be, lieutenant," Sullivan said. "But to me, they look more akin to folks spread on the march and searching. Like Wilcox spread his men out so they could look for our tracks as they make for the harbor. It's what I'd do."

Rumstick nodded. "Me too, I reckon. All right, it's a foot race, now. Let's get us back to *Falmouth* before they find us, or cut us off."

They headed off again, once more increasing their pace, once more making less of an effort to cover their tracks. They knew from the columns of smoke ahead that they were close to the village, and soon they could see the tops of the roofs, the brick chimneys. And then they were on one of the roads leading into Great Egg Harbor itself. They had no oxen, no logger's wheels, no spars, just the clothes they wore, but they had returned.

As to weapons, Ferguson and Kirby alone still had their muskets, and beyond that, there were just the four they had lifted from Wilcox's guards. Of those, Rumstick carried one and he gave another to Sullivan and the other two went to his two steadiest men.

They came in from the west, marching in a loose column into town, a dozen men and half as many guns, making for the waterfront. Rumstick, at the head of the column, had already passed a two-story house on his left when he heard a voice call out to him from the kitchen yard.

"I say!" the voice called. "Lieutenant Rumstick? I say!"

Rumstick held up a hand and stopped and turned. The fellow in the yard was dressed in an old coat and a wool hat and armed with an ax. In front of him, a stump, and around it a scattering of kindling, fresh-cut. He chopped the ax down into the stump and left it standing there as he crossed to the low picket fence that separated the yard from the road.

"Yes?" Rumstick said. He recognized the man's face. He could not place him, but he had to assume he was part of the Gloucester County Militia, because those people were the only ones in town he might recognize. Them and Barnett's pine robbers.

"Lieutenant, I'm Jonathan Mitnick... Captain Jonathan Mitnick. Gloucester County Militia. We've met...on a few occasions."

"Of course, captain, of course," Rumstick said, though if he was asked to recall any of those meetings he would certainly have failed. "What's acting around here?"

"Well..." Mitnick began, "I guess the question is more, what's acting with you? I know you and your men were off to the Pine Barrens..." He glanced down the road as if looking for the oxen and the logs and logger's wheels. "You have a couple of my oxen with you, in fact. Or did." He did not sound pleased by the apparent loss of his draft animals.

"Oxen are back up the road some," Rumstick said, nodding back the way they had come. "And we're heading back to *Falmouth*."

At that, Mitnick's eyes went wide. "Oh, no, you mustn't do that," he said. "Barnett and his banditti, they've laid siege to the ship. Set up camp right at the end of the wharf. No one's going on or off the ship. Locked up tight."

Rumstick frowned. "Siege?" he said.

"That's right," Mitnick said. "We thought...well, we knew Barnett sent some men off to take you and your men here prisoner. Rumor was he was going to use you as hostages, make Captain Biddlecomb trade the ship for you. Or hang the lot of you, right at the end of the wharf. To tell the truth, most of us thought you were prisoners already. That's why I was so surprised to see you come marching down the road."

"Is that a fact?" Rumstick said. "Well, we're not prisoners, not yet. And now we're going back to our ship."

"Listen, sir, Barnett had fifty men or more there at the camp." He looked over Rumstick's column. "And it looks like you got but half a dozen muskets. Of course, I have no say over what you do, but I would not recommend marching right into Barnett's arms. You'd be doing him the biggest favor you could do."

Rumstick frowned, not sure exactly what he should say or do with this information. "Very well, if this Barnett's invaded your town, why don't you and the militia drive him out? You got as many men as him, don't you?"

"Close on as many," Mitnick agreed. "But the thing of it is, Colonel Somers, he commands the militia. I don't have much say over what the militia does, any more than I have say over what you do."

I hope you at least have some say over what your wife does, you sorry bastard, Rumstick thought but he kept that to himself.

"So why doesn't Colonel Somers do something about these pine robbers?" Rumstick asked instead.

"Well...reckon you'd have to ask him," Mitnick said, and Rumstick could hear the mix of humiliation and anger in the reply. He had hit a sore spot here, he could tell, a matter of disagreement between the men.

"I would like to ask him," Rumstick said. "I would like that very much indeed. So, let us do this. Me and my men, we'll just slip into your barn, out of sight. And you can bring us some food and some drink, if you'd be so kind. And while we break our fast, you can go and fetch Colonel Somers and we'll all discuss this situation like the gentlemen we are."

Mitnick was not just willing to help, but eager to do so, and soon Rumstick and his men found themselves once again sprawled out on a stack of hay, eight hours after they had freed themselves from the barn in which Wilcox had been holding them. Their circumstances were much more amenable this time, however, with their hands not bound and not being under threat of death. They had jugs of beer and loaves of fresh, soft bread, and a ham and a cold roast, which they went at eagerly. Once those things had been consumed, leaving only a scattering of crumbs and two well-cleaned bones, they laid down and soon were fast asleep.

Rumstick meant to stay awake until Somers arrived, though in truth, he had no notion of how long that might be. He knew very little of the colonel, save that he was an amiable cove who was not much given to decisive action of any kind. He did not know if Mitnick would find him on a farm half a mile away or out on a fishing boat three miles off shore.

So, given that he did not know how long he might expect to wait, Rumstick figured it would do no harm to just recline onto the straw and rest his eyes for a moment. He could feel the fatigue behind them.

He woke in the twilight of the barn with someone shaking him. He had no notion of how long he had been asleep, and there was not much that might tell him the answer. He could see the gray November light through the cracks between the boards, so he knew it was still daytime, anyway.

Captain Mitnick was leaning over him, shaking his shoulder. Rumstick made a grunting noise to indicate he was awake and that Mitnick could stop shaking him. He sat up, then stood and brushed the straw off of himself. Colonel Somers was standing to Mitnick's left. The older man looked tired, and worried.

"Ah, Lieutenant Rumstick!" Somers said. "It's good to see you, good indeed. We had feared the worst, you know. That bastard Barnett, he's a great savage, and he has a damned lot of men under his command."

"You'll get no argument from me," Rumstick said. "But what's to be done about it? Why is he suffered to just decide who comes and goes on the wharf?"

"Ah, well…" Somers began. He glanced over at Mitnick for help, but it was clear that Mitnick was going to offer no assistance. "He has a damned lot of men, like I said. More than I have under my command. They're banditti. Pine robbers. Not family men, like the militia here. Those men, they're not the sort anyone here's too eager to tangle with."

"Most men are not too eager to go into battle," Rumstick said. "That's why their officers give them orders. And lead them." He looked from Mitnick to Somers. Neither man responded, or looked terribly comfortable with this line of discussion.

"What are you saying?" Rumstick demanded. "Are you telling me you and your men are too craven to fight?"

"Well, that's a damned thing to say!" Somers spluttered, and this time Mitnick, too, would not remain silent.

"I must protest, lieutenant," he said, clearly angry, eyebrows at a steep angle, face flushing. "I won't stand for being accused of cowardice, not by you or any man. The militiamen, us, we'll willingly lay down our lives for our country. Right now every man is on alert, sleeping on their arms, ready to turn out at a moment's notice. But we won't throw our lives away. We have wives and children, like the colonel said."

"That's right, *Lieutenant*," Somers said. "If we die just to play the hero, we leave our wives and daughters at the mercy of those bastards from the Pine Barrens. I don't even want to think about what would happen. And that's not a chance we're willing to take just to protect your damned ship, which we never asked to come here in the first place."

"Very well," Rumstick said, his voice calm, neutral. He had made a mistake and he could see that, and now he had to fix it. He wished Isaac Biddlecomb was there. Isaac was very good at this sort of thing, bending men to his will without infuriating them. Rumstick was not so talented in that department. He was more blunt, less diplomatic, and he had a number of impressive scars as a result.

"I see we have a problem here," Rumstick continued. "A mutual problem. But the men onboard *Falmouth*, they're a force to be reckoned with. Experienced fighting men, and disciplined, and Captain Biddlecomb has a knack for seeing himself out of corners like this. If we can make a plan with them..."

"Maybe you didn't hear correctly," Somers said. "Barnett has the wharf under siege. No one goes out to the ship, no one comes off. And he's collected up every boat for miles. Skiffs, fishing boats, all of them. There is no way to get word to *Falmouth*."

Rumstick frowned but he was not sure what to say to that, and no hint of a solution seemed to present itself.

"I don't see how there's anything more to discuss here, Lieutenant," Somers said, breaking the silence. "We have a stand-off. Stalemate. Barnett's set up camp but he hasn't actually committed any violence, or done much of anything. If he does something that warrants action on the part of the militia, well, we'll be there with guns blazing. Until then, we watch and we wait." He nodded his farewell to Rumstick and Mitnick, then turned and headed for the door.

Rumstick and the militia captain stood silent, watching him leave. Once he was gone, Mitnick said, "I'm sorry, lieutenant, but I'm afraid Colonel Somers has the right of it. Barnett and his banditti, they're too much for the militia. Maybe if we could get Captain Biddlecomb and the men on *Falmouth* to join in…but there's no chance of getting word to them. All we can do is wait and see what Barnett is planning."

"I see," Rumstick said. "You said the militia were on alert? Sleeping with their arms, ready to turn out?"

"They are," Mitnick said. "We're not insensible to the danger here. We're ready to defend ourselves."

Rumstick nodded. "And your militia, do you have an armory of some sort? Muskets and powder and ball you could issue?"

"Yes…" Mitnick said, not trying to hide the suspicion in his voice.

"I'm just asking because, well, it's pretty clear me and my men aren't going to rejoin *Falmouth* anytime soon," Rumstick explained. "So as long as we're on this side of the wharf, we should be ready to stand with the militia, in case something bad happens. We can add a dozen fighting men, experienced men, to your ranks, and that would certainly help. But not all my men are armed."

"Yes, yes, that would indeed be a help," Mitnick agreed. He considered the suggestion a moment more, and then said, "I suppose, as captain of militia, I could issue the weapons. No need to bother the colonel with this…" He did not sound any more eager that Rumstick was to ask for Somers's permission.

"Best to just go ahead and do it, I think, and quick," Rumstick agreed. "If Barnett gets it in his head, he might send men to break into the armory and help themselves to the firelocks and such that are there. Better to put them in our hands before that happens."

"That's a good point, lieutenant, a damned good point," Mitnick said. And he was right. It was a good point. And more importantly, it played right into the plan that was just starting to form in Rumstick's mind.

CHAPTER FIFTEEN

"Can't be but three bells in the first dog watch, and it's already black as pitch outside," Ferguson said. He and Rumstick and the rest of the logging party were still reclined on the straw pile in Captain Jonathan Mitnick's barn. No light came in through the chinks in the barn walls now, and the space was lit by a couple of lanterns that Mitnick had brought out as the sun was beginning to set.

"Every year, right about this time, seems it's always the same damned thing," Rumstick observed.

Most of the men had not left the barn since they had first secreted themselves in there, and they did not seem unhappy to just sprawl out on the straw and sleep. Like the true mariners that they were, they had no difficulty drifting off wherever they dropped, particularly not after the food and drink that Mitnick had provided.

Rumstick and Ferguson and Kirby alone had left the barn earlier, accompanying Captain Mitnick to the armory to gather muskets and powder and ball and bayonets for the six men in Rumstick's company who had no weapons. They had taken a detour first, on Rumstick's insistence, making their clandestine way down to the wharf by way of various kitchen yards, and sheltering behind outbuildings and other natural cover. If Barnett had posted men in the town, Rumstick did not want to risk being discovered.

But that was not a problem in the end. Mitnick, who had spent every one of his twenty-eight years of life in Great Egg Harbor, was perfectly capable of leading them down to the water unseen by anyone but the good people of the town. And when they were seen, Mitnick was recognized immediately and was greeted with a friendly wave or a nod of the head. No cry was raised.

"There," Mitnick said as they settled in behind a shed one hundred yards from the head of the wharf. "This is as close as we can get. But you can see from here that villain Barnett, he's pretty well settled in."

Rumstick nodded. There were tents pitched haphazardly over the ground all along the edge of the banking that dropped down to the water, and half a dozen stone rings with fires blazing and men huddled around. There were men standing slumped at various places beyond the camp, and Rumstick had to guess they were sentries, though such a poor excuse for vigilance would have earned them a flogging in any real army on earth.

"How do these bastards like camping out here in this damned cold, after having made themselves at home in the tavern?" Rumstick asked.

"Probably not much," Mitnick said, "though I haven't exactly enquired after their health. From what I can see, and what folks have told me, the lot of them are drunk all the time, at least when they're not sleeping. So that has to make things go easier."

"This Barnett, he allows that?" Kirby asked.

"I doubt there's much he can do," Mitnick said. "Scum like this, they'll only listen to orders for so long, and some things they just won't put up with. If they want to get drunk, they'll get drunk."

"You shouldn't tell Kirby that," Ferguson said. "Now he's gonna go change sides."

"I reckon all you drunken skipjacks would, if I let you," Rumstick said, but he was thinking about Barnett's men and their habit of being drunk the chief of the time.

Good...that's good... he thought. *That'll help.*

They watched for a few moments more but saw nothing else of interest, just a band of ragged, miserable, cold-looking men. They did not seem to be a particularly formidable force, but Rumstick knew well how deceptive that could be. These were men used to brutal ways and tough fighting. The drink might make them clumsy and dull-witted, but it would also erase any bit of fear they might harbor. They would not be easily put down.

From there, they made their way to the armory and collected up six muskets and a dozen bayonets and all the powder and ball they could carry and then returned to the barn. Mitnick left them there to attend to his chores, and Rumstick set his men to rolling cartridges and making certain their firelocks were in perfect working order.

"Say, lieutenant," Ferguson said. He was sitting next to Rumstick, adjusting the flint in his firelock, then cocking the weapon and pulling the trigger to judge the shower of sparks produced. "If you don't mind me asking, are we just going to hide out here and hope the militia does something?"

"Here's my plan," Rumstick said. "We'll wait here until Barnett and his men die of old age. And then we'll come out."

"We'll...we wait until they die of old age?" Sullivan, who was sitting nearby, asked.

"That's right," Rumstick said. "Or until I get bored. We'll see which comes first. The thing is, this situation, it's like a powder magazine in a ship. You got barrels of gunpowder over here. And you got cartridges over there, and priming powder over there, and some damned fool, he's let loose powder spill on the deck. One spark and the whole thing blows to hell. Well, that's like what we got here."

"Uh huh," Ferguson said. "Of course, as a rule you'd try not to make a spark. You know, with the felt slippers and the copper tools and such."

"Most times that's true," Rumstick said. "But sometimes the spark's just the thing that's called for."

Some time later, Captain Mitnick returned with a big pot of stew and several bowls and spoons and more bread and beer. "These are all the bowls we have, I apologize for that," he said, handing them out. "I hope you don't mind sharing."

"Sharing? Hell, no, we don't mind. With this lot, you could just pour the stew out on the ground and they'd eat it right up," Rumstick said. "But don't..." he added quickly, realizing Mitnick might not understand he was joking.

But Mitnick did understand, apparently, as he smiled and passed the spoons around and the men who had bowls set in to eating.

"I appreciate your generosity, Captain," Rumstick said. "And I promise, once we get back aboard *Falmouth* we'll pay you in full for all this. Hard money. Captain Biddlecomb, his father-in-law is rich as Croesus, and that can come in damned handy, I'll tell you."

"I reckon it can," Mitnick agreed. "Oh, but listen here. We have men watching the roads and the camp by the wharf and all, and I'm told that Wilcox and his men, those that were sent out after you, they came back in tonight. I guess they gave up looking."

"Guess so," Rumstick said and smiled. "I'd love to hear the report Wilcox makes to Barnett. I reckon he'll say he never did find us, rather than try to explain the truth of the matter."

Mitnick smiled as well. "I reckon you're right. I reckon telling Barnett you made a hash of something is probably not good for a man's health."

"Probably not," Rumstick agreed. "Say, Captain, you said the militia around here are ready to turn out at a minute's notice? How does that work?"

"Well, most of the men in the militia live within a mile or so of here. When we have a threat like we do now, with Barnett and his men, we keep our muskets and such by the doors, and boots and coats ready," Mitnick said. "And we have orders to muster on the green, if we get the signal."

"Signal?"

"The church bell," Mitnick said. "A couple of fellows are designated to ring it, if me or Colonel Somers sends word."

"I see," Rumstick said. "Sounds like a good plan. Does it work out all right?"

"Don't know," Mitnick said. "It does when we're drilling. We've never had to turn out like that for real."

"And the Good Lord willing you never will," Rumstick said, and Mitnick agreed with that. They spoke a bit longer, then Mitnick made his excuses and left them there in the barn, bedded down in the straw.

One by one they drifted off to sleep, save for Rumstick, who stared into the dark and let his mind work, let various scenarios play out in his head as the hours passed by. Sometime later, after midnight by his best estimate, he stood and brushed the straw off him, then slung his cartridge box over his shoulder. Ferguson was sleeping a few feet away and Rumstick nudged him with the toe of his shoe.

"Up and to arms," he said in a low voice. "And be quiet about it." He took a few steps and nudged Sullivan awake, and then Ewald, and soon all of the men were getting groggily to their feet.

"What's acting, lieutenant?" Kirby asked, the first to find his voice.

"There's a load of motherless bastards all sitting on the arses at the end of the wharf," Rumstick said, "and we're going to go make them get out of our way."

That met with a moment of silence. "How's that, sir?" Ferguson asked.

"By shooting the sons of bitches, if need be," Rumstick said.

Ferguson nodded. "You might recall, lieutenant, there's something akin to fifty or sixty of them," he said. "And a dozen of us, by my count."

"I wasn't aware you could count that high, Ferguson," Rumstick said.

"I can't, Lieutenant. I was just guessing," Ferguson said.

"Well, pretty good guess," Rumstick said. "But you missed some. The Gloucester County Militia…they must have fifty good fighting men under arms, or near enough."

"You mean them fellows that are abed and fast asleep?" Ewald asked.

"The same," Rumstick said. "But they'll wake up once the shooting starts, depend on it. And don't forget our shipmates aboard *Falmouth*. They're just at the far end of the dock, and you know they won't be drunk and asleep like them pine robbers."

In the light of the lanterns, Rumstick could see heads nodding, the men seeing this play out the way he did, and he hoped they were all correct. He could not imagine how this could go wrong, but then, one rarely imagined how something could go wrong until it did.

"Load up," Rumstick said. "Muskets on half-cock. Any man fires before I say, the next bullet goes through his heart. Understand?"

Heads nodded again and then the barn was filled with the small scrapes and clicks of a dozen muskets being loaded. Once the last ramrod was pushed back in place, Rumstick took one of the lanterns down from its hook and led the way to the barn door and out into the night.

It was a cold one, and in the lantern light, Rumstick could see the cloud of his breath in front of him. Once all of his men were standing in the frozen yard, he held up his hand for quiet and he listened to the sounds of the night. He could hear a dog barking, far off, and something creaking in the breeze. He could hear the low swish of dead branches swaying somewhere out where he could not see them. Beyond that, he heard nothing.

"Good," he said in a low voice. "Follow me, and keep your damned mouths shut." He shuttered the lantern and stepped through the gate from Mitnick's yard into the frozen street and headed off toward the waterfront.

He kept the column as much in the shadows as he could, but he was not terribly concerned about anyone seeing them. He doubted that Barnett's men would be that far from the camp, and he did not think any townsfolk would raise an alarm at the sight of a dozen armed men walking down the road. For one thing, they would not know if the dozen were friend or foe, and probably would not care to enquire.

We'll get those alarms raised soon enough, Rumstick thought as he walked past the dark and silent houses that bordered the road.

They came at last to the place where the buildings yielded to the open ground that ran to the waterfront and Rumstick led the men in behind a blacksmith's shop that hid them from view of Barnett's camp. Once they were well hidden, he peeked around the corner to see what he could see.

There was not much: a few fires burning in the pits, a handful of men huddled around them. Sentries, most likely, though staring into the fires as they were, they would be blinded to anything out in the dark. It was possible that Barnett had men posted farther away from the camp, watching for anyone approaching, but he doubted it. Even if Barnett had given those orders, Rumstick did not think anyone would obey. Too cold, too exposed and dangerous, standing all alone, far from the fires and their fellow banditti.

Beyond the fire pits and the huddle of men standing around them, Rumstick could make out the shapes of a few of the tents, and a pinpoint of light that must be a lantern hanging from some sort of hook, but he could see nothing beyond that.

"Ferguson, Kirby, to me," he said in a loud whisper. He heard a rustling sound, feet moving on frozen ground, and the two men were standing beside him. "Did you see that church, when we were here earlier?" He pointed off into the dark, in the general direction of the squat, white building with its short bell tower.

"Yes, sir," Ferguson said.

"Good," Rumstick said. He handed Ferguson the lantern. "You two, get over to the church. Figure out how to ring the bell. The moment you hear a gunshot, one of you start ringing like you're a man possessed. The other can find a spot to shoot from and start firing away at them banditti. Ring the bell for a couple of minutes, then whoever's ringing, you start shooting, too. Understand?"

Both men nodded.

"Good. Now go," Rumstick said, and the two men raced off into the dark. He waited a minute, then another, watching the pine robbers' camp, but there was nothing to suggest anyone there thought anything amiss.

"Sullivan," Rumstick whispered.

"Yes, lieutenant?"

"You the best shot here?" he asked. He could see Sullivan hesitate, unwilling to say as much, but Sullivan was a marine, and trained to shoot, which the sailors were not.

"Reckon so," he said at last.

"Think you can hit one of those men by the fire from here?" Rumstick asked next.

Sullivan peered around the edge of the building, took a quick look, and then turned back to Rumstick. "Don't know, sir," he said. "Kind of a long shot."

"Well, do your best," Rumstick said, nodding toward the camp.

"Do you mean…just shoot one of them fellows?"

"Yes, that's what I mean."

"But…they're just standing there," Sullivan protested. "They're not shooting at us."

"Not yet," Rumstick said.

Sullivan glanced over at the camp again, and then back at Rumstick. He half lifted his musket to his shoulder and put his thumb on the hammer and then paused again and frowned.

"Oh, for the love of God," Rumstick said, and thought *some bloody marine you are*. He lifted his musket to his shoulder, thumbing the hammer back as he did. He sighted over the top of the barrel, pointing the weapon in the general direction of the fire, and pulled the trigger. The priming in the pan hissed and a fraction of a second later the gun went off, slamming the butt back into his shoulder. He had no idea if he hit anyone.

"There," Rumstick said. "Now, just wait a second and I'll bet they'll be shooting at us and you can shoot back with a clear conscience."

He could hear shouting and the stamp of feet from across the open ground. He could hear yells of surprise and what sounded like orders being called, and questions demanding answers, though he could not make out any individual words.

Oh, well, Rumstick thought. *Guess one round wasn't enough.*

"You men, spread it out!" Rumstick shouted, the need for quiet now gone. "Load and fire, fast as you can! Sullivan, get up here and shoot at them bastards!" He reached down and pulled a cartridge from the box at his side and tore the end off with his teeth. He filled the pan and shut the frizzen and then poured the rest of the contents down the barrel. He looked to his right. The others were moving out past the wall of the smith's shop, taking a knee behind the low fence that enclosed the yard.

He looked back at the camp just as two of his own men fired. The open ground was lit up with the muzzle flash, and in the light of the banditti's fires, he could see men stumbling around. He jerked the ramrod from under the barrel of his gun as two more muskets went off, and that time he was all but certain he saw one of Barnett's men go down.

We'll see how drunk these bastards are… Rumstick thought as he replaced the ramrod and swung the musket up to his shoulder.

To his left, he heard a new sound, sharp and musical, the bell in the church ringing out, and he realized that in the excitement, he had forgotten all about Ferguson and Kirby. Luckily they had not forgotten their instructions, and even as the bell was keeping up its steady clanging, Rumstick saw a jet of flame come from one of the church windows, lighting up a patch of the building's wall, just for an instant. One man firing while the other tolled the bell.

He looked back over the barrel of his gun. It was indeed a long shot for a smooth-bore weapon so he found a knot of men and steadied the gun and pulled the trigger. He let the butt drop to the ground and reached for another cartridge. He had no idea if he had hit anyone, nor did he care terribly much. This was more about causing panic and raising the alarm. The real killing, he hoped, would soon start in earnest.

Hiss, bang! Hiss, bang! Two more muskets went off, priming and powder, the muzzle flashes like lightning bolts illuminating the ground ahead of them, just for an instant.

"Load and fire, fast as you can!" Rumstick shouted as he once again pulled his ramrod free. "Bastards'll be coming over the ground here any minute, you best be ready to meet them!"

He lifted his musket and sighted down the barrel and as he did he saw a muzzle flash from Barnett's camp, heard the sound of the firelock, the first return fire. He shifted his aim left and lined up with the place where the flash had been and pulled the trigger.

As he let the butt of the musket fall to the ground, he swung around and looked behind him. No militia racing toward the sound of the guns, no lanterns moving frenetically through the streets, no shouts of alarm.

Ready to turn out at a moment's notice, my arse, he though. *Hurry it up, you lazy sods...* He reached for another cartridge and tore off the top with his teeth. The taste of powder was strong in mouth now. He spilled the powder down the barrel and pushed the ball in after and looked off toward the waterfront. Two, three, four muzzle flashes as Barnett's men recovered from the shock of the attack and took up their weapons, sobered by cold and surprise.

Rumstick heard two of the balls strike the building next to him, but he had no idea where the others had gone. To his right, three more guns went off, and he saw Manning lean his ramrod against the fence, kneel, and take aim.

Barnett and those bastards, they'll be coming soon, he thought. The pine robbers were exposed, with no cover, and they were not the sort to stand and endure volleys of fire. They would want to get at their enemy, hand to hand, and while Rumstick and his men had bayonets, and he doubted that the pine robbers did, those weapons would only go so far. As it stood, Barnett had at least a five to one advantage in men, and bayonets would not change that.

The tolling of the bell had stopped and Rumstick heard more shots from the church, two in rapid succession, both Ferguson and Kirby joining in the volleys. That was good. It would make Barnett's men think they were facing more men than they were.

He could see Barnett himself now, walking fast down the line of tents, waving his sorry-looking sword, shouting orders. His men were tumbling into some sort of line, some loading and firing, some just looking across the open ground as if they had no notion of where they were.

"Stand ready!" Rumstick shouted. Barnett's men were like an ocean swell, ready to break on the shore. "We'll greet these bastards with a hail of lead!" It sounded good, but how much of a hail his dozen men could muster, he was not sure.

And then they came. Barnett, to his credit, took the lead, stepping off, sword raised, shouting as loud as he could, and behind him another forty men began to move forward, also shouting, muskets held across their chests.

"Hold your fire! Hold your fire!" Rumstick called. "Load and make ready, let 'em get close!" He'd heard enough accounts of Bunker Hill to know how effective this could be.

Barnett's men were moving faster now, their walk turning to a jog as they tried to get across the open ground in the face of an unknown number of muskets. They moved like men who were aware of just how vulnerable they were. Rumstick watched them come, trying to judge how close to let them approach. Close enough that the volley would tell, not so close that his men would not have time to reload.

"Fire!" he shouted as he lifted his own gun, leveled it, and pulled the trigger. The blast from his muzzle joined the other nine and Rumstick saw a number of Barnett's men flung back. And, more satisfying still, he saw the rest hesitate and slow in their advance, while Barnett continued to scream and wave his sword.

Rumstick looked to his right. His men were reloading as fast as they were able. Two more shots came from the church, and now Barnett's men had stopped completely, some taking a knee and firing, some just looking confused.

That's right…you just wait there, Rumstick thought as his hands went through the business of reloading his gun. He brought it up to his shoulder even as two of the other men at the fence fired and two of Barnett's men went down.

Rumstick looked over the barrel, swung it down the line until it was aimed directly at Barnett. He pressed the trigger in the same instant that Barnett lunged at one of his men, grabbed him by the coat, and pushed him forward. The man stumbled and Rumstick's ball missed entirely and then Barnett was pushing the next in line, and the next.

More of Rumstick's men were firing, but he could see that Barnett was getting his men moving forward now, getting the momentum back up. His own men would get in one, maybe two more shots before the pine robbers were on top of them.

"Fix bayonets!" Rumstick shouted. "Fix bayonets!" He looked right and left. The low fence would be an impediment to Barnett's advance; the banditti would die on the bayonets as they tried to get over it. But only a few. The rest would get over. Or around. Or they would stand back and fire into the struggling men.

We'll give them one go with the bayonets, Rumstick thought. *One go, then we run like the devil is after us. Those that still can.* Not exactly a bold stand, not exactly the battle of Thermopylae, but it was all that they could do.

Chapter Sixteen

Isaac Biddlecomb was exhausted, but he knew sleep would not come, so he did not even try. He sat at his table in the great cabin for some time, a candle flickering in the cold drafts coming in from a dozen places, a half-finished letter to Virginia spread out in front of him. He had managed to scrawl a part of a sentence over the course of the previous forty-five minutes, some ridiculous and barely coherent nonsense, and now he was trying to work up the energy to scratch it out.

Damn it all, damn it... he thought. It was maddening, infuriating, beyond endurance, the situation he was in. He felt helpless, immobilized, and there was no feeling, none, that he despised more than that.

They were trapped. Stalemate. As long as Barnett stayed where he was, as long as the Gloucester County Militia refused to act, then there was nothing he, Biddlecomb, could do. If he could speak to Somers he felt certain he could cajole, browbeat, threaten, or bribe the man into acting in concert with the men of *Falmouth* to drive Barnett away. But he could not speak to Somers. Because Barnett was where he was.

There was no getting to town by way of the wharf, that was clear, and there was no way to get there by water, either. A ship such as *Falmouth* would normally carry a minimum of five boats, but the partially built frigate had none. The only boat they had had been aboard *Sparrowhawk*. And that had disappeared with Angus McGinty.

So, it was not a fight they had there at Great Egg Harbor, it was an endurance contest. It was a race to see if Barnett's men would get fed up with bivouacking in the cold and leave before Biddlecomb's men ran out of food. The Lord alone knew how long it would take to find that out.

Biddlecomb felt suddenly that he would explode if he stayed in that cabin for a moment more. He stood quickly, nearly knocking his chair over as he did, pulled on his heavy watch coat, pushed his hat down on his head, and made his way up the ladder to the quarterdeck above.

Midshipman Gerrish had the watch, but by the time Biddlecomb reached the deck, he had retreated to the seaward side. From there, he touched his hat and said, "Evening, Captain," as Biddlecomb stepped through the scuttle, and said no more.

Biddlecomb nodded his reply. He stepped over to the rail on the landward side and looked out into the night. He was grateful, at least, that Gerrish had the good sense not to engage him in conversation or ask him why he was still awake at that hour.

He put his hands on the rail and stared out at the dark town beyond the far end of the wharf. Behind the scattering of tents he could make out the glow of several small cook fires and he pictured Barnett's rag and tag troops huddled around them as they kept some sort of watch. During the first few days of the siege, the nights had been filled with the sound of drunken revelry—shouting, laughing, guns firing at random—as the pine robbers tried to maintain the lifestyle they had come to enjoy while living in the tavern.

But that had dropped away quickly. Tents on the frozen ground were not conducive to revelry, and if the men were still drinking, which they likely were, then it seemed to be making them silent and morose rather than elevating their spirits. And that was good. Men who were silent and morose were men who would be slinking away soon. The only question was, would it be soon enough.

What Biddlecomb really wanted to do, of course, was to lead an attack against Barnett's camp. It was what Faircloth wanted to do as well, and Gerrish, and all the men aboard *Falmouth*. But they were too outnumbered to risk it, and that was made worse by the absence of Rumstick and his band of woodcutters.

*Rumstick...*Biddlecomb thought. Barnett could not have caught him yet. If he had, he would have paraded him and the other prisoners down the wharf already, eager to trade their lives for the ship. Since he hadn't, it had to mean that Rumstick and his men were still free. Or had indeed been taken prisoner and were on their way to Great Egg Harbor. Or were dead.

Biddlecomb thumped his hand against the rail in frustration and relished the pain of the hard wood against his half-frozen flesh. He did not know what was going on beyond those wooden walls, and he had no way of knowing, or of effecting any meaningful change in their circumstance.

"Rum," he muttered to himself. "A cup of rum, that's what I need." He pictured the half-empty bottle in his cabinet below. Even if he could do nothing else, he could at least have a drink. It would help him sleep, he figured, and that was excuse enough.

He straightened, turned, and had taken one step toward the scuttle when he heard the gunshot. It had come from somewhere behind him, somewhere ashore. He spun back quick, looking out into the night. Nothing had changed that he could see. If there had been a muzzle flash, then he had missed it, and in its absence, he was not entirely certain it was in fact a gunshot that he had heard.

Gerrish was stepping quickly across the deck, his shoes making a staccato sound on the planks, and a second later he appeared at Biddlecomb's side.

"You heard that?" Biddlecomb asked.

"Yes, sir," Gerrish said, staring out into the dark as Biddlecomb was. They could hear shouting now from Barnett's camp, and could see the shadows of a few men rushing about. "Are they drunk, do you reckon?" Gerrish asked. "Just firing off guns?"

"Perhaps..." Biddlecomb said. It seemed the most likely explanation, but it did not feel like the correct one. "Or perhaps..." he began when two more shots were fired. He saw the muzzle flashes that time, and they did not come from the camp, but rather from some place across the open ground that bordered the waterfront. He could hear more shouting among Barnett's people, the pitch and volume rising.

"Sir, I think..." Gerrish began and then suddenly the night seemed to be torn apart by sound. A church bell began to ring, loud and insistent, and more guns blinked in the dark, priming and charge making their double flash and bang. Men, barely visible, were stumbling around Barnett's camp, and now some of them were firing was well, shooting back at the dark place from where the shots had come.

"Turn out the marines, Mr. Gerrish. All hands to arms! Down on the wharf, now!" Biddlecomb shouted. He was moving as he spoke, stepping quickly to the scuttle, his feet on the ladder even as the last words left his lips.

He reached the great cabin and threw off his coat, grabbed his sword belt and buckled it around his waist. He slipped his coat back on and took his fine brace of pistols—a present from Virginia on his thirty-first birthday—from their polished mahogany box and slipped them into the pockets of his coat. He did not have to load them. He had kept them loaded since Barnett arrived at the wharf, kept them ready for this exact moment.

Up the ladder and out onto the quarterdeck, the cold air like salt spray in the face. The gangplank had been removed to make boarding the ship less convenient for potential attackers, but men were already swarming down the boarding steps and onto the dock, Faircloth's marines in their green regimental coats leading the way.

Son of a bitch...he must order them to sleep in those things, Biddlecomb mused. He could see no other way that the men had turned out in full uniform so quickly. Nor would it surprise him that Faircloth would do such a thing. For the lieutenant, being ready to go in an instant would mean being ready to go in all respects, and that meant full and proper uniforms.

Biddlecomb came down the quarterdeck ladder at a quick but dignified pace. There was no reason to hurry. There was still a crowd of men waiting to get through the gangway and down to the wharf: the rest *Falmouth*'s crew, who, with their blue jackets and short, heavy coats, and knitted caps pulled down over their heads looked decidedly less uniform than the marines.

But they, too, had done an admiral job of turning out quickly. Biddlecomb could see they wore cutlasses and carried boarding axes and pistols jammed in their belts and muskets in their hands. They were a lethal bunch. He just wished there were more of them.

"Make way! Make way for the captain!" Mr. Sprout shouted when he noticed Biddlecomb coming down the ladder. "Come along, make way!" Biddlecomb stepped into the waist and like the Red Sea, the men parted. He hurried through the gangway, turned to face inboard, and then went down the boarding steps and onto the wharf.

Lieutenant Faircloth was there to meet him, and like his troops, he did not look like a man who had just turned out of his bed. In the light of the single lantern on the wharf, Biddlecomb could see a hint of a smile on his face, half-hidden by his improbable mustache.

"Sir, some excitement, it seems," he said. "Do you know what's acting?"

"No, I don't," Biddlecomb said, looking down the wharf. He could see muzzle flashes like fireflies on a summer night, hear the cracking sound of muskets firing. "Perhaps the militia have finally worked up the courage to fight. That's my best guess. So we better go help them."

"Indeed, sir," Faircloth said. He turned and barked a few orders to the marines who fell into a line with muskets held at an angle across their chests. The sailors were on the wharf now as well, and Gerrish was getting them formed up as best as he could, though just on principle, they would never stand in as perfect order as the marines.

"Sir..." Faircloth said, taking a step closer to Biddlecomb and speaking in a low voice, "It occurs to me...if this bastard Barnett wanted to lure us into a trap, this would be a fine way to do it..."

Biddlecomb frowned. Excited as he was at the prospect of ending this stalemate it had not occurred to him that it might be a trick. He would not have credited Barnett with being that clever, but he had had lessons a' plenty in underestimating one's opponent.

"You make a good point, Mr. Faircloth," Biddlecomb said. He looked toward the town but he could not see much of what was going on, not nearly as much as he had been able to see from the vantage of the quarterdeck. "But there's naught we can do," he continued. "We have to go to the sound of the guns."

"I agree, sir, of course," Faircloth said. "But I beg, let me lead my marines in the vanguard. If it's a trap, we can bear the brunt."

"Of course," Biddlecomb said. He could hear the shouting getting louder, the firing more frequent and intense. "But we must go. Now."

With a few more shouts, the marines began to move, Faircloth at their head, Sergeant Dawes jogging alongside the first soldier. They would have looked intimidating indeed, advancing in good order, if only there had been a few more of them. Once the last of the marines passed, Biddlecomb turned to the rest and shouted, "Falmouths, with me! Listen for my orders! No one is to do a damned thing without my orders!"

He headed off at a jog to match the pace set by Faircloth in the lead, and he tried to imagine what they would encounter at the far end of the wharf: who was fighting, how they were fighting. If they were really fighting at all, or if it was all just play-acting designed to lure them away from his ship.

*We'll know directly…*he thought. They had no choice but to take the risk, to join the fight. If the militia had finally decided to go after Barnett, then this was their best chance at being rid of him. The son of a bitch had them trapped like fish in a weir, and now was their opportunity to break free.

Over the stamp of sixty shoes racing down the wooden wharf, Biddlecomb could hear the shouts, the call of orders, the gunfire, the scream of wounded men. It sounded like a real fight, he had to admit it. Two years of war had at least taught him what battle sounded like. If Barnett was staging this whole thing, he was doing a more than admirable job.

They were still moving fast as they came up with the camp and the haphazardly pitched tents. Faircloth's marines did not slacken their pace as they spread out at Sergeant Dawes's command, moving from column to rank and advancing with muskets leveled, bayonets fixed. They slowed as they moved through the tents, matching Faircloth's pace, muskets sweeping side to side as they looked for their enemy but found nothing.

Biddlecomb hurried forward, pushed his way through the line of marines and up to Faircloth's side. They had reached the far end of the camp now and come up with the cook fires burning in their stone rings.

They had encountered none of Barnett's men. But they could see them, a couple hundred feet away. They could see them in the muzzle flashes of their muskets, and those of whoever was shooting at them. The banditti had crossed halfway over the open ground toward what Biddlecomb recalled was a blacksmith's shop, and now they were advancing slowly, exchanging fire as they did.

"Halt!" Biddlecomb shouted, as Midshipman Gerrish came hurrying up to join them. "Everyone, halt!" He turned to Faircloth. "I don't think this is a trap," he said.

"Nor do I, sir," Faircloth said.

"Nor me," Gerrish said.

"Right at them?" Biddlecomb asked.

"Right at them, sir!" Faircloth said, and now he was definitely smiling. "Marines, forward!" he continued, half turning toward his men. "Advance and fire, one volley!"

The line of marines moved ahead, ten paces, then on Sergeant Dawes's orders they stopped and shouldered their weapons. "Take care to fire by division!" Dawes called.

"Hold up, hold up!" Biddlecomb shouted. "The sailors have muskets, too! You men, get up there with the marines!"

With a haphazard cheer, the sailors came racing past Biddlecomb on either side and joined the marines' line, extended it in ragged order. Sergeant Dawes looked left and right at them and he did not try to hide his disgust.

"Make ready!" the sergeant shouted, and the sailors shouldered their muskets as the marines were doing. "Take aim! Fire!"

Two dozen muskets went off at once. The flash of light lit up the ground and the backs of the men in the distance, but it was gone before Biddlecomb could see any reaction from Barnett's men, or see any of them fall. He heard the reaction, however: an instant of stunned silence at the shock of the unexpected volley from behind, and then, seconds later, the screams, the shouting, the panicked orders.

Faircloth was up with his marines once more, stepping in front of them, sword raised. "Bayonet charge!" he shouted and began to move forward, the marines following in their neatly dressed line. It was good to see that orderly advance, but it was irritating as well to have Faircloth lead the attack in that manner. It was only proper that the marines should go first, of course, and Biddlecomb was not proud of the petty annoyance he felt, but there it was.

"Falmouths! To me!" he shouted, rushing forward to get ahead of his men and drawing his sword as he did. The familiar wire-bound grip felt good in his hand, the finely balanced blade light and nimble. "Look to your bayonets! Take position either side of the marines!"

He turned again and hurried after Faircloth. He pulled one of the pistols with his left hand, cocked the lock with his other hand, and held the weapon low as he jogged on. Every bit of him wanted to break into a run, to get at the enemy in their front, but Faircloth was only walking fast, no more, and Biddlecomb forced himself to show the same degree of discipline.

He had heard of fearless men, of men who longed for combat, who seemed to never contemplate their own mortality. He was not one of those. Naval battles tended to provide ample time beforehand to consider what might happen when the iron started to fly, and his thoughts at those times had never been very comforting. His bravest act, he always thought, was not being unafraid, but appearing to be unafraid.

But this time, he was genuinely not afraid, this time he was simply eager to be at them, the damned pine robbers, Barnett and the rest. Maybe it was the wild frustration he had endured, the helplessness. Maybe it was how quickly this fight had come about. He did not know, did not care. He just wanted to drive his sword through someone's gut, put a bullet through a banditti skull.

And then he was on them, face to face, men turning to fight, men sprawled on the ground where they had been shot down. In the half a minute or so it had taken to close with the pine robbers over the open ground, part of Barnett's men and managed to turn and make ready for this new attack. Biddlecomb saw muskets go up, saw the blaze of gunfire, so close he could feel the heat from the discharge.

A bullet passed by his head with a deafening buzz. The marine to Biddlecomb's right was hit and flung back, arms going wide, musket flying off behind him. One of the sailors stumbled, staggered on for a few steps and went down, face-first. And then the two lines connected, and the time for long guns was over.

It was a strange fight in the darkness. The men in front of Biddlecomb seemed like moving shadows, seen and not seen as the wavering light fell on them—the light from the small cook fires some distance back, and a couple of lanterns that had come from somewhere and had been set on the ground.

Biddlecomb raised his pistol and pointed it at the man directly in front of him. He had a series of fleeting impressions: big man, several day's growth of beard, filthy Monmouth cap pulled down on his head, a tear in his homespun coat that showed the lighter cloth of his waistcoat below.

He was coming at Biddlecomb with a cutlass raised and appeared unaware of the pistol pointed in his direction. He was scowling, shouting, and his expression did not change, even when Biddlecomb moved the gun level with his head and pulled the trigger. The muzzle flash seemed to freeze the man in place: his scowl, his growth of beard, the hole blown through the front of his Monmouth cap, the back of his head bursting apart.

Biddlecomb shoved the gun back in his pocket—it was not a sea-service pistol to be flung aside—and stepped up with sword raised. To his left, one of Barnett's men was turning and bringing a pistol up as he did. His eyes, invisible in the dark, seemed to be fixed on Biddlecomb's. Too close to get the tip of his blade on the man, Biddlecomb took another step closer, wound up and drove the sword's metal hand guard with its three steel bands hard into his left temple.

The man's head snapped around and he stumbled back. The gun in his hand went off and Biddlecomb felt the bullet pluck the sleeve of his coat. The banditti would have gone down if he had not slammed into the man behind him, who was also trying to get into the fight. Biddlecomb thrust, felt the point of his sword drive through the man's flesh just below his shoulder, felt it deflect off bone as the man shrieked and spun away.

You're done, Biddlecomb thought. The man might live, would likely live, if the wound did not turn septic, but he was done with fighting and that was what mattered here.

Biddlecomb turned to his right. A cutlass was coming at his belly, straight and low and thrust with force, if not finesse. Biddlecomb swept his blade down and to the right and caught the cutlass a fraction of a second before it bit. He knocked it aside and once again struck with the handguard, struck straight up into the man's face, driving up from below.

He felt the man's nose crumble under the impact. A gun went off and in the flash, Biddlecomb saw the blood come pouring out. The man dropped the cutlass and doubled over, hands on his face. Biddlecomb brought his knee up hard, made a solid connection with the man's forehead that snapped him upright and sent him reeling back.

Biddlecomb swung left and slashed and felt his blade bite something. He slashed right and found air, then slashed again. There were men around him, and though he could not see much, he had the impression they were not his men. The marines, of course, were the most conspicuous of the lot, but Biddlecomb could see none of them nearby. He slashed again and struck something hard—a musket barrel or a cutlass blade—then took a step back.

Damn it, what's happening? he thought. It felt as if his men were being pushed back, overwhelmed by the weight of Barnett's numbers. He took another step back. He could see one of the marines now to his right. He had his musket leveled and he was slashing side to side with his bayonet.

Biddlecomb saw one of his sailors—Woodberry, he thought—also driving with his bayonet, hard-pressed and fighting three of Barnett's men. Woodberry raised his musket and trust it forward, but one of pine robbers grabbed hold of the barrel and wrenched the gun from his hands as another swung down with an axe. Woodberry twisted sideways, dodged the axe, and pulled his cutlass in one fluid motion, but then he was lost to Biddlecomb's sight by the press of men.

Biddlecomb turned to the threat in front of him. Two men, one with a musket held like a club, the other with a long knife, and in their eagerness to be at him they were slammed into one another. Biddlecomb's blade darted in, caught the man wielding the musket in the gut. He felt that familiar resistance in his arm as the blade parted flesh, heard the roar of the wounded man two feet away.

He pulled the sword free, took a step back, and let the man with the knife slash at the space where he had been a second before. Off-balance, the man was wonderfully positioned for Biddlecomb to give him an upward cut, slashing him right across the midsection. And Biddlecomb did just that, twisting the other way first, winding up to get maximum force behind the blow, letting the well-honed blade do its work.

Another step back and another as the wounded men served as an obstacle of sorts, keeping the men behind from getting at Biddlecomb, giving Biddlecomb a few seconds' pause to look around. His own men were nowhere to be seen, pushed back by Barnett's pine robbers, their lack of numbers finally working against them once the advantage of their surprise attack had worn off.

Damn it, damn it... Biddlecomb thought, taking another two steps back. He looked left and right. He could see Woodberry again now, off to his right, and several of the marines. A figure stepped up beside him and he recognized Midshipman Gerrish. His hat was gone and there was a dark mark on his cheek, which Biddlecomb thought was dirt but realized was blood.

"Sir! Sir!" Gerrish shouted. "Thank God! I thought you were... thought they had taken you down!"

"What's acting?" Biddlecomb shouted, his eyes moving from Gerrish to Barnett's men, who were advancing on them, bold but wary, men who had learned a lesson.

"There's too damned many of them, sir!" Gerrish shouted. "The militia...on the other side of Barnett's line...there's a handful, it seems, no more! Barnett's got the men to fight both ways!"

Biddlecomb nodded as he fished the second pistol from his pocket. At first, they had managed to catch Barnett's men between the militia on one side and the Falmouths on the other, squeezing them, pressing them. Killing them. But Barnett had men enough to fight back, despite all that. Fight back and prevail.

"We have to get back to the ship," Biddlecomb said. "That's our chief concern. Get the marines to form a rear guard..."

He was about to turn, to seek out Faircloth, when he heard another sound, another rush of motion, more voices, fresh voices, coming from his right. Barnett's men heard them, too. Biddlecomb saw heads turning, looks of confusion, the fighting men like dark shades moving here and there.

Then the line of pine robbers seemed to crumble, seemed to fall in on itself, and men were running and shouting, while other men stood and fought and died on the end of bayonets. It was a fresh wave, an attack right on the flank of Barnett's line, men shouting and driving forward with bayonets. A pistol fired, a flash that lit up the dark, and in that instant Biddlecomb saw a face he recognized, and it was Colonel Richard Somers of the Gloucester County Militia.

Where in hell did you come from? Biddlecomb thought. He had assumed that Somers had been there all along, that it was Somers who had started this fight, but now it looked for all the world as if the man was just now leading his soldiers into the fray.

No matter... Biddlecomb thought next, and in that he was right: it did not matter. What mattered was that they showed up when they did, that they rolled up Barnett's flank just as Barnett was about to drive Biddlecomb and his men back to the frigate, or worse, overwhelm them before they could reach it.

Men we running now, and guns were firing in the dark. It was chaos, and that could be a problem. In chaos, a man like Barnett might still find opportunity, he might still find a chance to get away, and Biddlecomb did not want that. He wanted an end to this, and that meant seeing Barnett in chains, seeing that he enjoyed his just deserts.

Biddlecomb whirled around and found Faircloth ten feet behind him, sword in hand. "Mr. Faircloth," he called, "get your men after these banditti, round them up, don't let them get away!"

"Yes, sir!" Faircloth called, and then waved his sword over his head and called, "Marines! After me!"

Biddlecomb turned to his right. "Mr. Gerrish, collect up some men, help Mr. Faircloth take those bastards prisoner! I want them all!"

"Aye, sir!" Gerrish shouted, and began waving his arms, gathering the sailors to him, as Biddlecomb raced off in the other direction. He could only just make out handfuls of his men, scattered around the open ground, and he called to them as he moved past.

"Mr. Sprout, Burke, Whitman, come with me!" He led his handful of armed men back toward where the line of pine robbers had been over-run. He could see men standing with arms raised, muskets and cutlasses lying at their feet. He could see men sprawled on the ground, some moving, some not.

"Colonel Somers!" Biddlecomb shouted. The militiaman was standing a dozen yards away, illuminated by a lantern that the man beside him was holding aloft. "Colonel Somers!"

Biddlecomb hurried over the ground as Somers turned to the sound of his name being called. Another man stepped up beside the colonel and Biddlecomb recognized him as Captain Jonathan Mitnick, a more active officer than Somers, certainly. He wondered if perhaps this had all been Mitnick's doing.

"Colonel," Biddlecomb said as he approached, hand outstretched. "Well done, here, sir. Boldly done."

Somers took Biddlecomb's hand and shook. "Thank you, sir, but we might have been a bit late to the ball," he said.

"Late?" Biddlecomb said. "But, surely you…" Another figure stepped up out of the dark, a big man, and the lantern light fell on his wool coat and his torn, dirty, blood-stained shirt and his utterly familiar face.

"Ezra?" Biddlecomb said.

Rumstick nodded his greeting. "Captain," he said, as casually as if he was bumping into Biddlecomb coming out of a tavern, but Biddlecomb could see he was smiling broadly.

"What the devil…damn me, man, it's good to see you here!" Biddlecomb said. He grabbed Rumstick's hand and shook, then pulled him closer and threw an arm around him, as best as he could, given Rumstick's size. It was indeed good to see him, and it was only then that Biddlecomb realized how much he had despaired of Rumstick's surviving the hunting party that Barnett had sent out after him.

Biddlecomb released his friend and stepped back. "You joined up with the militia, I take it?" he said. "I hope you didn't sign any articles or such."

"Not a bit of it," Rumstick said. "We were hiding out in Captain Mitnick's barn. Heard all the commotion so we come running down here."

Biddlecomb turned back to Somers. "So you lead the attack?" he asked. "You started all this?"

"No," Somers said, and he looked genuinely bewildered. "I...we... we heard the bell ringing, so we came. That's the alarm, you know. I reckoned Captain Mitnick rung it, but he says he didn't."

"Well, that's a damnable mystery, ain't it?" Rumstick said.

Biddlecomb tried not to smile. *Yes, a damnable mystery*, he thought, *to all but you.* He was eager to get the truth of it, preferably over a bowl of flip in *Falmouth*'s great cabin.

Lieutenant Faircloth stepped up into the circle of light. "Mr. Rumstick!" he said, and Biddlecomb recognized the same note of surprise and relief on seeing Rumstick that he had heard in his own voice. "Damned good of you to join us, sir!" He turned to Biddlecomb. "We've disarmed the rascals and rounded them up, Captain. They await your pleasure."

*My pleasure...*Biddlecomb thought. He could think of many things he might do to the prisoners that would give him pleasure, but for the time being he would confine himself to simply inspecting them.

He and Somers and the rest, followed by two militiamen bearing lanterns, crossed over to where the pine robbers stood, a sullen and defeated band of twenty or so men. Biddlecomb stopped fifteen feet away and for a moment the two groups, victors and their conquered foe, stood looking at one another.

"This is all of them?" Biddlecomb said at last.

"Yes, sir, all we could round up," Faircloth said. "Not counting the ones dead and wounded. And some that must have run off."

Biddlecomb nodded. By his estimate this was not even half of the vermin.

"Where's Barnett?" he asked next. "I don't see him. Is he among the wounded? The dead?" Biddlecomb would be disappointed indeed if Barnett had been killed in the fighting, as he had something more fitting in mind for the man. But his question was greeted with silence.

"I didn't see him there," Faircloth said and Biddlecomb could hear the mounting discomfort in the lieutenant's voice. "Pray, let me check again." He hurried over to where the wounded and the dead were being attended to by the men of the Gloucester County Militia. There were perhaps a dozen men on the ground: pine robbers, militiamen, Falmouths. Faircloth moved quickly from man to man.

"He's not here, sir," Faircloth called as he looked down at the last prone man.

"Damn it!" Biddlecomb said in frustration. If Barnett escaped then it would take the bloom off this whole victory. If the bastard was suffered to live, than there was no reason to think that he would not return to try again. *Falmouth* had become an obsession for the man, and surely one defeat would not put an end to it.

And then Biddlecomb had another thought, and it made his gut turn over.

"Oh, Dear God, no," he said. He turned quickly and looked down the length of the dark wharf toward where the frigate lay tied to the pilings. They had left no one onboard, not a single man. But even now, even from that distance, Biddlecomb could see a lantern moving along the quarterdeck rail.

Chapter Seventeen

For the second time that night, Isaac Biddlecomb found himself hurrying down the length of the long wharf at the head of a band of armed men. For the second time, he was desperately anxious, and wanted nothing more than to break into a run. But once again he restrained himself, keeping his pace to something quick but dignified.

It is not possible, it is simply not possible, Biddlecomb thought as he hurried through the dark, his shoes and those of the marines and the men of *Falmouth* behind him loud on the half-frozen wood. Somers's militia, unsurprisingly, had elected to stay behind and tend to the wounded and the prisoners.

There is no way that bastard slipped away from the fight. Or if he did, he could not have enough men with him to hold the ship. But even as he thought it, he knew it was not true. Barnett was a sneaky and clever son of a bitch; Biddlecomb had admitted as much to himself earlier. He might very well have pulled off something like that. And if he did, he would not need an awful lot of men to defend the ship. That was already well established.

One hundred yards away and Biddlecomb could see he had not been mistaken: there was indeed a lantern, and it was on the frigate's quarterdeck. It was sitting on the rail now, casting its light over the ship's side and down onto the mizzen channel. The rest of the ship was lost in darkness. If there was anyone onboard, Biddlecomb could not see them.

But he was quite certain they had not left a lighted lantern behind, which meant someone had put it there since.

He slowed a bit as they came closer, and Rumstick to his left and Faircloth to his right did as well.

"See anything?" Biddlecomb asked the others.

"No one aboard that I can see, Captain," Rumstick said.

Then the air was split with a long blast of flame, the concussion of a musket fired from the darkness at the after end of the quarterdeck. The flash illuminated the figure holding the weapon, but he appeared as nothing more than a dark shape behind the flash of light. Biddlecomb jumped in surprise, despite himself.

"Son of a bitch!" Rumstick said, loud and angry. He, too, had been startled, apparently, and he did not care for it.

"Captain Biddlecomb!" a voice called from the ship's deck, an unmistakable voice, gravely and mocking. Barnett's voice. "That would be close enough, sir."

Biddlecomb stopped and the rest of the men stopped as well. "Cleverly done, Barnett," Biddlecomb called. "But I don't see how you'll keep hold of the ship by yourself. Your men are prisoners, and we have Mr. Rumstick and his men back now. And the militia are with us."

"Oh, I'm hardly alone, Captain," Barnett called back. "How many of my men did you take prisoner? Twenty, maybe? You know damned well I have more than that. A lot more. And they're here with me now. Ain't that right, boys?"

Barnett's words were greeted with a chorus of shouts and hoots and calls of, "That's right, colonel!" Men unseen, hidden by the dark and the ship's rail. It was impossible to gauge exactly how many there were, but it was not an insignificant number. Two dozen at least, by the sound of it.

Damn it... Biddlecomb thought.

"You know what's so funny about all this, Captain?" Barnett called out.

"Don't know, Barnett," Biddlecomb said. "And I don't much care."

"Funny thing is," Barnett continued as if Biddlecomb had not spoken. "I actually thought about starting a fight myself, for just this reason. Thought if I could start something up, why, you'd be sure to leave the ship and join in. And then I could take half my men or so, the half I trust, anyway, and slip away during the commotion, and there...the ship's mine. But I didn't think it would work! I didn't think you'd be dumb enough to leave the ship, even if the guns were firing away. Fool that I am. Lucky, though, 'cause I had it all set up. Had the boats ready so we could row around the far side of the ship, board her from the water. Had the men ready. I just didn't reckon on you being so cooperative."

Barnett was enjoying this, Biddlecomb could hear it in his voice. He had no doubt been rehearsing this little speech from the moment he took possession of the ship. He would want to make the point as sharp as he could, then really drive it home.

Now what? Biddlecomb wondered. If Barnett's soliloquy had given him his moment to think, and it had not helped. Nothing had come to him.

"Captain, if I may," Faircloth said, speaking softly. "Let's just charge the ship, right now. We have the men here and under arms. We can attack along the whole length of the ship at once, climb aboard and overwhelm them."

Biddlecomb was silent for a moment, considering that. In fact, he had been considering it even before Faircloth spoke. The problem was that there were not so many places where a man could climb aboard. Up the boarding steps, of course, and over the fore and main channels, but that was about it. He pictured the men trying to climb aboard by those routes in the face of Barnett's muskets.

Then, as if he could hear the debate in Biddlecomb's head, as if he wished to reinforce Biddlecomb's doubts, Barnett spoke again. "Say, Captain, I got to say I was surprised at how many damned muskets you have onboard here! Of course, each of my men had a musket when we took the ship, and most got pistols, but damn me, if we didn't find enough firelocks so's to give two to each man. And with bayonets! Why don't you send your men up over the side, and we'll show you?"

Biddlecomb clenched his teeth and pressed his lips together. Barnett was not lying. Faircloth had seen to it that there were spare weapons for his men, and even more had been put aboard when *Falmouth* was launched, before Biddlecomb had even taken command. There were plenty of firelocks there, and that meant each of Barnett's men likely had two loaded weapons, at least, not counting their pistols.

"We can't attack the ship," Biddlecomb said to Faircloth. "Not now. It would be a bloody slaughter. That's why Barnett never attacked us before."

Faircloth frowned. He looked over at the ship and then back at Biddlecomb.

"Perhaps if we can find some boats," Biddlecomb continued, "launch an attack on both sides at once, but not now." He waited for the marine to make some protest but none came. Even Faircloth could see how unlikely they were to succeed.

Biddlecomb turned and faced the ship. "So, what do you want, Barnett?" he called out.

"Not a damned thing, Captain!" Barnett called back. "I got what I want! I got the ship. And once I see what we got onboard here, well, I'll take that, too."

"You're going to be disappointed, I fear," Biddlecomb said. "There's some ropes and some sails and some salt pork, and that's about it." And that was true, mostly. There were also some Continental bills, courtesy of the Congress, which were not worth much, and some Spanish gold, courtesy of William Stanton, which was worth considerably more, but Biddlecomb suspected that was all in Barnett's pocket by now.

"I reckon there's plenty you ain't telling me about," Barnett said. "But I got plenty of time to look things over, don't you worry."

"This is ridiculous, bloody, damned ridiculous," Biddlecomb said, just loud enough for Rumstick and Faircloth to hear, and no one else.

"It is that," Rumstick said.

"Listen here, Barnett!" Biddlecomb called. "You've put yourself in a trap, you damned idiot! You're on the ship but you have no way off, and you're dead men if you try!"

The same trap we were in, Biddlecomb thought.

"I reckon not!" Barnett shouted back. "We got boats, you see, which you didn't. And we got a damned lot of firelocks, and men who know the use of them. And you got what? The brave Gloucester County Militia? Ha!"

Biddlecomb wanted to shout in frustration, he wanted to fling curses at Barnett, he wanted to personally climb up the side of the ship and wring the man's filthy neck. But instead, he clenched his teeth even harder and squeezed his fists until the rage passed. Mostly.

"This is pointless," he said to Faircloth and Rumstick. "The son of a bitch is enjoying this. Let's be off."

"Just leave?" Rumstick asked.

"Yes," Biddlecomb said. "I feel no need to bid the man good night."

He turned and headed back up the wharf and heard the sound of the others following behind.

"You ain't leaving me, are you, Captain?" he heard Barnett call out. "Now, don't go away mad like that!"

He tried to ignore the taunts, tried to make his mind settle, to work through this problem in a methodical way, to reach some reasonable plan. But it was no use. His thoughts were nothing more than a jumble of rage and confusion and uncertainty, self-recrimination, and blame heaped on himself and anyone else he could think to blame.

Somers and Mitnick met them at the landward end of the wharf. The area was much better lit now, with a number of lanterns having appeared and the fires in the fire pits stoked up until they were several feet high.

The militiamen were going through the pine robbers' tents, looking for war _matériel_ or documents of some importance, Somers explained. Of course, the largely illiterate banditti were unlikely to have many documents in their possession, nor would such outlaws generally be hiding military secrets. In truth, the militiamen were simply looting.

"What of the ship, Captain?" Somers asked, happy to change the subject.

"Barnett has the ship," Biddlecomb said, his words clipped and short. He wanted to make it very clear he did not wish to discuss the situation. "I'll thank you to post some men here on the wharf to keep a watch, but I don't reckon Barnett or any of them will be going anywhere tonight."

Why would they? he thought. _They're exactly where they want to be._

"Ah…very well, Captain," Somers said. Biddlecomb braced for some argument, but none came. He suspected that the militia's late arrival to the fight, along with Somers' tacit permission for his men to loot the camp, and likely to loot the prisoners and the dead and wounded as well, was making the colonel a little less eager to protest.

"Where are the wounded?" Biddlecomb asked next. "And the dead? Were any of my men among the dead?" It was a dereliction, he knew, that he was only asking that now, but Barnett's coup had driven all other thought from his mind.

"No, Captain," Mitnick said. "None of yours among the dead. Three men wounded. They're in the church. Pray, come with me." He led them across the open ground and up the road a hundred yards to the small church with its short bell tower. Inside, a dozen lanterns and candles in sconces illuminated the space with a soft yellow light. Wounded men had been stretched out in the box pews, with armed militia standing near those that housed banditti, at least those banditti still able to cause trouble.

The three wounded among the men of *Falmouth* were housed in a single pew. Woodbury had taken a nasty cut to the arm, which someone had done a tolerable job of bandaging. Ephraim Kirby, who had been with Rumstick, had been shot through the lungs, and it was pretty clear from the blood and from the pallor of his skin that he would not be suffering long. A marine named Willard Lot had been stabbed in the leg and shot through the arm but he seemed hale enough.

Biddlecomb spent some time with each of them, and then it was time to go. "Woodberry, do you have strength enough to come with us?" he asked.

"Aye, sir," Woodberry said.

"Good. Lot, I think you had best stay here, what with that leg wound," Biddlecomb said. "They seem to be taking good care of you. We'll be by for you in the morning. No cause to move Kirby, I think."

Biddlecomb turned to Mitnick. "My men and I will be at the tavern," he said. "And we'll see this whole mess straight, come morning." He nodded his good nights and headed off without another word. He did not think he had to strength to say another word.

They walked in silence down the frozen road; Biddlecomb, Rumstick, Faircloth, and the thirty or so men of *Falmouth*. Less than a quarter of the men they would need to sail the ship. If they even had possession of the ship, which they did not.

They came at last to the tavern, which was dark now, quite unlike the last time Biddlecomb had been there, when the place had been lit up with the pine robbers' revelry.

"Please, sir, allow me to deal with this villain of a tavern keeper," Faircloth said as they walked past the gate with its pineapple finials and up the path to the door.

"If you wish," Biddlecomb said, but he was glad for the offer. Speaking to anyone was about the last thing he wished to do just then, and speaking civilly was even less appealing.

Faircloth knocked on the door, then knocked again and then shouted and knocked again, and finally, the door opened to reveal the tavern keeper in his nightshirt, blunderbuss in hand, and his wife behind him holding a lantern aloft.

"We'll need lodging for the night," Faircloth said, pushing his way in past the man and his lady. "Beds for thirty-eight, and we'll need refreshment before we turn in. Ale, meat, cheese." He spoke with that presumption of superiority and expectation of prompt and obsequious service that only a man of Faircloth's station could pull off. And the tavern keeper and his wife responded just as Faircloth expected them too, turning out the servants and the cook and seeing all in readiness to make the Falmouths as comfortable as they could be.

Biddlecomb remained below stairs long enough to see that his men were indeed properly fed and given drink and provided with beds for the night, with Boatswain Sprout and Sergeant Dawes to see that no one got out of hand or took advantage of the near-presence of great stores of alcohol. That done, he told the innkeeper to show him to whatever room he had available.

Lantern in hand, the innkeeper led the way up one narrow flight of stairs and then up another to the third floor. "Ain't a large room, sir, but it's private and the best private room we got," the man explained as he huffed up the steps. "All the quality who stay here, they take this room."

All the quality… Biddlecomb mused. He could just imagine the quality who passed that way.

They reached the third floor at last and the innkeeper opened the door. It was indeed a small room, but a fire had been stoked up in the fireplace, which took the chill from the air, and it seemed to be reasonably clean and there was a bed that looked tolerably comfortable. It was everything Biddlecomb dreamed it might be.

"Thank you," Biddlecomb said and the innkeeper nodded and said his goodnights and left, closing the door behind him. Biddlecomb stood for a moment, looking into the flames of the fire. Then he took his off overcoat, heavy with the weight of the pistols in the pockets, and hung it on a hook, then his sword belt and his waistcoat and breeches, and climbed gratefully into bed.

The storm in his head had not abated, the anger and self-recrimination. *Now what in all hell do I do?* he wondered as he lay with eyes open, watching the light from the fire dancing across the ceiling. He had no idea how he would get his ship back. He did know, however, that he would have all night to think on it. Sleep would not come anytime soon, he was sure of that. And even as those thoughts were still roiling in his head, he fell into a deep and dreamless slumber.

It was daylight when he woke to the sound of a fist pounding on his door. But it was not a fist at first, it was, in his dream, a loose plank on a boat that was banging each time the bow slammed down on a wave. He moved forward over the thwarts, trying to reach the plank and hold it in place so it would stop its slamming around, but every time he moved, a wave made the boat pitch and tossed him back again.

And then he was awake and the boat was gone and the fist was still pounding.

"Come!" he shouted and the door swung open and Ezra Rumstick came barging in. "Captain, you awake?" he asked. Biddlecomb looked at him. He did not bother to reply.

"Well, here's what's acting," Rumstick continued, ignoring Biddlecomb's irritated expression. "Got word at first light from down at the harbor that there were some ships standing in. More than one. So I sent Ferguson down to see what he could see. And he just got back and said there were three ships. One is a small man-of-war by the looks of her. Continental colors. The other's a brig, merchantman, mostly likely. And the third's a sloop. And Ferguson says he can't say for certain, but he's got a pretty good idea that the sloop is *Sparrowhawk*."

CHAPTER EIGHTEEN

Virginia Biddlecomb was waiting in the foyer, cloak over her shoulders, hat on her head, when Captain Richard Dexter knocked on the door. Little Jack was bundled up in a sling around her shoulder, thankfully asleep.

"That will be the Captain," said Mrs. Williams, who was hovering near the door, waiting for that particular knock. "And I'm sure he'll be able to talk some sense into you, even if I can't."

"Oh, I doubt it, mother," said Susan, perched on a small chair by the wall and enjoying every bit of the proceedings. "Our dear Virginia is far too headstrong for that!"

That is certainly true, Susan, dear, Virginia thought, but she said nothing as Mrs. Williams opened the door and gestured for Dexter to enter. He stepped in with his usual grace and ease, his cloak open, his elegant regimentals visible underneath. He gave a quick bow, more a nod of the head, and kissed Mrs. Williams's proffered hand, a gesture that never failed to charm the older woman.

"Dear Captain Dexter," Mrs. Williams said, taking her hand back from him. "We're in quite a state here! Mrs. Biddlecomb, it seems, intends to bring her baby, her dear Jack, with her on your outing! Can you countenance such a thing?"

"Ah, well…" Dexter stammered, searching for a diplomatic response. Virginia stood, a move made less easy by the weight of her growing boy, and crossed over to the captain.

"Riding and the out of doors and fresh air will always do a young man good, no matter their age," she announced to the company. "The vigorous life. I'm sure Captain Dexter would agree, would you not?"

"Ah, well…" Captain Dexter said again.

"You're not bothered by the presence of small children, are you, Captain?" Virginia asked.

"No, no, of course not," Dexter said quickly, and with an admirable degree of sincerity in his voice. "Whatever you think is best, Virginia, of course…"

This particular wrinkle in the plan came as a surprise to Dexter. Indeed, the whole thing had likely been a surprise. It was two days after their outing to the King's Arms that Virginia sent him a note, thanking him again for a fine evening, and thanking him, in particular, for their ride on the North East Square.

Let me say how delightful it was riding in your company, she had written, *and for that, I must thank you once again. And having thanked you, might I be so bold as to request an encore to that fine day? I would be ever so grateful if you might find the time (and horses!) so that we might enjoy a similar outing.*

She had spent a long time on the note, crafting it to sound as if it had been written on a whim. She did not doubt that the captain would be surprised by her forwardness. And she did not doubt that he would eagerly acquiesce to her request. And she was right on both counts.

But even before putting quill to paper, she had taken care to be as certain as she could be that her suspicions were correct.

She started the morning after the boozy carriage ride and dinner that Dexter and Cornwall had arranged. Head pounding, stomach in full rebellion, it had taken some time, as well as multiple glasses of water and a nap, before she felt able to advance her cause. Rising from bed for the second time, she made her way down the hall and knocked lightly on Susan's door.

"Who is it?" Susan called.

"Virginia."

"Oh, Virginia, dear, do come in!" Susan called, brighter-sounding now. Virginia stepped inside and closed the door. "I thought it was my mother, come to scold some more," Susan explained. "God, but that woman can be tiresome!"

On that we agree... Virginia thought, but she did not say anything, because she was not given to speaking ill of others. Besides that, she was grateful for Mrs. Williams's hospitality, and she knew Mrs. Williams to be a good and honest woman. If a bit tiresome.

"You're still abed, I see," Virginia observed. Susan was buried under a heap of blankets, the curtains on her four-poster bed drawn back.

"Oh, I just can't face the day! I can't bear the tedium, not after the magic of last night!" Susan said, adding a dramatic sigh for emphasis.

Virginia crossed the room to the small table near the head of Susan's bed. She turned the chair around and sat. "It's not always so tedious around here, surely," she said. "How about the afternoon I went riding with Captain Dexter? And your mother was out?"

"Oh," Susan said, and she smiled a bit as she thought back to that afternoon. "No, that was not tedious, I'll grant you that."

"Captain Cornwall paid a visit? Nelly didn't send him away?"

"I believe Nelly was out doing the shopping," Susan said. "But really, Virginia, dear, you need not be so coy with me. You know full well that Captain Cornwall was here. And being a married woman yourself, you might well guess at the entertainments I arranged."

"I might well," Virginia agreed. "But I also might wonder at the prudence of the thing."

"A subtle game," Susan said. "I give him a taste of the fruit, and then a bit of stand-offishness. And then another taste."

"It seems Captain Cornwall had more than a taste. A full meal from soup to nuts is more like it."

"As I said, Virginia, you're a married woman," Susan said, her tone less playful and insipid now. "Unless Captain Biddlecomb has quite failed you, you understand that there are...pleasures to be enjoyed. By women as well as men."

Virginia could feel her face flush a bit, and it annoyed her. "Yes, but is it worth the risk?"

"Captain Cornwall is a prize worth having," Susan assured her. "If he's only good for an afternoon's entertainment, then so be it. But if he is on the look-out for a wife, as frankly all men such as him are, then that is an office I should be happy to fill."

"Indeed?" Virginia asked. "He's such a good catch?"

Susan sat more upright and turned in Virginia's direction. "That he is," she said. "I don't rush blindly into such…*affaires de coeur*, you know. A captain's commission is not an inexpensive thing. A man needs money and patronage to purchase one."

"True," Virginia said. "But Cornwall might well have exhausted all his cash and patronage just to become a captain."

"He might have, but he did not," Susan assured him. "He's the third son of Lord Fairfax, a nephew of Lord Cornwallis."

"I see," Virginia said, and thought, *That explains a great deal…* "And his friend Captain Dexter?"

"Well," Susan said, "not that it's any great concern to a married woman such as yourself, but Captain Dexter has a respectable income and a good deal of patronage as well, though much of it is in the naval line. I do believe his uncle is that Sir James Wallace they spoke of the other night."

"Indeed?" Virginia said. She stared off to the far end of the room and tried to keep her face a blank slate though she felt as if she had been punched in the gut, as if she suddenly understood that she did not understand anything at all. Her suspicions had been just that—suspicions, vague and unlikely—until that moment. She looked back at Susan.

"On the day Captain Dexter and I were riding, Captain Cornwall was in your company all afternoon?"

"All afternoon," Susan said, and her coy, wicked smile was back. "Save for the odd moment when I sent him away so I might dress or such. A woman needs to maintain some secrets, you know."

"If she can," Virginia said. Susan had brought Cornwall into their home, given him opportunity to prowl around unseen, go through Virginia's personal effects, her correspondence. Virginia found it ironic to hear Susan speak about maintaining secrets, but she did not bother to explain. She would have to start maintaining secrets of her own, more assiduously than she had realized. She would have to start making plans.

She began immediately, considering options, thinking through each possibility: what might go wrong, and what would she do if it did? How could she salvage her situation, and, more importantly, protect her husband, after so much blind, foolish, vanity? The note to Dexter was the first step. His arrival that morning, his eagerness to once again accompany her on a ride, was the next.

"I'm a military man," Dexter said, his words couched in his usual good humor and agreeableness. "And I know little of children. If you say it's to your son's benefit to ride with us, I am hardly in a position to argue. Nor would I argue with the lovely and opinionated Mrs. Biddlecomb in any event."

"You have argued with me aplenty, sir," Virginia said, trying to keep her own words amiable. "With regard to horses in any event. I'm pleased that you'll yield ground to me in this."

"Humph," said Mrs. Williams, who had hoped she would find an ally in the army officer. Susan laughed out loud, delighted by the discomfort all around.

Captain Dexter, apparently, did not find the discomfort quite so amusing. He gestured toward the door. "Shall we, Virginia?" he asked.

"Certainly, Captain," Virginia said. She paused and took Mrs. Williams's hands in hers. "Fear not, everything will be fine," she said with a warm smile. "And thank you."

"Humph," Mrs. Williams said, but there was less censure in her tone than perhaps she intended. Virginia released her hands and stepped through the door into the bracing November air.

There were two horses standing hitched to a post on the edge of the sidewalk and she recognized both. One was the bay, Dexter's horse. The other was the spirited chestnut she had selected for herself on their first outing. A strong, fast horse, and Virginia felt as if she and it had come to an understanding. She was pleased that Dexter had brought that mount for her.

She was pleased as well that he had heeded her request in saddles: not a side saddle but a saddle for riding astride.

"I hope this is to your liking, Virginia," Dexter said as they made their way down the steps. "The chestnut seemed well suited to you. And the saddle…"

"Thank you, this is perfect," Virginia said.

"You'll have no difficulty riding astride with…your little one?" Dexter asked. He sounded like a man much out of his depth.

"None at all," Virginia said. "Much easier this way." She adjusted Jack in the sling and felt him stir a bit. She hoped very much he would stay asleep. If she had to stop and nurse him during their ride, it could get more than a bit awkward.

"Pray, allow me to…" Dexter stepped over to the chestnut's side and cupped his hands, then paused and straightened. "Are you quite able to mount? Or should I…" he asked, still flailing in the unusual circumstance.

"Just a hand up, if you would be so kind, sir," Virginia said. She spoke with confidence, but in truth, she was not so certain. She had never tried mounting a horse with her baby in a sling.

"Certainly, certainly," Dexter said. He bent over and cupped his hands again. Virginia placed her foot in them and took a grip of the saddle and Dexter lifted her up. She gave an involuntary and unlady-like grunt as she stood and swung her leg over the saddle, but that was the worst of it, and she settled herself into that familiar perch on horseback.

"I thank you, Richard. Very well done," she said, smiling down at him as he handed her up the reins. Jack thrashed a bit in his sling and Virginia bounced up and down and made cooing sounds, which seemed to settle both Jack and the horse. Dexter smiled, unhitched the reins of his bay, and swung himself up into the saddle.

"Shall we?" he asked, and his expression, which had been mostly one of uncertainty, was eager and enthusiastic now.

"Yes!" said Virginia. She tapped the chestnut with her cane and the two of them rode off north, over the cobblestones of Chestnut Street. This time, rather than riding past the State House, Dexter turned right on Fourth Street. Virginia wondered if he wished to avoid any possible embarrassment, or questions of political allegiance, but she did not ask.

On wide Market Street, the center of the city, east to west, they turned left and continued on. They rode past the brick homes that lined the way, and the sundry shops and stalls. A block east Virginia could see the trees that dotted North East Square and she reined to a halt.

"Richard," she said, looking for just the right tone to her voice: playful and suggestive, bold and adventurous. "We had a grand time riding in the square the other day. But honestly…it's so confining. No more than a couple city blocks. Just outside the city, however, there's open country. We could really give our horses their heads out there."

"Outside the city?" Dexter said.

Virginia could hear the uncertainty in his voice. Suspicion, perhaps? But she had given him no cause for suspicion. She had rarely given him anything but encouragement, and reason to believe in her good opinion of him.

"Nor far, mind you," Virginia said. "But as I recall there were some fields just a few miles north of here where Market Street runs into the countryside."

"Yes," Dexter said, drawing the word out as he considered Virginia's proposal. "But there are sentries as well," he added. "And barricades." There was no way to seal Philadelphia up completely, but Howe had at least ordered that the major routes in and out of the city be manned with checkpoints. The British army was in hostile country, and it would not do to allow civilians of uncertain loyalty to come and go as they pleased.

Of course there are sentries, Virginia thought. *That's why you're here. That, and to provide the horse.* She smiled at Dexter. "I should think a captain of the 17th Regiment of Foot, and a veteran of the fighting at Brandywine, goes wherever he wishes."

"Ha!" Dexter laughed, a genuine laugh. "Hardly! But yes, getting past a sentry post should be within my authority. We can certainly find out, in any event."

With that, he turned his horse north again and continued up chestnut, having apparently, in that moment, decided to give in to Virginia's request. The barricades come into view a few blocks later, two crude log and earth walls five feet high flanking the road, a dozen red-coats gathered in haphazard order around each.

A bored sergeant, twice Dexter's age, approached as they rode up. He asked their business in a voice that suggested he did not actually care, and when Dexter said, "Just exercising the horses, sergeant," he waved them through.

"Very good, sir," the sergeant said. "Just mind you don't go too far afield. Bloody rebels are everywhere. You can't tell them from decent folk, save that there ain't hardly any decent folk around."

"Thank you, sergeant, I'll bear that in mind," Dexter said as he led Virginia through the barricades and out beyond the edge of the city.

Virginia reached under Jack's bottom and shifted the boy a bit, settling him in a more comfortable position. She could hardly believe that he had not woken up and started in crying for the breast, but she guessed the gentle rocking of the horse's walk had lulled him to sleep.

We'll see how long that bloody lasts... she thought.

They continued walking their mounts north as the road turned from city street to wide country lane, one of the chief approaches to Philadelphia. Brick buildings yielded to farm houses scattered around brown, open fields with stands of timber here and there.

Very well, Virginia thought, *let's see how this plays out*. She adjusted Jack in her sling and turned to Dexter who was riding at her side. "Shall we give the creatures a chance to show what they're made of?" she asked with a grin that was for the most part genuine.

"What are you thinking?" Dexter asked but before he had quite finished speaking, Virginia slapped the chestnut on the rump with her cane and dug her heels into its flanks. The horse bolted ahead, an explosive move, but Virginia was ready for it and she rose slightly and bent her knees and took the motion in her legs.

She held the reins in her right hand and wrapped her left arm around Jack, supporting him and easing him from the worst of the jolting. She leaned forward as the tears streamed down her cheeks with the cold air rushing over her eyes. She could feel the first hints of burn in her muscles, muscles that had once been well used to this sort of thing, but which had grown weak from disuse.

Behind her she heard Dexter shout in surprise, and a moment later heard the sound of the bay's hooves on the frozen dirt of the road as the captain charged after her. She leaned further forward and urged her mount on. She did not think the chestnut could outrun the bay, nor did she mean to try, but she did intend to keep the race going for as long as she could.

Virginia could see the muscles in the horse's neck and shoulder flexing under the animal's brown coat as the road underneath them flew past. The mare ran with a beautiful, coordinated gait, pounding along, the fields flying past on either hand. Virginia smiled. She felt more alive than she had in a long, long time.

From the corner of her eye, she caught a glimpse of Dexter's bay behind her and to her right. She turned her head just a bit. He was half a length back but she could tell he was overtaking her. She urged the chestnut on. Over the sound of the hooves on the road and the wind whistling past her ears and her own increasingly labored breathing, she thought she heard Dexter calling to her, but she was not certain, and she did not care.

They reached the crest of a small rise and raced down the other side. Virginia could see Dexter coming more and more into view, until a moment later he was all but alongside her. She swiveled a bit and smiled at him, but he was not smiling back.

"Virginia!" he shouted. "Pray, let us stop a moment!" Virginia hesitated, wondering how much longer she could keep this up, what would happen, what Dexter might do, if she did not. He could probably reach over and take the reins from her, make her stop, and she did not want that.

She eased off a bit and let the chestnut slow its pace from a gallop to a trot and finally down to a walk, and Dexter, beside her, did the same. At last, Virginia reined to a stop, gasping for breath and smiling, genuinely smiling, all other considerations lost in the pleasure of the reckless ride. In his sling, Jack stirred a bit and Virginia bounced him with her left arm and said "Shhhh...shhhh..." between breathes.

"Virginia..." Dexter said. He was breathing hard as well, though not so hard as she was. Virginia could hear the admonishment in his tone, the scolding to come, as if she was an errant child.

"Wasn't that grand, Richard!" she said before he could go on. "Oh, what a fine horse! It's been far too long since I've just…galloped!"

"Grand?" Dexter said. "I'm not certain about grand. Reckless, perhaps. And we're getting damned far from the city, you know. You heard what the sergeant said."

Virginia turned her horse so she could look back over the way they had come, and she was surprised to see how much distance they had covered in that short burst of a gallop. *Bloody horses are faster than I'd imagined*, she thought.

"Oh, bugger the sergeant," she said with a wicked smile. "You redcoats see rebels behind every rock and tree. There's naught to be concerned about here." She could feel her breath returning to normal, the weariness in her legs easing a bit.

"Perhaps so," Dexter said, and Virginia could tell he had been caught a bit off guard by her words. "Still, it's best if we don't get too far afield. Best if we…"

"Am I too fast for you, Captain?" Virginia asked, turning her horse back in the direction of the open country. "Are you worried I shall outride you?"

"No, of course not," Dexter protested. "It's simply that…"

Before he could finish the sentence, Virginia whacked the chestnut on the rump with her cane once again and kicked its flanks. She felt the horse bolt forward as she half stood in the stirrups and took the jolting gallop in her legs.

"Damnit!" she heard Dexter shout from behind her but she was already flying down the road once again, relishing the feel and the sound and the smell of the horse under her, the dried grass and scrubby bush whipping past on either hand, the tears streaming down her cheeks.

She felt Jack shifting in the sling and she knew she did not have long before he would be howling to have his belly filled. She felt the burn in her leg muscles and knew she could not keep this pace up for very much longer.

Damn me for a weakling… she thought as she felt her breathing come harder with each furlough she and the chestnut covered. She could hear the hoofbeats behind her once again, Dexter having spurred his mount to come after her. She was smiling already at the thrill of the gallop, and she smiled more broadly still to think of how angry the Captain must be.

They raced on, over the wide, well-worn road, with farmhouses scattered around in the distance, trails of smoke rising up from their chimneys, past fields where cows looked on with their desultory expressions as they pounded past.

"Virginia...damn it..." she heard Dexter calling from behind her. He sounded out of breath, and she wondered if she would in fact outride him, leave him in the storm of dirt clots the chestnut was throwing up. It was tempting, just on principle, but it was not what she had planned.

Another hundred yards and she could see Dexter drawing up behind her. She could feel her legs burning and she was gasping for breath, and she knew that was as far as she was going to get. Once again she eased off and let the horse settle down into a trot and then a walk, and then with a tug of the reins, she brought her to a stop.

The bay came stepping up beside her, Dexter's face nearly as red as his regimental coat. He, too, was gasping for breath, and for a moment they both sat in silence, facing one another and sucking in air.

"Very well," Dexter said, as soon as he was able to speak. "This is quite far enough. I'll take your reins if I can't trust you to follow me back to the city." He was very angry, she could see, and doing his best to keep the anger in check.

"Actually, I don't think I will return to Philadelphia," Virginia said once she, too, had breath enough to speak.

"No?" Dexter said, amusement mixed with the irritation now. "And where do you think you'll go?"

"Whitemarsh."

It took Dexter a moment to work through the implications of that name. "Whitemarsh? Washington's camp?"

"Just so," Virginia said.

Dexter smiled. "Oh, indeed? That's rich! And how do you propose to get there?"

"On this horse. With you showing me the way."

Dexter's smile turned into a chuckle. "Well," he said, "If you wish to go to Whitemarsh, I certainly shan't stop you. But I won't show you the way. And you certainly will not go on that horse."

Virginia's hand was already resting on the butt of the pistol hidden in the pocket of her cloak. It was one of a brace of pistols her father had had made for her a few years earlier, lovely guns, well-crafted and fitted to her hands. Her biggest worry now was that in drawing the weapon she would get the hammer caught in the folds the cloak and thus ruin the dramatic impact of pulling it out, but happily, it came free unencumbered.

"I think you're wrong on all accounts, sir," Virginia said. She thumbed the hammer back to the firing position and leveled the gun at Captain Dexter.

Once again Dexter laughed, which Virginia found irritating in the extreme. She was not so foolish as to think he would shake in fear at the sight of the gun, but she had hoped for at least a hint of trepidation or uncertainty.

"Oh, please, Virginia!" he said, still smiling. "You are most certainly not going to shoot me!"

"Wrong again, Captain," Virginia said. "I most certainly am." And with that, she squeezed the trigger.

CHAPTER NINETEEN

Great Egg Harbor looked just as Angus McGinty remembered it. Just as miserable and bleak and unwelcoming as he remembered. He was not pleased to see it again.

It had been a long sail north, with baffling and contrary winds, and sometimes no wind at all. Once, they had spotted a half dozen sails on the horizon and altered course to the east, standing out to sea to avoid what in all probability was a powerful British squadron. One of the ships from that small, unidentified fleet had broken off and come sniffing after them, but after a tense twelve hours, it gave up the chase and returned to the rest, leaving *Oliver Cromwell*, *Sparrowhawk*, and *Hopefleet* unmolested but many miles off course.

In the end, what should have been a two- or three-day passage consumed a tedious thirteen days, almost two weeks of some of the most unpleasant time McGinty had ever endured. Captain Timothy Parker of *Oliver Cromwell*, the dog, seemed not to trust him, despite the utter sincerity with which he presented himself. Because of this mistrust, Parker did not allow McGinty to return to *Sparrowhawk* but rather insisted that he sail as a "guest" aboard the *Cromwell*.

To that end, the boatswain and the carpenter were turned out of the tiny cabin they shared and McGinty moved in, earning McGinty the warrant officers' blatant enmity. Worse, he was made to share the space with Captain James Finch, late of the ordnance brig *Hopefleet*, of all people. It was an awkward living arrangement, to say the least.

The two men dined in the gunroom with the other officers. McGinty sensed that it might have been a lively and convivial place were it not for the presence of the brooding Captain Finch, an Englishman among Yankees, a prisoner of war, and one who would remain a prisoner of war, regardless of how things played out between Parker and Biddlecomb. It was the fact he was clearly aware. Worse, perhaps, McGinty had seen among the papers that Finch was a major shareholder in the ship and cargo. For Finch, the loss of *Hopefleet* likely meant a huge financial loss for him as well.

Captain Finch did not hide his feelings. His sullen anger, which manifested both in dark silences and furious outbursts, was like a wet blanket over any pleasant times the gunroom might have enjoyed. Angus McGinty had dreaded the thought of reaching Great Egg Harbor, back when they had first set out for the coast of New Jersey. After two days of James Finch and the tedium of uncooperative winds, he was desperate to reach the place.

But now they were there, and the original dread was back.

"That's the *Falmouth*, I take it, Sergeant?" Captain Parker asked. He had stopped addressing McGinty as "captain" once he learned of the official rank he had held in the Third Company, Fifth Pennsylvania Regiment. It was clear enough to McGinty that Parker wanted desperately to claim *Hopefleet* as his own prize; anything he could do to minimize McGinty's legitimacy would help.

"Aye, that's her," McGinty said. Parker had at least done McGinty and Finch the courtesy of allowing them on the quarterdeck, and McGinty was there now, watching the landfall he had been anticipating with such mixed feelings for the past few weeks. Finch was there as well, but standing by himself, all the way aft in what had become his accustomed spot.

It was an hour past sunrise as they stood into the harbor with just enough wind to give them steerageway. The sky was grey, the water was grey, the shoreline was brown and grey. *Falmouth* lay tied to the wharf, just as McGinty had last seen her, with only her foremast and foreyard in place.

You ain't got too bloody much accomplished, did you Captain Biddlecomb? he thought. But much as he enjoyed seeing Biddlecomb's failure, he had to admit it was hardly Biddlecomb's fault. Thirty men on the crew and stuck in some backwater without the least facilities or materials, there was not much that anyone can do.

And remember now, Angus, old Captain Biddlecomb is your famous friend, McGinty reminded himself. *We're good partners, him and me.* At least that was what he had told Parker, and he hoped Biddlecomb would play along. McGinty's life might quite literally depend upon it.

With Lt. Little calling commands from the break of the quarterdeck, *Oliver Cromwell* rounded up into the wind until her topsails went aback and the best bower was let go in three fathoms of water. Astern of her, *Hopefleet* and *Sparrowhawk* followed suit.

Those ships were more ably handled now than they had been when McGinty commanded them. Parker had mixed up the crews, sending a number of his officers and men aboard the other ships, and placing some of the able-bodied English sailors from *Hopefleet* aboard *Sparrowhawk* and some aboard *Cromwell*.

Most of the lubbers of the Fifth Pennsylvania Regiment were shifted to *Oliver Cromwell*, where they were put to the simple tasks of hauling on lines when needed, or scrubbing decks or chipping rust off cannonballs. As a result, all three ships were decently manned, but none with enough hands who might wish to escape from Captain Parker's grasp that they could successfully retake their ship.

Lieutenant Little barked out an order and McGinty's men, standing in the waist and foredeck, ropes in hand, hauled away, and overhead the limp square sails were drawn up to their respective yards. Another order and those of the crew who were actual sailors raced aloft to stow the upper sails while McGinty's men made their slow, plodding, grudging way up and out onto the lower yards to stow those sails.

McGinty stared across the water at *Falmouth* and wondered what Biddlecomb would do. *He'll make Parker come to him,* he decided. Parker already had the upper hand—a functional man-of-war and two prizes— and Biddlecomb would not want to give him any more advantage by coming out to call. He would make Parker call on him.

"On deck!" the look-out called from the mainmast head. "Boat's putting out!"

Or maybe not, McGinty mused. He was surprised, but he was willing to admit, at least to himself, that he could be wrong.

"Would this be your Captain Biddlecomb?" Parker asked, handing his telescope to McGinty. His voice was calm, but there was something in it that McGinty could not miss, a slight catch, a slight hesitation. Like McGinty, Parker had been anticipating this interview for two weeks now. Like McGinty, he had quite a bit riding on it. Not his life, perhaps, but still quite a bit.

McGinty extended the tube and raised it to his eye and twisted it into focus. He would have expected *Falmouth*'s boat to be tied alongside the frigate, but it had not been, it had come from the wharf beyond. It was clearly a fishing boat of some sort, not a man-of-war's boat, but that was hardly surprising. The only boat Biddlecomb had possessed was the one aboard *Sparrowhawk* and McGinty had absconded with it.

As he recalled that fact, McGinty felt a twist in his stomach.

My dear friend Captain Biddlecomb…he has plenty of cause to want to see me hang, he thought. *But I'm sure he's over that by now, forgive and forget, and all that.*

McGinty, of course, was sure of no such thing, but he still hoped the riches to be found in *Hopefleet*'s hold would be enough to get Biddlecomb to play along. If Biddlecomb was smart enough and quick enough to assess the situation, which McGinty doubted.

McGinty held the boat in the lens. There were a half dozen men at the oars, *Falmouth*'s prime seamen, men who knew their business; the blades rose and fell in perfect syncopation and the boat surged ahead with each stroke. In the sternsheets, he could make out two figures. Each seemed to be wearing a cocked hat and heavy coat, as one might expect, but he could make out no more detail than that.

"I do believe it's Captain Biddlecomb, but I can't tell for certain, not from here," McGinty said. Parker made a grunting sound and said no more.

They watched for a few moments more as the boat pulled across the bleak, gray water for *Oliver Cromwell*'s starboard side, the side on which an officer would board. McGinty put the glass to his eye again and once again brought it into focus. The boat was close enough now that he could clearly see the men in the stern.

"Ah, yes, that's Captain Biddlecomb, to be certain!" he said. "You fight side by side as often as me and the captain have, well, you surely recognize your old shipmate when you see him!"

Parker grunted again and reached for the telescope and McGinty handed it to him without further comment.

"Lieutenant Little," Parker called to the first officer who stood at the break of the quarterdeck. "Do you have some sort of side party arranged?"

"Aye, captain, we'll show due honor," Little replied.

"Good," Parker said with a bit of a grudging tone, his high regard for the famed Isaac Biddlecomb having dimmed a bit, apparently. Part of it, McGinty guessed, was not knowing what to expect from this upcoming interview, and part was the prospect of losing the valuable prize. Both valuable prizes.

They watched the boat approach for another moment and then Parker made his way to the ladder and climbed down in the waist. Forward, *Cromwell*'s handful of marines came up from below, uniformly dressed in their dark coats and white crossbelts, muskets in their hands. They hustled over to the entry port where Lt. Little arranged them in two lines, as if the visiting officers were going to be made to run the gauntlet.

McGinty followed Parker down into the waist, wondering if the man would send him away, but Parker said nothing. Behind McGinty, Finch also made his way down. McGinty wished Parker would at least send the Englishman away, but still the captain said nothing.

The boat was fifty feet off the starboard side when McGinty took his place just behind Captain Parker. He could see Biddlecomb clearly now, and felt a bit of relief that it was indeed Biddlecomb, that he had not been mistaken. He recognized Midshipman Gerrish sitting beside Biddlecomb, his hand on the boat's tiller, and he recognized the men at the oars as well, most of whom he could name.

Two more pulls and the boat was lost from McGinty's sight. Lt. Little was standing by the entry port, watching it approach, and behind him the boatswain's mate stood ready with his call, the boatswain himself being off in command of *Sparrowhawk*.

"Attention!" Little called out and the marines snapped to attention in an admirable manner. They felt the boat bump alongside, and a moment later Biddlecomb's head and shoulders appeared at the level of the deck and the boatswain's mate set in with the high-pitched tweeting of his call. Then Biddlecomb stepped on deck and made his way between the lines of marines and the boatswain's call fell silent.

Captain Parker took a step forward. "Captain Isaac Biddlecomb, welcome aboard the Connecticut State Navy ship *Oliver Cromwell*. I am Captain Timothy Parker. I believe we met a few years past. In Newport, if I recall."

"Of course, captain, of course," Biddlecomb said with a bit of a smile, shaking Parker's proffered hand. "It's a pleasure to see you again, and congratulations on your command." If Biddlecomb genuinely remembered the man or was just faking it, McGinty could not tell. Biddlecomb's eyes flickered around the ship, settled on McGinty for a second, then moved on. His expression did not change at all.

Cool as a cucumber, that one, McGinty thought. He was impressed. But at the same time he could get no sense for what Biddlecomb was thinking, and he found it unnerving in the extreme.

Parker half turned and with a hand on Biddlecomb's shoulder led him back to where McGinty and Finch were standing.

"Captain Biddlecomb, I give you Sergeant Angus McGinty, of the Fifth Pennsylvania," Parker said, gesturing toward McGinty.

Ah, a test is it, you unsubtle dog, McGinty thought. Parker was trying to make the lie of McGinty's story even before McGinty could say a word. But to McGinty's surprise, and his relief, it was Biddlecomb who saved him.

"I know Sergeant McGinty of old, fear not," Biddlecomb said. "He had command of my sloop *Sparrowhawk*, and I'm pleased to see her come back, and none the worse for wear." His words conveyed nothing; not anger, nor delight, nor satisfaction at having McGinty again within his grasp. Nothing beyond the simple fact of his knowing the man and the ship.

"And this," Parker went on, turning to Finch, "is Captain James Finch, late of the brig *Hopefleet*, which is also at anchor astern of us."

Biddlecomb was about to speak when Finch took a step forward and cut him off. "Captain, or so you style yourself, I must protest this treatment, which is contrary to…"

He got no further. Parker held up his hand, and in a voice that did not allow for argument said, "Belay that, Captain Finch! All in good time. Captain Biddlecomb will have the truth of the matter."

"Aye, indeed," McGinty said. He nodded toward Biddlecomb. "It's my pleasure to return here with *Sparrowhawk*, Captain, and with a valuable prize to boot. Just we had planned, you recall, when last I…"

Parker's hand was up again and he cut McGinty off as well. "Yes, yes, there's much to untangle," he said. "Captain Biddlecomb, won't you join me in my cabin for some coffee, so that we might discuss all that has transpired here?"

"Yes, Captain, quite a bit to discuss," McGinty said, "I'm with child to tell you everything that's…"

Once again Parker's hand came up, a gesture that McGinty was starting to find truly annoying. "Captain Biddlecomb and I shall meet alone, I think, Sergeant," he said. "I'll send for you when we've come to some sort of understanding."

He turned his back on McGinty and put his hand on Biddlecomb's shoulder once more and gestured toward the door to the great cabin in the bulkhead under the quarterdeck. Biddlecomb made his way aft, with Parker right behind, leaving McGinty and Finch standing. McGinty could almost feel the rough cordage of the noose tightening around his neck.

Lieutenant Little dismissed the marines and the boatswain's mate. He leaned over the side and called down to the boat, "You boys can come aboard it you like! No need to sit in the boat." From below the gunnel, McGinty heard a chorus of voices call, "Thank you, sir!" and the rustle of men standing and the thump of shoes on the bottom of the boat.

Reckon I'll just go aft, McGinty thought as he turned quickly and headed for the quarterdeck ladder. He was certain that the men of *Falmouth* would recognize him on sight, but he was not so certain they would be happy to see him, or that they would treat him in any civilized way.

He made his way up the ladder and aft. He was tempted to stand by the scuttle over the great cabin and try to hear what was being said below, but he knew it would look too obvious, and he knew from experience that one could not hear anything from there in any event. Instead, he wandered over to the far side of the deck, where he was least likely to be seen from the waist, and leaned on the rail to wait.

Time…it's a damned odd thing, ain't it? he thought as he stared across the deck out toward *Falmouth* and the shore beyond. He glanced over at the half-hour glass. It had been turned just before Biddlecomb's boat had come along side, and six bells in the morning watch rung out. McGinty would have guessed it was ready to be turned again, but he could see less than half the sand had run out since then.

"Ah, damn my eyes!" he said softly. He had never been tried in a court of law. The few times he had been up for trial he managed to slip away before any proceedings began. But he had to imagine that this is what it felt like, at trial's end, waiting in some miserable cell for a jury of unfeeling strangers to determine your fate.

He looked around, wondering if there was some means of escaping this time, but there was none. He was on a ship. The only way off was in a boat or in the water, and neither option held much promise of success.

He stared out toward the shore. He thought about the hour glass. It had certainly run out by then, he was certain, and some poor midshipman would pay a price for letting that happen. He glanced over at it and saw that in fact there was still a quarter of the sand left to run.

"Ah, damn my eyes!" he said, a little louder that time and vowed he would not look at the glass again. He sighed and gazed aft at where *Sparrowhawk* and *Hopefleet* rode at their anchors.

"Sergeant McGinty?" The voice made McGinty jump, which only further irritated him. He turned. Lieutenant Little was standing at the top of the quarterdeck ladder. "This way, sergeant," he said.

McGinty pushed himself off the rail and ambled across the deck as if he had not a care in the world and followed Little down the ladder. Forward, the men from *Falmouth* were leaning on the rails and sitting on the hatches. McGinty glanced over at them, long enough to see the ugly looks they shot back at him, then turned and ducked under the quarterdeck and walked aft.

The marine sentry was at his station at the great cabin's bulkhead. He announced the men as the approached, and on Parker's order opened the door. Little went first and McGinty followed.

The great cabin was pleasantly warm, with the weak morning light coming in through the windows and a fire burning in a small iron woodstove. Parker sat behind his desk, papers spread out before him, a silver coffee pot and a cup set off to one side. He did not look particularly happy. Biddlecomb was seated across from him, a cup identical to Parker's in his hand. He did not look happy either, or angry, or amused. There was nothing on his face, no discernable expression, just a sort of pleasant blankness.

"Well, now, I trust you've worked this all out?" McGinty started in. He had intended to let one of the others fire the opening broadside, but he could not help himself.

"Worked it out, Sergeant?" Parker said, with something like a snort of disdain. "Well, I don't..."

"We've had an interesting talk, Mr. McGinty," Biddlecomb said. "You've been busy."

"Yes, well, to be sure," McGinty said, and thought, *what the devil did Parker tell him? What the bloody hell does Biddlecomb know, or think?*

"Busy he's been, captain," Parker said. "But as I mentioned earlier, at what I'm not quite sure."

"I understand you took a prize, sergeant," Biddlecomb continued, his eyes never leaving McGinty's. "Quite a valuable one, it seems."

McGinty looked at Biddlecomb, at his unreadable face. *Is the man fishing?* he wondered.

"Aye, that I did," McGinty agreed. "Loaded to the gunnels with military supplies. Cannon, powder, shot, muskets, everything dear *Falmouth* is crying out for. I'm sure the good captain told you that."

"Indeed," Biddlecomb said. "More or less."

"And I also said, as you will recall," Parker added, "that what Sergeant McGinty took don't matter so much as the manner in which he took it. Smacks of piracy, it seems to me. From what I've told you, I think you'd have to agree with me, Captain Biddlecomb."

"Piracy?" Biddlecomb said, sounding a bit shocked at the word. "I don't know about that." He turned back to McGinty. "Sergeant, I'd like to hear you tell it, pray. Your story. From when you first left us."

Damn my eyes, you're being damned coy, McGinty thought. Biddlecomb seemed like a man feeling his way in the dark. Why?

He's looking for a way to keep the bloody prize for himself, McGinty thought next.

And that was perfectly understandable, with avarice likely played just a small part in it. The brig, as McGinty had suggested, was loaded with exactly the matériel that Biddlecomb needed to outfit *Falmouth*. And *Falmouth*, McGinty knew, was the center of Biddlecomb's universe. He would be very eager indeed to keep hold of that particular cargo.

And McGinty was more than happy, delighted even, to help, because keeping *Hopefleet* meant excusing McGinty's behavior.

"I'd love to tell you the truth of the thing, Captain," McGinty started in. "It's what I've tried to do all along."

He turned to Parker. "Captain Parker, I've told you some of how Captain Biddlecomb here took *Falmouth* and *Sparrowhawk* right out from under John Bull's nose, and let me say, it was one of the boldest, and bravest acts I've every witness, and I've been around a bit, I can tell you. Your admiration for Captain Biddlecomb is well placed, sir, and I was damned proud to play my small part in that."

This next part was a gamble: McGinty didn't know what Biddlecomb had told Parker, or what game Biddlecomb wished to play: but McGinty was a gambling man at heart, and if ever there was a time to throw the dice, it was now.

"But as to what I've been about," McGinty continued, turning back to Biddlecomb, "after we arrived here in Egg Harbor and you took *Sparrowhawk* into the Continental service, as you recall, and you gave me the brevet promotion to captain of her, well, the boys and me we put to sea. Hunting prizes that would help with fitting out *Falmouth*, just as we'd planned, Captain. Not so easy, with the greenhorns I had onboard, but of course you needed the able-bodied seamen aboard *Falmouth*. So, we were on the hunt for a week or so when we run into the ordnance brig and took her with never a fight. And we were on our way back here when we run into dear Captain Parker and his fine ship."

"You were not on your way back here, Sergeant," Parker pointed out. "You were heading south."

McGinty gave a stifled sigh of exasperation. "We were sailing north until we saw you and took you for a British cruiser. Then we thought best to put about."

"We never saw you come about," Parker said, a note of frustration creeping in. "You want us to believe that you spotted *Oliver Cromwell*, put both your ships about, ships you could hardly sail, and were settled on a new course before we ever even noticed you? Is that what you're saying, Sergeant?"

McGinty shrugged. "I've no idea when you saw us, Captain Parker," he said. "But if you didn't see us until we had gone about, well, you had best have a word with the man who was on look-out."

"There's another matter that's of greater concern, Sergeant," Biddlecomb said. "Captain Parker says you had no papers when he took you. This is why he's come to the reasonable assumption that you're a pirate. What say you?"

McGinty looked at Biddlecomb. Parker must have asked him about the status of *Sparrowhawk*, about the legality of McGinty's taking vessels on the high seas. The entire question of who could claim *Hopefleet* as a prize rested on the answer. Could Biddlecomb have possibly deflected all of Parker's queries until he had a chance to hear McGinty's story? If so, that was some impressive verbal fencing indeed.

"I had no papers to show, that's no lie," McGinty said. "Sure Captain Parker explained to you that I threw them all overboard? The brevet commission you give me, the ship's commission, all the documents from the Marine Committee, the signal books, the written orders, all of it, I put 'em in a sack with a round shot and tossed it all over board."

"Why in the world did you do that?" Biddlecomb asked.

"We had no notion of what Captain Parker's ship was," McGinty explained. "Couldn't see his colors. We took him for British, as I said, and reckoned we were prisoners, for certain, what with him being so powerful and all. So, all the papers, over they go."

Biddlecomb shook his head in disbelief. He sighed and gave a bit of a smile. "Sergeant," he said, as if addressing a child who is more stupid than disobedient, "you don't throw everything overboard. The signal book, the written orders, certainly. Any official correspondence. But not the ship's commission. Certainly not your commission, or the logbooks or such as that. Dear God, man, Captain Parker would have been well in his rights to hang you from the yardarm, then and there. How could he think you were anything but a pirate? I hope you thanked the man for his forbearance."

McGinty turned to Parker. "I do indeed thank you, sir, for your wisdom in returning to this place, so that Captain Biddlecomb could put this all to rights."

"Humph," Parker said. "I'm not sure what exactly Captain Biddlecomb has put to rights." McGinty could hear the frustration in his voice, the sense that he was about to lose his valuable prize and he was not even sure how it had happened.

"I've kept my own council here, Captain Parker, I'll own that," Biddlecomb said. "I wanted to hear what Sergeant McGinty had to say, to reassure myself, at least, that there was nothing... untoward about this business."

"And?" Parker demanded.

"The sergeant has made some mistakes, to be sure, but I'll take responsibility for his actions."

"You'll...so you authorized this? What McGinty's done?"

"I take full responsibility, yes. Sergeant McGinty is under my authority. Isn't that right, sergeant?"

"Oh, yes, Captain, very much so," McGinty said.

"And now that you've returned, sergeant, and had some success, I reckon you'll be eager to get back to work with us here, help with fitting *Falmouth*, getting her to safety."

"Ay, captain, that I certainly am!" McGinty said with the enthusiasm of a man who could feel the noose being lifted from his neck. "It's what we were trying to do before, of course, before all this business began."

"Well, captain, there you have it," Biddlecomb said, turning to Parker. "I thank you for your assistance in escorting *Sparrowhawk* and her prize here. A damned valuable prize, I might add. Given the trouble you've gone to, I think it only fair that you should get Sergeant McGinty's share of the prize money, which will be substantial, I imagine."

"Oh...well..." Parker said and McGinty could see the man's demeanor changed for the better.

"Sergeant McGinty," Biddlecomb said, "that seems fair to you, isn't it?"

"Oh, fair indeed, Captain," McGinty said, his tone a decent facsimile of genuine agreement.

"Excellent," Biddlecomb said.

"Very well, then," Parker said next, "if that is all settled, then I guess we'll be underway as soon as the wind is fair."

"Ah, yes, as to that," Biddlecomb said. "Before you sail, I do have one request. It seems I have something of a tricky situation here, and I wonder if I might call on you and your fine ship and crew for some assistance."

CHAPTER TWENTY

It occurred to Virginia, as she pulled the trigger and felt the main spring trip the hammer, that the gun might not be as accurate as she had imagined, or her aim might not be as good.

*Too late...*was all she had time to think. And, in the end, she need not have worried.

The ball ripped through the sleeve of Dexter's upper right arm, and through the flesh and muscle beneath, as indicated by the spray of blood that followed in its wake. That was just where Virginia had intended to shoot him, and with only ten feet between them she was pretty much able to hit the mark. She could not tell whether she hit bone, but she guessed she would find out soon enough.

Several things happened at once in the instant after the discharge. Dexter shouted in pain and surprise and clapped a hand over the wound. Little Jack Biddlecomb shouted in anger and surprise and set it to wailing at an impressive volume. The horses shifted nervously, but, being army horses and trained to gunfire, they did no more than that.

Jack would not be put off much longer, but Virginia had other business first. She set the spent pistol down on the saddle, balanced between her legs, reached under her cloak and pulled out the second of the pair. She raised it and pointed it at Dexter's surprised, angry, pain-filled face.

"You bitch! You bloody shot me!" he shouted.

"I bloody told you I would," Virginia said. "Believe me when I tell you such things."

Dexter had dropped the reins of the bay, but now with his left hand, he reached for them where they hung.

"No, no," Virginia said. "Hands off the reins, and keep them up. The left hand, at least. And this time believe me when I tell you the next bullet goes through your heart."

It was getting harder to talk, or think, over Jack's insistent bawling. Caring for him would not be easy, but Virginia had played it out in her head many times, and had arranged her clothing to make it as simple as possible.

"Bind up your wound, best as you can," Virginia said. "I can't help you."

"Bind it? With what?"

Virginia glared at him for a moment as she considered this. For all her preparations, she was not ready to deal with bloody wounds because she had not really believed she would have to shoot the man. In truth, shooting him might not have been entirely necessary, had not her long-festering anger got the better of her.

She had no bandages, but she did have a knife, because she had been raised around sailors and sailors were never without their knives. She pulled it out her riding boot and handed it handle-first to Dexter.

"Cut some bandages from your cloak, just do your best," she said. He scowled at her and did not reply, but grudgingly took the knife from her hand, and with his one good arm and his one wounded, he began clumsily cutting strips of cloth from his cloak. Virginia undid the upper buttons of her jacket with her left hand, keeping the pistol more or less trained on Dexter with her right.

She adjusted her clothes and her semi-exposed breast and maneuvered Jack around. It was awkward at best, but Jack was well-used to nursing, no longer a newborn, but able to adjust himself. Soon the baby was feeding hungrily, his screaming replaced by a slurping sound, and Virginia felt the tension ease.

Dexter was just drawing the bandage tight around his arm when she looked up at him. "I hope I didn't break the bone," she said. "That wasn't my intention."

"I think not," Dexter said. "A flesh wound, it seems, but a damned good one." The shock of being shot had passed and Virginia could see the man's calm was returning. "Bleeding is an issue, of course. If you can't help me bind this wound, then I had best get back to the city where a surgeon can look at this."

"They have surgeons at Whitemarsh," Virginia assured him.

"You can't honestly expect me to ride to Whitemarsh," Dexter said, reaching for his reins once again. "I'll return to Philadelphia directly. I wish you joy of your stolen horse."

"Uh, uh," Virginia said, thumbing back the hammer, the click of the weapon being cocked making her point more effectively than any verbal warning. "I said don't touch the reins."

Dexter paused and looked Virginia in the eye, and to her relief, he slowly drew his hand back. Since first conceiving of this plan, she had feared that she would not be able to convince the captain of her sincerity, or her genuine willingness to kill him if need be. In truth, she was not convinced herself that she could do it. But Dexter's dismissive tone, his arrogant self-assurance, his apparent certainty that she would not be willing to pull the trigger, all on top of his betrayal, filled her with righteous fury. If ever she had felt able to put a pistol ball through a man's chest, it was then and there. And Dexter could hear it in her voice.

He sat straighter in the saddle, regarding her. He might consider her a genuine threat to his person, but he still did not seem terribly frightened or even concerned.

"I'll have my knife back, if you please," Virginia said.

"Of course," Dexter said, and using his left hand, he pulled the knife from his belt, where he had stuck it, and handed it back, handle first. Virginia took it and slipped it back into her boot.

"Do you know how far Whitemarsh is?" Dexter asked.

"I do," Virginia said. "A day's ride on a fast horse." She was fairly sure that was right—she had asked one of Mrs. Williams's servants about the distance—but she was not entirely certain. "Luckily we have fast horses."

Dexter glanced down at the bandage around his upper arm, which was already soaked through. The man was doing an admirable job of ignoring the pain, or at least appearing to. "I don't know if I have the blood in me for a day's ride," he said. "Even on a fast horse."

"Perhaps not," Virginia said. "But if I send you back to Philadelphia, then you'll send a patrol after me. I will most likely be caught, and when I am I will undoubtedly hang for shooting you."

Dexter was silent, his face expressionless, as he considered that. "And if I promise to see that no patrol comes for you?" he asked.

At that, Virginia actually smiled. "Oh, I am quite done believing anything you say, sir. But I think you know that. Which, I suppose, is you haven't even bothered to ask why I wish to go to Whitemarsh. Or why I shot you."

"Very well, I'll bite," Dexter said. "Why do you wish to go to Whitemarsh? Why did you shoot me?"

"In part because I despise redcoats of all stripes," Virginia said. "But mostly because you and Captain Cornwall contrived to read the letter from my husband so that you might send word to your uncle, Sir James Wallace, as to the whereabouts of him and his ship. Oh, and for plying me with drink so that you might ferret out that bit about David Weatherspoon." She could feel her face flush with anger and humiliation at the memory of that.

Dexter fell silent again, still looking her in the eye, and Virginia braced for the denials, the protests, the excuses.

"Cousin, actually," he said at last.

"What?"

"Sir James Wallace is my cousin, not my uncle."

"I see," Virginia said. The gun was growing heavy and she lowered it a bit, but the muzzle did not waver from Dexter's chest. It was Jack Biddlecomb, all twelve pounds of him, who was dictating their movements now, and the boy was clearly not done with his mid-morning meal.

"Stand bye," she added. "We'll cast off in a bit."

For some time, they sat there, silent, the only sounds the shuffling and snorting of the horses, the occasional call of a bird of the lowing of a cow, and the rhythmic sucking sound coming from Virginia's cloak.

"This is...a most odd situation," Dexter observed at last.

"It is that," Virginia said. "But while we wait on Master Jack, pray, tell me, sir, was Captain Cornwell's interest in Susan only about discovering the whereabouts of my husband, or was there more to it? In other words, are the two of you simply lying filth, or is there more to your miserable selves?"

Dexter did not reply at first, and Virginia guessed he was considering how to answer, how much to tell her. What truth he might feed her, and what lies.

"Captain Cornwall's interest in Miss Williams had nothing to do with me or your husband," he said at last. "I won't say his intentions were entirely honorable or driven by the noblest of motives, but they had nothing to do with anything beyond Miss Williams herself."

"I quite understand," Virginia said. "Miss Williams did not exactly cover herself with honor or noble intentions either."

"Just so," Dexter said. "In any event, Nicolas happened to mention that Susan had a house guest who was every bit as comely as she was. Married, and with a child, mind, but Nicholas never considered that sort of thing an obstacle."

"Charming," Virginia said. She could feel Little Jack starting to slow in his efforts. It would be time to get underway soon. "And you didn't consider my marital state much of an impediment either, I take it?"

Dexter raised an eyebrow. "More than an impediment," he said. "I should never consider seducing a married woman. Nicholas and I are brothers in arms, and I like the man, but we are quite different in that regard. When Nicholas told me your name, however..."

"Just my damned luck," Virginia said. "To encounter one of the few King's men in all of Philadelphia who knows who my husband is."

"You do your husband a disservice, Virginia," Dexter said. "He's quite well known among those of us in the military line. Sailing his ship right through the fleet as if it was a prize...that earned him quite a bit of respect. No one would say as much, mind you, but it's true. But I'm one of the few who understood that Sir James Wallace was the man most eager to find your husband, and most able to go after him. Being his cousin, and all. That was your bad luck."

Virginia nodded as she considered all of that. *Bad luck, indeed. So Dexter tells Cornwall and they look for a chance to find out where my husband could be found. They must have been astounded at how damned easy it was, in the end.*

"This is war, you understand," Dexter said next. "It's what we do. But please, believe me, Virginia, my respect for you...my feelings for you...that was genuine. A ruse at first, sure, but when I came to know you...our time together was a great joy to me. Truly."

Virginia raised the pistol and aimed it right at Dexter's heart and was rewarded with just the slightest flicker of concern on his face. "Turn your horse around and start riding, you miserable son of a bitch," she said.

Dexter nodded, winced as he shifted his right arm, then picked up his reins with his left. He flicked them across the horse's neck and tapped the animal's flanks with his heels. Horse and rider began to walk north, leaving Philadelphia in their wake, Virginia following behind.

For a mile or so, they continued at that pace, as Virginia tucked Jack away in his sling and adjusted her clothing, awkwardly, with her left hand as she maintained her aim at Dexter's back with her right. Once Dexter tried to swivel around in his saddle but Virginia told him in no uncertain terms to keep his eyes forward, and he obeyed. She did not want him to witness her various fumblings and uncertainty. It might give him unwelcome ideas.

Once Jack was tucked away and asleep once again and Virginia had the use of both hands, she carefully eased the hammer of her pistol to the half-cock position and secured the gun in the pocket of her cloak, arranging it for quick retrieval. She found the first pistol, the one with which she had wounded Dexter, and her small containers of shot and powder, and reloaded the weapon as quickly and silently as she was able.

"Captain Dexter," she called, once that business was done. "Pray, let us pick up the pace a bit." Once again he began to turn in the saddle, and once again Virginia corrected him. "Eyes forward, I did not say to turn around," she called, with enough menace to convince him she meant it.

"You seem fond of galloping today," Dexter called over his shoulder. "Shall we gallop, then?"

"A nice trot should suffice," Virginia called back. Dexter did not respond at first, and he did not increase his pace, and Virginia was about to speak up again when the captain gave his reins a flick and started building speed.

Arrogant bastard... Virginia thought as she, too, increased her horse's pace. She had her eyes set on Dexter's back, waiting for him to try something clever: race off across the fields, turn on her, rein up short in hopes that she might slam into him and drop her gun: but he did none of those things, just rode on at a steady trot.

Good, good... Virginia thought. She wanted to put as much distance as she could between them and Philadelphia, but not at the price of exhausting the horses. She needed the mounts sound enough to carry the three of them all the way to Whitemarsh.

They rode on like that for half an hour or so and then Virginia called for them to walk once more, and this time Dexter did not hesitate to obey. He reined his horse back and seemed to slump down in the saddle as he did, his whole frame bouncing with the horse's steps as if he did not have the strength to hold himself erect.

He's losing blood, Virginia thought. *Getting weak.* The bandage he had wrapped around his arm was dark brown, soaked through with blood that was starting to dry, and there was blood on his cloak and even on his right hand where it had run down his sleeve.

If he collapses and can't ride, what will I do? she thought next.

She considered the various options, and decided in the end that she would leave him on the road, ride ahead and look for help. Send someone back for him as she continued on. She would hope that he survived, but if he did not, it wouldn't break her heart.

God, I'm a cold one, she thought, but then she recalled how charming Dexter had been, how thoughtful and courteous, while his friend Cornwall rummaged through her things. She thought of their plying her with drink before Dexter had oh-so-subtly inquired after the whereabouts of David Weatherspoon, and she did not feel so cold or callous anymore.

They rode on that way for some time—an hour, two hours, Virginia really had no sense. The sun was lost behind a thick blanket of cloud and gave no hint as to how much time had passed. Ahead, Dexter kept his saddle though his body swayed more and more with each step and his head lolled as he rode.

He'll pass out soon, Virginia thought. *He'll fall right out of the saddle.* She had thought through this possibility, decided what she would do, but now, with the chance of Dexter's fainting seeming more likely than it had, she was not so certain. Could she just leave him where he fell and hope for the best?

What would Isaac do? she wondered. *What would he think of me if I did just leave him, if I couldn't find help and he died on the road?*

And then another thought came to her. *What if he's play-acting? What if this is a ruse? Fall off the horse and when I dismount to check on him, snatch my gun?*

And if he got her gun, what then? What if he managed to get her back to Philadelphia? With the crimes she had committed—horse theft, kidnapping, shooting an officer, spying—she would hang for certain, and they would likely capture Isaac as well. That thought made her angry, and erased her earlier worries.

But then she recalled that Dexter's condition might well be genuine. She had, after all, put a pistol ball through a good bit of his flesh. He had clearly lost a lot of blood.

"Oh, what the hell am I to do?" she said out loud, speaking in a whisper so Dexter would not hear.

It was Jack who decided what they would do next, Jack who had been sleeping and waking and sleeping since just after Virginia had shot Captain Dexter. His occasional quiet cooing and giggling had begun to escalate into yelps of irritation, which likely meant a soiled diaper and certainly meant an empty belly. The diaper would have to wait, but Virginia knew that the little one's hunger would not be put off.

"Hold up there, Captain," Virginia called and she and Dexter reined their horses to a stop.

"Might I turn around?" Dexter called over his shoulder. "Or are you still not to be looked upon?" His voice sounded smaller and weaker.

"One moment," Virginia said. She wanted to get a look at him, to see if he appeared to be in as bad shape as he sounded, but she did not want him to watch her fumbling with getting Jack on the breast. She tucked her pistol into a pocket and loosened off her jacket as Jack's fussing continued to escalate, rising quickly from a whimper to a full-throated cry. Finally, she maneuvered the baby around until he was able to latch on and his cries were replaced with his eager gulping.

Virginia covered up as best she could, pulled the pistol free and aimed it at Dexter. "Very well, you may turn around," she said. With a flick of the reins, Dexter turned his horse until he was facing her, ten feet away.

"How do you fare, sir?" she asked, with little sympathy, or any other emotion, in her voice.

"Well enough, thank you," he said, but she could see right off that that was not true. He was very pale and his eyes seemed to lack focus. The bandage and the fabric of the sleeve around it was soaked with blood, and there was blood on his right hand and on the horse and saddle where it had dripped off his fingers.

"We'll be in Whitemarsh directly," Virginia said. Dexter gave a weak smile and looked side to side.

"You know that for a fact?" he asked. "Do you know where we are?"

"You had best hope I do," Virginia snapped. "It's not me who'll bleed to death on the road if I don't."

Dexter nodded by way of answer. He did not seem to have the strength for more.

For some time, they sat their horses in silence, and Jack's efforts at nursing were the only sound they could hear in the frozen countryside on that winter afternoon. Virginia looked up at the sky, hoping for some sense of the sun's position, how much daylight they had left. If they could not reach Whitemarsh by nightfall, she did not know what she would do, and she added that thought to her long list of worries.

As Jack nursed, she kept the pistol pointed vaguely at Dexter and stared off in the distance, her mind racing. Then, slowly, she became aware of a new sound, a familiar sound, soft under the gulping from Jack's throat. She looked up, looked side to side.

*Horses...*she thought. There was no mistaking it: a dozen horses at least, coming over the ground at a trot. She looked at Dexter. His eyes were closed and he seemed not to have heard, but if he was just pretending she could not tell. She turned farther side to side, looking out over the open ground, but she still could see nothing.

Who the hell could this be? she wondered. Soldiers, certainly. A dozen riders, moving fast over countryside that separated Washington's army from Howes', they could only be soldiers. But whose? The answer to that would mean, for her, the difference between salvation and a noose.

She saw them at last, off to her right and about half a mile away. They came up over a small hill riding in a tight formation heading vaguely north.

"Now, who is this?" Dexter asked. Virginia looked over at him, surprised by his voice. His eyes were open and he seemed to be sitting a little straighter in the saddle, looking in the same direction that Virginia was looking.

"I don't know," Virginia said. "But we'll find out directly, I suspect." The horsemen would have to be very poor scouts indeed to not notice and investigate the two riders standing motionless on the road.

Dexter did not reply, but Virginia had no doubt his thoughts were moving along the same course as hers: the identity of these unknown riders would have an outsized impact on both of their immediate futures, and quite possibly beyond. With both armies sending mounted troops out to keep an eye on the other, there was no way to know who the riders were until they were on top of them.

The horsemen spotted her and Dexter a moment later, the rider at the head of the column turning to his left, the rest falling in behind like a flock of geese. A quarter mile away Virginia could make out the white plumes on the riders' leather helmets, the short jackets that looked black in the dull light but which she suspected were dark green or blue, the light-colored breeches showing about the top of black boots.

Dragoons, Virginia thought, but there was still no way to tell whose dragoons they were. She eased the hammer of her pistol to half-cock and tucked the weapon into a pocket. The gun would be unnecessary if they were American, of no use if they were British, and likely to get her shot either way. She looked over at Dexter. His face, as usual, showed little expression as he watched the riders approach.

He knows who they are, she thought. Dexter would certainly be more adept than her at recognizing troops in the field. And he did not look particularly happy or relieved.

Well, that's a hopeful sign.

And then the dragoons were on them, coming up over the last hill and down onto the road. A dozen, as Virginia had guessed, mounted on strong, fast horses. They spread out and formed a circle around her and Dexter. Their jackets were blue with white facings. Some wore leather helmets, some brass, but each had a blue cloth tied around it. A few of the men had long horse pistols in hand, a few had sabers.

While the others encircled them, their officer approached, a young man, early twenties, perhaps, a quizzical look on his face. He glanced at Dexter, looked him up and down, and then turned to Virginia.

"Ma'am," he said, nodding his greeting. "I'm Major Benjamin Tallmadge, 2nd Regiment Light Dragoons," he said. His accent was American, but that was no assurance of anything. There were plenty of Loyalist regiments formed in the United States.

"*Continental* Light Dragoons?" Virginia asked, and at that Tallmadge smiled.

"Yes, ma'am. Continental. I hope that's your preference."

"Very much so, Major, yes," Virginia said, and she could feel the relief wash over her, like slipping into a warm bath. "I'm Virginia Biddlecomb...Mrs. Isaac Biddlecomb, late of Philadelphia. This gentleman is Captain Richard Dexter of His Majesty's 17th Regiment of Foot."

At that, Tallmadge frowned. He turned his horse, took a few steps closer to Dexter and peered at his face while Dexter met his gaze.

"Dear Lord, so it is!" Tallmadge said, and he sounded delighted.

"You know the captain?" Virginia asked.

"We're acquainted," Tallmadge said. "We're in the same line of work, you might say." He turned back to Virginia, gesturing toward her and Dexter. "I suspect there's a fairly complex story behind all this."

"There is," Virginia said.

"Well, we must get to headquarters directly. The general will wish to hear all. And to speak with Captain Dexter, I should think."

"Very well," Virginia said. "But I can't tarry long. I'll need a fresh horse. And an escort."

"Escort? To where, Mrs. Biddlecomb?"

"Great Egg Harbor," Virginia said. "Do you know it?"

CHAPTER TWENTY-ONE

Things could change quickly, and often did. That was something Isaac Biddlecomb had learned after more than half a lifetime at sea. A dark squall could appear suddenly on the horizon. A granite ledge, unseen below the water, could tear out the bottom of a ship that a moment before had been sailing along untroubled. Rot, deep in the center of a spar, could send a seemingly sound rig tumbling down.

But sometimes things change for the better, he mused. *Not often, but sometimes.*

That thought came to him because he was experiencing such a rarified moment, standing at the head of the long wharf, reflecting on the nature of change, and watching *Oliver Cromwell* maneuver into position.

Ezra Rumstick, standing beside him, was apparently thinking along the same lines. "Well," he said, "this all's looking a damned sight more cheery than it was last night, wouldn't you say, Captain?"

"I should say so," Biddlecomb agreed.

Negotiations with Captain Timothy Parker of the Connecticut State Ship *Oliver Cromwell* had been pointed and brief. Once he had pulled Angus McGinty's sorry arse out of the fire, in part by offering to give Parker McGinty's share of the prize, Biddlecomb had gone on to explain his dilemma: Barnett and his Pine Robbers were hunkered down aboard *Falmouth* with no way for Biddlecomb and his men to dislodge them without considerable bloodshed. The men and guns of *Oliver Cromwell*, however, would easily change that balance of power.

Parker had been the very picture of sympathy, expressing particular sorrow that he and *Cromwell* could do nothing to help, as they had to get underway immediately. Biddlecomb had pointed out, politely, that the light breeze from the southeast would not allow them to sail anytime soon. Parker, equally polite, had then assured Biddlecomb that *Cromwell*'s company had far too much work to do in preparation for a favorable slant of wind to be of any assistance.

Oh, very well, you greedy son of a bitch, Biddlecomb thought, sitting across from Parker in the man's great cabin. He was disgusted, though he was not entirely certain he would not have done the same. He suspected that Parker, like himself, was a former merchant captain. Who else was there, after all, to command the men-of-war of the nascent United States? And as such, the man was used to wringing maximum benefit out of any negotiation.

"I know I'm asking quite a bit here, Captain," Biddlecomb said. "But here's how I reckon it. Sergeant McGinty has offered you his share of the prize money from *Hopefleet*, which is fair, but it's only an enlisted man's share, not a captain's. If you were you to help us with this... situation... however, I think we'd have to consider *Hopefleet* a prize of both our ships. You understand, divide the prize money between both our companies. In which case you get your proper captain's share. And given that we have damned few men aboard *Falmouth*, the money won't be spread too thin."

Biddlecomb glanced over at Lieutenant Little, who was listening quite closely now. This new offer might mean a greater share for Parker, certainly, but it would also mean prize money for Little and the rest of *Oliver Cromwell*'s men, whereas before they would get none. If Parker turned it down, the officers and men would hear about it and they would not be happy. And they could express that displeasure in a hundred subtle but effective ways.

"Yes, well, a generous offer," Parker began, and Biddlecomb wondered if Parker would try to bargain further, try to wheedle more out of the situation. It didn't matter. One look at the man's face, and at the face of Lieutenant Little, and Biddlecomb knew that the deal was done.

That had been just few hours earlier, and now Biddlecomb, standing, on the landward end of the wharf, could look beyond the mastless bulk of *Falmouth* and see *Oliver Cromwell*'s topsails come spilling off the yards as the men on deck sheeted them home. A moment later the yards began their climb up the topmast as the light breeze ruffled the sails. The wind was still foul for getting clear of Egg Harbor, but it would serve to bring *Cromwell* to a new anchorage, point-blank range from *Falmouth*'s side, and that was all they needed.

Biddlecomb pulled a telescope from his pocket, snapped it open, and held it up to his eye. He twisted the tube until *Falmouth* came into focus: her gun ports shut tight, the trail of smoke coming from the stovepipe over the galley, the foremast with its neat row of deadeyes and taut, black shrouds.

He ran the glass slowly along the edge of her bulwark. He could see a few heads above the rail, all turned toward *Oliver Cromwell*. He could see two on the quarterdeck and imagined that one was Barnett, though from that distance, and with the hats and coats the men wore against the cold, he could not tell.

"*Cromwell* has an audience, as you might imagine," Biddlecomb said.

"I would think so, sir," Gerrish said. The acting lieutenant was standing beside Rumstick, watching the activity. "They won't know what's acting, but they'll know it's not to their benefit."

"No it ain't," Rumstick spit. "As they'll find out."

Biddlecomb said nothing. He, more than any of them, would love to crush Barnett and the Pine Robbers like the vermin they were. But he still did not want to throw away the lives of any of his own men to see it happen.

For another ten minutes, they watched as *Oliver Cromwell*'s topsails filled and the ship drifted across the harbor. She was making for a spot a hundred yards or so from *Falmouth* side; too far for any of Barnett's muskets to be affective against her, but close enough for *Cromwell*'s twelve-pounder guns to do some very real damage. To maximize the threat, the guns were loaded and run out, or at least they were supposed to be. From where Biddlecomb stood, he could not see *Cromwell*'s hull, which was hidden behind *Falmouth*.

"She's there now, sir," Rumstick said. Biddlecomb saw the foretopsail yard come sliding down as the sail collapsed, and the main topsail come back as it was braced around to give the ship sternway. In the quiet of the day, he could hear *Cromwell*'s anchor splash down.

"Good." Biddlecomb turned and looked behind him. Faircloth's marines were standing in a neat file, muskets over their shoulders, as were McGinty's infantrymen, late of *Sparrowhawk*. The men of the *Falmouth* were gathered in a less-disciplined line, but they appeared formidable nonetheless, with cutlasses and muskets and boarding axes in belts. The cart stood ready, with a tired-looking horse standing in the traces and the barrels stacking on the bed.

"Mr. Gerrish," Biddlecomb said next. Gerrish held a long boat hook in hand with a white flag tied to the end. "Off we go, then."

Gerrish nodded and raised the boathook straight up so the makeshift flag flapped in the light breeze. With that, Biddlecomb set off down the dock, Gerrish at his side and the whole odd parade following behind. The clop of the horse's feet and the rumble of the wagon wheels on the boards of the wharf all but drowned out the sound of their footsteps as they advanced on *Falmouth*.

Barnett and the rest of the banditti had been distracted by *Oliver Cromwell*'s approach on *Falmouth*'s seaward side, but the sound of the marching men brought their attention back to the wharf. Biddlecomb saw a few heads peering over the rail at them, and then more and more heads appeared to join them. And soon after that, there were muskets as well, resting on the rail and aimed down the wharf at the advancing men.

Walls closing in, Biddlecomb thought. *That's how it must feel. Good, good.*

They were still a fifty yards away when Barnett's shout cut though the sound of the wagon's wheels. "That's close enough!" he called in his ugly, gravelly voice.

Close enough? Biddlecomb thought. *Are you nervous, you son of a bitch? You had best be.* But he just stopped where he was and held up his hand and heard the men and beast behind him stop as well.

"I've got a flag of truce, Barnett. Just came to talk." Biddlecomb had to shout to be heard over the distance between them.

"All right, then. Talk," Barnett shot back.

Biddlecomb half turned to the others. "Gerrish, with me," he said. "And bring the wagon up, too." The horse had been freed from the traces and now four men were standing ready to take up the effort.

He headed off down the wharf, Gerrish beside him, the wagon rattling along behind.

"I said talk, I didn't say come closer!" Barnett shouted, but Biddlecomb ignored him until he and Gerrish were forty feet from *Falmouth*'s side, close enough to be heard by all aboard, and then he stopped again. He could see Barnett on the quarterdeck, looking down on him, and thirty others at least lining the rail at various places.

Biddlecomb paused for a moment as he slowly took in the ship from stem to stern. When at last he spoke he addressed all of the banditti, and not just Barnett alone. "You might have noticed that ship off the starboard side," he called. "It's about a hundred yards away. Hard to miss."

"We seen it," Barnett shouted. "It don't change nothing."

"I'm not so sure about that," Biddlecomb called. "That's *Oliver Cromwell*. They have a lot of men, well-trained, well-armed. A lot more willing to fight than the Gloucester County Militia, I can tell you that. I got Rumstick's men back, and my men that were aboard the sloop. You're far outnumbered, you've got no escape by water, no escape by land. Seems to me a lot has changed."

"Well, you can feel free to take your *Oliver Cromwell* and all your armed men and shove them all up your arse, Biddlecomb, you son of a bitch," Barnett called back. "We still got men and we still got guns and we'll make a bloody hash of you if you try to take us, depend on it!"

"Oh, I do," Biddlecomb said. "If we try to take the ship, we'll lose a lot of men, I don't doubt it. But here's the thing. You'll be dead. The lot of you. No matter how many we lose, you'll all be dead."

"You think so, huh?" Barnett called back. "Well come and bloody try, you bastard!"

"No, I don't think so," Biddlecomb said. "I think it would be best if you were to give up. Leave the ship. We'll let you go back to whatever place you call home. Free passage."

"Ha! As if we'd trust you!"

"You might not, but the others…they can decide. You Pine Robbers, I know you like to make your own decisions. Like a town meeting. So I'll let you think on it. But just to show you I'm serious I brought you a peace offering." He turned and nodded to the men pulling the wagon. With a collective grunt, they moved forward, pulling the wagon the last dozen yard to the *Falmouth*'s side.

"Hold up!" Barnett shouted. "Hold up, or by God I'll shoot you down."

"That's good there," Biddlecomb called and the men left the wagon where it was and came trotting back.

"What in hell is this?" Barnett demanded.

"Peace offering, as I said," Biddlecomb called. "Four barrels of excellent Barbados rum. Just to show there's no hard feelings."

That was met with a pause, and then Barnett called back, "You haul that right back up that damned dock. We don't want nothing from you!" His words were insistent, but his tone sounded less certain.

"You gentlemen think on what I said," Biddlecomb replied. "Talk it over. I'll be back on the morrow to hear your answer." He turned and headed back up the dock, Gerrish and the others trailing behind.

"Son of a bitch, I said take that damned rum back with you!" Barnett shouted but Biddlecomb ignored him. He could feel himself bracing for a musket ball in the back, but he did not allow himself or the others to pick up their pace. He could still hear Barnett cursing, but he heard no more demands to remove the rum.

Enjoy, you damned bastard, Biddlecomb thought. *Drink it in good health.*

Chapter Twenty-Two

Colonel Shadrach Barnett stood with both hands on the *Falmouth*'s rail and stared at the barrels of rum resting in the back of the wagon. He stared with longing, and he stared with rage and uncertainty.

He and his men had searched the ship, from the bilges to the upper deck, the cabins and storerooms, the pantries, the great cabin, every inch they could access. They had found a bit of gold, which buoyed their spirits. They found muskets and powder and the personal effects of the men, mostly clothing but also some tobacco, which also cheered them. They found no rum whatsoever.

Barnett had been shocked and furious. It was his understanding that navy ships always carried a supply of rum. He had counted on it. But all they found onboard *Falmouth* was a few dozen bottles of wine, which had not gone very far when doled out among all the men, and now it was long gone.

Barnett needed drink the way he needed air, or near enough. It hurt to be without it, physically hurt. His hands shook and his head pounded and he would break out in a sweat regardless of how cold it was.

Nor was he the only one among them who needed hard liquor in that way. But they could not have it. Biddlecomb wanted them all to drink, and Barnett understood why, and he understood that they had to resist.

He looked forward and he could see the others staring at the barrels in the same way that he was, eager and desperate.

Ah, Biddlecomb, damn your eyes, you whore's son...

"It's a trick, you know!" Barnett shouted out so all the men could hear. "He's poisoned it, is what he's done."

"Tell you what, Barnett," one of the others called from the forecastle, "I'll go and have my fill from each of them barrels and I'll let you know is it poison!" That brought a laugh from the men, but not a laugh of pure mirth. There was an edge to it.

"Shut your mouth!" Barnett shouted back, but he knew this line of argument was pointless. The men would not believe that the rum was poisoned, any more than Barnett did. Biddlecomb did not need to poison the rum. The drink would do its work even without being tainted.

Barnett marched to the edge of the quarterdeck where he could look down at the men ostensibly under his command. "Come here, the lot of you, come over here, damn you all!" he shouted and slowly the company lifted their muskets off the rail and shuffled aft. He could see eyes glancing nervously over at Biddlecomb's retreating force and at the barrels in the cart, as if afraid Biddlecomb would return and take his offering back.

"See here," Barnett began, trying his best to sound reasonable, trying to appeal to the men rather than bully them, an approach he rarely if ever took.

"You know what that son of a whore Biddlecomb has in mind," he continued. "He reckons if he leaves us rum, well, we'll drink ourselves blind, and then he just walks aboard and cuts all our throats. Don't even have to fight us. He knows we'll bloody slaughter the lot of them if they come at us direct, so he thinks he can trick us. But he can't, I say. I say piss on his rum. Let's stave in them barrels and dump the lot of it on the ground. We won't fall for his tricks."

Even as he spoke, he could picture it all: the sledge hammer hitting the head of the barrel, the wood shattering under the blow, the dark rum gushing out onto the wooden planks of the wharf. The very thought of it gave him a jolt of panic.

He looked down at the men below him and saw little enthusiasm on their silent faces. A few glanced nervously over at the wagon.

"Come on, then!" shouted Wilcox who was standing at Barnett's side. "What say you? Let's bust them damned barrels open!"

Again there was silence. Then one of the Pine Robbers spoke up. "We ain't children, Barnett," he said. "We can have us a drink of rum, and it don't mean we're going to get insensible. Hell, get us fired up with some of that liquor and see if we don't fight like demons when Biddlecomb and that lot come for us!"

That was met with nodding heads and shouts of agreement. Barnett pressed his lips together. He could not muster the energy to make any further objections. He didn't want to make further objections. He wanted to dip a cup in one of those rum barrels and pour the contents down his throat. And though he would not even allow himself to think it, he knew he was relieved that the others had refused to follow his orders.

"Do what you will, and be damned with you!" Barnett shouted. "But if one of you sons of bitches gets insensible drunk, I'll cut his damned throat myself!"

He turned and walked aft, washing his hands of the business, confident that the men would get the rum aboard and the barrels open as soon as humanly possible. He stepped over to the starboard side of the quarterdeck and looked across the water at the ship Biddlecomb called *Oliver Cromwell*. She was not as big as *Falmouth* but she had cannons, not empty gun ports, and those cannons were jutting from her side and presumably loaded and ready to fire.

Biddlecomb…he ain't going to let them fire on his beloved ship.

But Barnett had always counted on the fact that he and his men could get in their boats and row to safety if things went against them, head up the sound or cross over to the barrier islands. And now they could not. *Cromwell*'s guns, loaded with grapeshot, would make short work of the frail, crowded things.

Nor were those cannons the only threat. *Cromwell*'s deck seemed crowded with men, more men, it seemed to Barnett, than a ship that size should need, and they would be trained and disciplined and well-armed. With them coming over the seaward side, and Biddlecomb's men attacking from the land, it would be damned hard to hold them at bay for very long.

Barnett spit into the water and turned and crossed the deck to the side facing the shore. He glanced forward as he did. His men had run the gangplank down to the wharf and were enthusiastically rolling the barrels aboard. He pulled his eyes away and looked inland toward the scattering of buildings and the brown, frozen landscape beyond.

Biddlecomb's men were nowhere to be seen. Once he had finished with his little show he had pulled them all back, out of sight. Barnett grunted. It was something that he would never say, and tried to not even think, but something he understood perfectly well: Biddlecomb's tactics had been damned effective. *Cromwell* coming along one side, guns run out, Biddlecomb's men under arms on the other...it had become very clear very quickly to Barnett and the others that they were trapped aboard *Falmouth*.

Maybe we should have given up... The thought came despite Barnett's best efforts to hold it at bay. But he could not give up. His men could not give up. What little pride they had left stopped them from doing that. Nor could they trust Biddlecomb's assurance that they would be free to go. All they could do was stay aboard the ship and wait for the inevitable. Which was another reason they were all so desperate to get their hands on the rum.

He could hear them now, his men, talking in loud voices, jovial voices, a marked change from a few moments before. He looked forward. One of the barrels had been set upright and the head stove in. Someone had brought up a sack-full of cups from down below and now the men were dipping rum and gulping it like water.

'*We ain't children*'...*my arse*, Barnett thought. Here was disaster, predictable and certain, unfolding before him, and there was nothing he could do but watch.

Well, I ain't a child...you won't see me getting insensible drunk, Barnett thought next. If he decided to have a cup of rum, he would have a cup of rum, but he would not become so incapacitated that he might be killed in his sleep.

He pushed himself off the rail and stomped forward, moving by instinct, not even thinking about what he was doing. He climbed down the short ladder to the gangway and walked over to where the rum barrel was set up, the men falling silent and parting in front of him as he moved. He snatched a cup out of a man's hand as he passed and dipped it into the dark liquid, waiting for someone to make some comment, some jest. He hoped they would. He hoped he might have an excuse to vent his rage, to give it free rein.

But no one said a word, as he knew they would not. He might have lost the debate over the rum barrels, and the others might be filling themselves with Dutch courage, but they still had a healthy and justified fear of him.

Barnett raised the cup to his lips and took a mouthful and swallowed it down. It was smoother and sweeter than the nasty kill-devil he was accustomed to drinking. He felt the liquid slide down his throat, felt it hit his stomach and spread its warmth like he was stepping up to a hearth. He felt his whole body settle, as if he'd been carrying a heavy load for hours and now he was setting it down.

He took another gulp, and around him, the various conversations started up again. He drained the cup and refilled it. His tolerance for drink was preternaturally high, but he could sense the rum starting to work on his head. He took another mouthful and felt his resolve to remain at least partially sober slipping away.

The afternoon wore on as the men emptied one barrel and with quite a bit of fumbling and cursing broke open another. Barnett was not the only one among them who could hold great quantities of drink, and so for hours beyond what most mortal men could endure the Pine Robbers swilled rum and ranted and shouted and fired muskets into the air and sang and laughed and wept.

At one point, they got the idea to fire small arms at *Oliver Cromwell*, and after a few clumsy attempts managed to load and discharge half a dozen muskets at the ship. But when *Cromwell* replied with a couple of swivel guns full of canister shot, they decided that shooting at the man-of-war was not as fun as they thought it might be.

The sun set and they kept on. The moon rose behind a blanket of cloud and the bacchanal continued, until slowly, one by one, the men staggered below or off to some corner of the deck, or just dropped where they stood, and let the rum wash away their waking thoughts.

Soon there were only a few clusters of men still on their feet, still valiantly pouring liquor down their throats, but Barnett did not join them. He leaned on the larboard rail and stared out toward the land and let disjointed thoughts of his life and death and Biddlecomb and all the injustices he had suffered tumble around in his head.

Bastards...bloody, bloody bastards... he thought, the words meant to encompass all of them, all who had wronged him, and their name was legion. But Biddlecomb, mostly.

Biddlecomb...bloody...coming for us...

The warning seemed to come from someplace deep inside, some part of his brain as yet untouched by the rum. He remembered. That was what this was all about, why Biddlecomb had left his "peace offering." They would be waiting for this moment, and then they would come.

He forced himself upright and staggered off across the deck. "Come along, you damned, drunk bastards!" he shouted. "They'll be coming, get up, get up!" He saw two men sprawled out in the scuppers and he stumbled over and kicked them, each in turn. "Get up, you damn rascals, get up!" But the men groaned and shifted a bit and did not move beyond that.

Barnett worked his way forward, kicking men as he came on them. He fell a few times but managed to struggle back to his feet. He shouted and cursed and got no response at all. Even the men who were still upright seemed not to hear him, or care.

*Whores' sons...*he thought. Here it was, playing out just as Biddlecomb had known it would. And now there was nothing left for Biddlecomb to do but stroll aboard and kill them all.

He felt the alarm in his head turn to a blinding rage. Damn the lot of them, he'd kill them as all, every damned one, his useless men, Biddlecomb's men. He did not care if he himself died. So be it. There were worse things. Far worse things than dying, if it meant taking Biddlecomb down with him.

And I'll take his damned ship, too... The frigate. It was what Biddlecomb wanted more than anything. What he, Barnett, had come to want more than anything. He had it now, but soon it would be taken away. That much was pretty clear, even through the thick fog of Barnett's mind.

No... It came to Barnett in a flash of inspiration. He could not let that happen. He could not let Biddlecomb take the ship back. He, Barnett, might not be able to keep it, but that did not mean Biddlecomb could have it.

With a renewed sense of purpose, he staggered off aft. He climbed carefully down the ladder to the waist and then made his way aft to the great cabin. He swung the door open and was pleased to see that the candle in the lantern hanging from the overhead was still burning. He stumbled across the deck and grabbed the edge of the table for support. His two pistols were still there, where he had left them, loaded and ready. He slid them into his belt and took the lantern and stepped back out into the waist.

He paused on the open deck and listened, but he could hear nothing alarming. No footsteps of men marching down the wharf, no splash of oars as men rowed over from *Cromwell* to swarm up the side. Only the bestial snoring of his dead-drunk banditti.

At the main hatch, he took care as he made his way down to the lower deck, holding the lantern with one hand and gripping the edge of the ladder with the other. He stumbled forward, looking for material with which to kindle a fire. He knew that a ship should have plenty onboard that would serve—tar and paint and barrels of gunpowder and old sails and oakum—but their earlier search had shown that *Falmouth* had precious little of any of that.

He held the lantern up as he moved slowly along the deck. There were heaps of clothes here and there where his men had rifled through the chests and seabags of the former crew. Barnett set the lantern down and collected up armfuls of clothing and piled it all around the base of the mainmast. He pulled an old sock from the pile and opened the lantern and lit the sock on fire, then tossed it on the heap. It sputtered and smoldered and Barnett feared it would go out, but then it flared and the flame spread to the cloth around it.

There, you bloody bastard...here's for your damned precious ship, Barnett thought, as he watched the flame spread, the cloth catching and flaring, the fire climbing up the pile of old clothes and wrapping around the mainmast. The lower deck, which had been cave-like in the darkness, was brilliantly lit now, and Barnett could see nearly all the way to the bow. He smiled with satisfaction as the fire grew brighter still.

The mast had been coated with some sort of oil, apparently, and it caught fire the moment the flames touched it and seemed to burn over its entire surface. Bits of flaming cloth drifted up and floated along the length of deck. It was beautiful to behold, and Barnett smiled. Then, suddenly, he felt as if his legs would not support him a moment more. It was time to just sit and watch the flames consume Biddlecomb's beloved frigate.

He set the lantern on the deck and started to ease himself down, but halfway to sitting his legs collapsed and he fell with a grunt. The flames were hot on his face but he did not have the energy to shuffle back away from them, so he stayed where he was and stared with blurred vision at what he had wrought. Soon after, and despite the brilliant light, the darkness washed over him and he slept.

Barnett woke sometime later, with no idea where he was. His eyes opened suddenly, and he could see a stretch of wooden deck visible in the weak light. He pushed himself up half-way and looked around. The lantern he had brought with him was sputtering its last bit of light, enough that he could see the ashes and charred cloth around the mainmast, the blackened wood, the few bits of glowing embers.

It started coming back to him. The fire, the resolution to burn the ship to the waterline. He must have passed out after setting the thing ablaze, but the fire did not take. It burned through the cloth and burned the oil off the mast, but it would not spread to the heavy timbers of the ship.

*Ah, damn it all...*he thought. He was less drunk than he had been, but he was far from sober, and his mind was not working as well as it might. He looked around in the gloom of the 'tween decks, wondering what he should do now. And then he heard the thump on the side of the hull.

It was not loud, or particularly unusual, just a soft thump against the fabric of the ship, as if someone had bounced their fist off of it, but it set an alarm bell ringing in Barnett's head. It was what he had expected. It was why he had lit the fire. They were coming.

He pushed himself to his feet, taking care not to make any noise as he strained to listen. There was nothing else, no other sound. The short waves on the harbor had been pushing the ship back and forth against the wharf all night, and Barnett thought maybe that had been the source of the noise, but he was not sure. He straightened and rested a palm on the butt of his pistol and then he heard something else, a soft creak from someplace outside and a bit forward of where he stood. His men had run the gangplank in, once they had rolled the rum barrels aboard, so that was not it.

Boarding steps... Barnett thought. It was the creak of the boarding steps as men came up the side, as quietly as they could.

And then there was another sound, another thump on the other side of the ship, lower down, not on the wharf side but on the harbor side. Barnett had no doubt as to what that was—a boat touching near the waterline. A boat from *Cromwell* filled with armed men ready to swarm aboard.

And that was it. Barnett knew it. His chance to burn the ship, to take it and his men and Biddlecomb all to hell was gone, lost. Now it would just be him, bound off to eternal damnation.

*No, no, no...*he thought. Oh, certainly, he would not avoid that destiny himself. He was resigned to that truth. But it was still possible that he could take someone with him on the voyage below, and he knew just the company he wished to keep. He turned around and stumbled aft once again.

Chapter Twenty-Three

Isaac Biddlecomb spent a good part of the day in the small church near the head of the wharf, which he had commandeered as temporary headquarters. His men were crowded in there as well, which at least helped to warm the place a bit. And it was not just his men, but McGinty's and most of the Gloucester County Militia, whom he had to browbeat into joining the coming fight.

Not that he expected much of a fight. That was what the rum was for. He had taken care to make sure there was more than enough loaded onto the wagon. The worst possible thing he could do would be to give the Pine Robbers just enough to get them fighting drunk. He needed them paralytic drunk, and he made sure that his peace offering was sufficient for that purpose.

Rumstick sent four-man squads out in rotation to keep watch. They positioned themselves near the end of the wharf, hidden from view of *Falmouth*, three men with muskets, one with a telescope. Per Biddlecomb's orders, the reports came in every half-hour unless something of note happened.

The first report came just as the men were settling themselves in the church and it was pretty much what Biddlecomb had expected. There had been some discussion among the banditti, or so it appeared, the men gathering in the waist, someone, Barnett, most likely, addressing them from the quarterdeck. Then the gangplank had been run out to the wharf, the barrels rolled aboard, and the gangplank brought back in.

Biddlecomb smiled as he listened. *No luck, talking them out of the rum, eh, Barnett?* he thought. He recalled Barnett's demand that they take the rum back, and he savored the memory. He wondered how vociferously the man had argued against bringing the rum aboard. Barnett might understand what a threat the rum was, but at the same time, he would be as desperate as any of them for his fill of drink

After that, word came only at regular half-hour intervals because there was nothing much more to report: the Pine Robbers were gathered around the rum barrels on deck and were not doing much of anything but drinking. The look-outs reported some singing and sporadic gunfire, but the latter was just drunk men shooting into the air. Another reported that *Oliver Cromwell* seemed to have fired a couple of guns, swivels by the sound of it.

"Hmm," Biddlecomb said. "I wonder if those blockheads had a notion to shoot at *Cromwell* for amusement. Likely Parker was letting them know it was a bad idea. But keep an eye and ear out for more."

The sun went down not long after, and then the reports became even less interesting, with nothing to see but blackness and little to hear as the singing and shouting and gunfire slowly tapered off. Still Biddlecomb kept his men in the church, waiting for what seemed just the right moment. The minutes crept by, and the hours, until finally, as midnight approached, he decided it was time.

"Mr. Rumstick, Mr. Faircloth, get your men ready. Quiet now, all quiet," he said. He turned to Colonel Somers and Captain Mitnick of the Gloucester County Militia. "I reckon it's time to go."

"Very good, Captain," Somers said. He seemed resigned to the task. Mitnick seemed enthused.

Biddlecomb turned to Gerrish. "Mr. Gerrish, the signal to *Cromwell*, if you please."

"Aye, sir," Gerrish said. He took a lantern down from a hook and headed for the church door.

By the time Gerrish closed the door behind him, the church was filled with the shuffle of men, many of whom who had been asleep, standing, stretching, putting on scarves and hats and taking up arms. Rumstick and Faircloth were moving among them, admonishing them to keep quiet, threatening them with dire consequences if they did not. Even the loud-mouthed McGinty was talking in hushed tones and making certain his men knew to do so as well.

Biddlecomb adjusted his sword so it hung properly at his side. He picked up one of the pistols that had been sitting next to him on the pew. He primed the pan and put the hammer on half-cock, then did the same with the second. They were sea-service pistols, fitted with long clips to hook on his belt, so he slipped them into place and stepped out of the box.

Once the others were ready Biddlecomb led them outside into the bracing night air where they sorted themselves out as they had been instructed to do: Faircloth's marines at the head of the column, the Gloucester County Militia fifty feet behind them in loose order and the sailors fifty feet behind them. They would advance down the wharf as silently as they could, with the marines ready to take the brunt of any resistance. They were the best trained, best disciplined, and Faircloth would not stand for anything else.

Biddlecomb walked the length of the column up to where Faircloth stood at the head of his men. He paused and looked up. The blanket of clouds that had covered the sky for days had not thinned in the least, which was fine. It made for a dark night. There was a bit of a breeze blowing but Biddlecomb could have wished for more, which would help mask the sound of their approach, but he knew he couldn't get everything.

He heard a slight huffing behind him and Gerrish appeared, a bit out of breath. "Signaled *Cromwell*, sir, and they acknowledged."

"Very good." He turned to Faircloth. "Lead on, McDuff," he said.

Faircloth half turned and raised his sword and stepped forward and his men followed behind, muskets held across their chests. They moved at something slower than a walk, taking each step with care, moving as silently as big men dressed for winter and armed for combat could move.

A few moments later they were on the wharf, their leather-soled shoes more silent on the wooden planks than they had been on the gravel-strewn ground, and that was a relief. Biddlecomb peered ahead into the dark but he could see nothing, and he reckoned it would be a miracle if they didn't all walk blindly off the edge of the wharf. He glanced over at Faircloth, who he could barely make out, but Faircloth seemed to be moving with confidence.

Hope he can bloody see more than I can, Biddlecomb thought. He concentrated on stepping as lightly as he could, listened for the steps of the others, and was satisfied that they were moving as quietly as they possibly could.

Soon a faint light was visible, a dull glow, low down, and Biddlecomb frowned as he looked at it, trying to imagine what it could be. Another dozen steps and he realized it was lantern light. The banditti must have lit lanterns and set them on *Falmouth*'s deck. The candles themselves were hidden behind the bulwarks but the loom of the light was visible above the rail. That would help.

They were halfway down the wharf, by his best guess, when Faircloth breathed the word "Halt!" and Biddlecomb and the marines came to a stop. Biddlecomb heard the word passed down the line and he tensed at the sound.

"What is it?" he said to Faircloth, his words barely audible, even to him.

"Heard something, sir," Faircloth said. For a moment, they remained frozen where they stood, listening. Then Biddlecomb heard it as well, a low rumble, and then another, a bit higher in pitch. A grunting sound, and then a cough.

"I think it's snoring, sir," Faircloth said at last. Biddlecomb turned his ear in the direction of the sounds and listened for a moment more.

"I think you're right," he whispered, and thought, *that's a hopeful sound.*

They moved on, and soon they could make out the looming bulk of *Falmouth* just ahead. The snoring they had heard was louder and more distinct, but still they advanced as quietly as they could. Just because some men were asleep did not mean they all were.

And then they were there, right at the frigate's side, her dark-painted gun ports standing out against her ochre-colored hull. Again they paused and listened and again they heard nothing but the sounds of sleeping men.

Faircloth stepped up to Biddlecomb, so close they were touching. "This might be a trap, sir," he said in a voice much softer than the ugly sounds coming from the deck above. "Might be they mean to let us come aboard and then shoot us down. Best if I go first."

Biddlecomb shook his head, though he doubted Faircloth could see him doing it. They had been over this before, several times, but Faircloth would not let it go. Biddlecomb did not doubt the man's motives—he only wanted to keep his captain out of harm's way—but that was not going to happen.

"No," Biddlecomb said in a voice meant to stop any further argument dead. "I go first." He stepped away from Faircloth and moved forward along the hull until he came to the boarding steps bolted to the side. With the gangplank run in that was the only way to get aboard. He pulled one of the pistols from his belt and cocked it, easing the trigger in as he did so the hammer would not click into place. He looked behind him. Faircloth was there with his marines, and he could just make out Somers and the militia farther back.

Once more unto the breach, dear friends, once more... he thought.

There was a bit of a chop on the harbor, enough that the frigate was moving with the swell, pressing against the dock, then surging away. Biddlecomb waited for the ship to come in hard against the wharf then set his free hand on one of the boarding steps and found another step with his foot. He slid his shoe inboard, looking for as much tread as he could get. He did not care to slip and tumble off the steps, not with all his men behind him and a cocked pistol in his hand.

His toe thumped softly against the side of the ship and he cursed silently and paused and listened but he heard no change from the deck above, no hint of alarm. He stepped up and took another step and another. His head came up above the edge of the deck and he looked side to side.

Just as he had guessed, Barnett's men had lit several lanterns and set them down and now they were casting a feeble light around the waist. Biddlecomb could see heaps of sleeping men, men sprawled out in the scuppers and on the forecastle head. He could see one rum barrel had been drained and was resting on its side. He could see the jagged remnants of the head of the second barrel where it had been imperfectly bashed in. He could see no movement at all.

Two more steps and he was through the gangway and onto that familiar deck. He walked aft, stepping carefully, and heard the sound of Faircloth and his marines coming up behind. He heard a soft thump low down to starboard and knew it was one of *Cromwell*'s boats coming alongside. In a moment men from the state ship would be swarming over the bulwark to add to their numbers.

It was not until he reached the break of the quarterdeck that Biddlecomb encountered any of the Pine Robbers awake enough to move. A grunt, a rustle of clothing, and one of the prone men rolled part-way over. He looked up and grunted something that might have been "Who the hell are you?"

Biddlecomb reached down with the pistol and pushed the muzzle against the man's forehead. "Shhh…" he said, softly, and the man's eyes went wide and he nodded, sober enough to understand the threat.

In the light of the lanterns, Biddlecomb could see the first of *Cromwell*'s men coming aboard, Lieutenant Little in the lead. Faircloth's marines were all aboard and spreading out along the deck, muskets pointed down at the men sprawled around, and the militia were coming up behind them. He looked down at the man at his feet.

"Stay here," he said. "Keep quiet. Don't move." The man nodded, his eyes still wide, and Biddlecomb left him and crossed back to the main hatch. He paused and eased the hammer of his pistol to half-cock and slipped the gun back into his belt. By that time the deck was growing crowded as the militia and *Cromwell*'s boarding party and then McGinty men and the Falmouths all climbed aboard.

There was no call for stealth now, and some of the Pine Robbers were starting to stir with the sound of dozens of feet stamping fore and aft. There were groans and dull shouts of surprise and sharp orders to keep silent and not move, orders that seemed to be readily obeyed.

Biddlecomb stopped amidships and from different directions, Rumstick, Faircloth, Somers, and Little all converged on him. "So far, so good," Biddlecomb said. "But this isn't all of them. Let's hope any men below are as paralytic drunk as this lot." He could see heads nodding at the sentiment.

"Colonel Somers, you and your men secure the upper deck here. Mr. Faircloth, take a squad and bring them down the after companionway and sweep forward. Mr. Rumstick, get some of your men and go down forward and sweep aft. Check the gundeck and then the hold. Anyone you find, bring them topside. Make certain Barnett is one of them. Mr. Sprout has the lashings?"

"Aye, sir," Rumstick said. The boatswain had brought three score lengths of cordage to bind the hands of the prisoners.

"Good. Give him some men to start lashing up everyone on deck, and those you find below as well. I'm going to inspect the great cabin, see how much damage these bastards have done." That last came out more bitterly than Biddlecomb had intended, and he realized he was angrier about this violation of his beloved frigate than he had realized.

His orders were met with a chorus of, "Aye, sir" and "Yes, Captain" and the men dispersed to carry them out. Biddlecomb looked around the deck and felt a deep sense of satisfaction. *Sometimes things actually work out the way you hope*, he thought. He picked up one of the lanterns and made his way down to the waist and then aft to the great cabin.

He stopped outside the door and listened, leaning close to the bulkhead, but he could hear nothing over the growing noise of the Pine Robbers being rounded up. With the ship well secured no one was trying to be quiet. Somers' militiamen were barking orders and kicking men awake as the marines and Rumstick's men went stomping down the companionways to the lower decks.

Biddlecomb gave up trying to listen and instead reached down and turned the doorknob and pushed the door open a fraction of an inch, then waited. Nothing. He drew one of the pistols from his belt and cocked it. He held the gun in his right hand and the lantern in his left. He pushed the door open with his foot and stepped inside.

He held the lantern high, the pistol straight out in front of him, and he turned slowly, larboard to starboard, as he scanned the inside of the cabin. There were a few pewter plates and remnants of food scattered over the top of the table and empty wine bottles strewn about. The doors of the sideboard were hanging open and its contents had been tumbled out onto the deck. Various storage lockers under the settees aft were also open, the things they once held pulled out and tossed around. The Pine Robbers had rifled the cabin well, but there seemed to be no damage beyond that.

This is not so bad... Biddlecomb thought.

He took another step aft and then another, looking behind him and then looking side to side once more. He wondered if any glass had been broken. The after end of the cabin was made up of the stern windows, and there were smaller windows on the sides in built-out sections called badges. On a larger ship, the badges would have housed the captain's private head, but on *Falmouth*, they were just windows. And Biddlecomb was pleased to see they were all intact.

Falmouth had the largest great cabin Biddlecomb had ever enjoyed, but it was still not particularly big and there were not many places for someone to lie in wait. One more look around and Biddlecomb was satisfied. He eased the hammer of his pistol to half-cock and set it on the table, then hung the lantern from a hook in an overhead beam.

His toe bumped against an empty wine bottle on the deck and he reached down and picked it up, and another beside it. He recognized them as having held a vintage that Faircloth particularly liked, and which he and the officers had enjoyed, sitting in that cabin. He pictured the banditti swilling it down like it was blackstrap.

Elisha will not be happy to see this, Biddlecomb thought. He was about to set the bottles down when he heard it, a shuffle from behind, a creak of wood, loud enough to make him start. He whirled around to see the far end of the table rising up from the deck as if it had been caught by a strong wind.

Just for an instant Biddlecomb stared in confused wonder. Then Shadrach Barnett came up from behind, lifting and flipping the table with his shoulder as he stood. He had a pistol in each hand and he shouted, "You bastard!" as he brought the guns up and aimed them at Biddlecomb's chest, ten feet away. Biddlecomb saw the black circles of the muzzles coming up level and he flung the bottles in his hands at Barnett and leapt sideways just as the guns went off.

The noise was thunderous in the confined space of the cabin. Through the blast of the discharge, Biddlecomb heard the balls buzz by his head, felt one tear through his coat and graze his side, but he gave it no thought. His hand was on the hilt of his sword and he drew the weapon as he turned back to face Barnett.

Barnett was shouting now, not words, just a bellow of pure fury. He flung one of the pistols at Biddlecomb. The gun hit him in the chest with surprising force, enough to knock him backward. He stumbled as went back and he felt the sword slipping from his fingers.

Then Barnett was up and over the upset table, holding the second pistol by the barrel, butt up, like a club. Biddlecomb tightened the grip on his sword and raised the blade just as Barnett swung the pistol at his head.

Sword and gun met a foot from Biddlecomb's face. Biddlecomb twisted his wrist and forced the pistol down and sideways, then lifted his right foot and drove it into Barnett's gut. Barnett flew back and slammed into the table, off-balance, stumbling, and Biddlecomb lunged forward, leading with the point of his sword.

Barnett reacted with a speed that Biddlecomb could hardly believe. He swung the pistol down in a wide arc and knocked the blade away, then pushed off the table and slammed into Biddlecomb shoulder first, driving him back. Biddlecomb was vaguely aware of footsteps outside the great cabin, voices shouting, but all his concentration was directed at keeping on his feet.

He had stumbled halfway across the cabin by the time he managed to regain his footing, and five feet separated him and Barnett. For the space of a heartbeat, the two men looked at one another, and then Barnett shouted again and charged.

Biddlecomb brought the tip of his sword up, or tried to, hoping the man would run right onto it. He was too late. Barnett knocked the sword aside with the butt of the gun, never slowing as he did. Biddlecomb heard the pistol hit the deck, and then both of Barnett's hands were up and his fingers were wrapped around Biddlecomb's neck.

The two of them staggered back and Biddlecomb felt the crushing force on his throat as Barnett squeezed. He slammed at Barnett's arms from below, again and again, but the man was powerfully strong and the blows made not the least impression on him.

Biddlecomb abandoned that, reached up, and punched Barnett in the face but still Barnett's grip did not falter at all. He punched him again and again, to no avail. He twisted and started to feel the air in his lungs running short. He kicked, hard, and felt his foot hit Barnett's knee. He wound up and kicked again, and this time his shoe made solid contact with the man's groin.

That, at last, seemed to have some effect, but it was just to make Barnett more angry still. Biddlecomb felt the grip tighten on his throat, felt those iron fingers pressing hard into his flesh until there was no chance of drawing breath. Barnett shouted again and pushed and Biddlecomb felt himself stumbling back, and back again, the two men, locked together, half-falling across the great cabin.

Biddlecomb's vision was blurring and he knew that with the next step, or the one after, his back would slam against the cabin side and he would be pinned there. Off to his left, he had a vague image of Ezra Rumstick pushing through the cabin door, pistol in hand, and more men behind him. The side of the cabin came into view as they tumbled backward and Biddlecomb knew they were about to hit.

And then they did. But they did not hit the solid planks of the cabin's side. Rather, they hit the badge farther aft. Biddlecomb felt his shins come hard against the low shelf that formed the structure's base. Barnett squeezed harder still and pushed him back, and then the stumbling became falling as their legs stopped dead and the rest of them continued on.

Over they went, Biddlecomb and Barnett, locked together. Biddlecomb felt his head and shoulders hit the glass windows, felt the frames give way, heard the sound of the glass shatter. The cold air embraced them as they went back through the broken space and then there was nothing under them; no deck, no wall, nothing but air.

Barnett's grip loosened as they fell, tumbling, and Biddlecomb had just enough time to think that they were going to hit the water and to consider the agony that that would bring when he hit the wharf. He came down on his shoulder and his hip, and the impact sent pain rippling through him and drove out what little air was left in his lungs. He thrashed and gasped and managed to get a breath, and then another.

Barnett... Two thoughts came at once: Barnett was no longer choking him, but if he was still alive, he was still a threat. Biddlecomb put his hand down and pushed himself up. He felt the pain redouble and he wondered if he had broken anything in the fall, but knew it would have to wait. He got his legs under him and pushed himself to his feet.

Twenty feet away and ten feet up Rumstick stood framed in the broken badge, his face a mask of fear in the light of the lantern. "Isaac!" he shouted but Biddlecomb did not have time to reply. Barnett. He had to find Barnett.

He looked side to side but the man was not there and it occurred to Biddlecomb that he had run off, that he had managed to escape, and the thought made him furious. Then he heard a sound, a grunting sound, animal-like, and down by his feet. He looked over and there was Barnett. Biddlecomb had landed on the wharf but Barnett had hit the wharf's edge and half tumbled over. Now he was clinging on, his fingers finding a tenuous grip on the worn planks, the rest of him, from the waist down hanging over the water in the narrow space between the ship and the wharf.

Biddlecomb took a few stumbling steps in his direction, unsure even as he approached what he would do. His first instinct: a kick to Barnett's head, the joy of watching him tumble into the water below. He took another step and realized he could not do that. That would be murder, pure and simple. Worse, if Barnett could swim he might escape.

Another step and Biddlecomb dropped to his knees and grabbed Barnett's arm and looked into his ugly, snarling face.

"Let go of me, you whore's son bastard, I'll kill you!" Barnett growled.

"Don't be stupid, Barnett," Biddlecomb said. He reached out for Barnett's other arm but Barnett pulled it out of the way and reached up for Biddlecomb's throat, fingers spread. He was an inch from getting hold when *Falmouth* surged against the wharf, driven by the unseen chop, pinning Barnett between the massive ship and the unyielding wooden beams. Barnett's eyes and mouth went wide and he made a grunting sound and Biddlecomb heard the sick crack of ribs and spine.

For a moment they remained like that, eyes locked, silent, Barnett's face frozen in surprise and agony as he was ground against the wharf by the terrific force of the ship. Blood erupted from his mouth like a dark waterfall. And then the ship surged back, leaving Barnett half draped over the wharf, alive or dead Biddlecomb could not tell. He hung like that for a second, maybe two, then dropped away, falling past the edge of the wharf, and Biddlecomb heard his body hit the water below.

There were footsteps on the wooden planks now, running, and lantern light bouncing over *Falmouth*'s side. Hands grabbed onto Biddlecomb's arms and shoulders and helped him to his feet. He straightened as well as he could and looked around. Rumstick was there, sword in hand, concern on his face, and Faircloth as well.

"Captain!" Rumstick said. "What...are you...?"

"Fine, I'm fine, Ezra," Biddlecomb said, making himself stand a little straighter, a little less like the cripple he felt. "Barnett's dead. Crushed."

Mitnick was holding a lantern over the edge of the wharf and looking down at the water. He turned back toward the rest of them. "Dead, for certain," he said.

"We can see if any of them banditti care enough to fish him out," Rumstick said. "If not, well, the tide's just starting to ebb. That should take care of it."

They went back aboard where Sprout and his men were binding the last of the Pine Robbers hands, at least those that needed binding. Three of the men could not be roused from their stupor and two more were dead, from either drink or cold of both. There seemed to be no enthusiasm among them for pulling Barnett's body from the water and giving it a Christian burial, so the tide was allowed to do the work for them.

It was well past midnight when Somers and Mitnick and the Gloucester County Militia marched the Pine Robbers off to whatever they would use for a jail and left the Falmouths back aboard their ship. The third barrel of rum had not been breached, so Biddlecomb ordered it open and a tot was called for each man. Rumstick set the watches, with half the men going below to sleep and the other half taking up muskets and positioning themselves around the deck. What they were guarding against neither they nor Biddlecomb knew, but Biddlecomb figured it was best to be ready.

At long last he dragged himself below and aft to the great cabin, where he found that someone had ordered canvas nailed up over the shattered badge to at least keep the frigid night air at bay. He shed his coat and sword belt and shoes and climbed wearily into his bed, his familiar bed. He let the memories of that day, that long, strange day, whirl around in his mind as he drifted into a deep and profound sleep.

It was past dawn when he woke, with sunlight, which he had not seen in some time, streaming in through the aft windows. He lay in bed for a moment, certain that something had woken him up, but not certain what it was. And then he heard it again, a knocking on his door, not too loud, but not tentative, either.

"Sir? Sir?" It was Gerrish's voice.

Biddlecomb sat up and winced in pain as he did. His shoulder and his hip, where he had hit the wharf, were in agony, and he knew there would be some impressive bruising to see once he removed his clothes.

"Yes, Mr. Gerrish?"

"Someone…ah…someone to see you, sir," Gerrish replied. Biddlecomb's first reflex was to tell them both, Gerrish and this visitor, to go to the devil. But Gerrish was no fool, and if he deemed this person worthy of waking the captain for, then he was probably right.

"Very well, just a moment," Biddlecomb called. He set his feet down on the deck and stood with care and received a new set of pains for his trouble. He remained standing for a moment, letting things settle, then made his way across the cabin and pulled the door open.

Gerrish was standing there, looking uncharacteristically unsure of himself, but Biddlecomb's eyes went to the person behind him. A familiar face, perfectly familiar, but one that somehow did not go with this setting, like two things juxtaposed that were not supposed to be. For a moment, Biddlecomb just stared, trying to reconcile the anomaly. And then he spoke.

"Virginia?"

CHAPTER TWENTY-FOUR

They met in *Falmouth*'s great cabin just a few hours after *Virginia*'s arrival: Biddlecomb and Rumstick, Faircloth, Captain Parker from *Oliver Cromwell*. Biddlecomb ordered Angus McGinty to attend as well. It was not an easy decision—he did not particularly want the man there—but he needed McGinty's men, and he was not certain he had any authority over them.

For that matter, he needed McGinty as well. The man had proved to be a skilled mariner, and Biddlecomb needed as many of those as he could get.

It had taken Biddlecomb some time to sort through the great tangle that Virginia and Jack's arrival had created: a tangle of information and emotions, of plans and rumors and suppositions and things left unspoken. They had arrived by carriage, a lovely vehicle with a good suspension, commandeered from someone of means, which had made the rutted, miserable roads of New Jersey as tolerable as they could be. They were escorted by a dozen mounted troops of the 2nd Regiment Light Dragoons, who remained just long enough to breakfast and see to their horses before riding off north again.

None of that mattered at first blush, or course, nor did Isaac even inquire as to how or why they were there. Rather, he pulled them into the great cabin and kissed Virginia, long and passionately. He was aware of

Gerrish quietly shutting the door but he did not look up, just continued kissing, continued to relish the feel of Virginia kissing him back.

He held her as close as he could. He wanted to squeeze her tight but could not because she was wearing Jack in her sling, so he pressed gently against his son and against his wife and kissed her again. And when Jack began to fuss, Isaac lifted him out of the sling and kissed him as well, as long as the young man would tolerate it. And when he would stand for it, no longer Isaac gave the boy to Virginia to nurse, ushered them over to the settee aft and sat them down. Then he sat down beside her and said, "I suspect you have quite a tale to tell."

That she did. She started with her arrival at the Williams' home in Philadelphia, described her time there, her time with Susan, the British officers whom Susan had befriended. She was not even halfway through her story when Rumstick knocked on the door, eager to see Virginia and Jack again, to express his welcome, to bring them breakfast, which Woodberry, behind him, was carrying on a tray.

Once he had greeted her and gushed over the baby (with Woodberry behind him trying not to laugh out loud at the sight), Rumstick took his leave and Virginia continued her story between bites of toast and egg and sips of coffee. She told him about the letter, how it had been discovered. She told him that the British officer, Dexter, cousin to James Wallace, had managed to get from her where it was that Weatherspoon had been killed, though she was notably vague as to how he had done it.

After that, the ride out of the city, the wounding of Captain Dexter, their discovery by the Talmadge and the Light Dragoons.

"I don't know if Dexter got word to Wallace about your where-abouts," Virginia said. "But he had the information for days before... we left the city."

Biddlecomb nodded. *Days...*

"I have to guess Dexter sent word as soon as he had it," he said. "There'd be little reason not to." He paused for a moment and considered that. "I need to call a meeting of my officers," he said at length. "And you need to rest."

That last, he knew, was pointless, but Isaac felt he had to say it anyway. Virginia would not rest, not when there was crucial business at hand, business of which she was a part. So, when she refused to take her ease, he did not argue, or at least not much.

Forty minutes later that they were all assembled in the great cabin.

"Mrs. Biddlecomb brings certain intelligence from Philadelphia," Biddlecomb said, once he had provided the others with the highlights of Virginia's saga. "She has reason to believe that Lord Howe knows where we are, where *Falmouth* is. Or, more specifically, Sir James Wallace knows."

"Wallace?" Parker said. "Wallace of the frigate *Rose*?"

"Late of the frigate *Rose*, yes," Biddlecomb said. "He commands a fifty-gun ship now, the *Experiment*. A more powerful beast, by far."

"*Experiment*, then," Parker said. "But just because he knows you're here, why do you think he'll come hunting for you? Are you quite that important to him?"

Biddlecomb did not have to form an answer, because McGinty answered for him. "Ah, Captain Parker, you'd best bet that James Wallace will be hunting for our boy here. Our captain, I should say. *Sparrowhawk* was tender to *Experiment*, and *Falmouth* was her prize. Captain Biddlecomb, he stole them both right out from under Wallace's nose. A fine caper, and I'm proud to say I had a hand in it meself."

"That's the truth of it," Rumstick said. "But this feud between Wallace and Captain Biddlecomb, it goes back a lot further than that, and a lot deeper. If Wallace has a chance to run us the ground, and get his sloop and his prize back, you can be damned sure he'll take it, and devil take the hind-most."

"Very well, then," Parker said, leaning back and setting his palms on the table. "Sounds like a hard lot. I wish you luck with it, but I must get my ship underway now, while the wind serves."

That gave the assembled group pause, all eyes on Parker. Rumstick broke the silence, an undercurrent of anger in his voice. "Do you mean to leave us, sir? Just run off?"

"Run off?" Parker said, his tone angry to match Rumstick's. "No, I mean to get underway and obey my orders, which are to return to New London. This all appears to be a Continental Navy affair. Frankly, it appears to be Captain Biddlecomb's private affair. And I think the

CHAPTER TWENTY-FOUR

Connecticut State Navy has rendered quite enough help, thank you, lieutenant."

"Humph," Rumstick said, sitting back, glaring at Parker. Biddlecomb readied himself to step in, rhetorically, before Rumstick made things worse, but the lieutenant managed to keep his mouth shut. It was, to no one's surprise, McGinty who spoke next.

"I think Captain Parker has the right of it," he said. "If old James Wallace learned of our whereabouts four or five days back, which well he might have, then there's a good chance that fifty-gun ship is just off the harbor mouth as we speak. He's looking for *Falmouth*, sure, and *Sparrowhawk*, but if he were to see a prize such as *Oliver Cromwell*, rigged and armed, well, he'd soon forget this half-built frigate. And Captain Parker can lead him off on a merry chase."

"A decoy, you're saying, Mr. McGinty?" Biddlecomb said.

"Exactly, sir!" McGinty said. "*Oliver Cromwell* leads *Experiment* off to kingdom come while we all slip away."

"*Experiment* is new built," Virginia said. "And copper-bottomed."

Biddlecomb waved a dismissive hand. "I don't think Captain Parker will have the least problem eluding her, will you, sir? No, I think this might work out excellently."

"There is no reason to think this *Experiment* is lurking just beyond the harbor, lying in wait," Parker said. "But...were I to delay sailing... what did you have in mind?"

"Well..." Biddlecomb said. He had had no chance to think too deeply on this, but some obvious ideas sprung immediately to mind. "First off, *Hopefleet* has cannon and powder stored down below, and it doesn't do much good there. We'll mount what guns we can aboard *Falmouth*, and bring the powder and shot aboard as well. We can transfer the bulk of the other cargo to *Cromwell*. That will keep it safer. We don't want to risk losing that lot."

Parker nodded. "That'll serve," he said. Biddlecomb had reckoned he would see the sense in that. *Hopefleet*'s chief worth was not the ship itself, but the cargo. If that was lost, then Parker would have gone to a lot of effort for nothing.

"Once that's done, we get underway as soon as we're able," Biddlecomb continued. "Make northing. Wallace might have leave from Lord Howe to operate as an independent command, but I doubt Howe wants him running off too far afield. So if we can just get past the coast here, and the approaches to New York, we should be safe as houses."

"Humph," Parker said with appropriate skepticism.

Biddlecomb had some other ideas as well, such as using *Cromwell* to tow *Falmouth*, and distributing some of Parker's men around the other ships, but he kept his mouth shut. He figured he had pushed Parker as far as he was going to push him for the time being.

"You say your orders were for New London," Biddlecomb added. "That seems as fine a place as any to bring *Falmouth*." Actually, Boston was the port he had in mind, but that seemed like another thing that was better kept to himself.

They discussed a few more details, haggled over some of the finer points, and then set to work. A crew was sent over to *Hopefleet* to raise anchor and half a dozen boats converged on the merchantman to tow her alongside *Falmouth*. It might have been a tricky business, keeping the two ships' rigging from becoming entangled, but *Falmouth* had virtually no rigging to get in the way, just the lower foremast and yard, and it was no great bother to get the merchant brig alongside.

They worked fast, and there were enough experienced hands that they could work efficiently, but there was a great deal to do, swaying the guns and carriages and powder out of *Hopefleet*'s hold and down onto *Falmouth*'s gundeck. Some of the other cargo, the uniforms and muskets and such, were lowered into *Cromwell*'s launch and brought aboard Parker's ship. Biddlecomb could think of no better way to gain Parker's trust and cooperation than by letting him carry a good portion of the booty.

As hard as they worked, and eager as they were to get underway, it was soon clear that they would not be ready by nightfall, and no one relished the idea of feeling their way through the narrow inlet in the dark. So they labored until the sun went down, and then they labored some more by lantern light, and when at last they were nearly done, and the men were staggering with exhaustion, Biddlecomb ordered supper and a tot and a night's sleep.

He himself dined in the great cabin with Virginia and Jack, and Rumstick, Faircloth, and Gerrish. It was only appropriate that he had his officers to supper on such an evening, as they prepared to sail into the teeth of a fifty-gun ship-of-the-line. But he had another, more cowardly reason for bringing them there. He had orders to give Rumstick, orders that Rumstick would not like, and he wanted the others there when he gave them.

"So, Ezra," Biddlecomb said as they pushed their plates away and took up their glasses. They were drinking rum, like the men. Faircloth's meticulously stocked wine cellar had been drained by the villains from the pine barrens.

"Yes?"

"I had a thought that I would put you in command of *Hopefleet*. I don't know who else I could choose."

Rumstick frowned. "Command of *Hopefleet*? You mean not be aboard *Falmouth* when we sail?"

"Well, if you can contrive to do both, you're welcome to it," Biddlecomb said, smiling. No one acknowledged the quip.

"That's...I'd much prefer to remain aboard the frigate," Rumstick protested. He had no fear of the responsibility of command, of that Biddlecomb was certain. But he also had no desire to leave the ship they had been fighting for for so long, to leave his shipmates with so vicious a battle looming.

"I understand, Ezra," Biddlecomb said. "But we might need *Hopefleet* to take *Falmouth* under tow, and for that we need a competent master. And there's not a lot of those around."

"Of course...I see your point," Rumstick replied. "So who stands in as first lieutenant? Mr. Gerrish?"

"Good Lord, no!" Gerrish protested. "I'm just a glorified midshipman as it is, and not too glorified at that. I'm in no position to stand as first officer." The unspoken point: in case of Biddlecomb's being wounded or killed, the first officer would take command. And there was a tolerably good chance that Biddlecomb would be wounded or killed.

"You are competence itself, Samuel," Biddlecomb said to Gerrish. "But no...I mean to make McGinty first officer..."

Rumstick's eyebrows came together and he frowned. Gerrish's eyes opened wide and Faircloth chuckled softly. Virginia looked on, confused, and Jack slept through it all.

"Are you serious?" Rumstick said. "You'd put that thieving son of a bitch in my stead?"

"I'm giving you a promotion," Biddlecomb said. "And McGinty's proven himself to be a decent seaman. Hell, he sailed *Sparrowhawk* and took a prize with that handful of infantry he had as a crew."

"Then why not put him in command of *Hopefleet?*" Rumstick demanded, then said, "Oh..." as he realized why not. The last time McGinty had command of a ship he had run off with it.

"This way I have a man I can trust on *Hopefleet* and I can keep an eye on McGinty, see that he doesn't get up to any more mischief," Biddlecomb said. "Anyway, it's decided." He was quite done talking about it. For that matter, he was done with talking in general. Damn the risk, damn the consequences, he was ready to act.

CHAPTER TWENTY-FIVE

The supper party broke up a short time later, the officers heading back to their Spartan quarters for the night. Lacking a cabin steward Biddlecomb took it upon himself to make up the bed in the sleeping cabin for Virginia and Jack, and piled blankets on the settee for his own bunk.

His body ached from the day's work, his shoulder and hip were a mass of bruises and the laceration left in the wake of Barnett's bullet was screaming in pain. If Virginia was hoping for anything beyond sleep, she would be out of luck; even months of abstinence were not going to rouse Isaac's ardor that night. But Virginia was exhausted as well and seemed no more inclined toward romance than he was, and soon they were all asleep in their separate berths.

They were roused before dawn the next day, per Biddlecomb's orders. Isaac built a fire in the small brazier to warm the cabin to the extent that it would, which was not much, then left Virginia and Jack there as he climbed up on deck. By the time he stepped out of the companionway, the others were already hard at it, preparing *Falmouth* for sea and swaying the last of the cargo out of *Hopefleet*'s hold and getting it aboard *Cromwell*.

McGinty and his men had been put to work on *Falmouth*'s gundeck, muscling the nine-pounder guns they had retrieved from *Hopefleet* into place behind the gun ports and rigging the breech tackles and gun tackles. Biddlecomb had been avoiding the man, dragging his heels about the new orders, but he knew he could put it off no longer, so he took one last look around and then headed below.

"Mr. McGinty," Biddlecomb called as he stepped off the ladder and onto the gundeck. He looked down the row of guns, the last of which McGinty's crew was heaving into position. They looked small—silly, actually—in place of the eighteen-pounders *Falmouth* was intended to mount.

McGinty left off his work and stepped over. "Aye, Captain," he said. McGinty never said *sir*, Biddlecomb noticed.

"How goes it?"

"Not so bad. Guns are in place, tackle rigged. There were fourteen of them aboard *Hopefleet* so I put seven on each side. Wee little things, them guns, for a great ship such as this. Not sure how much hurt they'll do a fifty-gun ship-of-the-line. But thing is, this Wallace won't think the frigate's armed at all. When those guns run out, won't that be a nice surprise?"

"Well reasoned, Mr. McGinty," Biddlecomb said. "I wish I had thought of it. But see here, Mr. Rumstick is taking command of *Hopefleet*, so when we sail I'll need you to stand in as acting first officer aboard this ship."

Biddlecomb could see the subtle amusement on McGinty's face and it annoyed him greatly. But why wouldn't he be amused? He understood perfectly well how little Biddlecomb wanted him to be second in command, and what little choice he had.

"Mr. Rumstick, he's happy with this plan, is he? His fine promotion?"

"Mr. Rumstick obeys orders. As I expect you to do. It's not too late to see you hanged for piracy."

"Oh, aye, Captain!" McGinty said, smiling. It was an empty threat and they both knew it. Biddlecomb was now as fully implicated in the questionable taking of *Hopefleet* as McGinty was.

"In any event," Biddlecomb said, "you seem to know your way around a ship, stolen or otherwise, so you'll have to do. Pray see this work finished up and report to me topsides."

Biddlecomb left him to it and climbed back up the ladder to the waist and then up to the quarterdeck. He looked over at *Oliver Cromwell* anchored nearby. Parker had brought her anchor to short stay and sent men aloft to start loosening off sail. A cable length beyond her, *Sparrowhawk*, now under the command of Mr. Sprout, *Falmouth*'s boatswain, lay at short stay as well.

Hopefleet was still rafted alongside *Falmouth*, the men in the waist battening the hatches down and getting her ready for sea. The brig's master, James Finch, had been turned over to the Gloucester County Militia, a prisoner of war. Now her crew was made up of a few of *Falmouth*'s men and a few of *Hopefleet*'s original crew who had been offered their freedom in exchange for cooperation.

Rumstick had taken command that morning and now he was all over the ship; back on the quarterdeck, stamping forward, bellowing orders, pointing at this and that, then back on the quarterdeck. He might not be happy about his exile to the brig, but he would not be found wanting. At the last moment, Biddlecomb had sent Gerrish as well, to serve as Rumstick's first officer.

Biddlecomb turned his face into the wind and felt it on his cheeks, cold, weak puffs of winter air. It had been flat calm when he first emerged from the great cabin, but now with the rising sun a bit of an off-shore breeze was filling in—no gale of wind but enough to move the ships, and blowing from the right direction to waft them out of Great Egg Harbor and out to the open sea. It made him desperately anxious to get underway.

He looked around again, looking for something, anything, that was not being done as quickly as it could be so that he could bark out some orders, get things moving along, but there was nothing he could see. McGinty emerged from the scuttle and made his way aft.

"Guns are secure," he said. He turned his head into the breeze that way Biddlecomb had done. "Wind seems fair to get us to sea."

"It does," Biddlecomb agreed. "So we should get to sea." He looked down at *Hopefleet* again. The last of the battens were being set in place. "Mr. Rumstick!" he called and Rumstick looked up from his spot on the quarterdeck.

"Aye, sir?" Rumstick called back, and he was thankfully too far away for Biddlecomb to see his expression.

"Are you ready to get underway?"

"Aye, Captain, we are!" he replied. Biddlecomb turned to McGinty.

"Get the boats manned and let's tow *Hopefleet* clear," he said. McGinty nodded and went forward, calling orders as he did. Biddlecomb listened to his instructions to the boat crews, and he could find no fault in the way he was going about the business.

He picked up a speaking trumpet and put it to his lips. "Mr. Sprout!" he called over to *Sparrowhawk* and Sprout on the quarterdeck looked over and waved. "Underway, if you will! Once *Hopefleet* is clear, pray lead us out!"

Sprout waved again and suddenly the activity of the morning doubled and tripled, with men on all four ships racing aloft to cast off sail and others placing handspikes in windlasses, or heaving capstans around, or securing the fenders aboard the ships that had been rafted up. *Oliver Cromwell* seemed in all respects ready to get underway, but for the sake of diplomacy, Biddlecomb did not care to issue orders to Captain Parker.

He put the speaking trumpet up to his lips. "*Oliver Cromwell*, halloa!" From *Cromwell*'s quarterdeck Parker waved to him.

"We're towing *Hopefleet* clear, Captain, then she'll get underway!" Biddlecomb called. He was stating the obvious, but he felt that it had to be stated.

"Very well!" Parker called back. He said a few words to Little and Little shouted orders forward and the men at the capstan began heaving the anchor up the last thirty feet. As they did, *Hopefleet*'s men passed tow lines to the boats gathered at her bow and McGinty ordered the *Falmouth*'s men to get the gangplank run in and the head-fasts and stern-fasts singled up.

Virginia emerged from the companionway that led up from the great cabin with Jack, as usual, snug in his sling. She had a wool cap pulled down over her head and a heavy cloak wrapped around her and the baby.

"Do I hear the sounds of ships getting underway?" she asked.

"You do," Biddlecomb said.

"Do you mind if I join you here?"

Biddlecomb looked around at the empty quarterdeck. "There seems to be room enough," he said. "You know, usually a man-of-war's deck is a very crowded affair, but not aboard this one."

"Well, being part of *Falmouth*'s crew, it's a very exclusive club," Virginia said. "Lucky you only have the one sail to handle."

"Yes," Biddlecomb said. "Lucky. That's just the word I was thinking."

The lines holding *Hopefleet* against *Falmouth*'s starboard side were cast off as the boat crews dug in and the brig was pulled clear, the gap between the ships quickly widening. Biddlecomb looked over at *Sparrowhawk*. Her big fore-and-aft mainsail was rising up the mast, and forward the men at the windlass were heaving the anchor up. A moment later the sail was set and drawing, the anchor hanging from the hawse pipe and the sloop gathering way.

Next, it was *Oliver Cromwell*'s turn. Her anchor broke the surface, dripping water and caked with mud. The fore topsail was sheeted home and hands tailed onto the halyard, hoisting the yard aloft. The sail flapped and filled in the breeze and the small man-of-war turned her bow east, falling in astern of *Sparrowhawk*, making for the gap in the barrier islands that would lead them out to sea.

"Mr. McGinty, let's loosen off the foresail, if you please," Biddlecomb called.

"Aye, Captain!" McGinty called aft. "But you know, you could just call it 'the sail' since we only have but the one!"

"Please see to your duty, Mr. McGinty," Biddlecomb replied. He turned to Virginia who was trying not to smile, but was smiling none the less. "Everyone seems to find great amusement in our having only one sail," he said.

"Just because your foremast is very short, that's no reflection on your prowess as a man," Virginia said.

"I'm relieved that you think so," Biddlecomb said. "A ship's master can get sensitive about these things."

Forward, a half-dozen men raced up the fore shrouds and spread out along the foreyard, casting off gaskets and coiling them into neat bundles as the heavy sail dropped into its gear. A moment later they were back on deck and McGinty ordered them to man clew garnets, buntlines and leechlines, and stand by the few remaining lines holding them to the wharf. From the gangway amidships, he turned and looked back at Biddlecomb on the quarterdeck.

"Send Ferguson aft to take the helm, Mr. McGinty," Biddlecomb called, "and then let's have the foresail and let go the head-fast. We'll hold the stern-fast for now."

"Aye, Captain!" McGinty called aft, then turning forward bellowed, "Let go clews and bunts! Haul away the foresheets!" Like a massive gray curtain, the foresail dropped from the yard and fluttered in the breeze as the sheets were hauled aft. Ferguson came hurrying up the ladder to the quarterdeck and back to the big wheel mounted just forward of where the mizzen mast should be.

"Hands to the braces!" McGinty called next and most of the men left off what they were doing and ran to those lines.

I feel like I'm commanding a merchantman again, Biddlecomb thought. A man-of-war of *Falmouth*'s size would normally ship a crew of a hundred and twenty men or more, enough that all the lines could be manned at once. What they were doing now was more akin to the merchant service, where cut-purse owners insisted on the smallest crews possible to run their ships.

"Brace up, larboard tack!" McGinty shouted and the men forward leaned into the braces. He could see *Falmouth*'s men instructing McGinty's soldiers when to pull the ropes and when to hold as the big fore yard came swinging around and the sail began to fill with the breeze.

"Mr. McGinty seems to know his business," Virginia observed.

"He does," Biddlecomb agreed. "Now, if he can resist stealing the ship out from under our feet we should be in good stead."

Slowly *Falmouth*'s bow began to swing away from the wharf, pushed off by the wind in the foresail. Biddlecomb crossed over to the larboard side and took the stern-fast off the cleat himself and hauled it back onboard. He could not recall the last time he had personally handled a dock line, but here was another price to pay for having so small a crew. He dumped the rope on the deck and turned to Ferguson. "We'll follow astern of *Hopefleet*," he said. "See that you don't run her down."

Ferguson smiled. "Aye, sir, I'll try," he said. They would be lucky if *Falmouth* would move at all with her one sail set. Running down one of the other vessels was the least of their concerns.

Biddlecomb stepped back to Virginia's side and looked forward, past *Falmouth*'s bow, as best as he could. McGinty had hauled away on the slablines to lift the foot of the foresail a bit, which made their view a little less obscured by the canvas, but not much. Bending over, Biddlecomb could see *Hopefleet* a couple of cable lengths ahead, her topsails set and drawing. Beyond her, *Oliver Cromwell* was well underway. *Sparrowhawk* he could not see, lost from sight behind the other vessels.

The breeze, which Biddlecomb feared would die away, was actually filling in, holding the foresail steady as it bellied out, and driving *Falmouth* along fast enough that he could hear a ripple of water down her side. The sun was climbing up above the horizon, and already he could feel the air growing warmer.

They stood on like that for half an hour or so, with the shoreline passing down the larboard side and a smattering of islands to starboard, before Biddlecomb walked forward to the forecastle head for an unobstructed view. Faircloth had his marines lined up on the leeward side and he and Sergeant Dawes were running them through the manual of arms. The men seemed to perform it flawlessly to Biddlecomb's eye, but either Dawes for Faircloth found some flaw with each step, and the men were made to do it again, and again.

Biddlecomb left them and continued forward, past the foremast—the only mast—and the foot of the foresail and up to the forward edge of the forecastle. From there, he could see the mile-wide gap between the barrier islands and the open ocean beyond. The local fishermen at Great Egg had assured him that he would encounter no sandbars if he kept to the north side of the passage, though to a man they declined his invitation to come aboard in the capacity of pilot.

Hopefleet was still on station, right ahead, with just her topsails set, but even under that reduced canvas she was drawing away from *Falmouth*. *Cromwell* was nearing the entrance between the islands and *Sparrowhawk* was nowhere to be seen. Sprout's orders were to head out to sea, off to the southwest, and scout around as best he could, to see if anyone was waiting for them.

Biddlecomb was looking out toward the open water when McGinty stepped up beside him. "I got me lads, the boys from the Fifth Pennsylvania, organized into the gun crews, Captain. I reckon they know more about guns then they do about pulling on ropes. I had to take some of the sailor-men, too, to make the numbers, but I trust I picked the ones who're least use on deck. Freeman's down their now, putting them through a drill."

"Good," Biddlecomb said, embarrassed that he had not thought to do that himself. "We'll want a good hand aloft on look-out as well."

"Beg pardon, but I sent that fine fellow Pip up to the foretop," McGinty said. "He's been up there this past half-hour or so. Got nothing to report, I reckon, which is why you've not heard from him."

"Good," Biddlecomb said again. For a moment they were silent, looking out at the horizon. "Very well, then, Mr. McGinty. Carry on." He could think of no other orders to give, nothing else that they should be doing. With so little rigging, so few materials or gear aboard, and so few crew, there was not that much for the men to do.

Biddlecomb made his way back to the quarterdeck and took his place at the weather rail. That spot was considered the exclusive domain of the ship's captain, but in this instance, there was one person aboard who could ignore that rule with impunity—the captain's wife—and she joined him there, watching the New Jersey shoreline move slowly past.

They stood on for another half an hour with the gap between the islands opening up ahead of them and the sun climbing higher off the starboard bow. Biddlecomb bent at the waist and looked under the fore-sail. *Hopefleet* was still right ahead, but now the distance between them had opened up to nearly half a mile off.

"Can you see *Hopefleet*, still, Ferguson?" he asked.

"Aye, sir," Ferguson said. "Mostly."

"Keep right in her wake," Biddlecomb said. With *Falmouth* nearly empty and riding high her draft was about the same as that of the brig. If *Hopefleet* didn't run aground, then *Falmouth* shouldn't.

"Right in her wake, aye," Ferguson said. And soon they were there, between the barrier islands, the northerly one a quarter mile off the larboard side, the southern three quarters of a mile away. Biddlecomb found himself bracing for the jarring shudder of the ship running hard on a sandbar, but the impact never came, and soon the islands were astern with nothing but open ocean ahead.

Cromwell and *Hopefleet* had already hauled their wind and made their courses just a bit north of west. The motley fleet would stand well out to sea, clear of the shipping around New York, before turning northeast for New London. Or standing on past Cape Cod and then making for Boston.

"Mr. McGinty," Biddlecomb called to the acting lieutenant who was standing forward on the gangway. A first officer would usually keep to the quarterdeck when they were not needed elsewhere, but McGinty seemed to prefer being elsewhere.

"Aye, Captain?" McGinty called.

"Pray see that Pip in the foretop has a glass, if he does not have one now."

"Aye, Captain," McGinty said again. A moment later Billy Burke was racing up the fore shrouds, bringing a telescope up to Pip in the foretop.

"Pip!" Biddlecomb called, once the man had had a chance to look around with the glass. "Do you see anything of *Sparrowhawk*?"

"Aye, sir!" Pip called back. "Three points off the starboard bow!" There was another pause as Pip collected more information. "She's on larboard tack and standing northeast!"

*Standing northeast...*Biddlecomb thought. He had sent Sprout off to scout things out to the west, but now Sprout was on a heading to rejoin the squadron. Perhaps he had found the horizon clear, nothing to report.

Then Biddlecomb heard a new sound, like a soft pop, muted and distant. He waited a moment, and then he heard another.

"*Sparrowhawk*'s signaling, sir!" Pip called down.

So I hear, Biddlecomb thought. Two guns. The prearranged signal. *Enemy in sight.*

Chapter Twenty-Six

The strange sail was hull-down when the man at the main topmast cross-trees reported it. He called it just that: a strange sail to weather, a small and irregular patch of gray on the horizon. There was nothing more to report. It was too far off to know what sort of vessel it might be—a sloop, a brig, a ship—or much of anything else about it.

Sir James nodded as he heard the words, but said nothing, not to the look-out, not to Lieutenant John Middleton, his first officer, or the smattering of midshipmen who were standing at the leeward side of the quarterdeck, waiting for orders. There was nothing that needed saying, no orders to give. Not yet.

Experiment was sailing comfortably full and by on a larboard tack, the coast of New Jersey stretched out to the north and west. If there was any change in the strange sail's course or the set of its sails, the man at the topmast would most certainly sing out; there was no need for Wallace to remind him of that duty. Indeed, reminding him might suggest that he, Captain Sir James Wallace, was anxious, and that was not a thing he wished to suggest. It was not even a thing he wished to acknowledge, even to himself. But he was indeed anxious.

They had been lurking off the entrance to Great Egg Harbor for the better part of three days now. They had kept far enough off-shore that they would not be seen by watchers on the beach, which meant they could get only occasional glimpses of the gap between the barrier islands, as seen from the topmasts. But that had not been any great concern. Over the course of those three days, the wind had been light and mostly southerly, which would have kept Biddlecomb bottled up in harbor.

That morning, however, the breeze had a westerly slant, good for the rebels to get to sea, so Wallace had brought his ship in close, close enough to keep an eye on the harbor entrance. If Biddlecomb was still at Great Egg Harbor, and was eager to leave, this would be a good day to do so.

"Deck, there!" the man aloft called again. "Strange sail's a sloop, and she's come about! Making to the northeast!"

Wallace nodded again. *Sloop*, he thought. What he really wanted to ask was if the sloop appeared to be *Sparrowhawk*, but he most certainly was not going to do that. He was not about to display any unseemly eagerness. They would find out soon enough.

Instead, he leaned back and looked up at the sails towering above his head. The breeze had been puffy and uncertain at sunrise, but it was filling in nicely now, and the fore and mainsails, the topsails and t'gan's'ls were all drawing well, the ship heeling to leeward under the driving pressure on the canvas. If need be, his crew could flash out the studding sails with truly impressive speed. He had seen to that.

Experiment was a beautiful vessel, and her copper bottom made fairly quick and handy as well, though none of the fifty-gun ships were particularly splendid sailors. She certainly didn't have *Rose*'s turn of speed or her quickness in stays, but that was no matter. With the massive 24-pounders on her gundeck and 12-pounders on her upper deck, she threw more than twice the weight of metal that his former command had done. Wallace was happy to exchange a bit of speed for that sort of firepower.

Finding nothing aloft to criticize, Wallace looked out past the weather bow toward the shoreline. It would be some time, certainly, before he could see the sloop from the deck: so small a vessel, they would have to be nearly on top of it before it was visible from that height of eye.

Sparrowhawk...he thought. He hoped very much it was *Sparrowhawk*. He wanted the sloop back. It was a great inconvenience to not have a tender. Even when he commanded the nimble *Rose*, he had one. He could have used *Sparrowhawk* now to keep an eye in Great Egg Harbor.

But the utility of having a smaller vessel was the least of it. *Sparrowhawk* had been stolen from him, and worse, stolen by the rebel Biddlecomb, and now he meant to have the sloop back and Biddlecomb in irons.

One of the midshipmen broke off from the gaggle and stepped forward to the belfry at the edge of the quarterdeck. He paused, eyes on the half-hour glass, and when the last of the sand ran out he flipped it over and rang the bell, six sharp strikes, three sets of two, six bells in the forenoon watch.

"On deck!" the look-out's call came from aloft.

"Deck, aye!" Lt. Middleton called in reply.

"Two more sail in sight, sir!" the look-out called. "A brig and a ship, looks like! All plain sail set! Bearing north by west!"

"Very good!" Middleton called back.

"Mr. Middleton," Wallace said, just loud enough to be heard. Middleton hurried across the deck.

"Sir?"

"You may beat to quarters. Clear for action."

"Beat to quarters, clear for action, aye, sir!" Middleton said crisply, keeping his excitement in check. The entire ship's company had been tensed and ready for this moment, like a hunting dog waiting for the command to go. Middleton turned forward and in a voice meant to carry the full hundred and forty feet of *Experiment*'s upper deck shouted "Beat to quarters! Clear for action!"

The drumsticks came down on the head of the drum even before the lieutenant had finished. The drummer beat out his familiar rhythm, his call to action, and the ship seemed to explode around him. Men raced up onto the weather deck, or raced below, depending on their assigned stations. Gun tackles were cast off, sand spread on the deck, chains rigged to the yards, buckets set down, chicken coops tossed into the boats resting on the booms and yard tackles brought inboard to hoist the boats over the side, the thousand or more tasks needed to turn *Experiment* into the fighting machine she was built to be.

James Wallace ignored it all. He put a hand on the quarterdeck rail and stared out past the bow and toyed with what little information he had. *A brig and a ship, looks like...* the look-out had said. Three strange sail to weather. They were in enemy waters, and whether these ships were Biddlecomb's or not, *Experiment* had to be cleared for action. They could be rebels. They could be prizes.

But where these ships Biddlecomb's command? The frigate they called *Falmouth* only had her foremast in place when Biddlecomb stole her away, but here the look-out was reporting a ship with all plain sail set. Could the rebels have rigged her completely in the few months they had been hiding in Great Egg Harbor? He did not know.

In truth, he knew almost nothing, save for what had been relayed to him by his cousin, Richard Dexter, a captain in the 17th Regiment of Foot. Dexter had sent word: Biddlecomb and *Falmouth* were at Great Egg Harbor, and the ship was not yet fit for sea. That was all he knew, and how Dexter knew it he did not say. Wallace had sent word back asking that they meet in person, hoping there might be more information to be gleaned. He'd had no reply by the time *Experiment* received orders to sail.

Those orders came curtesy or Captain Andrew Hamond, who commanded on the Delaware. They arrived just when Wallace was looking for a way to get his ship out of Philadelphia and out to sea where he could run Biddlecomb to earth.

You are then hereby required to proceed down towards the Capes of the Delaware, to prevent the Rebels from getting Supplies into any of the lower parts of the River; and to prevent Ships and Vessels from attempting to come up to the Town whilst you judge that Navigation to be impracticable.

When the Season of the Year shall be still more advanced, and it appears to You necessary for the safety of the Ship to quit the Delaware entirely, You are then to Cruize off of Egg Harbour, and along the Coast to the Southward at such distances from the Shore as circumstances and the Weather will allow of...

Hamond's instructions could not have been more perfect if Wallace had crafted them himself. He had wasted no time, had not waited for a reply from Captain Dexter, had not even waited for two of his midshipmen and a half dozen trusted hands who had been off on leave to return before weighting anchor, setting *Experiment*'s topsails, and dropping down the river and the bay to the Capes. Commanding officers had a disagreeable way of changing their minds, and Wallace wished to be well clear of Philadelphia as quickly as he could, lest Hamond decide to do just that.

And now it seemed to be playing out just as he had hoped. The Capes, Great Egg Harbor, the three strange sails… Save for that one part he could not explain: the presence of a fully rigged ship.

"Deck, there!" In the bustle of clearing the ship for action, the look-out had been all but forgotten.

"Deck, aye!" Middleton called aloft.

"Another sail, sir! Another sloop or such!"

"Mr. Middleton," Wallace called across the deck, "send a midship-man up there with a glass, if you would."

"Aye, sir," Middleton said. Most of the midshipmen had scattered to their assigned stations for quarters, but the signal midshipman was aft, readying the signal flags for hoisting. He was smart and quick—he had to be, for that duty—and since there was no one for him to signal in any event, Middleton sent him scampering aloft.

They waited long moments for the young man to make the long climb to the main topmast crosstrees, to settle himself and train the glass on the distant ships.

"Deck, there!" he called at last, his voice higher and more difficult to hear than the look-out's had been.

"Deck, aye!"

"Sir, the strange sail seems to be a larger vessel, but jury-rigged! Just a foresail set, sir!" Wallace could hear the edge of excitement in the boy's voice. Every man aboard *Experiment* knew what they were hunting for.

"Sir," Middleton said, turning to Wallace, "the young gentleman reports…"

"I heard him, Mr. Middleton, thank you," Wallace interrupted the report. "Carry on, if you please."

Wallace put his hand back on the rail and looked out past the weather bow, and with great effort, he forced himself not to smile.

Biddlecomb waited on the quarterdeck as *Sparrowhawk* ran down on them. He did not change *Falmouth*'s heading or adjust the set of the frigate's single sail in any way. He did not need to.

If the frigate had been rigged out the way she was supposed to be, he would have to heave to to allow the little sloop to catch up. Not one of the ships in the squadron could have kept up with *Falmouth*. Even the strange sail to leeward, her t'gan's'ls now visible from *Falmouth*'s deck, would have been left in the nimble frigate's wake.

But as it was, even *Sparrowhawk* was quicker than *Falmouth* with just her single lower sail set, and Sprout had no difficulty swooping down astern of Biddlecomb's ship and coming up within hailing distance of the leeward side.

"Mr. Sprout!" Biddlecomb called through his speaking trumpet. "What say you?"

"Man-of-war, Captain!" Spout called back. He had no need of a speaking trumpet; boatswains generally did not. "I daren't get too close, sir, but she's a man-of-war, for certain! British colors! A big bastard... beg your pardon, Mrs. Biddlecomb...might well be a fifty!"

"Very good, Mr. Sprout," Biddlecomb replied. "And her heading?"

"Making a rhumb line for us, sir! Never a doubt, like a hound on a fox!"

"Thank you, Mr. Sprout!" Biddlecomb called back. "Pray, take a place to weather, keep an eye on this fellow, but keep well out of his grasp, even if you have to run off to the westward!"

"Aye, sir!" Sprout called. "And Godspeed to you, sir!"

"And you, Mr. Sprout," Biddlecomb called back. He did not entirely care for the sound of that. It had a finality that did not sit well.

Sprout gave an order that Biddlecomb could not hear and *Sparrowhawk*'s bow swung away from *Falmouth*'s side. The little ship spun around through three quarters of a circle, tacking smartly and coming up under *Falmouth*'s transom as Sprout charged off to take his station to weather. Biddlecomb envied the man his maneuverability.

"Godspeed, is it?" Virginia asked, with her hint of a teasing smile, a look that Biddlecomb generally adored. "Is that not what one says on parting forever?"

"Yes, sometimes," Biddlecomb said. "And sometimes it's when one plans to meet up again, unscathed, in an hour's time."

"Well, I hope it was the latter that Mr. Sprout had in mind."

"I'm sure it was, my dear," Isaac said. McGinty was standing at his now-familiar place on the weather gangway and Biddlecomb called to him. "Mr. McGinty, pray pass the word for Mr. Faircloth, and then I would speak with both of you, if you please."

"Aye, Captain!" McGinty said and rather than pass the word, he hurried below himself. A moment later he was back, leading Faircloth who had donned his immaculate uniform. They climbed the quarterdeck stairs and stepped over to the weather side as Virginia moved discreetly to the leeward.

"I have no doubt you gentlemen heard what Mr. Sprout had to say," Biddlecomb said. "All the ship's company did, I'll warrant."

Heads nodded and the officers mumbled, "Aye, Captain."

"Good," Biddlecomb continued. "Mr. McGinty, is the ship ready? Cleared for action?" He could see McGinty starting to smile again, but this time he managed to suppress it, with some visible effort.

At least the man had sense enough to keep his jokes to himself just now.

"Not too much onboard that needs clearing, Captain," McGinty said. "The lads left the guns secured by their tackle, after their wee drills. I suppose we could sand the decks, get out water buckets and the like."

"Very good," Biddlecomb said. "Whatever you can do to make proper preparations, do it. Mr. Faircloth, I need not ask if your marines are ready."

"Ready they are, sir. Uniformed, guns inspected and loaded. Cartridge boxes full."

"Good. We'll probably want half of them in the foretop and the other half aft on the quarterdeck. Small arms are like to be more effective than the 'great guns' on the gun deck. But right now I want you to roust out every musket or pistol we have onboard. Have your men inspect the locks and replace any flints that need it, or anything else that needs doing. Pray see that anything that can fire a bullet is ready to go."

"Very good, Captain," Faircloth said, and he and McGinty went off to see to their duties. Biddlecomb walked to the aft end of the quarter-deck and brought his glass to his eye, and then swept the ocean around him with the lens.

Falmouth and the other ships of his little squadron were spread out over a mile or so of ocean. The wind was still steady from just south of west, and the ships were sailing northwest on a broad reach, the wind just over their larboard quarters. *Oliver Cromwell* and *Hopefleet* were both sailing under topsails alone, but even with that reduced canvas, they were having a hard time not sailing away from *Falmouth*.

Biddlecomb swiveled to the south. *Sparrowhawk* was there, having positioned herself somewhat between *Falmouth* and the strange sail to leeward. Biddlecomb continued his scan until the glass came to rest on the ship following astern. Her topsails were visible now, which meant she was rapidly overhauling them. And she was indeed big; Biddlecomb could see that clearly. Bigger than a frigate, certainly, though not as big as a seventy-four. So, a fifty? *Experiment*?

McGinty stepped up onto the quarterdeck and came aft. "Guns are as ready as they're going to be, Captain," he reported. "The men are at quarters. We've a dozen or so left for sail handling and such, but that should do us."

"Very good. You have gun crews to work both sides at once?"

"Aye."

"Mr. Sprout reported just one sail," Biddlecomb said. "If there is indeed but one enemy ship, let's pull the men from the unengaged side and get them on deck with muskets. If this son of a bitch decides to get close, muskets will be worth more than having a crew for each gun."

"Very good, Captain," McGinty said. He turned to leave but Biddlecomb stopped him.

"This ship in our wake," he said, "It'll most likely prove to be *Experiment*. She's certainly Royal Navy, whatever ship it is."

"Aye, Captain," McGinty said.

"You were in the navy, weren't you, McGinty? The Royal Navy?"

"Aye, for a bit. Got bloody tiresome, all the piping and the flogging and such. Boatswain's mates…bloody boatswain's mates."

"So you joined the army? The Continental Army?"

"Might have been in His Majesty's Army too, for a spell," McGinty said. "It all gets a bit hazy."

Biddlecomb shook his head. "Loyalty doesn't seem to be your strongest trait."

McGinty smiled at that. "Not true, Captain, not true at all. The lads who are with me, I'm loyal to them. I'd die for them. I reckon I could say the same for the other fellows on this bark, now that they've welcomed me like the prodigal son. Or near enough."

"Your king? Your government? No loyalty there?"

"My *king*?" McGinty smiled broadly. "I'm Irish, you'll recall."

"Hard to forget," Biddlecomb said. "But I do believe George the Third is King of Ireland."

"And king of his American colonies. How well is that working, boy-o?"

"Captain," Biddlecomb corrected.

"Captain, then. Captain in a rebel navy. You'll be a hero if you win this thing, but I'll warrant it's a rope's end for you if you don't."

"Well, I have that advantage on you. At least there's only one country looking to hang me."

"Ah, as for me, let 'em try!" McGinty said. "But tell me, are you worried about my loyalty to you? To the ship? Is that it? Are you afraid that I'll…I don't know…desert in time of battle?"

"Something of that nature," Biddlecomb said.

"Here's the truth of it, Captain Biddlecomb. When you grow up in Ireland, you learn pretty damned fast that it's your people…family, village…they're the ones deserve your loyalty. The rest…government, kings…the devil take the lot of them. Because, Captain, they'll bugger you every time, and first chance they get."

"We're not your people," Biddlecomb said.

"Whoever I decide to fight alongside, they're my people, Captain, never you doubt it. As long as they'll have me."

"Well, we seem to have no choice this time," Biddlecomb said. "Either of us. So pray, carry on."

"Aye, sir, that I will!" McGinty said, then saluted and hurried forward. Biddlecomb stepped over to the aft corner of the deck and picked up a canvas bag that lay there. Inside were the smattering of flags that *Falmouth* had aboard. He fished around until he found a red flag, tightly bundled and ready to run aloft.

He carried it forward to the break of the quarterdeck. A few of the older hands were standing amidships and he called out, "Manning!" and Manning broke off from the rest and hurried aft.

"Take this and run it up to the weather yardarm," he said, handing the flag to Manning. "Make certain it'll be visible to *Hopefleet*."

"Aye, sir," Manning said and hurried forward. Biddlecomb retreated to the weather side of the quarterdeck and Virginia joined him there.

"What is it that's Manning's up to?" she asked.

"Signal," Biddlecomb said. "One of the few we worked out. It's for Rumstick aboard *Hopefleet*. It means 'take *Falmouth* in tow.'"

"I see," Virginia said. "You reckon *Hopefleet* can tow us clear?"

"No," Biddlecomb admitted. "No, I don't." In truth, he did not think *Hopefleet*'s taking them in tow would accomplish one damned thing. It was just something to do, something other than simply waiting for death to come rolling down on them. They would still die, certainly, but at least they would die doing something.

Chapter Twenty-Seven

Ezra Rumstick was being more quiet than was his wont, but then again he was more aggravated than he could recall being in some time, so there was good reason for it. If he opened his mouth, if he spoke to anyone around him, it would probably not end well. He knew it, so he opted to keep his mouth shut.

Nor was there much need for him to speak. Biddlecomb had sent Gerrish to act as his second, and Gerrish was competent enough to handle things just then, with *Hopefleet* sailing before an easy quartering wind under topsails alone. A monkey could have sailed the ship in those conditions. McGinty could have sailed the ship in those conditions.

Even Gerrish was somewhat superfluous just then. Biddlecomb had also sent some of the most experienced hands: Woodberry, Burke, Ewald, and some others, and none of them needed to be told what to do to keep the brig underway and making way.

Rumstick wondered at Biddlecomb's reason for sending such good men. Certainly, *Hopefleet*, having all her rig intact, needed them more that *Falmouth* did. That was one of the reasons, no doubt. Another, probably, was that Biddlecomb was trying to placate him, knowing he would not be pleased with his exile from the frigate. And that only made Rumstick more irritated still.

"Mr. Rumstick?" Gerrish asked, approaching Rumstick with caution, as if he was a dog of unknown aggression, yet another thing he found annoying.

"Yes, Mr. Gerrish?"

"I was just...I wasn't certain...if there was more that needed doing just now, sir..."

Rumstick looked around the deck. "Are we cleared for action?" he asked. "Great guns loaded and run out? Magazine made ready? Powder monkeys ready to go?"

"Ah...well...we don't actually have any great guns, sir, as I suspect you know," Gerrish said.

"Right...of course..." Rumstick said. "We're an empty, useless shell. I quite forgot." He was disgusted with himself for being so petty, but he seemed unable to stop.

"We do have small arms, sir," Gerrish said. "I could see those distributed. Have the men check the flints. See that cartridge boxes are filled."

"Very good, Mr. Gerrish, please do so," Rumstick said, then turned and looked out to leeward once again.

He had been watching the distant ship grow closer all morning, and doing so quickly. If she was *Experiment*—and Rumstick very much believed she was—then she would be up with their little squadron within the hour, it seemed, a bear among hounds. Largely toothless hounds.

"Deck, there!" Woodberry called down from aloft.

"Deck, aye!" Gerrish called back.

"*Falmouth*'s signaling, sir! Red flag at the yardarm!"

Hopefleet to take Falmouth in tow... Rumstick thought as Gerrish came hurrying aft. He wondered if Gerrish would remind him of what that signal meant, on the assumption that he, Rumstick, could not keep it in his head. But luckily for the acting lieutenant, he did not, but said simply, "Shall I slack away the boat, sir?"

Rumstick looked astern. *Hopefleet* carried two boats, and they had been cradled on the main hatch when he had come aboard. Once underway he ordered them swayed over the side and towed astern. Boats were notorious for turning into deadly splinters with the application of round shot, and Rumstick did not want them on deck when the iron started to fly.

Now they following behind the brig, pulled along at the end of ten fathoms of light hawser. There was another line as well, running from *Hopefleet*'s afterdeck and through a chock to the second boat in line. Rumstick had anticipated this, having to get a tow line to *Falmouth*, and he reckoned the easiest way would be to tie a light messenger to a boat and let it drift down to the ship astern.

He looked up at the set of *Hopefleet*'s sails and then back at *Falmouth*. Despite his best effort at sailing as slow as he could, the brig was still pulling ahead, foot by foot. But *Falmouth* was almost directly in their wake, and it seemed to Rumstick that the boat should drift just about where they wanted it to go.

He turned to the helmsman. "Fall off, just a point or so," he said.

"Fall off, aye," the helmsman said, giving the tiller a slight nudge.

"Mr. Gerrish, let's have the main topsail clewed up and then we'll send the boat off."

"Aye, sir," Gerrish said. He called a few orders down the deck and a moment later the main topsail was hauled up to the yard where it hung flopping in loose folds and *Hopefleet*'s speed dropped off noticeably. For a few moments, they stood in silence, watching *Falmouth* slowly closing the gap between them.

"That should do, Mr. Gerrish," Rumstick said at last. "Let's slack away on the tow rope now, drift the boat down to them."

Gerrish sent a few men aft to the boat's tow rope and they took the line off the cleat and let it pay out astern. Every hundred feet or so a float was attached to keep the weight of the line from pulling the boat forward. At the same time, another gang of men wrestled the bitter end of the hawser aft to where it could be run out from *Hopefleet*'s stern.

It was only a minute or so before the boat bumped up against *Falmouth*'s bow, a hundred yards astern, and hands climbed down her side to retrieve the messenger.

"Very well, haul the boats back," Rumstick said and a half dozen men began pulling the boats back with the line they had used to drift them down to the frigate.

CHAPTER TWENTY-SEVEN

"Bitter end of the hawser bent on?" Rumstick asked next.

"Aye, sir," Woodberry said. Rumstick looked down at the line on the deck. The light messenger, which was now running from *Hopefleet*'s stern to *Falmouth*'s bow, had been securely fixed to the end of the heavier rope with which they would actually tow the frigate, and Rumstick could see it was ready to go.

"Good. Dip the ensign, Mr. Gerrish."

The ensign was flying from the peak of *Hopefleet*'s gaff and Gerrish was already holding the halyard in his hands. He hauled the flag down halfway and kept it there for a moment before hauling it up again, the signal that they were ready for *Falmouth*'s men to start heaving away on the messenger. And, indeed, the flag had not even returned to the end of the gaff before the messenger came taught and the hawser was pulled out over the water astern.

Eager, ain't you... Rumstick thought. Gerrish stepped up beside him. "Will this work, do you think, sir?" he asked.

"If the messenger doesn't break, should do."

"No, I mean towing the *Falmouth*. Will we be able to tow her clear of *Experiment*?"

"Oh," Rumstick said. "I see what you're asking. No, this won't work. There's not a damned chance we can get away."

"I see..." Gerrish said. He thought about that for a moment. "So why are we doing it?"

"We have to do something," Rumstick said. "Forgive me, are we inconveniencing you?"

"Oh, no sir," Gerrish said. "I'm happy to help. And when it comes to pointless labor, well, I'm something of a prodigy."

They watched as the hawser made its laborious way over the water and disappeared onto *Falmouth*'s deck. A moment later, the red flag at *Falmouth*'s yardarm came fluttering down, the signal that the tow hawser was made fast at their end.

"Mr. Gerrish, let us set all plain sail, if you would," Rumstick said, and Gerrish turned and called out the long-anticipated order. Soon the main topsail was set again, as was the foresail and the t'gan's'ls and the fore-and-aft main. *Hopefleet* surged ahead, pressed down a bit by the wind, and the hawser rose dripping from the ocean as the strain came on it. In their wake, *Falmouth* pitched a bit in the chop as she, too, picked up speed.

Absorbed as he was in this neat bit of seamanship Rumstick had all but forgotten the man-of-war coming down on them, the very reason they were making all this effort. He turned and looked to leeward and felt like he had been punched in the gut. In the short time, it had taken them to pass the tow line to *Falmouth*, *Experiment* had halved the distance between them.

She was at most a mile and a half astern now, her hull clearly visible. Wallace, if it was Wallace, was carrying every bit of sail he could, including studding sails aloft and alow. *Experiment* was not a particularly fast ship, Rumstick suspected, but she was fast enough. Faster than their little squadron by far.

"Well," Rumstick said, "at least we won't be hanging on these tenterhooks for very long."

From *Falmouth*'s quarterdeck, Biddlecomb watched *Hopefleet* set all the canvas she could: main topsail sheeted home, foresail, t'gan's'ls, mainsail. The hawser that Rumstick had drifted down to them on the ship's boat came rising up from the water as the strain came on, and he felt the change in motion underfoot as the brig took the frigate in tow and *Falmouth*'s speed began to build.

He had let McGinty oversee getting the hawser aboard and making it fast. It was a tricky business, but McGinty had proven himself sufficiently competent so far, and he handled the task with never a hitch.

"I suppose I should go below, when our caller arrives," Virginia said, nodding toward *Experiment* a mile and a half astern. "Me and Jack."

"I suppose," Biddlecomb said. "The breadroom, I think, would be safe. It's below the waterline, and there's precious little bread in it. Some of the fellows moved a chair down there, and Jack's crib."

Virginia smiled. "You think of everything."

"I wish it was true, but actually it was Ferguson who thought to do that." The men worshiped Virginia, and adored Jack, and they did not miss a chance to put that on display.

Virginia appreciated their concern, but Isaac knew she would have found it irritating in the earlier days. He could recall another time, before Jack was born, before they were married, when their ship had been under fire from a British frigate and he had ordered Virginia to get below, repeatedly. She had ignored him then, choosing instead to stand on the quarterdeck and pepper the enemy with pistol fire.

He suspected she would do the same again, were it not for Jack. If Virginia had not been a mother, then she would not consider hunkering down in safety while her husband and his men stood in harm's way. But her priorities had shifted now. Jack changed everything.

"Well, that's very kind of Ferguson and the others," Virginia said, "to turn the breadroom into a nursery. But I think I'll wait until this fellow gets a bit closer before I retire."

It would not be a terribly long wait, that much Biddlecomb could see. *Experiment* was charging down on them carrying all the canvas that she could set, and it had taken an astoundingly short time to set it. Biddlecomb had been watching her on and off as she came on under plain sail. He had been distracted by the process of floating the messenger down from *Hopefleet*, had looked away for just a minute or so, and when he looked back the man-of-war had studding sails set, aloft and alow.

At first, Biddlecomb was not sure of what he was seeing. He trained his glass on the distant ship and saw that that was indeed what he was looking at. He shook his head at the sight. *Experiment* probably carried more men that Biddlecomb had in his entire squadron; well-trained and disciplined men. Here was an example of what such a crew could do. Soon, when *Falmouth* was under fire from twenty-five heavy guns at once, they would get another.

And then there was nothing to do but wait, which every fighting man knew was the worst part of such a day, but an inevitable part as well. McGinty found a couple of musicians among the men, a fellow with a fife and another with a fiddle, and he had them strike up some tunes, which helped, but not much.

Biddlecomb looked over the ship's side at the water running past and the wake forming astern, trying to gauge what speed they were making.

Three knots? he thought. Maybe four, but he doubted it. He considered tossing the chip log over and measuring their speed more accurately but he dismissed the idea. He didn't really want to know, and whatever it was, it was half of what *Experiment* was doing.

The first shot came half an hour later. McGinty's ad hoc band had managed to get through *Farewell and Adieu*, *The British Grenadier*, *Yankee Doodle*, of course, and half of *The World Turned Upside Down* when they heard it, a soft *pow* off to leeward. Biddlecomb turned in time to see the puff of smoke from *Experiment*'s bow and then the jet of water, a hundred yards short, as the ranging shot fell into the sea.

"I think Captain Wallace is telling me I should go below," Virginia said.

"I think he is," Biddlecomb said. He put his arm around her and hugged her softly. He kissed her and kissed Jack and sent them below, then pushed all thought of them to the back of his mind. He had done everything he could to protect them, little as that might be, and he knew they could easily occupy his every thought if he allowed it, but he had other things that required his attention.

He looked out at *Oliver Cromwell*, maintaining station to windward, off the larboard quarter. No doubt she was cleared for action and ready to go. At least Biddlecomb hoped she was. He had no authority over Captain Parker and his ship, could do no more than suggest a course of action, which he had done, clearly and emphatically.

His suggestion, such that it was, had been that *Cromwell* stay with the squadron and engage the enemy when and if the time came. He could make no more definite plans than that. They had no notion of who the enemy might be, or indeed if there would even be an enemy at all.

Parker had been lukewarm to that suggestion, as well he might be. He had agreed only to accompany the squadron only as long as it was "convenient," and "in keeping" with his instructions. And now that the enemy was actually in sight, now that the iron had started to fly, Biddlecomb expected *Oliver Cromwell* to come about and make for the far horizon. Doing battle with a fifty-gun ship, he imagined, would be neither convenient nor in keeping with Parker's instruction.

He turned and looked out over the starboard side. *Sparrowhawk* was nearly abeam, sailing a parallel course with *Falmouth*, keeping ahead of *Experiment* and clear of her broadsides. There would be no role for her in the coming fight. A direct hit from just one of *Experiment*'s 24-pounder guns would be enough to send her to the bottom. The best that Sprout could do now would be to sail off while he still could and let the world know what had become of *Falmouth* and the rest.

Another shot from *Experiment*'s bow chaser, and this time the water plume was no more than fifty feet away, though the shot was wide. McGinty's band had folded their tent and McGinty himself was coming up the ladder to the quarterdeck.

"Holiday's over, I reckon, Captain," he said, looking out at *Experiment*.

"I reckon," Biddlecomb said. "Get the gun crews below. Load and run out. Can Freeman take command down there?"

"I'd think so," McGinty said.

"Good. Put him in charge. Tell him to fire as he bears."

"Now there's an order your land soldier would not understand," McGinty said. "He'll be looking for bears to shoot at. I'll tell him to fire when he sees something he might hit."

"Whatever makes sense to him," Biddlecomb said. "Then you take charge forward, I'll stay aft here. All we can do is wait and see what Wallace intends, and then try to stop him. Not much of a plan, is it, McGinty?"

McGinty shrugged. "I for one can't think of better," he said. "You mean to keep towing like this?"

"Yes," Biddlecomb said. "There's naught else *Hopefleet* can do, with no guns, and if Rumstick isn't kept busy at something, he'll do something stupid, I'm sure of it."

"Is he a stupid man, then?" McGinty asked.

"No," Biddlecomb said. "Stupid is the wrong work. Reckless. Foolhardy."

"Ah!" McGinty said. "That sounds more like the Ezra Rumstick I know!" He turned and hurried off forward.

Another shot and this time the ball passed over *Falmouth*'s deck and landed in the water off the larboard side. Biddlecomb turned to look at the ship coming up behind and was shocked to see that their studding sails had been taken in, their t'gan's'ls as well, and the courses clewed up, all in the brief time he had been speaking to McGinty. It was like a magician's illusion. Biddlecomb shook his head at the sight.

Fighting sail he thought. *Experiment* was reduced to fighting sail, the canvas a man-of-war generally carried into battle. He was oddly happy to see that Wallace took this seriously enough to make that preparation. He would have to take in even more sail, though, if he wished to go slow enough to keep along *Falmouth*'s side.

Biddlecomb felt the deck rumbling beneath his feet and he knew that Freeman below was running the guns out, making ready for the coming fight. But *Experiment* was still astern of *Falmouth*; none of *Falmouth*'s guns would yet bear on the British man-of-war.

A sailor named Tolpin was at the wheel now, his eyes fixed forward. He and Biddlecomb were the only men on the quarterdeck, and that was profoundly odd, particularly for a man-of-war heading into battle. But the others were needed elsewhere, and with no main or mizzen mast and no guns on the quarterdeck, there was not much reason for anyone else to be aft.

"Tolpin, fall off a bit," Biddlecomb called. "We'll see if we can get these guns to bear."

"Fall off, aye, sir," Tolpin said. He sounded skeptical. The tow rope from *Hopefleet* would force the bow back, but Biddlecomb had an idea that there was slack enough for a bit of maneuvering.

Tolpin turned the wheel to starboard and *Falmouth*'s bow began to turn, lifting the tow rope higher out of the water as it did. Biddlecomb hoped that Rumstick would notice, that he would turn *Hopefleet* as well so that *Falmouth*'s guns could bear for as long as possible. He hoped that Freeman on the deck below would also notice and open fire. He was about to call to someone forward to pass the word when he felt the deck planks jump under his feet, heard the blast of the nine-pounder almost directly below him.

He was too surprised by the sound to notice where the shot fell, but he was ready for the second and he kept his eye on *Experiment* as the gun went off. The man-of-war was no more than half a mile away and coming on fast, and Biddlecomb saw the spout of water as the shot fell. It had nearly reached the ship but was well to the right.

Once the guns are warmed up, they'll do better he thought, but even as he thought it he knew it was absurd. These were infantrymen, not artillery. They might know how to load and fire a cannon, which was no great art, not much different from loading a musket, really, but they would not understand the finer points of aim, particularly not aboard a moving platform aiming at a moving target.

Well, it hardly matters, he thought next. *It's not like we're going to do any bloody damage to that beast anyway.* They might as well hurl pebbles at *Experiment*, for all the good firing nine-pound balls would do. There were just two reasons Biddlecomb was bothering at all. One was the hope of a lucky shot: a nine-pounder could take out a topsail yard or a topmast, or smash a channel and knock the shrouds free from a mast, or maybe take out the bowsprit. But that would have to be a very lucky shot indeed.

The other reason to make some effort at fighting back. Like the tow rope, it was something to do.

Another gun and another went off, and Biddlecomb felt certain that one at least had hit. It was getting harder to miss, with the massive man-of-war charging down on them. *Experiment* fired again with the single bow chaser that would bear, and this time the ball slammed into *Falmouth*'s side with a shudder that Biddlecomb could feel through the ship's fabric.

He leaned over the side and looked forward. A section of planks was stove in and the ball was still lodged in the divot it had made. The impact had damaged the ship's side, but it had not broken through. Biddlecomb was happy to see that.

The bow chaser, of course, would be a smaller gun, a nine- or twelve-pounder, not the twenty-four pounders *Experiment* carried on her lower deck.

The forward-most of *Falmouth*'s guns went off and a second later the aftermost, the one just under Biddlecomb's feet, fired again, and this time Biddlecomb was certain he saw splinters flying up from *Experiment*'s bow. She was close enough that he could see the elaborate, painted figurehead under her bowsprit, though what it was supposed to be he could not tell. He could see the water curling white around her stem, her taut, black rigging, the barrels of her guns run out on the gun deck and the upper deck.

One by one *Falmouth*'s guns went off again and each seemed to find its mark, sending up sprays of splinters from *Experiment*'s rounded bow, but she did not waver in the least as she raced down toward *Falmouth*'s side. A hundred yards away *Experiment* began to turn, bringing her course more parallel with *Falmouth*, presenting her powerful broadside.

Biddlecomb stood transfixed, his eyes on the wooden wall half a cable length away, on the round muzzles of the heavy twenty-four pounders staring back at him.

Which, like dumb mouths, do ope their...raven...lips, To beg the voice and utterance of my tongue... he thought, pointlessly. But he had no words to utter, no orders to give. There was nothing he could do but sail on and blast away with his nine-pounders and wait for Wallace to do what he would.

And then *Experiment* let loose, a ripple of fire that had to have come from a single command. The side of the ship was lost in an eruption of smoke, the morning was torn apart by the cannons' blast, and, in nearly the same instant, the scream of round shot overhead, the shudder of the deck underfoot as iron balls slammed into *Falmouth*'s side.

The fury of the broadside seemed to obliterate thought, and for a second Biddlecomb just stood there, staring at the cloud of gray smoke swirling around *Experiment*, watching as it was torn apart and whirled away by the breeze. He braced for the sound of screaming, which so often came on the heels of such a fusillade, but thankfully none came.

*They didn't fire the big guns...*Biddlecomb thought as his head cleared like the smoke. He pictured the broadside he had just witnessed, tried to freeze the image as if he was examining a painting. He realized that Wallace had fired only the guns on the upper deck, the smaller guns, twelve-pounders, maybe, not those on the gun deck. They were deadly enough, particularly at that range, but they certainly did not have the ship-killing power of the twenty-fours.

Falmouth was firing again, the guns going off in random order as the gun crews loaded and ran them out. Freeman was keeping them at it, and that was good. Biddlecomb could see bits of wood flying off of *Experiment*'s side as the shot struck, and one of the main shrouds was shot through. But he could also see *Falmouth*'s iron balls bouncing off *Experiment*'s thick hull and falling impotently into the water.

Why does he not fire the big guns? Biddlecomb wondered. A few broadsides from that range and *Falmouth* was a wreck. A few more and she would be on the bottom. And then he cursed himself for an idiot.

He wants a prize, he doesn't want a wreck, he thought. *He wants to take me prisoner...wants to hang me, not let me die in battle...*

He was certain that he was right. And that meant Wallace might give a few more broadsides with the smaller guns, loosen things up a bit, and then he would be bringing his ship alongside, driving it right into *Falmouth*, and sending his hundreds of men over the side in a boarding party.

And there was not one damned thing that Biddlecomb could do to stop him.

Chapter Twenty-Eight

Experiment's guns were firing at will now, going off in random order as fast as they were loaded and run out, and that was very fast. The two ships were close enough that Biddlecomb could see the swarm of men around the mainmast hauling the huge main topsail up to the yard. The fifty-gun ship was sailing too fast under both topsails, starting to head reach on *Falmouth*, and Wallace would not want that to happen. He would want to stay alongside, right up until the moment he ran his ship hard against *Falmouth*.

Twelve-pounder balls were slamming into *Falmouth*'s upper hull and screaming over the deck. A section of bulwark just aft of the forecastle had been smashed flat, and the starboard gangway was now three times wider than it had been. The whole scene was sometimes obscured by the thick choking smoke, and sometimes not, with each fluke of the wind.

*They're aiming high...*Biddlecomb thought. Wallace must have passed the order. No shots at the waterline. They did not want their prize on the bottom of the sea.

He saw McGinty coming up the quarterdeck ladder, saw him put a foot on the deck, just as the bulwark beside him exploded in a great spray of splinters and flying sections of planking. The big Irishman was knocked sideways, sprawled out on the deck like some rag doll a child has tossed aside.

"McGinty!" Biddlecomb shouted. He hurried forward, stepping over shards of bulwark, but by the time he reached the man, McGinty was already pushing himself up to a sitting position.

"Jesus, Mary and Joseph!" McGinty said as he sat upright. He shook his head to clear it. There was a gash across his cheek that was bleeding down his jaw, but nasty as it looked it did not seem too great a threat.

"Are you hurt?" Biddlecomb asked. It seemed like a stupid question, but McGinty shook his head.

"Not so bad, Captain, not bad," he said. He started to stand and Biddlecomb hooked an arm under McGinty's and helped him to his feet. McGinty looked at the gaping section of bulwark and the debris scattered on the deck and shook his head.

"I was..." he began, then paused as another shot passed overhead and about ten feet aft, shrieking as it went by. "I was coming aft to say we've had precious little damage, despite the great beating we're taking," McGinty continued. "Some of the lads handling sail took some splinters, none too bad. One of the guns was hit and overturned, no one hurt there, thanks be to God. That's the worst of it."

"They're shooting high," Biddlecomb said, nearly shouting to be heard over the continuous thunder of the guns, British and American. "I think they mean to board us."

"They don't want to hurt their lovely prize, is that it?" McGinty asked, shouting as well.

"I reckon not," Biddlecomb said. They both turned and looked over at *Experiment*, just in time to see her point up a bit higher, turn her bow more toward *Falmouth*. Soon, very soon, the two ships would meet, bow to bow, and then the British sailors would swarm down from the 50's high sides and onto *Falmouth*'s deck.

"They've run in the lower battery!" Biddlecomb said. The twenty-four pounders, which had been run out and ready to fire, were now hauled back in and the gunport lids shut up again. That told Biddlecomb two things: Wallace, as he suspected, did not mean to batter *Falmouth* into a wreck, and he meant to use the hundred or so men who had manned those guns as a boarding party instead.

"I trust you've thought of some clever way out of this?" McGinty said.

"Then your trust is misplaced," Biddlecomb shouted. "We'll keep at it with the great guns, hope for some lucky shot to carry something important away. The guns must be at their maximum elevation even now, am I right?"

"You're right, Captain!"

"They'll be useless soon. They won't reach *Experiment*'s rig, and hitting the hull is pointless. Another broadside or so and then get all the men on deck and get muskets in their hands. We'll see what we can do to hold the boarders off."

"Very well, Captain!" McGinty said. There was, of course, a great deal that was left unspoken. *Falmouth*'s small crew would not hold the boarders back for long. They would certainly not win in a stand-up fight. There was no means of escape with the man-of-war looming right alongside. But if they surrendered, Biddlecomb would likely be hanged on some pretext, and McGinty would most certainly be hanged as a deserter, so they, at least, had little to lose in trying.

I should give the others the chance to strike, Biddlecomb thought. *McGinty and I could take a boat, make our escape, give the others a chance.*

"Captain! *Oliver Cromwell*'s hauling their wind!" It was Tolpin, back on the helm, who was calling to him. Biddlecomb and McGinty both turned and looked astern, over the larboard quarter, where the Connecticut State Ship had been keeping station. She was turning away from *Falmouth* now, turning west, her sails bracing around as she changed course.

*There she goes...*Biddlecomb thought. *The first rat to leave the sinking ship.*

The rebel frigate was lost to Wallace's sight by the blast of smoke from the twelve-pounder directly under his feet. The smaller guns were on the weather deck, just below him and stretching forward through the waist to the forecastle. They were firing as fast as the men could load and run out, creating a continuous fog of smoke that was whisked away by the breeze and then quickly replaced.

Wallace waited for this new wall of smoke to clear and when it did, he could see a section of the frigate's bulwark had been flattened, a good shot. Most of the round shot was passing high, over the American's deck, but he was willing to tolerate that. He had given the order: no shots at the waterline, and since the ship had no great expanse of freeboard, and there was virtually no rigging to shoot at, the gunners had a very narrow target indeed.

No matter... he thought. The guns were just to unnerve the rebels, and maybe thin them out a bit. He would take the ship by boarding, and the less damage the better. That was why he had decided to house the twenty-four pounders. At this range, they would have battered the frigate to a wreck in three broadsides.

More gun smoke obscured his view, and when it cleared, he put his glass to his eye and scanned the length of the frigate, bow to stern. There were perhaps a dozen men on deck to handle the single sail that was set, as many as were needed for that task. The frigate was barely making way, it seemed, even with the brig towing her. Wallace had ordered *Experiment*'s main topsail clewed up just so his ship did not shoot ahead of the American.

Gunfire rippled out from the rebel's lower deck, the cannons firing as fast as they could be loaded. Wallace had been surprised, he had to admit, when the gunports open and the guns were run out. He had not figured the frigate would be armed at all. But they were small guns, nine-pounders he guessed, and they were doing no damage at all to *Experiment*'s thick sides. Even a very lucky shot would do no more than inconvenience them.

*Seven guns...*Wallace thought. There were seven guns in the rebel's broadside, and he imagined there were seven on the other side as well. If each gun was manned, then that meant about seventy men down below, though Wallace did not think the guns would be manned on the unengaged side.

*Say they are...*he thought. *That would put the total at about a hundred men that Biddlecomb has under his command.* The boarding party he sent over would outnumber them by nearly two to one.

He continued to sweep his glass aft until he came to the rebel's quarterdeck, their very empty quarterdeck. There was a helmsman and one other, whom Wallace assumed was the captain, and he assumed that captain was Isaac Biddlecomb. He smiled a bit.

*You look lonely, sir…*he thought. *Experiment*'s quarterdeck was crowded with men: four men at the wheel, the signal midshipman and his mate aft, the quartermaster, a gaggle of midshipmen, the second officer, and more coming and going. *Experiment* was not some hopped-up Yankee Doodle bumboat. She was what a proper man-of-war was supposed to be.

Lieutenant Middleton appeared on the quarterdeck. Along with the sword he generally wore into battle, he now had two sea-service pistols thrust into his belt. He saluted and started right in.

"Armorer's getting the men from the gundeck kitted out with their boarding gear, sir," he said. "We have about a hundred and fifty to two hundred men told off for boarding. I reckon we'll be going over just aft of the cathead, marines in the van."

"Very good, Mr. Middleton," Wallace said. He had given Middleton command of the boarding party, to the lieutenant's relief and gratitude. It was the sort of action that helped boost a man from lieutenant to master and commander, and then on to post captain, if he lived and was lucky.

"Shall we keep on firing with the upper deck guns, sir?" Middleton asked.

"Another few rounds, I think, and then we'll house them," Wallace said. "But keep the men at the guns, larboard and starboard. There's still this sloop-of-war, we don't know what he means to do." The smaller rebel ship had thus far remained on the far side of *Falmouth* and shown little inclination to get into the fight. Wallace did not imagine that would change, but it would not do to be unprepared.

"Very good, sir," Middleton said.

"One other thing, lieutenant," Wallace said as Middleton was turning to leave.

"Sir?"

Wallace had been wrestling with this question, the choice between doing what he should do and doing what he wanted to do, with the former finally winning out.

"When we draw alongside the rebel, before we send boarders away, I'll ask that they strike their colors."

"Oh," Middleton said. Wallace could see the conflict in the man's face, the same question he himself had wrestled with. Of course, any bloodshed should be avoided if possible, and given the choice, there was every reason to think the Yankee would strike. Still, neither man much cared for that outcome. Middleton did not want to lose the chance for glorious action, and Wallace did not want to miss inflicting maximum pain on Isaac Biddlecomb.

"Of course, sir," Middleton said at last. "It only stands to reason." He saluted again and hurried off forward to organize the boarding party he still very much hoped to lead.

"Sloop-of-war's hauling its wind, Captain!" the quartermaster called, breaking into Wallace's thoughts. Wallace turned and looked aft. He could not see the hull of the smaller man-of-war, it was blocked from view by *Falmouth*, but he could see the masts well enough. Like *Experiment*, she was sailing with topsails alone to match her speed to the jury-rigged frigate. Now she was spinning on her heel, turning through a hundred degrees to run off in the other direction.

Wise choice... Wallace thought. He had hoped, of course, to make a prize of that ship as well. She was small, but seemed well armed and fitted out. Still, he had never really held out much hope of catching her. He had only one ship under his command, and *Falmouth* and Biddlecomb were his target.

He was about to turn back to *Falmouth* when he realized that the sloop-of-war was not settling on her new course at all but was still turning. Her foretopsail began to flog and was braced around as she came head to wind. Then her main and mizzen were braced around as well as she came up on the opposite tack.

What the devil... Wallace thought, then a moment later the smaller ship emerged from behind *Falmouth*, her gunports open, her guns bearing on *Experiment*'s stern.

"Why, you impudent little bastard," Wallace said, and with that the Yankee sloop-of-war opened up, smoke jetting from the muzzles of her guns, and in the same instant, Wallace felt the deck tremble under him as the round shot slammed into *Experiment*'s transom.

Son of a bitch! Wallace thought. The small guns would do no serious damage, but they were firing right through the stern windows, right into his own great cabin. With the cabin cleared for action all of his furniture and personal effects were stored safe below and there was not that much that could get injured, but still Wallace did not care to have the cabin itself battered to pieces. The sloop-of-war would blow the windows clean away, and they would be damned hard to replace, and the round shot would make a mess of the cabin sides.

And then he heard a different sound—screaming. It was the sound that often followed a broadside, the sharp, unnerving noise that came right on the heels of gunfire, but Wallace had not expected to hear it now. The shot must have flown down the length of the upper deck and taken out men working the guns.

He glowered at the sloop-of-war as it sailed past and considered what he might do. *Experiment* had no stern-chasers; the small ship had chosen its place well. There were no British guns that could reach it where it was.

Well, you've had your fun, now be off with you, Wallace thought. He would not lose sight of his goal, which was *Falmouth*, always *Falmouth*. He would deal with the sloop-of-war once *Falmouth* was his, though he reckoned the ship would be long gone by then.

"Wearing, sir!" the quartermaster called out, pointlessly. Wallace could see the ship in their wake was wearing, turning her stern through the wind and bringing her other broadside to bear.

Do you have the actual gall? he wondered and then the sloop-of-war fired again, one gun at a time, forward to aft, the balls slamming into *Experiment*'s stern and making the deck jump underfoot.

Damn him! Wallace thought, and at the same time, he made a decision. No quarter for *Falmouth*. No quarter for this impudent little bastard.

Rumstick slammed his fist down on *Hopefleet*'s rail. He pressed his lips together. He did not curse out loud, but it took every bit of willpower he had to not do so.

"Wait, sir!" Gerrish said. "I don't think..." He was standing next to Rumstick, training his glass aft, looking beyond *Falmouth* at the masts of *Oliver Cromwell* astern of her.

They had been watching the exchange of gunfire between *Falmouth* and *Experiment*, the lopsided exchange. They had been watching *Experiment* inch closer and closer to *Falmouth* as she prepared to send boarders away, when they saw *Cromwell* make her move. She turned to the northward, her sails bracing around as she changed course, leaving the place she had been holding at *Falmouth*'s side.

"You don't think what, Mr. Gerrish?" Rumstick asked. "You don't think that bastard Parker has the stones to stand up and fight?"

"No, sir...I don't think he's sailing off, sir," Gerrish said.

Rumstick's eyes were fixed on *Cromwell*'s sails, and a moment later he could see the truth of what Gerrish was saying. Rather than sail off to the northward, the ship continued around, tacking smartly through the wind and settling on a heading to pass astern of *Falmouth*.

"What the devil is he about?" Rumstick asked. They still could see only *Cromwell*'s masts—the rest of her was hidden by *Falmouth* and the great mass of *Experiment*—but they could see she was sailing to pass astern of them both.

"Could he be..." Gerrish began, and then they heard the sound of a broadside going off, a note different from the guns aboard *Falmouth* or *Experiment*. "I think he's raking *Experiment*, sir!" Gerrish called with delight. "He's firing right up their arse, sir!"

Rumstick frowned and squinted in the direction of the three ships. He could see a billow of smoke from behind *Experiment*, a cloud that could have come from *Cromwell*'s broadside.

"Well, damn my eyes..." Rumstick said. "Guess that bastard Parker's not so craven as I thought." Rumstick felt a great cross-current of emotions tossing inside him as he watched the dance of the three ships. It had been brewing for some time now, as he stood impotently watching *Falmouth* take a beating from the fifty-gun ship and him unable to do the least thing to help. He was still towing *Falmouth*, his single contribution to the fight, and that was not worth a pile of horse dung.

It was true, certainly, that there was nothing he could conceivably do, battle-wise, with the unarmed merchant brig. Still, it drove him to distraction to have to watch, helpless, at the end of a tow rope. At the same time, Parker with *Oliver Cromwell* had also stayed out of the fight, and he had guns and a proper man-of-war. It was petty, it was stupid, which Rumstick knew full well, but somehow because *Oliver Cromwell* was not in the fight, it did not feel so bad that he was not, either.

"Parker's wearing ship!" Gerrish reported eagerly.

I bloody see he's wearing ship! Rumstick thought, but he limited his reply to, "So he is."

Sparrowhawk was standing off, clear of the fighting, but she was the smallest of vessels, and one well-placed twenty-four pounder would put her on the bottom, so Rumstick gave her no mind. But here was *Oliver Cromwell*, plunging into it, joining the battle. He could hear her guns going off as he watched her charging along on the new heading, firing into *Experiment*'s stern, one gun after another.

"Very well, Mr. Gerrish, cast off the tow rope," Rumstick said. Gerrish lowered the glass and looked at him with a dumb and confused look on his face.

"Cast off the tow rope, sir?"

Once again Rumstick resisted the various caustic responses that came to mind and said simply, "You need not do it yourself, Mr. Gerrish, but yes, have the damned tow rope cast off." Gerrish knew better than to ask again and he set the glass aside and raced off, calling for the men nearest by to start taking the tow rope off the bitts by the mainmast and letting it go overboard.

Rumstick had been considering this plan for the past fifteen minutes, and in that time, it had gone, in his mind, from pure madness to a possibility to perhaps the best course of action. Now, with *Cromwell*'s joining the fight, and his own sense of uselessness no longer tolerable, he made his decision.

"All of you, come aft!" Rumstick shouted. "Everyone aft, here!" and the dozen or so men of *Hopefleet*'s crew made their way back to the quarterdeck.

Rumstick heard a splash behind him and Gerrish called, "Tow rope's away!" He could feel *Hopefleet* surge ahead without the drag of the frigate astern. A moment later, they were joined by Gerrish and his men.

"We ain't staying out of this fight, not a moment more," Rumstick announced to the assembled crew. "Now, some of you, you're English, you were part of the brig's company from before, and I know you were promised your freedom, and you were promised you wouldn't have to fight Englishmen, and that holds."

"I plan on taking this ship and driving her right into the bow of that fifty and devil take them all. But I won't make you help. There's two boats towing behind and you can take the small one and head for shore and do your best. You have until the count of ten to decide. Mr. Gerrish, please count to ten."

"One," Gerrish said. "Two, three, four…"

He only made it to eight before one of the English sailors, a thick-chested fellow with impressive whiskers said, "We'll take the boat." On either side of him, the others nodded.

"Very well," Rumstick said. They were good sailors and he was sorry to lose them, but a promise was a promise. "Get the boat up here and get aboard. We're going to change course directly and you best be gone by then."

With that, the men on the quarterdeck raced off in every direction possible on that small ship. The Englishmen ran aft and clapped onto the rope made fast to the smaller boat and pulled with a will. Others ran to braces and sheet and tacks, clewlines and bowlines. Rumstick took his place by the weather rail and looked aloft, then looked aft. The last of the English sailors was swinging himself over the taffrail and sliding down the tow rope into the boat below.

"Ready sheets and tacks, ready braces!" Rumstick called. He turned to Whitman on the tiller. "Port your helm! Bring her around to a beam reach!"

"Port your helm, aye!" Whitman called out and pushed the tiller to the larboard side. *Hopefleet* turned sharp under the pressure of her rudder, heeling over as she did. Bowlines were cast off and braces hauled and slacked and the yards swung around as the wind kept the sails full and driving.

"Stand bye, we'll tack directly!" Rumstick shouted. He looked over the larboard side. The other ships were upwind and two or three cable lengths off. *Oliver Cromwell* had worn around again and was still dogging the fifty-gun ship, pouring shot into her unprotected stern. Whether it was doing any real damage or not, Rumstick could not tell, but it had to be driving James Wallace to madness, and that was good enough.

The gap between *Experiment* and *Falmouth* was a mass of gray smoke punctuated by flashes of orange and a continuous rolling thunder as the two ships pounded away at one another. *Experiment* was closing the gap, inching toward *Falmouth*, ready to send her men over the frigate's rail, but it seemed that *Cromwell*'s broadsides were distracting her from that mission.

Rumstick kept his eyes on the ships, gauging the distance and the angles. This would be a tricky thing, indeed. He meant to sail away from the two ships, then tack and retrace his course. If he gauged it right, he would meet *Experiment* nearly head-on as he did. If he got it wrong, the ships would sail past him, and he could never hope to catch them again.

"Ready about! Rise tacks and sheets!" he called and the foresail was hauled up to the yard above. "Let go your headsails! Helm's alee!" he called and *Hopefleet* turned up into the wind, her fore topsail flogging as she did.

There was something comforting and familiar about the vessel: for years Rumstick had sailed as first officer under Biddlecomb aboard the *Charlemagne*, their beloved *Charlemagne*, which was also a brig of similar size. It was nice to be tacking a brig once more. He would continue to enjoy it, he knew, for the next fifteen minutes or so.

"Mr. Gerrish, lay aft!" Rumstick shouted as *Hopefleet* settled onto her new heading, retracing her path through the water. The other ships were still to windward, but closer now, with *Hopefleet* converging on them.

Gerrish came hurrying aft.

"Mr. Gerrish, pray take the con here," Rumstick said. "We're aiming for *Experiment*'s starboard bow. Just keep us on course for that."

"Starboard bow, aye, sir!" Gerrish said. "But, sir..." he added, his voice dropping to a more conspiratorial level, "Sir, I don't see how running this brig into *Experiment*...she's a damned big ship... I don't see how that will do her much hurt."

"It won't," Rumstick admitted. "But I mean to set this brig on fire as well. Did I not mention that?"

Chapter Twenty-Nine

Rumstick hurried forward. "Burke, Ewald, Gosbee, with me!" he called to some of the men in the waist as he dived down the main hatch to the lower deck below. Despite the constant fear of fire, it was no easy thing to get a ship blazing, and he had little time to do it. Minutes, in truth.

He heard footsteps behind him and the men he had called to join him were there.

"We're going to set the brig on fire and we're going to drive the son of a bitch right up Wallace's arse," Rumstick said. "Well, actually, right into his bow, but that should work just as well. I think there's some spare sails aft. Burke, Ewald, get those and bring them here to the mainmast, and any other damned thing that'll burn."

"Aye, sir," Burke said and the two men ran off.

"Gosbee, with me," Rumstick called and he and Gosbee went charging forward. *Hopefleet* had been stripped of nearly everything of value, but she still had plenty of material onboard that would work well for this purpose. Rumstick had inspected the brig and he knew that the boatswain's stores were well stocked and stowed in a small cabin forward. There, he and Gosbee grabbed buckets of tar and linseed oil and turpentine, all they could carry. They raced aft once again, where Burke and Ewald were piling canvas around the base of the mast.

"Good, good!" Rumstick said. He picked up a bucket of tar and dumped it on the canvas and Gosbee followed with a bucket of turpentine.

"There's a pistol in the great cabin, go fetch it!" Rumstick said and Ewald raced off and Rumstick sent the other two aft for more canvas while he raced back to the boatswain's locker for more tar and turpentine.

They met again at the base of the mainmast and doused the new canvas with another bucket of tar and sloshed turpentine all over the deck. Rumstick ran up the ladder until he could see over the bulwark. *Hopefleet's* bow was making a rhumb line for *Experiment* and there was a half a mile between them, maybe a bit more.

"Damn me!" he shouted, suddenly afraid that he was too late. He dove back down again and grabbed the pistol from Ewald's hand. He pointed the barrel at a likely looking spot and pulled the trigger.

The report was loud and the muzzle flash brilliant in the dim lower deck. It blinded Rumstick, and for a moment, he could not see if the shot had caused ignition. He was about to curse himself for a fool when he saw the turpentine flare up and the canvas start to catch.

"Good, good," he said. "You three, stay here, keep the flame going, feed it what you can. I want this son of a bitch burning! I'll call for you when need be!"

He left them there and hurried up and aft to the quarterdeck. "Mr. Gerrish, get some men and pull that boat up under the transom, then get a pilot ladder and put it over. When we're ready to quit this brig, we'll want to do it fast."

"Aye, sir!" Gerrish said, sounding relieved to no longer be in charge, and hurried off forward.

Come along, come along... Rumstick thought, but he was not certain at whom or what that thought was directed. All of it. *Hopefleet. Experiment.* The fire. It all had to come along, and it all had to do so at just the right time, or this was all a colossal waste.

And then, to his surprise, he smiled.

"Ha!" he shouted, his eyes on *Experiment.* "Damn you for a miserable rascal!" He was filled with the joyful recklessness of the whole thing, the absolute absurdity. He would take them all down, every damned one.

And then he saw a puff of smoke jetting out from *Experiment's* starboard battery, and then another and another as the man-of-war opened fire. Round shot screamed overhead and a hole appeared in the foresail but Rumstick's jubilation did not diminish. He turned around, bent over, and directed his hindquarters at the fifty-gun ship.

"Right here, James Wallace!" he shouted, slapping his arse for emphasis. "Put your damned round shot right here, if you have the stones!"

"Mr. Faircloth!" Biddlecomb called down the deck. The marine officer turned at the sound of his name and hurried aft. Behind him, Biddlecomb heard *Oliver Cromwell*'s guns going off again, one after another, and he took a grim pleasure in the sound.

Parker had been wearing back and forth, pouring gunfire into *Experiment*'s stern. It was unlikely that his shot was doing much damage, but he certainly had destroyed Wallace's stern windows and no doubt made a mess of the cabin's interior. It was even possible he had done some slaughter among the gun crews as well. Raking fire, coming in through the stern, was a deadly as it came.

Faircloth came up the quarterdeck ladder and hurried aft as quickly as dignity would allow.

"Sir?"

"My guess is that Wallace means to board us," Biddlecomb said, still speaking loud over the almost continuous gunfire. "Parker's fire seems to have given him pause, but I still think that's what he means to do. Our..." he paused as a round shot passed overhead, obliterating all other sound. They could feel the wind of its passing.

"Our great guns are useless now. I mean to get all the men on deck with small arms, see if we can hold the boarders off. We'll send all the marines up into the top. They'll do the most good there, firing down on *Experiment*. Bring grenadoes, if you have them."

"Yes, sir," Faircloth said. "But..."

"Tow rope's loose!" a voice came shouting aft, cutting through the sound of the gunfire. "Tow's gone!"

What the devil... Biddlecomb thought.

"Did *Experiment* shoot it away, you reckon?" Faircloth asked. The two of them had turned to face forward so they might see what was going on.

"Most likely," Biddlecomb said, and then McGinty appeared on the quarterdeck and hurried back to join them.

CHAPTER TWENTY-NINE

"Tow rope's been let go, Captain," he said, huffing from having run aft.

"Let go?" Biddlecomb asked. "Or shot away?"

"Let go," McGinty said. "*Hopefleet* let it go, just dropped it right into the water."

The three of them were silent for a moment as they looked past the bow to where *Hopefleet* was visibly gaining speed. "Some miscommunication?" Faircloth said. "Did Rumstick think some signal had been sent?"

"I can't imagine that," Biddlecomb said. "Red and yellow flag to the yardarm. That was the signal to let go the tow. I don't see how Rumstick might have thought he saw such a thing."

They were silent again as *Hopefleet* continued to sail away from *Falmouth*, away from *Experiment* and the fighting.

"You don't reckon...well...that ol' Rumstick..." McGinty began, but Biddlecomb cut him off.

"No, Mr. McGinty. I do not."

From the look of it, it would seem obvious what was going on. Rumstick had decided that the fight was lost and figured he could at least save his own ship and crew. He was not happy about his being put aboard *Hopefleet*. Everyone knew it.

But it was simply not possible that he was abandoning them. It did not even bear further thought.

Then *Hopefleet* turned, coming around on a beam reach, starboard tack, sailing a course perpendicular to the fighting ships.

"Now what the devil..." McGinty asked.

"I don't know," Biddlecomb said. "But Rumstick's up to something. What it is, I suspect we'll find out directly. Meanwhile, Mr. Faircloth, please get your men aloft."

"But, sir, if the marines are in the foretop, they won't be able to repel boarders."

"Ha!" McGinty laughed. "There'll be no repelling borders, boy-o! Once they're coming over the side, we're done for. Best listen to the captain. Our only chance is to shoot them all before they come aboard!"

"I must agree with Mr. McGinty," Biddlecomb said. "Now, please, aloft with you. You may open fire when you're within range. And feel free to use those grenadoes. Mr. McGinty, let's leave off with the great guns. Get all the men on deck and ready with small arms. As you say, we'll try and shoot them all before they get onboard."

The two officers hurried off to organize that defense, that forlorn hope. Biddlecomb looked out past *Experiment*'s bow. *Hopefleet* was half a mile away, but she was coming about now, tacking to get back up with the others.

Ezra, what in all hell are you about? Biddlecomb wondered.

"Get everyone aft, here! Everyone aft!" Rumstick bellowed down the length of the deck. "And someone get the men on the lower deck!"

A cable length, no more. *Experiment* was a cable length away and pouring a furious fire into *Hopefleet* as she charged for the fifty's side. Round shot was screaming over the deck and slamming into the brig's frail hull, twelve-pounders and even twenty-four pounders that punched in the larboard side and went clean out the starboard. The leeward end of the main yard had been shot away and the main topsail was flogging and beating, but the ship was still driving on.

Running, staggering, the men came aft and up onto the quarterdeck, as protected as they were going to get from *Experiment*'s guns. Gosbee and Ewald came up through the hatch. Ewald's arm was hanging limp and he held it against his side. Gosbee's slop trousers were soaked with blood and he was limping.

"Where's Burke?" Rumstick asked but Ewald shook his head.

"Round shot done for him, sir," he said.

"Bloody horrible," Gosbee added, which was all Rumstick cared to hear.

"Fire?" he asked.

"Burning good, sir," Gosbee said, brighter. "Mast's caught, and the overhead, too. Spreading all over the deck, and forward. It ain't going out anytime soon."

"Good," Rumstick said. He looked forward. Smoke was roiling out of the main hatch and he could see more coming out of the smaller hatch toward the bow.

Half a cable length now. Most of *Experiment*'s guns would no longer bear on them, unable to train around far enough, and that offered some relief. The bow chaser went off and the shot flew by, leaving a massive rent in the mainmast and spraying the deck with splinters. Wallace might have guessed what *Hopefleet* was about, or he might not have, but certainly, he would consider a rebel ship charging down on his as something he should stop, and he was making a real effort to do so.

Experiment's two forward-most twenty-four pounders were the next to fire, going off at nearly the same instant, and the bulwark just aft of the mainmast was blow apart in blinding cloud of shattered planks. Rumstick felt the rush of one of the balls pass, so close it spun him around and dropped him to the deck. He felt splinters like a hundred little knives jabbing into him, felt something more substantial slam into the back of his head as he hit the quarterdeck with a numbing thud.

There was screaming now, and he could feel *Hopefleet* turning, her angle of heel changing. He pushed himself up onto his elbow.

*Get up, get up, get up...*he told himself. He got a knee under him and reached up and grabbed the binnacle box and stood.

Gerrish was leaning up against the far bulwark as if he had been tossed there, eyes open, staring numbly at the place where his right foot had once been. A splinter like a spear was jutting out of his side. Rumstick could not tell if he was alive or dead. A forecastle man named Anders was writhing and screaming on the deck, his arm shot away at the elbow, splinters stabbing him in a dozen places.

Rumstick looked aft. Whitman at the helm had been cut right in two at the waist. His legs were sprawled under the abandoned tiller, his torso further aft, a string of entrails between the two.

*Tiller...*Rumstick thought. He staggered aft, kicking Whitman's remains aside, and grabbed the tiller that was swinging off to starboard. He pulled it amidships and looked forward. *Experiment* loomed ahead and Rumstick was looking at her foremast now. *Hopefleet* was turning to windward so Rumstick pulled the tiller farther over and watched her bow swing back.

*Not too late, it's not too late...*he thought. He could still hit just where he wanted to hit, and *Hopefleet* was moving with a good turn of speed. He heard a thump, thump, thump all around him and he realized that *Experiment*'s marines were firing down on them with their muskets, but that would not stop them. Smoke and flames were gushing out of the hatches, and even if every man aboard the brig was shot down, this collision could not be avoided.

"Stand ready, get ready!" Rumstick shouted to his stunned men. *Experiment* was like a cliff right ahead, rising impossibly huge in front of them. Rumstick could see men running on her deck, could see the massive anchor on her side, the gold-leafed lion face on the end of her cathead, the bright painted figurehead, and then *Hopefleet* struck.

It was not like one ship running into another. Rumstick knew what that felt like. It was like a ship hitting a rocky ledge, an immovable object, one as permanent as the earth itself. *Hopefleet*'s jibboom and bowsprit crumpled as if they were sticks and her bow drove into *Experiment*'s with a force that made the brig shake with a death rattle.

Rumstick, despite bracing himself, was flung forward and just managed to catch himself on the binnacle box, while half a dozen others went galley-west on the deck.

For a moment, Rumstick just stood there staring as the foremast leaned forward, twisting and cracking, the rigging tearing apart and whipping off in every direction, shrouds snapping or pulling the deadeyes clean out of the sides of the ship. He was reminded of cutting trees in the pine barrens not so long ago: the slow downward arc of the falling timber, then faster and faster as it dropped.

It seemed to take a very long time for the mast to go over, though Rumstick knew it had to be a few seconds, not much more than that. The foresail draped over *Experiment*'s bow, the topsail covering her beakhead and forecastle. As the foremast fell, it dragged the main topmast and topgallant mast down with it. They crashing onto *Hopefleet*'s deck with a shudder, smothering the waist in canvas.

But not for long. The fire was already roiling up through the hatch, and the sails caught as soon as they dropped onto the flames. In a flash, the foresail was a sheet of fire, a blazing swath of canvas as the flames clawed their way up the torn, tarred rigging and ignited the topsail that was draped over *Experiment*'s deck. Soon all of *Hopefleet*'s shattered rig was ablaze, hiding *Experiment*'s forward end behind the flames and smoke. The roar of the fire was loud as any gunfire, the smoke more thick and acrid than that of a ship's broadsides.

*No guns...*Rumstick thought. There were no guns. *Experiment* was no longer firing, not at *Hopefleet*, not at *Falmouth*. Even the musket fire had stopped. In its place, Rumstick could hear frantic voices shouting from the deck above him, the cries of men hidden behind the flames that were clawing at the British fifty-gun ship.

"Mr. Rumstick!" Ewald was standing there, blood dripping from the cuff of his slops, a nasty splinter in his arm. "We better go, sir!"

Rumstick looked around as if suddenly aware of the ship he was standing on. Ewald was right. *Hopefleet* would either sink or burn very shortly; it was a race to see which one would happen first.

"Right," Rumstick said and he found his thoughts building up speed once again. "Start getting men aft, help as best you can. Who here's still able? Gosbee, Marks, get the wounded ones and get them aft, we'll pass them down to the boat." He ran over to where Gerrish was leaning against the bulwark.

"Gerrish, Gerrish, you alive?" he asked, kneeling beside the midshipman, and to his relief, and surprise, truth be told, Gerrish turned his head and looked at him.

"Good, good," Rumstick said. "That's a start." The stump of Gerrish's leg was sitting in a spreading pool of blood, and that would not do. Rumstick pulled his knife from its sheath and cut a length of rope from the main topsail clewline and set to work binding Gerrish's wound tight.

"See, Captain Biddlecomb, he always chides me for carrying my sheath knife," Rumstick said as he worked. "Says I think I'm still in the forecastle, but I reckon I got the laugh of him now? What do you say?" He was rambling, he knew it, and he was not sure why. He pulled the lashing tight and Gerrish gave a half-stifled shout of pain.

"Good, that's good," Rumstick said. He looked at the splinter jutting from Gerrish's side. It might have pierced his bowels and condemned him to a long and agonizing death, or it might not have. They would know soon enough. But Rumstick did not want to just pull the thing out—that did not seem like the best idea—so he broke it off short. Once more Gerrish screamed in pain as Rumstick stood.

There was nothing to see but fire from the main hatch forward: blazing sails, blazing rigging, blazing spars. The paint on *Experiment*'s side was blackened and burning in spots, and Rumstick could see that the man-of-war's fore staysail and spritsail were fully engulfed.

There's a little taste of hell for you, he thought. He bent over and grabbed Gerrish under the arm and hefted him up so he was standing on the one foot he had left. He crouched down a bit so Gerrish could put an arm over his shoulder, then Rumstick half carried, half dragged the midshipman aft.

The survivors were there, all wounded to various degrees but ready to go. The smoke from the flames was rolling down on them like dense fog, making them choke, making their eyes water. They could feel the heat all the way aft, and the roar made it difficult to talk.

"I'll get in the boat first, and you can pass the wounded down to me!" Rumstick shouted, then swung a leg over the transom and climbed down the pilot ladder to the bow of the launch. It was a substantial size, twenty feet long and stable, which was a blessing. Rumstick looked up at Gosbee, who was looking down at him.

"Sent the first man over!" Rumstick shouted and the few still able to do so lifted one of the others and eased him over the rail. Rumstick held up his arms and because of his height and his strength, he was able to get hands under the wounded man's arms and ease him down into the boat, then aft to where he could sit out of the way. He went back to the bow for the next man, who was already being eased over the rail.

It did not take long. The crew was small and smaller still after *Experiment*'s broadsides had ripped through them. Gerrish was last, and then the fit men came down and cast off the painter and took their places at the oars. They brought the blades down and pulled. Rumstick pushed the tiller away and the boat swung clear of *Hopefleet*'s transom.

The brig was starting to settle in the water, Rumstick could tell. No doubt the planks in her bow had been stove in by the impact. But she had done her job, and was still doing it, her forward end a mass of flames that were spreading over *Experiment*'s bow.

And then *Hopefleet* and *Experiment* and the flames were behind them and the men at the oars were pulling for open water. Rumstick wondered if the marines on *Experiment* would be saluting them with musket fire, but none came, and he imagined they were well occupied with other concerns.

"On this heading, we're bound for Spain, Mr. Rumstick," Ewald said. "Do you mean for us to row there?"

"I just might," Rumstick said. "Let me think on it." He had not considered where they would go. Back to *Falmouth*, he supposed, but they would have to come around the far side, clear of *Experiment*. And of course *Falmouth* was still underway. Slow as she was, he did not think they would overtake her.

They might have to row back to New Jersey.

He turned and looked to the west. The smoke was pouring off of *Experiment*, obscuring a great patch of ocean. And out of that smoke, like some ghostly ship from an ancient legend, came *Sparrowhawk*, a cable-length away and running down on them.

EPILOGUE

His Majesty's fifty-gun ship *Experiment* did not burn to the waterline. Not even close. That was a disappointment to Biddlecomb, and to Rumstick, but it was not really a surprise. Still, the fire did what it needed to do, and they both lived to enjoy that fact.

At first, the fighting played out just as Biddlecomb imagined it would. Faircloth's men scrambled aloft into *Falmouth*'s foretop, the rest of *Falmouth*'s crew lined the rails forward where Biddlecomb guessed the two ships would come together. Wallace had his boarding party assembled on *Experiment*'s forecastle head, well over a hundred men massed and ready to go over the side as the two ships drew closer and closer.

But what *Hopefleet* was about, no one knew, *Hopefleet* charging down on *Experiment* under all plain sail. Biddlecomb could only guess that Rumstick meant to slam the brig into the man-of-war's bow. He could not imagine what good Rumstick thought that might do.

Wallace could not have known either. He certainly did not see *Hopefleet* as any real threat. He made no attempt to fend her off, save for opened up with his starboard battery. He was determined to send boarders over *Falmouth*'s side and he did not waver in that. *Oliver Cromwell* was wearing back and forth, pouring round shot into *Experiment*'s stern, *Hopefleet* was driving to collide with her bow, and still Wallace closed with *Falmouth*, still his men stood ready to sweep the frigate's deck.

Then everything seemed to happen at once. With a call from Faircloth, the marines in the foretop opened fire, raining musket balls down on the men on *Experiment*'s deck, and an instant later the men lining *Falmouth*'s side opened up as well.

Biddlecomb could see men on *Experiment*'s deck dropping where they stood, or clapping hands on bloody wounds. He heard shouts and orders passing along and then the British marines were firing back, aiming up at the foretop and at the men hunkered down at *Falmouth*'s rails.

Experiment's bow swung closer to *Falmouth* as Wallace, eager to get his men onboard before they were cut down by Faircloth's marines, drove his ship through the gap that remained. Biddlecomb pressed his lips together, waiting for the impact of the massive man-of-war slamming into *Falmouth*'s bow. Once they hit, once Wallace's men could get aboard, then it would all be over quickly.

He looked past *Experiment*'s deck, out to where *Hopefleet* was still running down on them, and that was when he saw the smoke. It was pouring up from the brig's main hatch and whisking away down wind. So much smoke had to mean that the entire lower deck was engulfed in flame.

"Rumstick...son of a bitch..." Biddlecomb said out loud. He was not sure if he was angry at such recklessness or impressed. Either way he knew Rumstick might well have pulled his bacon out of the fire.

Wallace, or one of his officers, seemed to see the smoke at the same time that Biddlecomb did. There was suddenly a great swirl of activity on the fifty's expansive deck, men pointing to the starboard bow, some running forward or aft, some shouting orders. The boarding party, assembled and standing ready, broke apart as *Hopefleet* slammed into *Experiment*'s bow and her fore and mainmast come down in a smothering tangle.

There seemed to be no thought of boarding *Falmouth* from that instant on as the men on *Experiment*'s deck turned to clear the wreckage of *Hopefleet*'s masts and yards and sails, all tangled up with the man-of-war's headrig and bow. They began slashing at the shrouds, shoving spars back overboard, and Biddlecomb was just starting to think that they would clear it all away before it could do *Falmouth* any good when the whole mass burst into flames.

It started with *Hopefleet*'s foresail. The flame spread quickly up to the topsail and its attendant rigging. Soon the fire was consuming *Hopefleet*'s broken yards, and then *Experiment*'s spritsail and spritsail yard and her fore staysail and then the forestay itself.

Faircloth's marines did not let up, nor did the men on *Falmouth*'s rail. They continued to pour small arms fire into *Experiment*'s men, even as the men were fighting the mounting flames, bringing confusion and near-panic to *Experiment*'s foredeck. Men beat at the flames with wet bedding, they formed chains with buckets, while others fired back at *Falmouth* or fell wounded under their shipmates' feet.

For some moments, Biddlecomb stared, transfixed, at the scene, before he regained his senses. He turned to Tolpin who was still at his place at the wheel. "Tolpin, bear up, bear up!" he called and Tolpin turned the wheel to larboard, swinging *Falmouth*'s bow away from the burning *Experiment*.

Biddlecomb hurried to the break of the quarterdeck. McGinty was pacing back and forth behind the line of men firing over the bulwark.

"Mr. McGinty!" Biddlecomb shouted over the gunfire and the roar of the flames. He pointed up at *Falmouth*'s one sail. "We're bearing up! See to bracing the foresail!"

McGinty looked back at him, looked up at the foresail, looked over at *Experiment*. He waved and started directing men to the sheets, tacks, and braces.

Experiment was dead in the water, her topsails clewed up, the entire ship's company fighting the blaze. *Falmouth* swung clear of the man-of-war as her foresail continued to drive her ahead, and even as slow as she was it was not long before the jury rigged frigate had left *Experiment* well astern.

Biddlecomb watched the activity through his glass as the man-of-war receded in their wake. He could see buckets of water moving man to man up to the foredeck, could see the heavy canvas hoses pulled forward. *Experiment*'s crew was trained and disciplined and well-led, and already the flames were coming under control. This would not be the end of her.

No, she was not dead, but she was wounded. Her forestay and the spritsail and the rigging on her bowsprit and jibboom were all burned away, and Biddlecomb suspected there was a lot more damage he could not see. The fifty-gun ship might not burn and sink, but neither would she be getting underway again for some time to come.

Experiment was a mile astern of them before *Oliver Cromwell* came up along *Falmouth*'s leeward side and Parker offered to take the frigate in tow. A half-hour later, the hawser had been passed between them and *Cromwell*, with all sail to studdingsails set, was underway, making a good four knots with *Falmouth* dragging behind. *Sparrowhawk* was with them as well, Rumstick and the remains of his crew safe aboard, to Biddlecomb's enormous relief.

For all of that day and most of the next, they made their heading northeast, with *Cromwell* towing *Falmouth* in her wake. The wind backed from south of west to all but southerly, but that still served them well. *Sparrowhawk* stayed to the north of them, between the two ships and the coast of New York, keeping a weather eye out for British cruisers, but the horizon remained blessedly empty.

The sun was past its zenith and heading for the horizon on the second day of their passage when they spotted Montauk and Block Island off the larboard bow. Those waters were Biddlecomb's, he knew them as well as he knew any home he had ever lived in, and he could have easily navigated them in the dark or in any weather if need be. But there was no need, because Captain Parker aboard *Oliver Cromwell* knew them just as well, and the approaches to New London even better.

On Parker's signal, both *Cromwell* and *Falmouth* tacked together, though in truth *Falmouth* did not so much tack as she was dragged around by the tow rope. With the wind over the larboard beam, they stood into Long Island Sound and at daybreak the next morning dropped anchor at New London, at the mouth of the Thames River. McGinty assembled a boat crew and they rowed over to *Oliver Cromwell*: Biddlecomb, McGinty, Faircloth, and Ezra Rumstick, who had come back aboard *Falmouth* the moment the anchor was set.

A proper side party was in place to welcome Biddlecomb aboard as he climbed up the steps on *Oliver Cromwell*'s side. The boatswain's mates let loose with their calls just as his head reached the level of the deck, and the marines, in two rows, presented arms. Biddlecomb stepped aboard and walked down between the lines of marines and shook Parker's outstretched hand.

"Welcome to New London, Captain," Parker said. He was smiling broadly. Biddlecomb realized it was the first time he had seen the man smile.

"Thank you, Captain. And thank you for pulling us the whole way here."

"I suspect you'll want to visit your wounded first?" Parker said.

"Yes, very much," Biddlecomb said. *Oliver Cromwell* carried a surgeon onboard, to Biddlecomb's great relief, and the wounded from *Falmouth* and from *Hopefleet* had been transferred to the Connecticut ship so they might be under his care. Parker led Biddlecomb below now, where the men were recovering in the sickbay: Ewald and Gosbee, Manning, McGinty's men Bellows and Foster, and a few others.

The splinter in Gerrish's side had not pierced his bowels, as it turned out, and the surgeon was able to cut it free and to dress the stump where his foot had been. He had been given laudanum for the pain. He was sleeping when Biddlecomb stepped up to his hammock, but his color looked as good as one might hope for a man who had endured what he had. The surgeon felt that Gerrish's chances of survival were decent, much better than fifty-fifty. Maybe seventy-thirty, which he reckoned good odds.

They breakfasted in *Cromwell's* great cabin, guests of Captain Parker, who, it turned out, could be quite gracious when the mood struck him, which it certainly did at that moment. They had a fine time of it, recounting their experiences during the fight and the ponderous sail to New London. When the plates were cleared away, Biddlecomb turned to business.

"Well, Captain Parker," he said. "This is your home, you know who's who here, so I reckon it would be best if you were to arrange the sale of the materiel we took from the prize. And I think it would be appropriate if you were to keep *Sparrowhawk* as tender to *Cromwell*, if you like."

"Most generous, sir," Parker said. "And yes, I would like that very much."

"And perhaps you could assist me further," Biddlecomb continued, getting to the real reason for his generosity. "If I don't miss my guess, you probably have some influence in this state. Any help we might get in procuring masts, yards, boatswains stores…I would say just about everything a ship might need…that would be most appreciated."

The talk continued on like that for a bit more, amiable negotiations, though negotiations nonetheless. Biddlecomb and his officers took their leave at last and were rowed back to *Falmouth*. There Sprout also had a proper side party ready, though somewhat less impressive than the one Parker had assembled.

Virginia and Jack were on the quarterdeck when Biddlecomb climbed up the ladder. They had come through the battle unscathed; *Experiment*'s twelve-pounders were able to flatten sections of bulwark but they could not punch through *Falmouth*'s hull, yellow pine planks over frames of white oak. Despite that fact, her time below, huddled in the dark, feeling the impact of the round shot against the hull, Jack screaming in her arms, had been the worst experience of Virginia's entire life, surpassing even her long ride while holding the wounded Captain Dexter at gunpoint.

Biddlecomb kissed her and kissed Jack on the cheek.

"How did you fare with Captain Parker?" Virginia asked.

"Well enough. He can be gracious when he cares to be, but he's still a tight-fisted Yankee merchant captain at heart."

"I know the sort well," Virginia said. "I'm the daughter of one. The wife of one."

"Perhaps the mother of one," Biddlecomb said.

"Will you get what you need to finish *Falmouth* out?" Virginia asked.

"Parker agreed to help," Biddlecomb said. "We need masts, spars. Cordage. Guns. Men. Mostly we need men. And even with Parker's help, we still have shortages to contend with, and no hard money to spend, and the privateers are first in line for stores and the best seamen."

"You're making me quite melancholy, Captain Biddlecomb," Virginia said.

"On the other hand, there's little danger of me sailing away anytime soon," Isaac replied.

"Ah, now that does my heart glad to hear!" Virginia said. She put her arm through his and they looked out to the east where the sun was climbing up over the sound and the low hills of Fisher's Island.

*Little danger...*Biddlecomb thought. There was every reason to believe that. He, Rumstick, Faircloth, McGinty, they were well out of harm's way now.

It's an odd thing, though, he thought, *how harm has a way of hunting us down.*

GLOSSARY

able-bodied a rating applied to a sailor that indicates he entirely proficient in all the sailors' arts, in particular working on a ship's rigging.

aft toward the back end of a ship, the opposite of *fore*.

athwartships from one side of a ship to the other.

backstay a heavy rope running from the top of one of the masts aft to a place near the deck where it is secured. The backstay prevents the mast from falling forward.

belaying pin a wooden pin resembling a long billy club and mounted through a hole in a *pin rail*. The lines of the rigging are hitched to the belying pins to secure them.

bend to attach one thing to another. A sailor *bends* a sail to a *yard*.

block pulley.

bow the front end of a ship.

bowline a line attached to the edge of a square sail and used to prevent the sail from curling over when the ship is sailing *close hauled*. This when a ship is sailing on a taut bowline, she is sailing close hauled.

bowsprit a type of mast extending at an angle up from a ship's bow to which the stays for the foremast are attached.

breeching a heavy rope running between the sides of a ship and the back end of a cannon to limit the distance a cannon can recoil when fired.

bulwark the low wall around the outer edge of a ship's deck.

buntline line attached to the lower edge of a square sail and used to haul the sail up prior to furling.

cable a nautical unit of distance, about two hundred yards.

capstan a vertical manual winch turned by the use of horizontal bars like spokes inserted into the capstan's upper part. Used for very heavy lifting.

cast to turn a vessel's head away from the wind when getting underway.

ceiling planking on the inside of a ship.

clewgarnet line used to pull the lower corner, or clew, of a course sail, the lowest square sail on a mast, up to the yard above.

clewline line used to pull the lower corner, or clew, or any sail above the course up to the yard above.

close hauled point of sail in which a ship is sailing as directly into the wind as she is able. A square-rigged ship could sail at best about forty-five degrees toward the wind, a fore and aft rigged ship somewhat better.

course the lowest square sail on a mast.

crossjack yard the lowest yard on a ship's mizzen mast. Pronounced *cro'jik*.

end for end to run a piece of rope in the direction opposite of how it has been run to more equally distribute the wear.

fife rail a three-sided, free-standing *pin rail* at the base of a mast where running rigging from that mast is belayed.

fore in or toward the forward part of the ship.

fore and aft running along the centerline of a ship, the opposite of *athwartships*. Also used to denote the entire expanse of the ship.

fore stay a heavy rope that runs from the top of the foremast to the bow and supports the foremast.

forecastle the compartment in the bow of the ship. In merchant vessels, it was traditionally where the sailors lived. Pronounced *fo'c'sle*.

freeboard the part of a ship or boat's hull from the waterline to the edge of the deck.

futtock shrouds short ropes extending from the edge of the *top* to the mast below. These secure the upper shrouds and are used by sailors to climb around the edge of the top.

girtline a line extending from the deck to the top of a mast and back to the deck, used for hoisting aloft whatever needs hoisting. Also called a gantline.

gripe special line used to secure a ship's boat to the deck. Also, the process of setting up gripes.

halyard line used to raise a sail. The halyard is attached to a yard in the case of a square sail, or to the sail itself in the case of a jib or staysail. The line on which flags are raised is also called a halyard.

handing stowing a sail by means of pulling the sail up in bunches by hand and securing it. The same as *furling*.

hanging knee a heavy, right-angle bracket that reinforces the junction of a ship's frame and the deck beam above.

hawser a large rope used for various purposes such as warping.

heave to to adjust the helm and sails of a ship in such a way that she will remain stopped in the water, making no headway or sternway.

helm the machinery by which a ship is steered, including the wheel, tiller, and rudder.

in irons when a ship is caught pointing directly into the wind and unable to make way.

jibboom an extension to the *bowsprit*.

keelson a timber sitting on top of the keel on the inside of a ship and running the full length of the ship, a sort of inner keel.

league a distance of three miles.

leech the vertical edges of a square sail.

leeward downwind.

lightering to take cargo or supplies on or off a vessel by means of placing it in another vessel, called a lighter, which moves between the ship and shore.

linstock a wooden staff on which is carried smoldering match used for igniting a cannon's priming powder to fire the gun.

lowers a shorthand term for lower masts, the lowest part of a ship's mast extending from the keelson up to the junction with the topmast.

main mast the largest mast on any ship. On a three-masted, ship-rigged vessel it is the mast in the center.

main-wale plank on a ship's side that is thicker than the rest and serves as a sort of fender. A ship might have more than one wale, the main-wale being the most prominent.

mizzen mast the smallest, after most mast on a three-ssssssmasted ship.

ordinary the intermediate rating a sailor might achieve, between *boy* and *able-bodied*.

pin rail a shelf-like structure mounted on inside of a ship's *bulwarks* and pierced with holes into which *belaying pins* are set.

quarter the aft corners of the ship.

quarterdeck the deck at the aft end of the ship from which the captain commands the vessel.

rammer a wooden pole with a wooden head used to push the gunpowder cartridge, ball, and wadding down a cannon's barrel.

ratline thin lines tied horizontally to the shrouds to form a rope ladder used by sailors to climb aloft.

relieving tackle block and tackle hooked to the tiller in rough weather to take pressure off the wheel and to steer the ship in case the wheel suffers damage.

rolling tackle block and tackle used to steady the yards when the ship is rolling in heavy seas.

scantlings the thickness of a given piece of timber, in particular those that make up a ship's sides.

scud to run before a gale with little or no sail set.

scuttle any hole cut in a ship's deck, such as a hatchway.

scuttlebutt a cask with a hole cut in it, kept on deck and filled with water for general use. The equivalent of a modern water-cooler, hence "scuttlebutt" meaning casual talk.

sheer the curve fore and aft of the upper edge of a ship's side as seen from a broadside view.

shroud heavy, tarred ropes running from the head of a mast at an angle athwartships to keep the mast from falling over. *Lower masts, topmasts and topgallant masts* each have their own sets of shrouds.

slush fat skimmed off the surface of the water after meat is boiled. It was used for various purposes such as lubricating the masts so the yards would travel up and down more easily. Cooks would often sell slush to the crew as a butter substitute, hence the term "slush fund."

slushing down to rub slush on the masts to allow the yards to slide more easily. Not a pleasant job.

snow a type of two-masted, square-rigged vessel.

soundings water shallow enough that the depth might be measured.

spar general term for all masts, booms, yards, any of the poles in a ship's rig.

spritsail a small square sail carried under a ship's bowsprit.

stay 1. a line running from a mast forward to prevent the mast from falling back. The foremast is supported by a forestay, the mainmast by a main stay, etc. 2. To turn a ship's bow through the wind in order to change direction. The same as tacking.

stay tackle a heavy block and tackle hanging under the mainstay used for lifting objects in and out of the hold.

stay sail a *fore and aft* sail attached to a stay. The fore staysail is attached to the *forestay*.

step to put a mast in place. Also, the slot into which the base of a mast fits.

stretcher a pole lashed to the lower end of a set of *shrouds*.

strop a piece of rope spliced around a *block* to hold it together and to attach it to something.

swab a wooden pole with sheepskin or the like wrapped around the end. It was dipped in water and run down a cannon's barrel to extinguish any sparks leftover from firing.

sword mats a type of mat woven from old rope and secured in certain places to prevent chaffing.

tack to alter a ship's course by turning the bow through the wind.

taffrail a rail around a ship's stern.

t'gan'sls standard pronunciation of topgallant sails.

tiller a horizontally mounted bar, attached to the head of the rudder, by which a ship is steered. A tiller is either turned directly by the helmsman or is attached to the ship's wheel by means of ropes.

tompion a plug to stopper the mouth of a cannon, chiefly to keep water out.

top a platform at the junction of a *lower mast* and a topmast.

topgallant sail the sails above the *topsail*. Used in light to moderate wind.

topsail the second sail up from the deck of a square-rigged ship, just above the *course*. By the eighteenth century, the topsails were the primary sails used to propel a ship.

'tween decks corruption of "between decks" the space between any two decks of a ship.

warp to move a vessel by means of running a hawser to a fixed point and hauling the ship up to it. Also the line used in warping.

warping post a piling some ways from a dock to which a vessel is warped.

wear to alter a ship's course by turning her stern through the wind.

weather 1. to windward of something. 2. to pass to windward of something.

worm a corkscrew type device set on a long pole and used to pull wadding or cartridges from a cannon's barrel.

yard horizontal spars from which square sails are suspended.

yardarm the outer ends of a *yard*.